The Drums of December

The Drums of December

SHARON SALVATO

A DELL BOOK

Published by
Dell Publishing Co., Inc.
1 Dag Hammarskjold Plaza
New York, New York 10017

Printed in the United States of America

The Drums of December

Part One

Elizabeth

1

The air in Robert Dillon's Tavern was close, hazed with cigar smoke, palpitating with the sounds of many male voices in eager conversation, heated and scented by the crush of damp, winter-clad bodies, and the pungent smell of beer, brandy, and whiskey. Drew Manning sat back in his chair, tilting it precariously onto two legs, as comfortable in this noisy atmosphere as he was in his own parlor. Over the years he had often been in this tavern listening to the Liberty Boys talk and drink and relax after a meeting. He had come to know them all, and to share in their concerns.

He remembered one night very well. There had been a celebration commemorating the beginning of the John Wilkes Club. In honor of it the Liberty Tree had been decorated with forty-five lights, one for each of the original members. Forty-five skyrockets had been fired into the evening sky. At about eight o'clock that evening the whole company, which was far greater than the original forty-five men, marched in regular procession to town. Forty-five members of the John Wilkes Club were in the lead carrying a candle each. They led their procession down King and Broad Streets to Robert Dillon's Tavern. There they placed the forty-five candles on the table. With forty-five bowls of punch, forty-five bottles of wine, and ninety-two glasses, they spent a few hours in a round of toasts.

Drew pulled himself away from the memory, and once more began to attend to the bits of talk that came his way.

Across the round, scarred oak table from him sat his cousin and good companion, George Manning, a few years younger than Drew's twenty-seven years. George's attention, however, was not on the other men in the room, but on Drew. The look on his face was one of admiration with a tinge of harmless envy, for George would always come out second best when compared to his Upcountry cousin. George was stocky and stood no more than five feet eight inches, even with his back ramrod straight and his barrel chest thrust out, to Drew's easy six feet. The color of his hair was brown; the color of his eyes was brown. No adjective would ever come to mind to make the color more distinguishable, or romantic. Some said that God was the ultimate jokester, and George wasn't sure the saying was false. Drew's hair and eyes were brown, too, but his hair was a deep mahogany brightened by rich auburn highlights, and George had seen too often the reaction of both men and women to Drew's magnetically deep brown eyes not to know how different they were from the brown of his own. He smiled to himself, wondering how many times he had sat as he now was and tried to understand what made one man outstanding, and another ordinary.

Ever since George had been a young boy, he had been fascinated by his older cousin. It certainly wasn't perfection that he saw in Drew. Of all the family members Drew came closest to being the black sheep, and deservedly so. He had caused more discord, more contention, more divisiveness in the family than anyone else, and he had suffered the bitterest of consequences as a result of his errant ways, but regardless of that, Drew had a standing in the family and a respect that was unequaled. Whatever unkind things could be said about Drew, it could never be said that he was ever malicious, or deliberately cruel. Drew Manning was essentially an honest, sincere man, and he was shrewd. He always seemed to be one step ahead of the rest of the Mannings. Even now George could only wonder what Drew was hearing in—and learning from—these barroom conversations that he was not himself hearing.

George sighed and unwisely downed the remaining half-mug of ale. He was feeling philosophic, worldly wise, and fatalistic as he recognized that there were certain things in life that never changed. No matter how circumstances altered, there were a few things that would always be. He and Drew could walk along a beach at any time, in any place in the world, and George would see sand, while Drew would see the gold coin buried beneath it. He always seemed to be a step ahead, knowing and sensing what was to come before others did. He had a great deal riding on his admiration for Drew. In a way he was placing his life in the hands of Drew's foresight and judgment.

The Manning family had for some time been divided in loyalty between the King's royal government and the emerging desire of the colonists to govern themselves. Drew, because of the problems in the Upcountry, where he owned a plantation, had sided with the radicals. Only their grandmother, Elizabeth Manning, and Drew's wife, Gwynne, had stood by Drew—and George. It had been one thing for Drew to risk being ostracized by the family, for he had had many personal involvements with the changing times and mores, but it was not the same for George. George didn't have Drew's judgment or sense of history, he had only Drew and his deep respect for him.

He sighed again, wondering about the soundness of his own mind. He looked into his empty mug, slammed it down on the table, and smiled amiably as a serving girl noticed him and came over to the table. "Polly, m' dear, I'm in need of fortification. I'm in danger of better judgment altering the course of my life. Save me," he said, and grandly thrust his mug out in front of him.

Two men came up to the table and stood nearby, smiling. "You don't look as though you need help, George," Tyrus Kincaid said.

"Looks are deceiving," said George, and nodded at the girl.

With a smile and a boldly flirtatious wink, Polly took the pewter mug from him and headed toward the bar.

George grinned after her. He knew he was becoming more addlewitted with each swallow, but what did it matter? Better judgment had lost. Drew was here. Drew would see that he got home in one piece, and with all his possessions in his pockets. Drew always took care of everything, and now there were friends joining them!

Tyrus Kincaid drew up a chair and sat down, his elbows on the table, his large, handsome face highly colored from the heat and excitement. The man with him, Daniel Cannon, a carpenter and one of the original group forming the John Wilkes Club, smiled and said, "I trust you have seen the circular we have put out today?"

Drew laughed. "I have indeed. I was easily offered a dozen as I made my way from my grandmother's house to here. How have they been received? Are you expecting a large turnout?"

The two men looked at each other; then their attention was drawn away as another man joined them. Edward Weyman, clerk of St. Philip's Church, upholsterer, and avid Liberty Boy, smiled a greeting and pulled up a chair. Daniel said, "Drew was asking what we thought the turnout would be in response to the handbill."

Edward laughed gently. "Any man who isn't going to attend is a fool. The *Planters Adventure* is sitting in the harbor, her belly full of two hundred and fifty chests of tea. We couldn't ask for a better time to resolve the question of nonimportation than now, could we?"

Drew played with his mug. "That doesn't exactly answer my question. There has been no doubt that the more radical of us have wanted to enforce nonimportation for some time. But what of the other townsmen? The merchants, for instance?"

Weyman shrugged. "We'll see," he said, then turned to George. "How will your family stand on this, Manning? You have something of a nest of king's men in your house, haven't you?"

George made an effort to clear his muddled mind. He smiled rather vacantly. "We are a fine mix in my house," he said happily. "You can count on Drew and me to be there, and doubtless my grandmother."

"We don't need women cluttering up the Exchange," Cannon said.

George straightened to full height, his chest out. "My grandmother does not clutter—"

Drew smiled. "Don't get angry, George, they don't know Grandma," he said, and turned to Daniel Cannon and Edward Weyman. "And it's a pity you don't. She could teach you all a thing or two about strategy."

"I'm sorry. I didn't mean to offend," Cannon said.

"And you didn't. Now, let's get back to the topic at hand. Will the planters and the merchants back this plan that is essentially of the mechanics' design, to prevent importation of goods—in particular this tea?"

All three men shrugged. "I don't know, and I wish like hell I did," Tyrus said. "But the only way to find out is to test it, and if nothing more comes of tomorrow's meeting than a show of power, it is still progress."

"But we must make a firm stand soon, or the colonies will not hold together," said Drew. "If all of us do not agree to policy, then we shall always be prey to Britain's divisive policies."

"Exactly," Tyrus said, his ruddy face more highly colored than ever. "That is why it is so important for men like you—and George—to be present. Even if only a few planters are present, it is better than none. We are making headway. Many more support us now than did a year ago. We can count on the Rutledge brothers more often than not these days. Edward told me he'd be there tomorrow when I gave him his circular."

"What is to keep Captain Curling from off-loading the cargo regardless of what happens tomorrow?" George asked.

"He wouldn't risk it. Our men have already talked to him," Cannon said, and gave a knowing look to Weyman. "He understands it would be an unwise action for a healthy man to take. He'll keep his tea aboard the *Planters Adventure* until word is given."

George nodded and looked unhappily into his once again empty mug. "I think you forgot to fill this, Polly love."

Polly sidled over to him, her hip thrust out. "I did nothing of the sort. Shall I fill it for you again, Mister Manning?"

George looked up at her as he handed her the mug. His eyes followed her to the bar and back. His grin became slightly lecherous as she provocatively leaned across him to place the mug at his right hand. "Wouldn't want you to be spilling it," she said. Momentarily his befuddled brain tried to tell him that she had indeed deliberately touched his shoulder with her breasts, and then he spoiled it all by blushing so hard his cheeks were pink and his eyes watering.

The men at the table watched in amusement, then burst out laughing. Tyrus stood up and his companions followed. "Drew, George, give my best to your family. I'll see you tomorrow," he said, and moved through the crowded room to join Joseph Verree, John Hall, and some other men engaged in heated conversation.

Hurriedly, too hurriedly, George drank his mug of ale and ordered another. This time, seeing the futility of teasing George, Polly was not provocative, merely efficient. George felt more comfortable now that the other men had left, and he was not forced to try to keep up with the conversation or understand what they implied. All he needed do now was sit back, pleasantly warmed by Polly's previous attention, pleased with himself, pleased with the world, and suddenly talkative. "You should have been a lawyer, Drew."

Drew looked at his cousin, took in his general tipsy condition, and chuckled, but said nothing.

"No, I mean that sincerely," George insisted, leaning far across the table. "You thrive on . . . on all this talk you hear, forget nothing, and twist it all around to make a sense particular to yourself." For a moment George leaned back in his chair, a triumphantly smug look on his face. He took a long drink, then leaned forward again, his plain earnest face pink from liquor and his eyes bright. "I've been thinking about that all evening long."

Drew laughed.

"Don't laugh at me," George said seriously. "That's the mark of a truly legal mind."

There was amusement in Drew's expression, but his voice betrayed no levity. "You confuse the legal mind with the practical mind, George. I am a practical man."

That gave George pause for thought. He blinked at Drew, his mouth open for speech, but nothing came.

"Think about what was said at this table tonight," Drew said. "These men are talking about your future—and mine."

George's face was completely blank. "They were talking about the shipment of tea that came in today, and the meeting tomorrow. In the short run, of course, it has practicality for us—we'll be at the meeting, but what practicality is there in the long rum . . . run?"

Drew raised his eyebrows slightly. George normally drank little, and he wasn't certain how sensible a conversation George could carry on, but he, too, wanted to talk. Saying his thoughts aloud clarified them for him. "George," he said in a low voice, "shipments of tea have been coming into port regularly, and no one has bothered about them. There has been talk, but nothing has actually happened. Now we have two hundred and fifty . . . two hundred and fifty-seven chests of tea, to be exact, consigned by the East India Company to prominent merchants of this city sitting aboard ship, and no one clamoring to unload it. Instead the taverns are abuzz with talk and speculation, and Charles Town is plastered with handbills calling for a meeting on December third to decide what shall be done with the tea. Don't you see the import of that?"

"Well, frankly, no—we seem to have nothing but meetings these days, with everyone expressing his views, but—"

"Mark my words that this meeting will be different. There should be three major groups present there—the planters, the mechanics, and the merchants. If ever those three agree, then we shall see a concerted and unified move against English policy. If that should happen tomorrow— nonimportation will become the policy of all the colonies." Drew placed some coins on the table and stood up, satisfied that he was correct. He wasn't certain how far reaching such a move might be. England would most certainly take steps if the colonies ever became united in their own policy, but what those steps would be, he wasn't certain. He did know that this latest incident meant that a good portion of South Carolinians were prepared to take rebellious action against the mother country, and that was important. Once such a step was taken, there would always be another step, and it was not easy to stop a movement once it had momentum.

He and George walked slowly down the darkened streets of the city, making their way back to their grandmother Elizabeth Manning's large house on Legare Street. Drew loved this walk. Actually, what he loved was coming home to his grandmother's house. She was his best friend, Drew mused. Even when he had made his worst mistakes, and there were few friends or relatives who wanted anything to do with him, Elizabeth had stood by his side. She had done more than that. She had placed all the weight of her position as matriarch of the family behind him. If the Mannings refused Drew, she had made it clear that they would have to refuse her as well. He laughed.

George turned to look at him. "What's so funny?"

"Nothing," he said lightly. "I was just thinking of Grandma—her spunk."

"Hrmmph," breathed George. "You call it spunk, but that's because she likes you. Mostly she's an old harridan to the rest of us."

"That's because you don't try to understand her."

"Ho-ho," George hooted. "That's because she has a streak in her that is as wild and reckless as your own. Daddy told me that. He said that when he and your father were boys, Grandma went out hunting and riding right along with Grandpa, and that he used to brag that she was a better shot than half the men he knew . . . and she wore breeches!" George added in a lower voice.

"She would," Drew agreed. "You really ought to get to know her better, George. You say I hear things and put them together in such a way that I know what others don't, but when I want to know what is really happening, I talk with Grandma."

George said nothing, but he agreed with Drew. Grandma was always sending her servants out onto the streets to chat with others, and she always did seem to know what was happening in Charles Town and all the surrounding plantations long before his father or his brothers heard of the news. But, unlike Drew, he had never found his grandmother's fascination with politics and other matters in the male domain appealing. Having a grandmother as knowledgeable as Elizabeth complicated life terribly. For one thing, he could not recall one of his youthful didoes that she had not discovered. And for another, he never knew what to say to her. When he treated her as he did other women of his acquaintance, including his own mother, she was very likely to turn a razor-sharp tongue on him and cut his fragile pride to ribbons—but how did one speak to a lady about manly things? Drew seemed to have no difficulty, but then everyone was aware that Drew Manning followed his own peculiar rules in everything. George Manning was not very good at that. He sighed as they turned into the drive to Elizabeth's house.

Lamplight still shone in the windows. Drew smiled. Elizabeth's home always seemed to radiate warmth and welcome. More than anyplace else, even the plantation on the Wateree River where he had grown up, Elizabeth's house was home to him. He always had a sense of excitement when he returned here.

When he and George entered the house, they found Elizabeth and George's father John, and Gwynne, sitting in the parlor. Elizabeth smiled as they came into the room, her eyes twinkling. "You seem to have enjoyed yourself liberally, George," she said, then looked at Drew, her amusement complete as George began to bluster and make apologies. Drew gave him a push. "Sit down, she is teasing you." He walked over to his grandmother and kissed her on the cheek, then sat down beside his wife. Gwynne moved a bit closer to him, and hid her hand in the warmth of his.

Elizabeth talked on. "We have been waiting impatiently for your arrival, gentlemen, and in your absence have delegated all manner of tasks to you."

Drew made a face and looked at Gwynne. All he got was a return smile, and a look that said he should have been present to volunteer rather than allowing Elizabeth to delegate.

"You realize, of course, Drew, that there are going to be some awkward moments with the arrangements we have made for this Christmas season. I have just this afternoon received a reply from your father and mother regarding my invitation to them for the holidays. Of course, phrasing it the way I did, they could hardly refuse. Joseph has not forgotten that he is my son. So your parents and Arthur and his fiancée shall be here both for Christmas and the christening of your daughter."

Drew looked at her in amazement. "How did you bring that about? I have great faith in you, Grandma, but I thought that beyond even your inestimable powers."

John laughed. "I would have agreed with you, Drew. But when Mama sets her mind to something, well . . . Joseph is coming. I don't suppose anything else need be said."

"But does he realize that I shall be here, too?" Drew asked.

"He would hardly suppose that you would not be present at the christening of your own child," Elizabeth said with a touch of acid. "And anyway, I'd hear none of his excuses, and he is aware of that. It is one thing to stand on pride, but quite another when a man has never so much as set eyes on his own grandchildren. I let him know how and what I felt about a Manning who did not attend to the welfare of future Manning generations."

"I see," Drew said mildly, and tried to imagine what his father was thinking. It had been nearly six years since he had seen his father. Joseph Manning had disowned his son when Drew had refused to honor a marriage contract Joseph had made with his cousin William Templeton when Drew was a child. He hadn't loved Joanna Templeton, nor had she loved him. Drew had followed his own heart, but had paid the price of being exiled from his own home and family. It had been Elizabeth who had kept him close to herself and his cousins, but even she had not been able to heal the rift between father and son—until now. This would be a memorable Christmas, for it would include a battle between titanic wills.

Elizabeth was petite and very feminine to look at. Her white hair and advanced years had not diminished her beauty, or her own awareness of it. She delighted in taking full advantage of the privileges age gave her, and combining her femininity and a brilliant, well-tutored mind to produce some truly outrageous behavior. Elizabeth Manning might be seen in the midst of a street rally, or at a ball at the St. Cecilia Society, listening in at an Assembly meeting, or out horseback riding before sunrise with only a groom for escort. Much to the consternation of her mostly conservative and Tory family, Elizabeth had definite leanings toward the rebellious and perhaps revolutionary ideas of the Liberty Boys, a fond appellation given to the John Wilkes Club. She now looked up at Drew and said, "I hope you are prepared to place yourself at my disposal for the next few days. We have many preparations to make, and I shall need the assistance of all of you. The servants already have more than they can manage."

George groaned. "That means we are going to have bachelor quarters again."

"But, of course," Elizabeth snapped. "We have barely enough room to sleep everyone with the use of the bachelor quarters over the stables, let alone without them. It would be impossible. Next year we shall plan better and have Christmas at Willowtree. We could do it this year, John, if you were not so negligent about that plantation. You must learn that an overseer cannot replace a master. I don't believe you spent a full three months at Willowtree this year."

"I didn't, but there is no need. I know far less about rice than Milo Sayers does. He is a good overseer, and he is very good about bringing the books here to me. Everything I need do, I can do from my study here in the comfort of my preferred home," her son said complacently.

"There is something decadent in what you say, John," she said.

"There is nothing decadent, Mother. The plantation always shows a healthy profit, and supports us very well."

"I think, in my will, I shall leave it to someone else. Neither you nor any of your sons takes proper care of that plantation."

John chuckled. "You know perfectly well, Mother, that you can't do that. Father left it to me in his will. It is not yours to take away or give."

"I can certainly threaten and wish. If nothing else, perhaps I can shame you into caring for it."

"Mother, George is falling asleep in his chair. Tell the dear boy what you want of him tomorrow and let him get to bed," John said.

"George!" she said sharply.

"Yes, Grandma," George said quickly, his eyes roving around, trying to focus. "I'll do it first thing in the morning."

"Do what?"

George stared at her, then cleared his throat. "What you asked of me."

"I haven't asked anything yet, you fool! Wake up, and pay attention. I want you and Drew to take out that old carriage and have John Laughton see to its repair. Make certain he gives me a good price. I'll also be needing new harness and fittings for both carriages." She poked at George with her finger. "Are you awake?"

"Yes, I'm awake. Drew and I will see to the carriages first thing."

"Good! Now, go to bed and sleep. You can't do a good job if your mind is all fuddled with drink."

George made his apologies and went off to bed as though he were an obedient child. Drew looked at his grandmother. "You are too hard on him, Grandma."

"I am not! Do you suppose you and George would have time to stop by the chandler's before you go to the meeting? You are going to attend the meeting in the Exchange, aren't you?"

"You know I'll be there. I wouldn't miss it for anything."

"Neither will I," she said impishly, and looked to see if he would offer to take her or join with her son in advising her to stay at home where ladies belonged. Seeing his smile, she went on. "There is no need for your frown, John. You must admit that at the very least it should be amusing. Imagine —all this fuss over tea and we in the colonies, even with the new tax, can buy tea less dearly than they can in England. Doesn't it seem to you that the bone of contention might have come over something a little more controversial?"

John said tiredly, "Mother, it really doesn't matter what item is used to base the argument for nonimportation upon. The real issue is that there are elements of this colony that want a fight with the mother country no matter what. For their purposes tea is as good a subject to fight over as any other."

"Achh!" she scolded. "You are such a cynic!"

"Nonsense! I am a realist," said her son. "We have nothing to gain by all this agitation, except of course, to focus Parliament's attention on us, and remind them constantly that perhaps we should be giving more revenue to England. It would seem to me that the colonies would prosper better by being quiet and going about their business. What harm does it do us to make England prosperous, if we, too, reap the benefit?"

"Then you have chosen your side and will stand with the Tories?" his mother asked.

"I have taken no side, Mother. Theoretically, at least, there are no sides. We are all British subjects—all of us."

"But we all know that theories are usually brilliant pieces of speculation, and seldom applicable to life."

John sniggered. "Mother, I give up. You have a knack of making pure nonsense sound profound and true. I am going to retire, and pray on bended knee that you have not wished upon me nightmares."

Elizabeth sat quietly for a moment. "He certainly isn't in a very good humor tonight," she said.

Drew stood up and put his hand out for his grandmother to take. "Come on, Grandma," he said, and reached his other hand toward his wife. "Let me escort two of my favorite ladies to their bedrooms."

"Two of your favorites?" Gwynne said in mock anger. "Who, may I ask, are the others?"

He kissed her on the nose. "My Mary, Susan, and little Elizabeth."

Gwynne smiled happily.

Elizabeth held tightly to his arm as they walked three abreast to the staircase. "I have longed for the day your father would be made to acknowledge his family again, and now it is almost here. Imagine his face, Drew, when he sees his four grandchildren for the first time."

"Georgina hasn't seen them, either," Gwynne said quietly, then added, "And my mother and father haven't seen Elizabeth . . . or the other children."

"I am still working on that, dear. I have written to your parents, and to Joanna, as well. I thought that if we were going to try to bring the family back together, we might as well go all out. I haven't received a reply yet. But I shall."

2

On Friday, December 3, 1773, Elizabeth Manning was dressed in a deep wine velvet afternoon dress, and waiting impatiently for her grandsons to take her to the meeting in the great hall of the Exchange building. Her eyes gleamed with the snapping eagerness of a young girl's. She had no idea how she had managed to raise two such conservative sons. John was ready to shift from side to side, depending on who was winning, and Joseph, Drew's father, was holed away on his plantation in the Upcountry preaching the glories of English rule and of maintaining things exactly as they were. Neither of them seemed to have the keen eye or the appetite for the adventure of watching a new, raw country emerge from its European beginnings. She wasn't any more certain than John or Joseph that rebelling against England, even in small ways, was best. But it certainly was exciting. It was change. It was adventure. It was a testing of the mettle of a new nation. She found thrilling the idea of these thirteen colonies perhaps forging themselves into a nation. She couldn't understand why her sons did not. Thank God for her grandson Drew. At least he had some sense of destiny and a willingness to leap into his future. And now it seemed that George might follow in his steps. Despite his bumbling and his shyness, George was showing definite signs of becoming the sort of man Elizabeth could admire. But, of all her family, Drew was the only one who reminded her of her late husband Walter. How she missed him! She knew that if he were still alive, Walter Manning would be at this meeting today, and he would be on the side of America. He would most likely have spoken to the assemblage, and she could imagine him telling his fellow planters, and the artisans and mechanics and merchants who would be gathered there, that it did not matter whether they went as far as revolution, or even if they succeeded in some of their rebellions, but that what was important was their development as a people with their own country and their own philosophy. Walter would have said that if people chose to form communities it was then important for them to take the responsibility and the privilege of governing those communities. How she missed him!

She took a deep breath and stood up, pacing in the front parlor, impatient for Drew and George to return from the errands she had sent them on. She knew it was early, but she wanted to be on her way. She couldn't sit still another minute, and hurried to the window looking over the stable. She spotted the Manning coach and tugged at the servants' bell. When Aaron, her butler, came in, she hastened to him. "Tell Master Drew that his grandmother wants to see him immediately."

Drew did not even get to enter the parlor. As soon as she heard his step in the hallway, Elizabeth was out the door, taking his arm and heading for the front door of the house. "I don't want to be late," she said waspishly.

"I doubt very much you will be, Grandma," Drew said, laughing softly. He slowed her down then turned her to face him. "But you will have to be patient for a few more minutes. George and I just came into the stableyard, and the carriage is still loaded with boxes of the candles you ordered, and several other items. Aaron and Millie were helping us put the packages away when you started pulling on your bell."

"I suppose you think I should apologize," she said, slightly mollified, walking with him toward the back of the house and the activity. "Well, I shan't. I want to be on my way, so I shall supervise the unloading of my carriage so that I can see for myself that no time is being wasted."

Drew rolled his eyes heavenward, then laughed. "I am sure your presence will expedite matters."

They were on their way in less than half an hour. Finding no place to leave the carriage, Drew instructed the driver to come back for them later in the afternoon. A large crowd milled about outside the Exchange building as every planter, landowner, merchant, and mechanic had been requested to attend the meeting. There were few men left in Charles Town who felt that the colonies could ignore English policy any longer, so the streets were clogged with carriages, and the sidewalks cluttered with men dressed in garb from the very fashionable to everyday work clothes. The two main topics of conversation were the questions of what should be done, and if this was the right time to join with the extremists, or if it was still the time to maintain a wait-and-see attitude. A large portion of the people did not enter the building, but remained outside curious, concerned, and waiting for the decision of those who had entered the Exchange.

Elizabeth was nearly trembling with excitement, her bright eyes darting this way and that, afraid that no matter where she looked she might miss something taking place elsewhere. She noted those men whose shops she patronized, and nodded approvingly to each of them when she could catch their eye. Even before the crowds had completed entry into the hall, and the gavel that would call the meeting to order had fallen, she knew that among those men were the Carolinian leaders who would command during the next years, no matter what decision was made here today.

Flanked by Drew and George, she put her hands on their arms and let them lead her through the throng into the hall. With a good deal of gentle shoving the two men managed to find seats near the front where she would miss nothing. The three of them waited for another fifteen minutes or so. Drew looked around the hall, then turned to George, saying in a low voice, "There are too many of the extremists here and too few of the conservatives. I think we are seeing a preliminary to the real event."

George nodded. "I heard a group of planters talking outside. They are to hold their own meeting later and in private."

Elizabeth smiled and said sweetly, "So are the merchants."

Before either could ask how she knew that piece of information, their attention was drawn to the front of the room. Edward Weyman, Christopher Gadsden, Peter Timothy, George Flagg, and Daniel Cannon were conferring; then they turned to the crowd at large. They were an impressive group of men, but all of them represented the interests of the mechanics, and they began to speak of those interests.

"We must have control of our home markets, and as long as the King pursues the policy of mercantilism, we shall not have that control. We shall always find ourselves subordinate to English commerce and manufacturing. Articles of English manufacture come into the colony at such a rate that we shall never compete and establish ourselves, nor does Mother England desire that we should. Tea may be the focus of our defiance, but it is not our only target. It is essential that we Americans, we who comprise the thirteen American colonies, stand as one and refuse the constant pouring of English products on our shores. We must begin to protect our own.

"Coaches, clothing, shoes, saddles, pistols, hardware, all manner of things are sent to us, and what then comes of our own artisans? With the products being shipped, and the tight-fisted control over the value of money in the colonies, we are being squeezed dry, with England taking from us what she wishes, and giving to us what she says we wish. The time has come for us to make our stand, and the issue is tea!" Edward Weyman said.

A man near the middle of the hall stood up and shouted toward the front. "What does it gain us if we make a stand on tea, or any other damn product, if England decides to teach us a lesson and remove the subsidies she has given us? If we feel squeezed now, what shall we feel then? We are better off telling our tale through our representatives to Parliament. It does us no good to antagonize so mighty a nation as England."

Another man stood up. "If we make no stand, then we must begin to accept that there will never be cheap currency in the colonies, and we planters require that. If we haven't our own issue of paper money at a fair exchange, the cost of tools and material and labor becomes so dear that only the largest and wealthiest may prosper."

The debate raged on for well over an hour. Voices of all persuasions from the very conservative to the very liberal were heard, but it became more and more apparent that the greatest number of men in attendance were extremists.

Drew kept his eyes on Christopher Gadsden, one of the first, most vocal, and most dedicated of South Carolinians to the cause of independence. Gadsden seemed to be waiting confidently, patiently, for all the talk and argument to subside. Finally it did. The meeting resolved not to import or purchase any tea taxed by Britain for the purpose of raising revenue in America.

Elizabeth, along with most of the others in the hall, was on her feet applauding as the consignees for the tea shipment resigned.

In short order Christopher Gadsden was appointed to chair a committee to secure signatures all over the province promising not to import or use tea. It was also agreed that those who refused to sign the agreement would be threatened with boycott.

"We shall now hear some squealing and complaining," Elizabeth whispered.

A portly man stood and spoke with a booming voice. "This action is being taken in too much haste, and does not in any fashion serve us well. The East India Company is a private concern. We are agreed not to be punitive to private enterprise—our target for objection is the use of British tax upon the colonies, and British policy regarding enterprise."

Another man stood, and said, "Why should we take such precipitous action? We would be better off to wait and see what action is taken in the North. They are far more stirred by British policy than we are. I say we should wait."

"And if we wait, what then? Better we should take action now!" Tunis Tebout cried. "We know what we want for South Carolina. Let's make it clear to King George that we will not stand having the colonies looted by his taxes."

The arguing went back and forth for some time with the crowd dividing into their three major groups. Just as Elizabeth, Drew, and George had heard in the conversations taking place outside before the meeting, the planters banded together and decided to hold a meeting of their own. The merchants, being creditors, were not as much in favor of nonimportation as the others, and agreed to hold their own meeting in private. The meeting of December third ended with the resolution that the tea should not be landed, and that another public meeting of all interested parties would be held on December the twentieth. With that solution seeming to be the only acceptable one, the meeting was adjourned, but few people left the hall. The argument and talk continued with the lines drawing tighter and more firmly between conservative and liberal factions. The three Mannings waited for a time, until Drew said, "I think we've heard enough. A very equitable meeting with a small victory for everyone, and perhaps a very large one in the offing for the Liberty Boys. Are you ready to go home, Grandma?"

All of them were silent on the way home. There had already been too much talk to warrant discussion of the discussion. As George helped Elizabeth from the carriage, she looked at both her grandsons and thanked them, then smiled. "I think I shall take a tiny little nap before supper. I am sure we shall have to give full report to John and Leo and Rob this evening, and I find I am a bit tired."

Drew walked up the stairs with her, then turned down the hall toward the suite of rooms he and his family were using. "Gwynne!"

Gwynne Templeton Manning stepped out into the hall, a look of exasperated amusement on her pretty face. "Your daughter *was* taking a nap, Drew! I hope you notice I use the past tense."

His deep-brown eyes sparkled, and he grabbed her by the waist, pulling her against him. "I heard your use of the past tense. We'll take them all out for a long ride. I'll run the three older ones through fields and over hills and under bridges until they are all exhausted and ready for a long night's sleep. All you need do is hold the baby and watch us. Are you satisfied now, woman? Will you kiss me and ask me how the meeting came out?"

She pushed at his chest and laughed. "How did your meeting turn out?" She laughed again. "Oh, Drew, this is ridiculous. I know perfectly well how the meeting came out. You told me what would happen before you went. It was no different from what you expected, was it?"

"No," he said, and rubbed the tip of his nose against hers.

Nathaniel, Drew's only son, came to the door and watched his father and stepmother with curiosity. He had seen them kiss many times, and except for being left out, he liked the feeling he got when they were together. But what was this new thing his father was doing with Gwynne?

Drew looked at the perplexed expression on Nathaniel's face. "Are your sisters awake?"

"Yes, sir. Susan and Elizabeth are crying 'cause you woke them up."

"Then go see what you can do to quiet them, because we are going to the country for a long ride."

"Where are we going?"

"I don't know," Drew said, his eyes twinkling. "Where do you think we should go?"

Nathaniel began to smile, then, uncertain, frowned. He wasn't sure of his father today. He was being very silly, Nathaniel thought, but then it was hard to tell. He decided to do as he was told, and hope that his father figured out where he wanted to go by the time everyone got into the carriage.

As Nathaniel disappeared back into the suite to find Penny and tell her to dress his three younger sisters, Drew and Gwynne went to their sitting room. "Drew, you really shouldn't be so flippant with him. He is a very serious child. He doesn't understand what is happening when you tease him with nonsense," Gwynne scolded.

"Perhaps not, but it is time he did. He is turning into a proper little stuffed shirt. Much as I love being here, I shall be glad to get back home to Cherokee. It is time I started teaching Nathaniel about the land. He's old enough now to learn what a field is for and how to plant and tend the tobacco. I want him riding at my side."

"Drew Manning! He is too young!"

"He's five years old, and can sit a horse. That's all he needs to do."

Gwynne shook her head, not sure if Drew had simply gotten a notion into his head, or if this was something he was serious about. She knew how much Drew loved the little boy, and how eager he was for some sign that Nathaniel was truly his son. Drew, of course, would never admit, even to her, that he had any doubt, but she knew he did, and wished there were some way she could reassure him. But there was not. There would never be a time when all doubt was removed.

Nathaniel Dancer, named after an Indian woman, was the child of

Drew's first wife, Laurel. The boy had been born right after Laurel had escaped from the outlaws who had stolen her, and no one would ever know if Nathaniel was Drew's child or the child of the outlaw Albee. Gwynne sighed. Those memories had their own special pain for her as well as for Drew. Now she said, "You cannot rush the child into something he is too young to be ready for, Drew. If you do, you are going to make him hate the very things you want him to love."

Drew's eyes narrowed a bit. "My son could never hate the soil. Love of the land is in his blood. It must be, for it is in mine."

"Oh, dear Lord, you can be stubborn and unreasonable!" Gwynne fumed.

"And you would coddle him and turn him into a citified little prig."

"How dare you! Drew Manning, I have never—"

He pulled her into his arms quickly, and tried to soothe her. "I didn't mean that, Gwynne. I spoke in haste and ire, forgive me. But it is true that you have been raised in the Low Country. You don't know what it means to be an Upcountryman. My son is one. He . . . he will be ready to do a man's work before—"

"Nonsense! Five years old is five years old, and it doesn't matter if one is raised in the hills or along the seashore."

"I was clearing my father's land at ten years of age."

"Yes, ten! Not five. Talk to me when Nathaniel is ten years old."

Drew started to reply, but Gwynne put her hand up to his mouth. "Drew, I will not hear another word about this. He is too young, and we'll not discuss this again." She looked down, wondering whether to risk saying what she was thinking, then decided she would. "I know how deeply you care, and how much you want Nathaniel to prove himself . . . to prove to you that he is your son . . . but you will destroy the very thing you seek if you persist in forcing him to grow up too soon, Drew. Please, allow me my way in this."

As she had thought, he was angry. He didn't like being reminded of the stormy days with Laurel and the doubts and uncertainties of that time. He said, "Have I any choice?"

Gwynne leaned her head against his chest, her hand moving gently across his shoulder. "You always will have the last word for me, Drew. I want you to listen to me. I want you to promise you will not force Nathaniel, but if you do it anyway, and you cannot wait for him to grow into the task you have set for him, I'll help you. You know that, my darling. You must know that."

Drew put his finger under hers chin and gently lifted her face to his. Her lips were soft and moist beneath his. He didn't know what got into him sometimes. If he never knew another thing, he must know, as she said, that she would always stand by him. The familiar feelings of fear and guilt swept over him. He had failed Laurel so often in their brief time together, and now he was failing Gwynne. He didn't know what came over him, nor did he know what he would do if Gwynne were not there for him. He held her tight against him, then sought her mouth again, kissing her hungrily.

Penny Webb, the children's nurse, had had quite a time dressing two infants, a three-year-old and Nathaniel, in outdoor clothing. Now she struggled getting the four of them into the sitting room, only to turn back hastily with her cheeks flaming. Nathaniel looked at her wide eyed. All the big people of his world were acting very strangely today. "Aren't we going in the carriage, Penny?"

"Yes, Master Nathaniel, we are . . . but your daddy isn't quite ready to leave yet. I'll just be a minute. Why don't you be a big boy and knock on the door for me, as my hands are full right now."

Nathaniel hesitated for a moment, then did as he was asked.

There had been a time right after Laurel Manning's death that Penny had imagined herself the next Mrs. Manning. It had been no more than a dream, she realized now, but it had been pleasant while it lasted. It had seemed so natural, she being the one who had taken care of the children almost single-handedly since they were born, and he with no other woman in the house. But then Gwynne had come, and Penny's dream had gone. Now she thought of herself as a spinster, and the most she would have out of life would be the care of the Manning children, and the privilege of being around him and Mrs. Gwynne. At least this wife got herself out of bed in the day and cared for the little ones. Penny coughed loudly and entered the sitting room again. Drew and Gwynne sat on the couch, near each other, but not touching. Why, a body would never know that just a moment before, they had been hugging and kissing like there was no one else in the whole world! "The children are all dressed and ready, sir," she said primly, still unable to look either Gwynne or Drew right in the eye without blushing.

Drew smiled and took one of the children from Penny. "You're a bit loaded down there, Penny. You should have called for me to help you."

"Yes, sir," she said, blushing despite herself. "I'll keep that in mind, next time. Now that Miss Susan has gained her health, she is becoming quite heavy."

Drew handed Elizabeth to Gwynne. Elizabeth was a month and a half old, the first child born in their marriage. Gwynne's eyes were a deep blue as she gazed at her lovely little daughter named for Drew's grandmother. "Look at her, Drew, I believe she is smiling at me."

Mary, nearly three years old, relinquished the hold she had on Penny's skirts and clung to her father instead. Drew could never refuse Mary. She was his happy child, always smiling, a dazzling little bundle of color and merriment. Mary's hair was an unfortunate carrot red, which all of the Mannings hoped would tone down with age, and she had the vivid light blue eyes of her mother. Drew handed Susan back to Penny. "You take her, and I'll give my little Mary a ride in the sky," he said, hoisting her up onto his shoulders. He took Nathaniel's hand and the group of them paraded down the stairs and out to the carriage.

The children were too impatient and squirmy for Drew to take them far, so he settled for a pasture just outside of the town. With a flurry of unpacking blankets and lap robes, and some bread and cheese Gwynne had taken from the kitchen on their way out, the Mannings settled down on the grass and watched the older children play.

As Penny ran after a fleet-footed Nathaniel, Gwynne turned to Drew and asked, "Are you worried about your parents coming to the christening?"

Drew said nothing for a long time, his eyes following the progress of Penny and Nathaniel. "I don't know how wise Grandma is in trying to bring us all back together—especially not all at one time. Did she tell you she has invited your family as well? Including Joanna and Bert?"

"She told me. If you're not frightened and worried about this grand meeting, I can assure you that I am. My sister has not spoken a word to me since you and I were married, and Lord knows what Papa and your father will have to say to each other when they meet. I think you and I are going to be dragged over some hot coals."

"It won't be the first time for me, but I am sorry you are going to have to experience it, too," he said, and leaned over and kissed her. "In spite of all the stupid things I say to you, I love you more than anything else in this world, Gwynne. You once accused me of hurting those I love in grievous ways, and I fear I am about to do it again."

"Not at all," Gwynne said, and touched his cheek. "This is none of your doing, and if Cousin Elizabeth should be successful, well, then . . ."

Drew stared across the pasture for a moment. "My father is not going to give in so easily as that."

"But your mother . . ."

Drew smiled. "Yes, Mama will do all she can to mend fences. She wants to be near the children . . . and us." He suddenly smiled. "No matter, if

Grandma cannot make my father accept me again, we shall at least see them, and be together for the holidays and the christening. It will be good to see Arthur again. We haven't been together since he took over the plantation and I helped him in secret."

Gwynne blinked back tears. She would never understand how people's lives got so tangled, and she remembered a day long ago, when she had talked to Drew on the lawn of her own family home, and had said that people who had easy lives never seemed to be happy, and those who had to struggle did seem to find happiness. She had told him then, that she wished for a hard life. She had gotten it, and she had to admit that she was happy with Drew, but she also knew now that the cost had been great, and underlying that happiness was always the shadow of past grief. Yes, it would be good to have the whole family under one roof, if only for the Christmas celebration.

3

Georgina Manning was taking great care with her packing. It was difficult for her to believe she was actually going to see her son again, and see her grandchildren for the first time, and perhaps the only time. "I wish I knew more about the size of the children," she said to her husband. "As it is, I cannot make anything personal like a sweater, or a little dress." She held up the intricate blanket she was knitting for his inspection. "Do you like it?"

Joseph looked at the delicate blue blanket. "You are very pleased with the turn of events."

"I can't help it, Joseph, I am," she said. "I'm afraid that I never felt the bitterness you did when Drew broke the marriage contract with Joanna. I know it was terribly wrong of him, and it caused you great pain . . . and it was a disgrace to the family name and honor, but . . . he's my son."

Joseph was silent for a long time, a troubled look on his face. "Georgina, I know how much this trip means to you, but I don't want you to get your hopes up and begin to wish for something that is not going to happen. Even if I wanted to, which I do not, I could not forgive Drew for the breach of that contract. I have made my decision, and I shall stand by it. I have accepted Mother's invitation, because I could not refuse without causing more dissension in the family. You know my mother, and when her mind is set on something, she will have her way whatever the cost."

Georgina smiled, and silently thanked God for her mother-in-law. "I know, dear," she said mildly.

"But . . . she shall have her way only to a point. We shall be at her home for Christmas, but I promise nothing beyond that."

Georgina looked up from her knitting in alarm. "You will talk with Drew, won't you?"

"I shall do whatever is demanded by courtesy. I just don't want to see you looking at me with those doelike eyes of yours hoping for more. I cannot embrace Drew as my son again, Georgina. I will not!"

Arthur came into the room, looked from one parent to the other, and chuckled. "I take it we are having another discussion about the momentous trip to Charles Town."

"We are," Joseph said. "If you are on your way to the Madeira, please refill my glass as well."

"What I don't understand is, if Grandma is asking the entire family to gather together for the holidays, why are we going to Charles Town? We will be packed in like a bedful of oysters. Why hasn't she chosen to have Christmas at Willowtree?"

Joseph laughed. "We don't actually know where we'll be. It is always dangerous to assume anything with your grandmother. We may all end up at Willowtree yet."

"But she specifically said we were to come to her house in Charles Town," Arthur insisted. "Surely she would not say one thing if she meant another."

"If I were to guess, I would say that my dear mother awakened one morning, and decided her best course of action was to invite the entire family for Christmas, or should I say order the family to gather round her —royal command, or something like. She would then have gone immediately to her writing table, and sent out the letters. Since that time, however, my mother, one Elizabeth Manning, will have been plotting, planning, and scheming. It would be impossible to guess how elaborate her plans are by now, or where she envisions this happy reunion."

"Joseph, I really don't like it when you sound so cynical. It is unbecoming, and unfair to your mother. She has a perfect right to want her family to be united, and you might show a bit of shame when you consider that you have four grandchildren, and it is your responsibility to see they are raised proper Mannings. That is and always has been important to her."

Joseph made a sound in his throat, but said nothing. Georgina had touched upon a tender spot. He didn't, himself, know how to reconcile that. He felt as strongly as his mother that there were certain traditions and standards that all Mannings should adhere to, but without recognizing his son, he didn't see a feasible way of being a part of his grandchildren's lives. And then there was that boy, Nathaniel. No one even knew if he was a Manning or not.

"We don't even know if little Mary has begun sewing and piano lessons yet," Georgina said.

"Isn't she a bit young, Mother?" Arthur asked.

"Oh, my dear, no! She must be three or near to it. Of course, she wouldn't be able to do fancy work, but it is certainly time she know how to handle a needle, and she could make little kerchiefs."

"I'm sure Gwynne would not neglect the children's education. I remember correctly, of all the Templeton girls, it was Gwynne that her mother worried most about, for she had a tendency to be brainy."

Georgina thought for a moment. "Yes, I believe you are right, Joseph. Oh, don't you see, dear, we have just proved Elizabeth's point. We have been removed from the family for so long, we have difficulty remembering the characteristics of our own cousins! Why, we are not even certain of the ages of our grandchildren."

"Perhaps," Joseph said, weakening for a moment; then he scowled again.

"What is wrong, dear?" Georgina asked.

"I was just thinking. Do you realize what my mother is doing? She has invited me and William Templeton for Christmas. She has thrown in Drew and Gwynne, and not satisfied with that, she has also invited Joanna and Bert Townshend. What can she possibly hope to accomplish? We shall all be at each other's throats before the second day. I am sure William has never forgiven Drew for the humiliation he caused Joanna, and he has never spoken to me since that contract was broken. Joanna loathes Drew, and from what Mother has told me there are some strong feelings between Gwynne and Joanna, and for good reason. . . ."

Arthur laughed. "I have always found Gwynne marrying Drew in her sister's place a source of amusement and an act to be admired, if for no other reason than the courage it took. Drew seems to have a way with women that is to be envied."

"I think the past should be put behind us," Georgina said. "No one ever claimed that Joanna wanted to marry Drew any more than Drew wanted to marry her. And now she is settled with a family of her own, why should she mind if her sister marries Drew? After all, when the contract was originally made no one ever knew that Gwynne might be the one to love Drew."

"Well, something could have been said!" Joseph blustered. "If it had been, William and I might have been able to negotiate the terms of that contract, and Drew could have married Gwynne, and still honored the contract, making Riverlea safe in the hands of the family. The only reason

Joanna was designated as the bride was that she was the firstborn. All William or I ever really wanted was to be sure Riverlea stayed in the family and had a good man to run her."

"You might have done a bit better—both of you—if you had thought more of the people involved and less about a rice plantation. I often think that it is the loss of Riverlea to the family that neither you nor William can forgive."

"That, my dear, is something you would not understand," Joseph said patronizingly.

Georgina wrinkled up her nose. "That, my dear, is something you do not wish to talk about for you have no suitable answer. And now, while I have the last word, I am going to retire. Don't be too long, please," she said to both men. "We have a very busy day tomorrow."

Georgina kept the household in turmoil for the next few days. Gifts were wrapped, unwrapped, and wrapped again as she changed her mind from minute to minute. She worried over every gown she was to take with her and fussed with equal pickiness over Joseph's wardrobe. She finally sat down in a pile of clothes and looked dreamily up at her frazzled husband. "You know, Joseph, I do hope Elizabeth does decide to move us all down to Willowtree. I'd love to go there again . . . and remember how it was when you and I were both children."

He sat down beside her and took her hand in his. They were both well into their middle years, and just of late he found that he had lost sight of who they had once been. Perhaps it was the invitation from his mother that had stirred up old memories and feelings. Or perhaps it was that he had been in the Upcountry too long and had lost sight of the outside world. He had become self-satisfied during these last few years. Now he looked at Georgina and stroked the soft skin of her hand. "I had forgotten you are a Santee River girl."

"You had forgotten!" she said in mock anger.

He smiled. "No, I have never forgotten—I just don't think about it. I don't always like what I think when I remember all that I took you from. You were a great one for the balls and barbecues and soirées and the theater, and I brought you out here, and—"

"Joseph, I have never wanted to be anywhere else. I have always been happy with you."

"And never lonely for society?" he asked, eyebrows raised.

"Well . . . on occasion."

"I wasn't fair to you."

"Joseph," she began in a low, serious voice, "the only time you have not been fair to me was the day you took my son from me. You disowned him, but I did not, and yet I have not been able to see him."

Joseph put his head down. "I know that, but I don't know what to do about it."

"You can make a promise to me."

"I told you last night that I would do all that courtesy demanded but could promise no more."

"But I am asking you to do just that, Joseph. I want you to promise you will go beyond courtesy, and talk to your son, and spend time with his children . . . even Nathaniel . . . try to love them, Joseph."

He looked at her, and saw her heart shining through her eyes, and he couldn't refuse her. "I'll try," he said quietly, and felt a great relief inside himself. Honor was a cruel taskmaster. He wanted to be with Drew again, but he didn't know how. At least now he was obligated to Georgina to make an attempt.

They left for Charles Town with a retinue of servants and baggage on December the seventh. If all went well, and they found suitable accommodations along the way, they would arrive in Charles Town by the twentieth or twenty-first.

Elizabeth had her household even more disordered than Georgina's had been. As her son had suspected, she had decided her Charles Town house would never be adequate for all the people who would be arriving. She had really not taken into account the number of children and spouses, and how that would swell the family. She had cornered John at the breakfast table, waited until he had a mouthful of waffles, and said, "John, I want you and Leo and Rob to go to Willowtree and see that it is opened and ready for us."

"Mother!" he sputtered. "That's impossible! It has been closed up since spring, and we haven't had guests down there in years."

"I am aware of that. That is why I am sending you down. Eugenia is perfectly capable of setting a house to rights—in fact she is very good at it, and she will have Bethany to help her, and she can take whatever of the staff from here she needs, all but Pelagie, that is."

"Eugenia has her own plans for the holiday season, and Bethany has been invited to many Christmas balls, which I am sure neither she nor her mother will want to miss. And, as a matter of fact, I don't want her missing them."

"Then, what do you suggest?" Elizabeth said, as though there were no other solution in the world.

"A good inn. We do have them, you know."

"That's unthinkable!" Elizabeth snapped. "I will not have my guests—my own family, mind you—shunted off to an inn."

"While you're busy saying what you won't do, have you considered how difficult this will make the christening? All the plans for that will have to be changed, too."

"I have arranged for that," she said sweetly.

"Oh, you have. In other words whatever I say, the house at Willowtree will be opened and we will have Christmas there."

"Yes." Elizabeth said, smiling. "If you refuse to help me out, then I shall simply have to go myself. Gwynne can help me, and of course, Pelagie."

John's mouth was clamped shut. "Mother, you are an impossible woman. I do not know how father managed to live with you all those years."

"This conversation would never have taken place if your father were alive. He would have foreseen the problem, and never have allowed me to make my original mistake."

"You mean inviting all these people who would prefer to shoot each other on a field of honor than sit around a Christmas tree together."

"I mean that he would have realized there were too many of us for this house. I might add, he would never have neglected Willowtree in the first place. That house was always prepared for guests when he was alive."

John laughed. "I recognize defeat when I see it. You are now going to bombard me with the heavy artillery of father's virtues and my shortcomings. I will send someone down to open the house and go down myself later in the week. But, Mother, I am not sending my wife or my daughter to do your work. Now, tell me what you have decided about the christening, and have you told Drew and Gwynne you have changed their plans?"

"No, I haven't told them yet, but I am sure it will be acceptable. If no one else is pleased, Drew should be. I saw Reverend Woodmason in town the other day. He is returning to the Upcountry around the twenty-second, and has agreed to stop by Willowtree and perform the christening. We shall have it in our own parlor."

"Woodmason . . . isn't he the man who held services for the Regulators?"

"He is, and a fine man, too."

"Well, you're right, Drew will like that, but I don't know about Gwynne. She seems to have her heart set on the baby being baptized in St. Philip's."

"Don't worry about it, dear, it will all work out. You just see to Willowtree," said his mother as she gave him a maternal pat on the hand before bustling out of the room.

John shook his head. He remained at the table for some time, and found he liked the idea of going home to Willowtree. He couldn't have said why he had never made real use of the plantation house. It no longer seemed like home to him, perhaps for the very reason that his family was no longer there. Perhaps this was one of his mother's better ideas. He daydreamed for a moment of the days long ago, when he and Joseph as small boys had ridden and run and rowed their way through every byway of that plantation. Quite suddenly he felt an old, rusty excitement course through him. For this one holiday season, at least, Willowtree would be home again.

The air around Elizabeth Manning's house was alive with excitement. Elizabeth was in her glory. She loved the activity, and there was enough of it to satisfy even her. After an initial wave of complaint everyone in the household agreed that going to Willowtree was a wonderful idea. Added to the clamor about the Christmas celebration and the christening, the family was full of talk about the nonimportation agreements.

On December the twentieth the planters, mechanics, and merchants met. Each of the three parties had met privately, and entered the meeting with their positions determined. The merchants had decided to reject nonimportation and accept the tea that had now been sitting in the harbor for nearly three weeks. However, after some talk, the planters and the mechanics joined forces and agreed that the tea should not be imported and that the cargo now in the harbor should not be landed.

The merchants maintained their position, but did nothing to try to sway the decision. From there the talk went to other matters such as what would be done if Captain Curling tried to unload the tea despite their order not to do so.

"We'll throw his damned tea in the harbor!" a man yelled.

"And him with it!" said another.

The talk was wild and not terribly serious for a time, then it calmed down and the men got to talking seriously about what action would be taken if Captain Curling did not recognize their authority. The radicals knew that if they were ever going to be able to determine their own right to rule, or even have a say in it, this decision had to be backed up with action if it became necessary. At this point several men left the meeting, among them George Manning.

He burst into the house seeking Drew. "They've done it!" he exclaimed. "The planters and the mechanics have banded together and passed a non-importation!"

Drew's face broke into a huge grin, and he grabbed George by the shoulders, giving him a bear hug. "Have they decided how they will take the tea—or will they order the ship back to England without off-loading?"

"I don't know. I didn't wait to hear." George frowned. "I'll never get the hang of listening for the right things. I was so sure that this time I would have a full report to give you, and I left too soon."

"Don't give it a thought! We'll know the answer in the next few days."

"If I weren't such a fool, we'd know now," George said.

"And if you hadn't gone, we'd know nothing, so there you are," Drew said.

No one had time to dally. Lieutenant-Governor Bull was given reports of threats to Captain Curling, and took action immediately. By the time the meetings had been held and a decision made, the ship had been in the harbor for twenty days and the collector was empowered to seize the cargo and store it for nonpayment of customs. Bull ordered Captain Curling to perform his duty. He then ordered the sheriff and several of his men to protect the ship and her captain. The collector supervised the unloading of the tea and placed it in the Exchange building.

"Well, Bull certainly got the better of you upstairs this time," John said with some relish.

Drew grinned. "Everyone must win once in a while, but I can assure you that the victory is a temporary one."

"And not a very significant one," George added. "The important matter is that our people agreed to a course of action, and just because that action was thwarted this time, does not mean it will be the next time. Anyway, the merchants haven't the tea."

Leo, George's older brother, who had just arrived home the day before, gave George a scathing glance. "Since when have you become an expert on politics?"

"I'm not an expert," George said pleasantly, and with a smile. "But it doesn't require an expert to see the obvious. It only take eyes and ears."

Leo started up, then sat back down again, and looked to the young woman on his right. He had only been married five months, and Eloise had not yet had the chance to become accustomed to his sometimes raucous family. Her family, the Miltons, were far quieter and more staid than the

Mannings were even when on their best behavior. Leo nearly blushed when he thought of the many near fights that had happened over heated dinner debates in this house. He smiled at her now and said quietly, "You must pay no attention, my dear. My brother loves to bait me. It means nothing."

Eloise lowered her eyelids and said demurely, "Of course, Leo, I understand. It is just that I am not yet accustomed to the gentlemen talking politics while the ladies are still at table. I find the talk terribly confusing, and beyond my abilities."

"We do it only because my grandmother affects a liking for politics. I am afraid it has become a bad habit of my family's."

As Leo and Eloise gazed into each other's eyes and talked privately, the conversation about Lieutenant Governor Bull's action and the counteraction of the planters and mechanics went on.

"There have already been several public meetings held, and there will be more," Drew said. "The important thing about these meetings is that with each one the unity is forged a bit tighter, and the ideas they have of enforcing nonimportation become more clearly defined."

"I sincerely hope you young men know what you are about. It would be a tragedy to have these radicals get their way only to discover it is not what we want at all."

"What do you mean by that, John?" Elizabeth asked.

"I mean that once action is taken against English policy, we have no way of knowing what counteraction the mother country will take. While I understand that most of the radicals want a say in their—our economy, there are others who will not be satisfied until they have driven us to war with England, and that is a prospect I doubt any sensible men truly wants. The subsidies that keep up a wealthy colony will be gone. The British Navy could close our ports before we knew what happened to us. And we have no army to speak of . . . we would be ordinary men fighting one of the greatest powers on earth."

"You don't think we could win a war?" George asked.

"I do not wish to see it tested," John said.

Leo looked up from his new wife and said, "Well, perhaps the merchants will yet become more forceful, and split the coalition of the planters and mechanics. Sense must prevail sometime. After all, the mechanics are very different people from the planters, and sooner or later places will be kept again. This coalition may work to everyone's advantage as soon as some of the mechanics get too outspoken, or their heads get too befuddled by power. The planters won't stand for it."

"Ohhh, I don't want to hear anymore of war or of coalitions," Eugenia said. "Let us think of pleasanter things. After all, nothing is happening right now. No one is at war, and no real decision has been made, has it?" She looked around the table and got no dissent, so she went on, "When will William and Ruth and Joseph and Georgina be arriving? I do so look forward to seeing everyone again. It has been too long! No one has said a word about Meg . . . will she be coming with her parents?"

Gwynne smiled. "Yes, Meg is coming. Do you know it has been nearly a year since I have seen her. Cousin Elizabeth, I want to say right now for all to hear, that no matter how this gathering turns out, I am grateful to you for bringing us all together. We have been apart too long . . . and no matter what has passed between the families, we do love each other . . . and respect each other."

"Bravo! Well said," George declared loudly. "I think we should all toast to that."

Georgina and Joseph and Arthur were the first of the guests to arrive, coming the following day late in the afternoon. Georgina hesitated for a moment before allowing Joseph to help her down from the carriage. She sat still looking at the house, a sweet smile on her face, but her lips trembled. "I think I am afraid, Joseph. I have longed for this moment so long that now that it is here, I don't believe I am capable of anything but tears."

Joseph squeezed her hand. "If you promise not to tell a living soul, I shall confess to a little trepidation myself. Now, come, dear, or they shall all be peering out the windows wondering what we are doing."

Arthur had gone to the door ahead of them, and when Georgina and Joseph stepped into the entry hall, he was already being passed from handshake to embrace among his aunts, cousins, and uncles.

"Georgina!" Eugenia squealed, and pushed her way to her sister-in-law. She hugged her fiercely, then stood back looking at Georgina's fashionable cloak, and the gown peeking from beneath it. "Why! I think I am jealous already. I didn't realize you could come by such fashion out there in the wilderness!"

Georgina hugged her sister-in-law close to her. "Oh, Eugenia, it is so good to hear you chattering on in that delightfully catty way of yours. I have missed that!"

Eugenia had the good grace to smile shamefacedly. "I suppose I am a bit catty, but you know I mean no harm."

"I do indeed, dear." Georgina's eyes were no longer on Eugenia, nor was her attention. At the back of the hall near the staircase stood her son. Around him were his wife, his son, a little girl clinging to Gwynne's skirts, and two infants. Drew looked so much older to her! No more the boy she had chastized and coddled for so many years of her life. She remained where she was, for she didn't know what to say or do. It had been such a long time since she had seen him, and so many harsh words had been said. She wasn't even certain he would want to talk with her. Perhaps never again would he welcome a motherly kiss from her.

Joseph was equally hesitant at approaching his son. The two men stood in silence, several feet of space dividing them. Neither of them knew what to do. The others in the hallway, one by one, fell into silence and turned their attention to Joseph and Andrew. Finally the quiet in the hallway was worse than the uncertainty between the two men, and Drew smiled tentatively and took a step forward, Susan sitting like a curious little bird on his arm. "Hello, Father," he said a little stiffly.

Joseph's voice sounded like a rusty hinge being forced open after years of disuse. "Drew," he croaked, then squeezed his eyes shut and lurched forward, his hand out for his son's. The two men embraced with Susan crushed between them. With her piping little voice she broke the nearly unbearable tension between father and son. With her tiny fists she hit at Joseph. "Go 'way, man," she ordered, one hand clinging to her father's neck, the other pushing and hitting at the strange man.

Joseph stepped back, a smile on his face. "She is already a woman, wanting full attention for herself."

"This is Susan," Drew said, and turned her fully to face her grandfather for the first time. One by one the older children came forward, and Drew took his time acquainting Nathaniel and Mary with Joseph. He had just brought Gwynne forward with the baby Elizabeth, when he looked up to see Georgina standing to the side watching, tears in her eyes.

Drew handed Susan to his father and went to his mother. There was no uncertainty about his welcome with her. "Mama," he breathed, and held her close.

Georgina sniffed, then gave in to the tears that had been threatening ever since she and Joseph had left Manning days before.

"Well!" Elizabeth said smartly, when she judged there had been enough emotion. "Shall we all move from the hallway and sit more comfortably in the parlor? I, for one, would love something refreshing to drink," she said, and gave the bell inside the parlor door a mighty tug. Aaron appeared almost immediately, and Elizabeth ordered tea and a light repast to be served.

Many things could be said about Elizabeth Manning and not all of them complimentary. She had often, and with good cause, been accused of meddling. She had been criticized for her domineering ways on occasion, and she had too often been said willing to sacrifice anyone or anything to achieve her own ends. But Elizabeth had never been accused of lack of cleverness, lack of planning, or stupidity. As soon as the Templetons had arrived, Elizabeth hustled everyone into the carriages and began the procession to Willowtree. There, she knew, she could keep everyone busy and active all through every day, and with a bit of cooperation she could keep them engaged in games and lighthearted activities long enough into the evening hours to assure that this rather tentative peace among some family members would last through the holidays.

The trip to Willowtree was not a long one. As it grew, Charles Town kept reaching out toward it. It might one day be just on the outskirts of the city, Elizabeth mused. When she and Walter had first settled on the land that was Willowtree, it had seemed isolated and far from all civilization. Now she thought of it as a pleasant drive in the country.

As they turned into the gates, Elizabeth marveled, as she always did, at the size to which the live oaks had grown in her lifetime. They had been mere twigs when she and Walter had planted them in stately rows on either side of their plantation road. Now they towered above the carriages, their gnarled limbs reaching across the road to intertwine with sister trees on the other side. The road was dappled with spots of sunlight that had sneaked through the foliage to dance on the golden earth. Clumps of Spanish moss hung like veils from the trees, waving gently in the wind. A creature of the moment, given to enjoying all of life's little pleasures fully, Elizabeth leaned against the seat, her head to the side looking out the carriage window at the trees that were so much a part of earlier years. Often she and Walter and their two sons had walked down this road after supper and enjoyed the night songs of the birds.

As the road turned to the left in a gentle curve, she looked out upon the lawn and the pond that had given the plantation its name. In this one section were willow trees clustered about the long narrow pond. In earlier days her friends and her family had played lawn games near that pond. The children had sailed small boats the plantation carpenter fashioned for them. The men had raced horses down on the track behind the stables, and the small boys had raced their toy boats. It had been a glorious time, and now she wanted it back. She turned her head slightly and looked at Georgina beside her. "Do you remember the wonderful times we had here?"

Georgina smiled. There was a sadness in her eyes, Elizabeth noted, and thought she had seen that look too often in recent years.

"I have been thinking about little else ever since Joseph and I received your invitation, Elizabeth," Georgina said. "I have always loved the rice paddies. Of course, indigo is a fine crop, and Joseph and I love the Up-country, but . . . this was my home for so long. I suppose there will always be a part of me that is Lowland."

Elizabeth agreed, then said, "I know it hasn't been easy for you, Georgina. I wish there were something I could do."

"You have," she said brightly. "Whatever the outcome of this little venture of yours, Elizabeth, I shall always be grateful that you made the effort. For a long time I have thought that I might never again see Drew, and might never meet my grandchildren at all. Now, at least, that has happened, and perhaps will again."

"They are beautiful children," Elizabeth said. "Are you pleased with Drew's marriage to Gwynne?"

Georgina didn't answer for a time. "They seem happy," she said finally. "But it has made healing the rift in the family all the more difficult. Did you notice that Joanna did not say a word to Gwynne when she arrived at your house? And she would not permit her little Rebecca near Mary or Susan? That is no way for sisters to be."

Elizabeth's lips were drawn tight. "I may have made a mistake in including Joanna and Bert and their family in this invitation. Joanna is a very rigid woman, and she has not forgotten any injury ever done her."

"Then she is still bitter toward Drew?"

"Extremely. She never misses an opportunity to denounce him as a country bumpkin, or cast doubt on his judgment. And she still swears that there will come a day when she will pay him back in full for not honoring that marriage agreement."

"Well, fortunately women have little power, so that is mostly talk, I hope," Georgina said.

"Perhaps," Elizabeth said, then pointed as her attention was caught. "Oh, look, Georgina, the darkies are lining up to greet us as they used to do when Walter and I would come home after the summer in Charles Town."

Georgina squeezed Elizabeth's hand. "Do you suppose they did it of their own accord, or did John think to tell them?"

"I can hardly imagine any of the old ones would remember, or even care . . . unless Pelagie . . ." Tears came to Elizabeth's eyes. In so many ways Pelagie was her dearest friend, and perhaps she alone would know what having the entire plantation waiting for her would mean. She sniffed and bit, and was forced to search for her handkerchief as the sounds of singing came to her.

At the final curve of the drive as it swept past the white pillared front of Willowtree the slaves stood dressed in their colorful Sunday finest.

With no small amount of confusion the twenty-two Mannings, Templetons, and Townshends stepped, were lifted, or tumbled from the six carriages now parked in front of Willowtree. Adults were laughing, or shouting orders to children and servants, and children and infants were squealing with laughter, hunger, or fright. For a moment it seemed they would never make any greater progress than to mill about the drive trying to sort out families and possessions. Then one person mounted the front stairs, and the rest followed in orderly fashion, taking their children and confusion into the cool open foyer of Willowtree.

Elizabeth stayed behind, for at the front of the line of servants stood Pelagie, and next to her, her sister Unity. Elizabeth came forward into the ample embrace of Unity.

"I wants you to meet her family, Miz Lizzybeff," Pelagie said proudly.

Elizabeth turned her head slightly and smiled at a tall, lean black man, whose hair was beginning to gray at the temples and around his forehead. "How are you, Jehu?" she said in a choked voice. Jehu had been Walter's personal man, and he was Unity's husband. "Pelagie tells me I have you to thank for having Willowtree ready for us today."

Jehu's smile broadened. "When I got word you was all comin', I say to myself, Jehu, Mastah Waltah he roll in his grave you doan have dis place in ordah fo Mizzy Lizzybeff. So I gets it in ordah. Now, iffen you 'cuses me, I git inside an' he'p yo' guest fin' they rooms."

"Pelagie did tell you to use both wings and keep the two families separate?"

"Yes'm. De Templeton's goes in de wes' wing, an' de Mannin's goes in de fambly wing."

As she spoke several young people had edged closer to her and to Pelagie and Unity. "Miz Lizzybeff, this be Unity's chilern," Pelagie said, and brought forth a young man, who looked very much as Jehu had when he had first come to Willowtree. He had a fine round skull, and beautiful dark wide-set eyes. He stood about five feet ten inches tall, his back straight, his carriage proud. "Dis be Toby." Without pause she reached behind her and grabbed the skirt of the girl standing there. Misjudging, she managed to pull two girls forward. "Dis be—" Pelagie stopped, looked at both girls, then said, "Wheah be Daisy?" Daisy came forward, and Elizabeth met the three girls. All of them were slender, attractive young women. Daisy had already been mated with Rufus, and Pelagie had plans of her own for Hedy, which she meant to reveal to Elizabeth later, but it was Folly, fourteen years old and the youngest, that caught Elizabeth's eye. The girl was an elfin creature of unusual beauty. Pelagie watched the interest flare in her mistress's eye and said. "Dis Folly girl got de right name. She cause her mama no end o' griefs."

"Is that so, Folly?" Elizabeth asked, placing her hand beneath the girl's chin and raising her face.

"I 'spec's it is, mistress."

"What has she done?" Elizabeth asked and looked at Unity for the answer. "I can't imagine a daughter of yours being ill behaved."

"She been 'roun' that Seth. He de new man Mastah Leo brung here. That man ain't no good, Mizzy Lizzybeff. He doan wan' to fit in with de res' o' us. He allus talkin' 'bout how it was back his home."

"Perhaps he misses his home, Unity. That doesn't sound too bad."

Dark looks passed between Pelagie and Unity, and several of the slaves nearby shifted uncomfortably.

Elizabeth nodded almost imperceptibly. "Perhaps this is something we should think about." She caught Pelagie's eye, and they both understood they would talk later in private.

On Thursday morning, December 23, 1773, Jehu announced after the family had had breakfast that the Yule log had been cut and hidden on the plantation. The hunt would begin within half an hour. "It be a nice crisp day, so y'all bettah dress wahm," he added, smiling.

Beth looked dreamy eyed at her relatives sitting around the table. "Oh, I hope I am the one to find it. Wouldn't it be wonderful to be the one who would bring good luck to the plantation for next year?"

"I am certain you have a very good chance, Bethany," her Uncle Joseph said. "For one thing you are far fleeter of foot than most of us."

Hedy was designated to assist Penny in caring for the Manning children too small to participate in the search, and Daisy was asked to assist Delia with the Townshend child, Rebecca. As the grown-ups put on their outdoor clothing and gave last-minute orders regarding those to be left behind, Joanna took Delia aside. "Under no circumstances is Rebecca to be permitted with Nathaniel, Delia. Heed me, for I'll accept no excuse should you disobey. You see to her meals and to her playtime."

"Mistress Manning say the chillen were to tek they meal togedder, miss."

"I do not care what Mrs. Manning said, Delia! You will not allow Rebecca near Nathaniel! We know nothing about that child. No one can be certain what he might do."

Delia looked puzzled. "He sick?"

"There is no way of telling," Joanna said with a sigh. "It isn't decent the way my sister forces that little waif on everyone. Just do as I say, Delia.

Mister Drew is something like white trash, and you know we would want nothing to do with that sort."

Delia's eyes grew large with understanding, then disgust. "No, ma'am! I see to Miss Rebecca. He not get his filthy han's on her, no, sir! Delia keep him away."

Joanna smiled and patted the woman's shoulder, saying, "I know you will, Delia. I never worry when you're in charge."

The family poured through the doors and out onto the lawns accompanied by several guests invited from neighboring plantations. George caught up with his eighteen-year-old sister. "Beth! What do you say we join forces and find the old log?"

"No." She giggled and ran from him. "I want to be the one to bring the good luck, and I want all the credit myself!"

"What a pig, you are!" George howled, and ran after her, nearly knocking Meg Templeton to the ground as payment for having got in his way. George grabbed her arms before she fell. "Meggins! I'm so sorry. I was trying to catch my ungrateful little sister. I have made her the grand offer of finding the Yule log, but she has turned me down flatly. Wants all the credit for herself—and the bottle of wassail wine, too, no doubt. Shall we thwart her? Perhaps you would join me in the search?"

Meg laughed. "How could I refuse such a gallant offer, George?"

Though he did not know it, George had done his kind deed for the day. Through what Meg considered a nasty turn of fate, she seemed to have been designated the Templeton sister who was doomed to remain a spinster, and dutifully take care of her parents in their old age. It was not a role she preferred, but one that was already so widely accepted in the neighborhood of Riverlea Plantation that no one ever selected her for their partner. For today, anyway, she had a partner, and was not one of the outsiders always wishing she was part of the fun. She picked up her skirts and began to run. "Hurry, George! Everyone will beat us to the woods!"

"Oh, damn!" George howled as Drew and Gwynne rode past on horses. "There goes Drew! He always cheats! Why didn't I think of the horses?"

"Never mind! Hurry!"

"I bet they put it in one of the paddy ditches," he said, puffing beside her.

"No! The woods! It's always hidden in the woods! The darkies don't like to carry it so far," she panted back.

Gwynne and Drew, having the same idea as George, that the Yule log might be hidden in one of the ditches along the rice paddies, made a quick sweep across the rice fields. Each one had taken a different route around the field to save time. When they met again Gwynne shook her head. Drew laughed. "Whoever finds this Yule log will find it by accident. Pelagie says Jehu was—and still is—part devil. He and my grandfather got along fine. Where would he hide it?"

"The woods?" Gwynne offered.

"Everyone is headed for the woods . . . what about the willow pond?"

They found no Yule log by the willow pond, but they found something that was perhaps rarer these days, a moment alone. Drew helped Gwynne dismount, then remained standing with her in his arms. She was a strong woman, his Gwynne, but she didn't look it. He gazed down at the fine creaminess of her skin, and then lost himself in the blue depths of her eyes. "Drew," she murmured, clinging to him, her knees trembly. It was as though she never saw him, she thought. But then, they had never really had time alone together. First there had been Joanna, and Gwynne hadn't dared tell Drew of her feelings for him. She had been certain he was going to marry her sister, and then had come the devastating news of his intention to marry Laurel Boggs, an Upcountry girl so different from everything and anyone the Templetons and Mannings considered their equals. She had told him then that she loved him, but it had been too late. After that she had wandered about England living with her sister, going to plays and concerts and balls and longing for Drew. No matter how hard she tried, she could not forget Drew. The ache did not grow less, it intensified, until she had finally returned home and thrown her pride and her self-respect to the wind. She had become his mistress. But even that hadn't been the same as the brief moment at the pond, for he had been a borrowed man, and she had always known there would come a day when Drew would not continue to live a dual life. He was too honest a man for that, and she had awaited that day with dread and a kind of anticipation. And finally the time had come when she was left alone, her only ally the indomitable Elizabeth. It had been a long, lonely time for her, the endless hours stretching out as she pondered the wisdom or the folly of having taken of Drew the small bit she could have. She had traded her own life for that small share in his, she thought at the time. And it had nearly been so, for when Laurel died, Drew had been too proud and too guilt ridden to ask her to come to him. Once more she had had to decide on her own and go to him. And now they had their first child.

"Whatever are you thinking about, love?" he asked, smiling. "You are thousands of miles away from me."

"No, I'm not. I was thinking of you . . . and of me. I was thinking of a

Christmas years back, when you caught me putting gifts under the tree, and . . ."

"And that night you gave me the most precious gift of all."

"I gave you nothing. I told you that you hurt those you love, and that I loved you."

"That was the gift," he said, and kissed the tip of her nose. "You had no idea what that meant to me." He kissed her eyes, his lips warm and moist as they lingered on the soft delicate skin of her eyelids. "I didn't, either—then. I was too stunned."

"And went home and married Laurel—that's how much it meant."

"Timing has never been our best suit, Gwynne," he said, and laughed.

"I will admit that," she agreed, putting her arm around his waist. Together they walked around the end of the pond and up the long side of it. At a spot where three willows grew so close together that they looked to be one tree, there was a bench. It had been Walter and Elizabeth's spot, and now Drew took it for his and Gwynne's. "Drew," Gwynne said softly, "I overheard Joanna telling Delia to keep Nathaniel away from Rebecca. We will have to see that Nathaniel does not understand that he is being singled out and separated."

"How like Joanna," Drew said, and stiffened beside his wife. "I'll have a word with her when we get back. If she dares . . ."

"No, Drew, please don't say anything to her. It would give her just the excuse she is looking for to discuss Nathaniel's parentage to every adult here. Please, say nothing. Nathaniel is very young. As long as we're aware of what my sister is doing, we can avert the damage she might cause. Please. I know Joanna."

"Unfortunately I do, too, and must agree with you. Good Lord! Must we always be confronted with one problem or another?"

"Now that we have talked about it, we have no problems—except to find the Yule Log."

"I somehow have lost my interest in the Yule log. Anyway, I hope your cursed sister trips over it! A pox on her!" He slipped his hands beneath her coat, finding warmth and the full soft curves of her waist and breasts. "I have already found what will bring me good luck for the following year," he murmured, and kissed her, his mouth first barely touching her lips, then with greater pressure and warmth. His breath became shorter and his kisses more urgent. "Gwynne, my darling, I love you."

Gwynne touched his face, her fingers moving lightly across the strong broad planes of his cheeks, down along the hard line of his jaw. His eyes were a deep brown and filled with wanting. Gwynne shivered. She would never get over the wonderment she had at being with him. She would rather die herself than have to live in a world that had no Drew Manning. Whatever she was, and whoever she was, she would give to him. "Could we go back to the house, Drew?" she asked.

He kissed her hungrily again. "Do you want to?"

"I want to be with you. . . . I want you to love me . . . now."

He took her hand in his and kissed it. Then he picked her up and carried her back to the horses.

The others were tramping through the woods searching in ridiculously unlikely places for the log and having no success. Georgina was out of breath from running and from laughing. She couldn't remember when she had had such fun. "Where is it?" she asked of Joseph, still laughing and trying to catch her breath.

Joseph leaned over, his hands on his knees; he, too, was breathless. "It's probably one of mother's jokes—there is no Yule log. She is just keeping us all busy and out of trouble. You know, she used to do that when John and I were children. She'd send us after something—an errand, only there would be nothing. It would take us hours to figure it out, and she had peace and qui—"

"Joseph! Look!" Georgina cried. "The log! There it is! We're all but sitting on it."

Not two feet away from the tree stump Georgina was sitting on was the Yule log carefully cut and marked with the four seasons. Both of them began to shout. "It's found! Yule log! Come!"

Georgina jumped up and down like a young girl, then hurled herself at Joseph. "We found it! It is an omen, Joseph! Our lucky year."

Joseph put his head back and laughed heartily. "My God, what a woman I've got," he said appreciatively.

"Ah ha! What have we found here? It doesn't look like a log to me, it looks more like my aunt and uncle kissing," George said.

"We found it," Georgina bubbled again as soon as she could talk. "It was so exciting, George—I nearly sat on it!"

"And now you shall," he said.

"Oh, no! I had forgotten!" Georgina's hands went to her face. She had never found the log before.

The others shouted the news down the line, and soon all of them had gathered greenery in their hands. Each of them touched the sprigs of green to the log for good luck, and then Georgina was placed on the log and carried back to the house. As they neared the quarters, the blacks came out bearing their own sprigs of green, and they, too, all touched the log.

Elizabeth nodded at Jehu to run to the cellars and bring forth their best bottle of wassail wine. The troop of Mannings and friends tumbled into the house in a flurry of coats and scarves and laughter. Glasses appeared on trays carried by servants, and Joseph was given the bottle of wine, since he had lost to his wife the privilege of riding on the log. He held the bottle high. "To a merry Christmas, a blessed christening, and a prosperous year to come!"

Amid cheers and salutes, all toasted, and drank and toasted again. Several bottles of wine had disappeared before the ladies and gentlemen went upstairs to change for dinner.

Elizabeth entered her bedroom with her cheeks rosy from the nippy air, and her eyes bright with the success of the day.

"You mus' be 'bout to drop," Pelagie said sympathetically. "I got a hot tub jes' waitin' fo' you."

"Pelagie, I don't know if I could manage without you. Today has gone well, and tomorrow the baby will be christened, and it is doubtful that anyone would be so tasteless as to cause trouble on a day like that."

" 'Lessen it be Missy Joanna. She jes' itchin' to cause trubble. Why, she got that Delia girl o' hers thinkin' she too good fer the likes o' us," Pelagie grumbled as she undressed Elizabeth and helped her into the porcelain tub.

"What's this about Delia?" Elizabeth asked.

"She so uppity, she can't see where she goin'—her nose dat high in de air. Missy Joanna tell her she ain't to let 'Becca near Massa Nathaniel 'lessen he gib de li'l girl somethin' nasty. She tell Delia dat Massa Drew an' Missy Gwynne white trash, an' not to 'sociate wif dem."

"Dear Lord, the girl has brass! I think I shall have to nip this in the bud! I knew I was mistaken in inviting them, but I didn't see a decent way to invite every other member of the family and omit Joanna and her family. Since she has proven she doesn't know the meaning of decency, I shall not be bound either. I think the Townshends might enjoy a short stay here, and then return to town or Riverlea—wherever they wish."

"What'm I gonna do with dat Delia? Li'l Nathaniel he hear everythin'. Someboddy doan shut that no-count woman up, she gonna be sayin' somethin' we doan wants Massah Nathaniel to be hearin'.'."

"Tell her I have said that she will be polite and courteous to everyone in this house, particularly the Drew Mannings, or she can spend the remainder of her stay here in the quarters with the field hands—the lowliest of field hands."

"I sure do like tellin' miss uppity Delia that!" Pelagie chuckled. "You

got time fo' fifteen minutes catnap. I wakes you up in time to dress." With
that said, Pelagie hurried out of the room.

Elizabeth smiled as she closed her eyes, knowing exactly where Pelagie
was headed. Poor Delia.

Elizabeth's table was lavishly filled with platters of roasted oysters,
crabs and mussels, pheasant, yams, broccoli, and baby potatoes fired to a
golden crisp on the outside, succulent and tender on the inside. The easy
camaraderie of the early afternoon continued throughout the dinner.
Though William Templeton and Joseph exchanged a few hard looks across
the table, nothing was said, and both men avoided finding themselves alone
with each other. There was much on each man's mind, but neither of them
wanted to be responsible for ruining the holidays or the christening.

After they had been served a selection of pies, the pecan being the most
popular, Elizabeth said, "I suggest we play some parlor games, and keep
ourselves alert and moving, or I swear we shall all be napping in half an
hour."

"You feed us too well," Ruth Templeton said. "I for one would like to
play the Christmas candle game. It is always so funny."

"You just like to watch everyone else be the fool. You never join in,
Mama," Meg said.

"But I do have fun watching all you young folk," Ruth said.

"Not tonight," Elizabeth retorted. "I am going to play, so you must.
You haven't the excuse of watching the young, and I'm sure Eugenia and
Georgina will be participating."

"Well," said Ruth, "I surely don't want to be left out, now, do I?"

They sat in a facsimile of a circle in the parlor, and a large red candle
was brought out and lit. "Who will go first, or shall we draw lots?" John
asked.

"Lots!" was the consensus, and a deck of playing cards was brought
forth. Each person picked a card. "Highest card goes first, and so on to the
last," John said.

Joanna drew the ace of spades and held it aloft. "I have the highest card
in the whole deck!"

John placed a silk blindfold over her eyes, then turned her around three
times. Joanna staggered a bit when he released her. Her hands out in front
of her, she took a tentative step, then reached for the blindfold.

"No peeking!" hooted the others.

"But I can't see! Bert? Help me . . . where is the candle?"

"To your right," her husband said.

"Boo! Boo! No coaching," the others called out, laughing.

Joanna moved to her right, but another voice cried, "No! Watch out. Go to your left . . . turn round!"

Drew nudged Gwynne. "Don't torment her."

But Gwynne's eyes were twinkling. Drew had forgotten how, when they were children, Gwynne had loved to bait Joanna's temper, and how she had usually gotten the best of her older sister.

"To your right!" Bert called.

Other voices joined in, everyone calling different instructions.

At first Joanna moved aimlessly back and forth, her hands seeking the warmth of the flame, then slowly her temper began to get the better of her as the laughter increased. "Where is the candle!" she demanded. "I must take a small look."

"Nooo! That is cheating," came a chorus; then they began to give her legitimate instructions, which at first she ignored, then began to follow. She moved closer to the circle of people, moving cautiously along. "A little farther," Joseph said. "Just a bit more."

She moved slowly, tapping with the tip of her toe to be certain she would not bump something. Gwynne pulled her feet back well under her chair as her sister neared. Joanna took a step and came in front of Gwynne, then another, and was nearly past when she lurched forward and dived headlong into Leo's lap with a scream.

Gwynne jumped up from her chair and walked across the room, taking the seat vacated by Bert as he rushed to his wife's rescue.

Joanna yanked the mask off her face and glared into the empty chair next to Leo's, then at Bert. "Were you sitting there? You tripped me, you fool! You could have injured me. Why can't you keep your big feet in!"

"But, Joanna . . ." Bert began helplessly, then glanced over to his own seat to see a sweetly smiling Gwynne daring him to say anything. He looked away and took Joanna's arm, helping her into the chair. "Are you all right, sweetheart? Shall I take you upstairs to rest."

She pushed his hand away. "Oh, do leave me be! Of course I am all right. It is only a game, and I would have been successful if you could have managed to keep your feet out from under mine!"

Five other people attempted to blow the candle out before the company tired of that game and called for blindman's buff. Blindman's buff was usually a tame sort of entertainment, but not at the Manning household. All the male Manning cousins called for Drew to be blindfolded. Knowing well that this would be a bruising ordeal, Drew grinned and gave each one of them a mischievous look. "How I wish Rob had arrived—then I could get all of you!"

George and Leo both laughed and sang out in chorus, "But not before we get you!"

The blindfold was in place and Drew was turned around and given a cane. As Joanna had, he stretched his arm out, flailing at the air, then moved rather quickly forward, pointing with the stick. Though in a fairer game the others would have remained in place, George moved quickly and slid a footstool into Drew's path. With his next step Drew fell over the footstool, rolled twice, and managed to bump against someone's legs. "Ah, ha! I have someone. Tell me the color of my breeches!"

Leo pinched his nose to give himself a nasal sound, and spoke with a high squeaking voice. "They are ugly green, kind sir."

Drew burst out laughing at the ridiculous voice. "I have four more questions. Are you a man or a woman?"

"Why, sir! I'm the prettiest woman here, and I'll thank you not to call me a woman in public, for certainly I am then a lady," Leo squawked.

"My God, it's got to be one of my cousins! Are you tall and thin?"

"Only in the right places."

"Leo Manning!" Drew crowed, pulling off his blindfold. "You are so easy to guess!"

"Why?" asked Leo, insulted. "I had a very good disguise for my voice."

"Yes, but you are the only one here whose knees are sharper than the edge of the table."

"Hah!" Leo said, putting on the blindfold. "I hope my bones have done you grievous injury, Drew. You deserve it! All right, everybody, here I come!"

The parlor games went on well into the night, and came to a halt only when Elizabeth protested the overturning of a lamp. "Enough!" she cried. "You boys are entirely too rough, and we older people shall be breaking bones before the night is out. Play fairly, or not at all."

Drew, George, and Leo grinned at her, and said, "If we must play fair, we'd rather not play. We've always cheated, Grandma."

"Then I suggest Bethany play for us, and we shall sing a few carols and retire for the night after."

The house was slow to quiet down that night. Long after the lamps on the lower floor had been extinguished, the sound of talking and an occasional laugh could be heard on the second floor. Elizabeth lay in her bed, weary and content, listening to the sounds of her family. They were good sounds, and she wished they were as true as they seemed, but she knew she would have to keep them busy all the time, or soon enough talk of broken promises and criticisms of behavior would begin, and the pleasant sound of laughter would be gone for good. She had but one opportunity to bring them together and this was it. If she succeeded, there might come another time, but if she failed now, even she would not be able to call them together again.

Just before she fell asleep, she remembered that Pelagie and Unity had wanted to talk to her about something, but there hadn't been time. Tomorrow or the next day she would have to make time. Pelagie did not engage in idle chatter. If she wanted Elizabeth's ear, there was good cause. Drowsily she reminded herself again she must find time.

Reverend Charles Woodmason arrived at Willowtree early the following morning and joined the family for breakfast. As the result of a brief conference he had had with Elizabeth before he met and joined the others, he performed a small service at the breakfast table and blessed all those present. "And be it remembered that the Lord God Himself has placed us in the bosom of our family. These members of a man's family are his loved ones, and those by whom he is loved. That is the will of God. Let us all heed and take to heart His word. Amen!"

Heads all around the table were bowed, and the "Amen" that sounded like a chorus of music came from the heart of all those present. But several of the family were not in agreement, and avoided looking at those with whom they were disillusioned and could no longer trust as father, brother, cousin, or friend.

The christening was held late in the afternoon, after all the young children had awakened from their naps. The infant Elizabeth was dressed in a gown of handmade French lace that had once been her great-grandmother's at her christening. Elizabeth had been the first to wear it, and since then every Manning child to be christened at the Manning home had also worn it, male and female children alike. The lace was yellowed with age, and it had been mended many times over, and had lost some of its original delicacy as a result, but it had become a Manning tradition, and with all the mending came also all the fiber and character the Mannings wanted their name to stand for.

Elizabeth watched Gwynne carry the baby down the broad front staircase of Willowtree, with Drew at her side carrying Susan. Mary toddled along holding onto Gwynne's skirts for balance, and Nathaniel walked manfully alone, his small head high, his eyes wide with curiosity and perhaps a little fear. Elizabeth knew full well she carried the family banner and that it was she who remained responsible for the moral fiber of her family. She also knew that, as so often happened, that banner and responsibility were going to skip a generation. The next person who would be head of the Mannings and responsible for their collective welfare was Drew, her grandson. Neither of her sons would take that position, for somehow they had become content with their own lots and no longer looked to the welfare of the whole. Only Drew seemed to have that sense of the whole, and unfortunately he was a tarnished man in the eyes of the others. His would be a difficult leadership, and Elizabeth closed her eyes for a moment and asked that as God blessed the infant Elizabeth, He also bless Drew. She prayed for his strength and his courage.

She didn't see or hear much of the ceremony, for her eyes were filled with tears and her mind was filled with disturbing thoughts. War and peace were both strange states of being, and human beings sensed the approach of each long before they actually came. Elizabeth sensed disruption in the air, and she labeled it war only because the word was being used more and more frequently. She was seventy-five years old, didn't feel it, and didn't look it, but she knew she could not count on many more years. It shook her and saddened her to know that these last years she would have would be tragic ones.

As Reverend Woodmason poured water over Elizabeth's head, and the startled child squalled, Elizabeth slipped out of the room. Pelagie was standing in the hallway, waiting, almost as if she had known Elizabeth would need her. The old black woman put her arms around her mistress and they walked together out into the garden.

"I don't know what came over me in there, Pelagie," Elizabeth said, gulping in great gasps of fresh air. "I was having the most awful thoughts. Why, I swear, I was feeling almost desperate . . . I so want this family to hold fast to each other, and recognize our strength is in our unity, and I am so afraid. . . ."

"You done all a human body kin, Miz Lizzybeff. Cain't mek nobuddy do what they don't want."

"But why can they not understand that their private disagreements are so petty when seen in the light of what may befall us soon?"

" 'Cause mos' folks don't see like you an' Mastah Waltah an' Mastah Drew see things. All dey sees is what's happenin' to them right now. Mos' folks in de worl' is like that. All dey be wantin' is dey creature comforts. Dey don't look out to see what's comin' 'roun' the corner."

Elizabeth took another deep breath. "I suppose so—but these are Mannings! We were raised to *know*, Pelagie!"

Pelagie's great dark eyes were sad. "Even the bes' don't allus learn what dey's taught, Miz Lizzybeff. My daddy was impo'tant man to my people, but when him an' another man got to warrin', I got took, an' sent on a ship. Now my daddy shoulda knowed somethin' like that would happen 'cause dat other man was knowed fer doin' things like stealin' li'l girls, but it happened."

Elizabeth blew her nose noisily. "What is it, Pelagie? Is the curse of mankind perpetual stupidity? Or selfishness, or blindness, that we must always fall prey to shortsightedness no matter how we strive to avoid it?"

Pelagie shook her head. "It be dem creature comforts. A humun bein' do almos' anythin' to git a li' relief from his miseries, an de snake he allus temp' us wiff de creature comforts. Gib a man a lovin' bed, an mek him think he a king, an' he be happy even as he walkin' 'roun' dat corner where de bad man's waitin' to chop his head off."

"Oh, dear God! We can't all be like that," Elizabeth groaned.

"Not all, but mos' is, an' nothin' you an' me kin do to change dat."

"Well, we can try. We can make them feel like kings and perhaps lead them away from that corner."

"We kin try," Pelagie agreed, but without much conviction.

The two of them turned in accord to enter the house, when Elizabeth touched her friend's arm. "Pelagie, I haven't forgotten that you wished to talk with me. We will find a time soon."

"Yes'm, I knows dat. It jes' be more o' what we talkin' 'bout. Foolish folks tryin' to fin' a way out o' their miseries."

All of the people in the parlor were crowding around Gwynne and Drew and the baby when Elizabeth reentered the room. She watched for a moment, then saw Nathaniel standing alone against the wall. She walked over to him, and without saying anything took his hand and led him to the dining room and a bowl of creamy French mints. "Don't tell your mama I let you have one before the others are allowed in here."

Nathaniel smiled and dug his hand into the bowl, trying to get a yellow one.

"Why were you standing all alone, Nathaniel?"

"Mrs. Townshend said I was to keep away from Rebecca. She told me to stand there, Nonnie. Wasn't I supposed to?"

"Well, I don't know. Where did you want to be? Did you like it there?"

"No. I want to be with Mary . . . she keeps getting knocked down, and I want to be with her."

"Good! Then you go take care of Mary, and if Mrs. Townshend says anything to you, you tell her Nonnie told you to stay with Mary, and she should talk to me." She leaned down and kissed the little boy on his cheek, then whispered, "You are quite the handsomest man here, my dear. Now, go forth and be your little sister's escort as well."

Elizabeth scanned the room, located Joanna, and moved toward her. "Joanna, I would like a word with you, please," she said.

"Of course, Elizabeth. It was a lovely ceremony. Of course, I prefer these things to be done in church, but this was very nice—quaint."

"Thank you, Joanna. I shall also thank you right now not to give orders to my great-grandson again. If you have a complaint with him, you may feel free to talk with me about it privately, but do not give him orders, and never again try to exclude him from the doings of his own family."

Joanna's face paled. "Cousin Elizabeth, I can't believe I am hearing you correctly."

"You are hearing correctly, Joanna."

"But surely, you don't actually consider that . . . that little . . . that child your great-grandson! Why he's—"

"My great-grandson!" Elizabeth snapped.

"Well, I suppose for appearance sake, you might—"

"Not for appearance sake, Joanna. He is my great-grandson! And a great favorite of mine. Do not deliberately misunderstand me again, Joanna. I have tolerated too much of your behavior toward that child already. I will stand for no more!"

Joanna remained silent for a moment, her lovely face marred by a frown, her mouth drawn in a hard line. "Courtesy does not permit to say what I feel, Cousin Elizabeth, nor do I have the advantage of advanced years to excuse my lapses, but rest assured Bert and I will be leaving here as quickly as we can ready ourselves."

"That is agreeable. However, as it would upset your parents, and your father is not a well man, I suggest you wait until the day after Christmas. Bert will be able to provide you with an acceptable excuse by then, I am sure. There must be some urgent matter he must attend to with all the agitating going on in Charles Town. I am informed that the meetings of the mechanics are still being called, and that their strength is growing."

Joanna laughed in an ugly way. "You certainly have given this some thought, haven't you? I always knew you didn't want me to marry Drew. You have always been my enemy."

"You are wrong on both counts, Joanna. This required virtually no thought at all, and I have never been your enemy. You are your own enemy, Joanna, and a formidable one at that," Elizabeth said, then added, "You'll excuse me, please. I wish to see Georgina. She seems to be quite overcome with happiness. I would choose to be with her."

That night after the evening meal the slaves and the guests of Willowtree joined the owners in a candlelit procession through the grounds. The whole population of Willowtree, nearly sixty strong, moved slowly across the lawn down toward the pond singing Christmas carols.

To Penny Webb, the children's nurse, and Nathaniel and Mary huddled beside her at the upstairs window, the long snaking line of flickering candles was an awesome sight. Nathaniel Dancer had been told the story of Christmas by his Nonnie, so he was certain that the sounds he heard this Christmas Eve were the sounds of a chorus of angels proclaiming the birth of the Son of God. He put his small hands on the glass of the window and pressed his face closer so that he might see more. The line of lights and the wavering sounds of song kept moving. Sometimes the sound seemed near at hand, and then it seemed to come from far away. The lights moved back toward the house, then went on to where he knew the slave quarters were. He wondered if that was where the Babe was, and if his Nonnie would take him there in the morning.

He was up at false dawn, unable to remain still in his bed. Still in his nightdress, he crept past Penny, sound asleep on her cot, and into the hall. He wasn't sure which room was his great grandmother's. With all the doors shut the rooms looked alike, but he closed his eyes and tried to remember how he walked when he was allowed to sit with Elizabeth in her sitting room.

He hesitated for a moment, then chose a door and opened it as quietly as he could. He tiptoed into the darkened room, his fingers to his lips, as if that would make him quieter. Unknowingly he let out a giggle of relief as he recognized the hazy, grayish forms in Elizabeth's sitting room. He was halfway across the room when a mound rose up off the chaise. "Who dat?" came a low, frightened voice.

"I want to see Nonnie," Nathaniel said in an equally frightened voice.

"Nathaniel? Dat you, chile? What you doin' heah? It ain't even daylight yet," Pelagie said. "You git on back to your bed, heah?"

"I want to see Nonnie," he repeated.

"Honey chile, you cain't wake Miz Lizzybeff up. She need her res'. You be a good li'l boy an' git on back to yo' bed."

"Please, Pelagie. I want to see Nonnie."

From in the other room came Elizabeth's voice. "Pelagie, what is going on? Who are you talking to?"

Pelagie hissed at the little boy and waggled her finger at him. She got up off the chaise, and went to Elizabeth's door. "It ain't nothin'. Mastah Nathaniel be wantin' his presents, an' he—"

"I don't want my presents," Nathaniel said indignantly. "I want to see Nonnie."

Elizabeth laughed sleepily. "Come here, my little man. What is it you want of me?"

Nathaniel bolted past Pelagie and ran to Elizabeth's bed. With a leap he was on the bed beside her. "I heard the angels singing last night—the ones you told me about—and I want you to take me to see Baby Jesus now. I watched and I know where they went. I saw them. They went to the quarters."

"Lord a' mercy," Pelagie breathed. "In de quahters! Whatever will dat chile come up wiff nex'?"

"There is a similarity, Pelagie."

"Ain't no such thing!" Pelagie said.

"Is a manger in a stable so far from a house in the quarters? Are there any newborns among the people?"

"I knows of one 'bout a week ol', but he mama jes' some ol' fiel' han'. You ain't thinkin' of goin' down there an' takin' this chile, is you, Miz Lizzybeff?"

Elizabeth laughed again. "Don't you want to give up your creature comforts for a walk to the quarters, Pelagie? After that talk you gave me yesterday, I think you would be ashamed to say you didn't want to join us."

"I ain't never tellin' you nothin' agin, an' that's a fac'!"

"Nathaniel, you go back to your room and dress, dear. You must give Pelagie and me a chance to dress as well; then we shall go together to see the child at the quarters."

Elizabeth dressed quickly and listened patiently to Pelagie's grumbling. "Dis be a sacrilege, dat's what. Dat chile gonna grow up thinkin' he see de Christ child in dese quahters!"

"Is that so wrong? Most of us grow up thinking we have never seen him."

"Well, we hasn't!"

"He said we would," Elizabeth said. "He said we would see him in the least of us. If Nathaniel thinks this is the Christ child, who are we to say he is not?"

"Mizz Lizzybeff, dis gonna come to no good! When your fambly hears you let Nathaniel think a li'l black baby be the Christ chile, dey gonna put tar an' fedders all over you!"

"Bosh and twiddle to my family! Are you ready? We must go downstairs and find suitable gifts for this child. We cannot go empty handed."

Pelagie was still grumbling, but she had tried her best, and Elizabeth was still determined, and Pelagie began to allow some of her deeply reserved enthusiasm surface. It pleased Pelagie that she would be part cf seeing this, but at the same time she was worried. She had told Elizabeth the truth when she said the family would be angry, and there was another reason. The only child she knew that was newborn was Seth's son. Seth was only a boy of sixteen, but he was proud and fierce, and he hated the white man. As the white man looked upon Seth as an inferior being, a kind of highly intelligent beast of burden, so did Seth look out upon his white captors as inferior beings given to prancing about in ridiculous clothing, wearing wigs upon their heads and ridiculous little pigtails for their limp hair. Seth was part of the problem Pelagie wanted to speak to Elizabeth about, but hadn't had the chance yet.

The three of them left the house just as the sun was rising. The morning bell was ringing in the quarters as they walked down the path. Elizabeth was smiling, breathing deeply. "It is a beautiful morning! I cannot remember a better Christmas morning. I thank you, Nathaniel."

The whitewashed house was about sixteen feet long and ten feet wide. It was raised off the ground and had a planked floor, for neither Elizabeth or Walter felt it was healthy for the slaves to live on earthen floors in the damp seasons. Elizabeth knocked on the door, and waited until a young woman came to the door, still in her shift. She glanced out sleepily, then as she realized who it was, her eyes grew wide, and she tried to cover herself. "Missy heah," she said in poor, broken English.

This house was inhabited by six slaves, all of whom had come from Africa in the last ten years. They stayed together, refusing to be separated, although John, Rob, and the overseer had complained it was not decent that unmarried men and women be housed together. The problem was finally solved to the men's satisfaction by decreeing two men married to two of the women in the house, and closing their eyes to whatever else might take place. The Africans did not understand the ceremony anyway, and had no idea they were married by the white man's law.

"We have come to see the child of this house," Elizabeth said. "May we come in?"

The woman stood dumbly, not understanding what was said to her. A man came to the door and took her by the shoulder and pulled her aside. "Come in, Missy. Chile ober heah."

"What is your name?" Elizabeth asked.

He looked at her for a time, as though confused, then said, "Dey calls me Sam. Dis be called Seth," he said, and pointed to a boy Elizabeth recognized. The women were designated as Annie, Bess, Lily, and Pansy, and for the first time Elizabeth was made to realize that these people, the ones she called her people, did not truly consider those to be their names. But she could not even pronounce the names they thought of as theirs.

Elizabeth Manning had always been comfortable on her plantation. There was not a nook or a hidey-hole she didn't know about or feel at home in, until today. Today she felt an alien. These people were all one, and she was the strange one. Yesterday, when she had been so quick to criticize the shortsightedness of her own family for their attention to petty personal quarrels, she had thought herself very wise; but today, this Christmas morning, she felt very humble and ignorant. "We have brought the child gifts. I hope you will like them," she said, and handed the woman she called Annie, but who was not Annie, a baby blanket and a silver spoon, and allowed Nathaniel to give her a beautifully decorated fruitcake for the house to enjoy.

Nathaniel walked over to the pallet where the baby lay. The child was naked. Nathaniel had seen babies before, and he knew to be gentle. He cooed at the child and put his finger in the palm of the infant's hand, so its tiny fingers wrapped around it. "I like him, Nonnie. He is beautiful."

"Yes, he is," Elizabeth said, but her attention was on the young man called Seth.

Seth had been moving restlessly about the cabin behind them, his eyes darting this way and that. He was filled with pent-up anger, and his looks were hostile and bold. Now he picked up the blanket, crushing it in his fists. At first Elizabeth wasn't sure if he were feeling the softness of it or smelling the fragrance of the talc it had been wrapped with; then with a flash of insight she realized he was exercising all the control he had not to tear the soft, lovely blanket to shreds. He threw the blanket to the ground, and then, as though he hadn't noticed it, walked across it and came to stand, arms crossed over his chest, by the baby.

"Dat my baby!" he said.

His words were so unclear, Nathaniel hadn't understood him. The boy smiled, then the smile faded as he saw the look in Seth's eyes. He backed away from the pallet and sought the safety of his Nonnie's hand.

"We wish you a blessed Christmas," Elizabeth said. "We will have Christmas dinner sent down from the house. God bless you all . . . and give you peace."

She turned to leave the cabin, knowing they had not understood the language of her words or wishes any more than she and Nathaniel had understood theirs.

6

With the holiday celebrations over, the various family groups began going to their own homes. Joanna and Bert Townshend had left the day after Christmas. Her parents, Ruth and William Templeton, and Meg had left on January second. John Manning wanted to get back to the more civilized comforts of his Charles Town house. Eugenia, and his daughter Bethany, missed the parties and balls. They went home on the sixth of January, 1774. Joseph, Georgina, Arthur, and Drew's family were the only ones left with Elizabeth.

"We will accompany you on the road as far as the Wateree branch," Drew said to his mother.

"I don't think your father would object if you and Gwynne visited at Manning for a time, Drew. Can't I persuade you?"

"No, Mama, not this time. We have not really had a chance to talk to each other with all Grandma's plans keeping us busy, but I can assure you, we would if I were at Manning, and that would undo all the good that has been done."

"You are that far apart in your views?" Georgina asked sadly.

"I am afraid we are, Mama. I wish it weren't so, but it is. Just know that I love you both, and always shall."

"Oh, Drew," Georgina sobbed. "How did this ever happen to us? We were once all so happy . . . how did it turn so wrong?"

Drew looked away from his mother. How often had he asked himself the same questions? He had been raised by Joseph Manning and had loved and admired him as only a son could. He believed he held to the same beliefs and values as his father, and yet somehow they had ended up enemies who were tied by blood and loved each other. How could that happen? Would he ever know the answer? Was there an answer? He said nothing to his mother, for he had nothing to say.

Georgina dried her eyes, took a deep breath, and smiled bravely at him. "Well, we shall all pray that we be given another time such as this one. Perhaps then . . ."

Drew leaned forward and clasped her to him.

He left his mother and went upstairs to help Gwynne prepare the children for the trip back to their own plantation, Cherokee, in the morning.

Gwynne looked up from the trunk she and Penny were loading with children's necessities and toys. "There you are! Cousin Elizabeth was just in here looking for you. She would like to talk to you before we leave."

"I wonder what she has up her sleeve now?" Drew said, smiling and bending to kiss his wife. "Do you know where she is?"

Elizabeth was in her sitting room. As Drew entered, she motioned for him to sit down. "I hope you don't mind my taking a bit of your time, Drew, but there are several matters I wish to talk with you about."

"The pleasure is mine, Grandma. You have rescued me from packing—a task that has never been a favorite of mine."

"Well, dear, I suppose I may as well begin with my own trespasses. I seem to always have at least one to confess, don't I?"

"You wouldn't be my favorite grandmother if you hadn't. What have you done this time?"

"I told Nathaniel the story of Christmas, and the night we had the candlelight procession, and the caroling, the child thought we were angels heralding the birth of the Child. He also saw the line of candles disappear in the direction of the quarters, and believed them to be the guiding stars—Nathaniel thought this time there were many instead of the one large Star of Bethlehem. He came to my room and awakened me before daylight, and asked that I take him to the quarters to see the Christ child. Pelagie told me there was indeed a newborn in the quarters, so Pelagie and Nathaniel and I made a dawn visit to the child in the quarters."

Drew began to nod his head. "Ahhh, a few remarks he has made are now clear. Gwynne and I thought he was talking about the babe in the crib set by the Christmas tree, but he actually did mean that he had seen a child."

"I must say he has been admirably quiet about our whole venture. I expected him to talk to everyone who would listen, and cause a whole big thing over my allowing the child to believe the Christ was a quarters baby. Can you imagine what Joanna would have made of that? As a matter of fact, I'm not sure anyone would have approved—not even you and Gwynne."

"Why did you do it?"

"I don't really know, Drew. Perhaps it was the time—at the break of dawn it seemed perfectly reasonable to me—even something of a spiritual experience. There was this angelic little Nathaniel asking me to take him to see the Christ. He was so sure. . . ."

"But that doesn't seem to be all he saw there. He has also asked me what is wrong with the man who guards the Child."

"Oh, yes. Seth. It is actually due to Seth that I have made my confession. You see, I wasn't certain how much Nathaniel understood. Seth barely speaks English, and that he does speak is hardly comprehensible. But he was very disturbed, and came to stand by the child's pallet. Nathaniel, I think, was frightened of him—at least he backed up and sought the refuge of my skirts and hand."

"He told me the guardian man was very unhappy. Again I assumed he was speaking of the plaster figures downstairs. You know what dour faces the artists always put on those statues."

"No, he meant Seth. He said he was unhappy?" Elizabeth mused. "I wonder that he didn't say angry. That is what I would have said." She sat silent for a long time, then looked up at Drew. "But I think the child is correct. Seth's anger is one born of sorrow, Drew."

"Isn't he one of the new bunch of slaves Leo bought a few months back?"

"Yes, but more than a few months. It has been nearly a year."

"Well, in any case, Seth apparently hasn't had time to adjust. It is very difficult until they have learned a few words. I think it is a mistake not to educate them. Seth may be a bit slow, but he'll come round, and when he can speak and understand a bit better, I think you'll find him more tractable. You might suggest to Uncle John, or Leo, that they work with him a bit."

"I shall do that, but, Drew, I have never felt before as I did that morning. I am afraid that, with the exception of Pelagie, Unity, and a few of the others, I have always looked upon the darkies as . . . human in a different way than we are human. But on Christmas morning, it was not them I found so strange, but myself. I was more than a little afraid, and it seemed that I could see myself as they must see me." Elizabeth fell silent again. "It was not an attractive sight, Drew. I was looking at that plump little brown infant, and thinking how soft his nappy hair was, and then I looked up and Seth was staring at me with those dark hostile eyes of his, and I saw that he was looking at my hair and thinking what flimsy limp stuff it was." She folded her hands, unfolded them, then stared at her grandson. "Drew, are they people just like us, only so different in custom and appearance that we do not recognize them?"

Drew said nothing. He had wondered the same thing many times, but had never been able to break through the tangle of language and custom, and the position of master to slave.

"Do you know what a horror we are committing if that be the truth, Drew?"

"I know, Grandma, but I have no answer."

"Pelagie is my best friend. She is no different from me . . . she is just as intelligent, perhaps more so. She laughs and cries and feels pain as I do. I've always thought of her as an exception, but is she? I think not."

"All right, Grandma, supposing you are right. What can be done about it? We cannot simply turn these people loose. They have no place to go . . . they know no trade, don't speak the language, and would be caught as runaways before they went a day's ride. Nor can we send them back to Africa. They would merely be caught again and sent back if they survived the trip across to begin with. There is no answer, Grandma. Those in Charles Town who have been trying for years to stop the trade are the ones who have the answer, but that will not work, either, for there are Englishmen and northerners who want to make their fortunes in the slave trade, and will bring them in whether we want them or not."

"Then, what will happen to them, Drew? What will happen to us?"

"I know you are not talking idly. What is it you have in mind?"

"I don't know exactly. . . . I mean I don't have this well thought out. But Pelagie wanted to talk to me about Folly. She is Unity's youngest daughter. It seems that Folly is enchanted with Seth, and Seth in his own tongue and a bit of broken English is preaching freedom. He speaks of their homeland, and the pride of the African. Folly is committed to him, and has joined her voice with his. Folly is but fourteen years old, but Pelagie and Unity say she is quite hostile toward us, and is doing her best to stir more of the darkies to anger."

"Grandma, no matter what you may believe are the injustices done to these . . . people, you can't allow an uprising to happen. That can accomplish nothing but bloodshed . . . for us and the darkies. Every plantation in the area would take action against their blacks, and there is no way of telling how many would die if Seth is allowed to form a band."

"I know that, Drew. This is why I am talking to you. I want your advice." She paused again, then said, "If it is possible, I would like to circumvent trouble in a manner honorable and just to Seth as well as us, and yet I also realize that we may not put the plantation or any of its people in jeopardy."

"Have you spoken to Leo or Cousin John about this? It is their decision rather than mine."

"I have. Both of them feel Seth should be isolated, disciplined—his rebellious spirit broken by whatever means necessary. And if that does not bring about the desired results, he should be sold." She rubbed her hand across her forehead. "Never before have we taken a whip to a slave on this plantation. I don't like the thought, and though John and Leo did not specifically say what they meant by discipline, I know."

Drew got up and walked to the window and looked out. He stood, his broad shoulders nearly filling the frame, his hands clasped behind his back. "There was a slave at Manning who may have been much like your Seth. His name was Topper, and it was he who made me question much as you are now. Topper was angry, proud, and mean. He was quite possibly the most able indigo man I had, but I could never get him to work consistently, and he was always what I would describe as mutinous."

"What did you do with him?"

"I didn't do anything. He was one of the crew—I kept on him, had him work at my side sometimes . . . but then I left, and I had accomplished nothing with him. Arthur had trouble with him. He got into several serious fights, and finally Arthur took the whip to him, and found it did no good. Topper was more belligerent than ever, so Arthur sold him. I heard he attacked a white man, escaped, and was later hanged. I don't know what should have been done with Topper. I don't know what to tell you about Seth."

"Would you think me a silly old woman if I suggested that Seth and a few select others be tutored—taught the language, and then a trade suitable to their own interests?"

"It is considered to be a dangerous course," Drew said mildly.

"That is no answer. Do you think it has merit?"

"It gives you no protection."

"Jehu says he can keep the slaves in line and maintain order no matter what Seth does."

"Then try it—for a time, anyway. Have Jehu select good men to keep an eye on Seth, and listen to what he tells the other darkies. If he continues his agitating, Grandma, carry your experiment no further, or you shall be endangering both whites and blacks on this plantation—and in the neighborhood."

"Then you do not think it an entirely foolish idea?"

"Not at all, but that is not to say I am convinced you will be successful. You must, above all, be cautious."

"I shall, Drew. I shall."

Drew smiled and took Elizabeth's hand. "So we are to conspire together again, Grandma, and this time to give words and knowledge and training to the child named for the prophet who brought forth the dream of mankind. A heady conspiracy."

"It may be, Drew, and yet it may be no more than the folly of an old impressionable woman and a young impressionable boy. But I believe your son understood something this Christmas Eve that the rest of us did not."

On January 23, 1774, the radicals succeeded in calling yet another public meeting at which the people set up an Executive Committee which was to enforce the nonimportation of tea. Often in the past, violence had been threatened if nonimportation were not observed, but matters had never gone beyond threats. This was no longer to be true. The mechanics, the planters, and some of the merchants' parties were beginning to feel their growing power, and some made misuse of it.

Elizabeth sent regular reports to Drew and Gwynne at Cherokee. Once the first letter had arrived, they could expect one almost weekly. The news was always a week or so old, but it kept Drew abreast of all the developments in Charles Town while he remained in the Upcountry preparing his crop for the coming season.

Elizabeth also gave him regular reports on her progress with the education of Seth and the welfare of the infant Isaiah. Drew was a little surprised to find that he was as eager for that news as he was for news of the political situation.

However, the letter that arrived on the first of March that year was not welcome, and its news was bad. He and Gwynne read the letter together and then sat back in silence.

Finally Gwynne said, "Cousin Elizabeth would not have written about this if Daddy were not very ill."

"You can pack just the necessities, and we can leave tomorrow morning, Gwynne. Ned can have everything else sent to you later."

"I'm not going," she said in a small voice. "They don't want you there, and I'm not going without you, Drew."

Drew took her hands, turning them over in his larger ones, marveling at the smooth whiteness of her skin, and her small well-formed fingers. How often had these hands touched him, soothed him, excited him? He kissed each hand in turn, then looked at her closely, observing the sadness and pain in her eyes. It wasn't right that she always had to choose between him and her family. "This is no time to worry about your family's feelings about me Gwynne. They have good cause for their ill will, but you are needed there, and you need to be there. Go to Riverlea, and be with your father now. As you said, Grandma would not be writing this sort of letter to us if William's illness were not serious. I want you to go—and I will stay in Charles Town and see to something I have been thinking about for a long time. I will be nearby, if you should need me, and I shall be busy."

She smiled, but shook her head. "I love you for being so understanding, but I am not going, and I know that you do not want or need to be in Charles Town at this time . . . and . . . and there are the children to consider."

"Nathaniel and perhaps Mary are old enough to go with you, and Penny is perfectly capable of taking care of Susan and Elizabeth. There is no need to worry. If it would make you feel better, I can take Penny, Susan, and Elizabeth to Charles Town with me."

Gwynne was silent for a long time before he realized she was crying.

He pulled her close to him. "My darling, what is it that is making you so sad? We can manage the problems—please go to see your father and don't worry about me or the children."

"Oh, Drew," she wailed, turning her face against his broad chest. "Why is everyone so hateful! I can't take Nathaniel with me. . . . I don't know what Joanna might say or do to him while we were there . . . you know how she feels about you, and about Nathaniel . . . she . . . she can be so cruel."

Drew kissed her and wiped the tears from her face, but they kept streaming down. "Hush, my love, this is not the time to think of Joanna. I'll take the children with me to Charles Town. Penny can manage—and Pelagie will help out. Perhaps we could bring that girl Hedy from Willowtree to help."

"But, Drew . . ."

He kissed her on the lips, stopping her words. Her lips were warm and slightly swollen from crying. The warmth and the softness of her stirred him, and his breathing became ragged. "Gwynne, promise me . . ." he began, then lost his concentration as his hands moved along the curve of her waist down across her hips.

"Take me upstairs, Drew," she murmured, her arms around his neck.

He moved reluctantly away from her, then stood up, deliberately looking away so that he could say what he wanted like a rational man. "Gwynne, I want you to leave for Riverlea tomorrow . . . and trust me to see to the children. Do I have your word? No backward glances, or regrets about how things should be rather than what they are?"

"Take me upstairs to our bedroom, Drew," she repeated; then after a pause she added, "I shall answer you there."

He picked her up from the sofa, marveling anew at the smallness of her. He often thought of her as a big woman, but it was only her heart that was big. He carried her up the stairs and into their bedroom. There was but a single light lit in the room, and it cast a mellow shadow across the walls and ceilings, making them both look larger than life. Her skin glowed golden in the candlelight as he opened the front of her bodice and savored each step of their undressing. He pulled her dress from her shoulders and ran his hands across the creamy smoothness of them.

Gwynne stood perfectly still, reveling in the feel of his touch. As long as she lived she'd never tire of the touch of Andrew Manning's hands on her body. Even though she had been with him for nearly three years, there was still a fire that burst into hot flame every time they came together. Her head was back, her eyes closed as he bent to kiss her breasts, his hand fastened tightly at her back, pulling her hips against his.

Drew let out a great shuddering breath, holding her tight against him, then he picked her up and took her to their bed, and laid her gently down. He watched as she undressed, and then stood up to remove his clothing. Naked, they stood looking at each other as though this were the first time they had ever seen one another, and then he moved a step toward her and she put her arms out to receive him. As one, they lay down on the bed, wrapped in each other's arms and desires.

Early the next morning Gwynne and Drew packed their necessities in three carpetbags—two for her, one for him—and prepared to leave for Charles Town. Worry over her father and excitement over Drew's plans warred within her.

"Why didn't you tell me sooner that you have been thinking of buying a house in town for us?" she asked, as she hurriedly went over the room searching for things she had neglected to pack.

"I haven't decided. I wanted to be certain before I said anything. And I haven't had the time to look for the right place. I don't want just any house."

"But now I shan't be able to help choose it," she complained good naturedly. "Cousin Elizabeth will be pleased . . . and perhaps we'll be able to spend the summers there."

Drew laughed. "You have it all backward, dear. If we spent any appreciable amount of time there, it would be the winter. Summer is fever time. You can certainly tell you are a country girl."

Gwynne laughed, too. "We all have our little failings. Daddy would never consent to buying a house in the city, so anytime I get to go there it is a treat. Fever season means little to me, I'm afraid."

"That's because you have never had it . . . nor have any of the children, or you wouldn't say that." He came and put his hands around her waist, looking at both of them in the mirror. "I keep you hidden out here too much. I shall have to remedy that."

"I happen to be very happy here. Cherokee is my home, and I can think of no place I'd rather be."

He kissed her lightly, but said nothing. He hadn't been aware of his first wife's needs for his time and attention and understanding, and he had lost Laurel both in mind and body. He would not allow that to happen to Gwynne. He smiled suddenly and released her. "Well, finish up here. I must talk with Ned and be sure he can manage the planting."

"And I must talk to Penny. Drew, are you sure she and the children will be safe following us next week? Are you sure we shouldn't wait until we can all leave together?"

"Ned will send a suitable and able escort with them. They will be safer than we are, I promise you. No more worries. Hurry and be ready to leave in an hour. We have a lot of traveling ahead of us."

Gwynne looked apprehensively at him. "I have never traveled so far by water before," she said.

Drew was already out the door as he answered her. "It will be much faster."

As Drew stepped out of the house, he noticed that there was still a chill in the morning air. He hurried to the shed near the slave quarters that served as Ned Hart's office. Cherokee had come a long way in just the few years since he had started it. He and Ned had been working almost alone in the first days, and now he was the owner of fifteen slaves and the employer of five part-time white laborers. Harley Boggs, Junior, a nine-year-old bundle of devious cunning, was one of those who were classified as white laborers. He had hired his very young brother-in-law out of guilt and a sense of duty to his wife's memory. Harley was one of the reasons he wanted to talk to Ned before he left. He opened the door and was greeted by the warmth and good smell of a wood fire in the stove.

Ned glanced up from his paper and smiled. "Coffee's hot an' strong, Drew. Pour yourself a cup and come set a minute whilst I finish this work sheet." He wrote laboriously for a minute or two longer, then sat back, taking a sip of hot coffee himself. "Thought I'd try a work schedule this season and see if we do better. Basil Robinson tells me he's got his people on a quota system an' it's workin' fine fer him. Thought we might give it a try. If it ain't no good, I can throw it away."

"Basil has a fondness for the whip that you and I don't, Ned. That may make a difference."

"Might, but I been thinkin' of an incentive system to take the place of the whip. I been meanin' to talk to you about it, but jes' haven't got aroun' to it. Mebbe we could chat a bit tonight."

"I'm here to tell you I've got to go to Charles Town. Gwynne's father is very ill, and if I'm any good at reading between the lines of Grandma's letter, they don't expect him to live. I'll be taking Gwynne to her parents. You're going to have to get along without me."

"That's a damned shame about ol' William," Ned said. "I ain't seen him in a dozen years, I 'spect, but he was a good man, as I remember. Not too handy in the field, but his heart was in the right place regardin' everythin' 'ceptin' you." Ned chuckled. "But then, he had a bit o' right on his side in that matter, too." He glanced up, his eyes filled with mischief as he checked to see how Drew would react to that. He saw no reaction, so went on. "Well, if you're worryin' that we can't manage without you, you can stop frettin' right now. The seedlings are doin' fine, an' if the weather ever makes up its mind to stay springlike we'll have them planted by the end o' the month or beginnin' o' April. We're goin' to do the sterilizin' in the sunniest fields today—accordin' to my task sheet."

"Isn't that a little early?" Drew asked, frowning. "We may not get the new plants in for two or three weeks yet."

"My bones, and the birds, and the plants, is tellin' me we're gonna have a good an' early spring once it makes up its damn mind. You let me tend to things. When've I ever failed you?"

"Never—and the worst that would happen is that we'd have to wait for some new seedlings."

Ned grunted. "You're a hard man, you are. You mark my words, we'll have the biggest, finest tobacco harvest this year you ever saw."

"Now, what's this incentive system you want to try out?" Drew asked.

"Well, I haven't thought it all out yet, but you know how damned careless those darkies are about their mealtime fires. They damn near set fire to the whole back section of the woods field and the woods last fall, so

I was thinkin' that if we gave each of them a patch of his own, they could clear that woods back from the field a bit, and start their own patches along the south border. They aren't so likely to burn up their own patches. Those boys aren't goin to risk their womenfolk givin' them what-for for ruinin' the family patch. What do you think?"

"How much land are you thinking of?" Drew asked.

"Start with a quarter acre apiece, an' allowin' them to git it up as high as an acre for themselves if they earn it. They can grow what they please and keep it for themselves. If they should have enough to sell, they can take it into Camden on a Sunday, or we'll buy it from them at a fair market price."

"Sounds all right to me, but I don't like the idea of their patches bordering on the tobacco field. Give up a strip in between. If anything is going to get damaged, you're right, it won't be their patches, and I don't want it to be the field."

Ned laughed. "You may have a point there. I'll do some thinkin' on how to protect us better. Anythin' else?"

"Just a word or two about Harley . . ."

Ned rubbed his hand across his forehead. "I don't, fer the life o' me, unnerstand why you keep messin' with those Boggses. That boy is the image of his good-fer-nuthin' daddy in mind an' body an' spirit. The little cuss ain't but nine years ol', an' he'd cause a fight in an empty store-room. He mixes up the tools, pesters the darkies til they cain't git a lick o' work done, an' he's the damndest, meanest little thing when it comes to the mules I ever did see. He plagues those poor animals day an' night lobbin' rocks at their legs."

"That's what I wanted to talk to you about. Try to find something for him to do where he's away from the bondsmen . . . maybe put him under Lena's eye. She'd box his ears for him if he doesn't work."

"Set the kid to the laundry?" Ned asked, and began to laugh. "Now, why in hell haven't we thought about that before? There ain't a meaner soul on Cherokee than Lena when she's got that ol' laundry tub a-steamin'. If anyone can handle little Harley, it's Lena. I'll do it first thing."

"As soon as he's old enough, I plan to apprentice him to someone in Charles Town—after that I'll feel my responsibility has ended."

"You never had no responsibility to begin with."

"Laurel always dreamed of her family being something. Ben proved it is possible, Ned. You can't find a better man than Ben Boggs. The least I can do is give Harley his chance . . . what he does with it is his business."

Ned shook his head. "Ben and Laurel were mavericks in that herd. The rest o' the Boggses is dirt, an' always will be dirt—'cept maybe that little Mandy. She puts me a little in mind o' Laurel, 'ceptin' she's a lot tougher. Got a lot more o' Mathilda in her."

Drew nodded, musing as he thought of Mandy; then he stood up and put his hand out for Ned to shake. "Well, I've got to be moving, Ned. I told Gwynne to hurry, and here I sit. We're taking the pettiauger—I want to get her there as fast as possible. We'll pick up horses, and maybe a carriage at the Trainers. I've given Penny instructions about sending the children after us. Make certain she has a good escort coming in—I want the children well guarded. I'll send the men back home as soon as they've had a day's rest."

"Godspeed, Drew," Ned said, giving his hand a long and warm clasp. "Give my sympathy to the Templetons . . . and my best to Mrs. Manning."

By the time Drew got Gwynne settled in the long plantation boat, the excitement had died out of Gwynne and she was subdued and quiet. She had never been away from the children before, and though she would never permit Drew to know she felt any differently about any of the children, it was her own baby Elizabeth she was going to miss most. The infant was less than six months old, and even though it had only been minutes before that Gwynne had held the child and kissed her good-bye, she was already missing her, looking ahead to the many days and perhaps weeks that would pass before she held the child again.

They rode in silence for nearly an hour before Drew said anything. "Are you going to tell me what is troubling you? Is it your father, or are you fretting about the children?"

Gwynne tried to look up at him, but the bright sun in her eyes, and the tears that were threatening, defeated her. "I don't know what it is, Drew— it's everything. I miss the children. I miss Elizabeth. She is too young to be without her mother. I am worried about Daddy. And I don't want to go to Riverlea without you. And I hate letting Joanna have her way like this. She has dictated that I may not see my own father on perhaps his deathbed unless I do so without the solace and comfort of my own family with me. You know this is all Joanna's doing! Mama would never do this, and neither would Daddy. It is all Joanna! My spoiled, vindictive sister . . . and no doubt she is relishing every moment of her newfound power!"

"That is quite a plateful you have given yourself, my love."

"But it is all there, Drew! I can't ignore it and pretend it isn't so. You won't be with me, and neither will the children. It isn't right!"

"I'm sure Grandma will accompany you. Whatever Joanna might wish to do, she won't go against Grandma."

Gwynne gave him a doubtful look. "I wouldn't even be too sure of that. From what Meg told me, Cousin Elizabeth put a bug in Joanna's ear at Christmas time, and my dear older sister has added that to her long, long list of grudges. It is no wonder Joanna thinks herself so busy, she has so many people to exact retribution from, it must take up her entire day."

Drew chuckled. "Do you realize you have made your cheeks red and your eyes nearly green with all that ire directed toward your sister?"

"To be honest I'd like to sink my teeth into her," Gwynne said viciously, then burst out laughing. "I was five years old when I last did that, and got a spanking for it, but I'd still like to do it. And believe me, childish as it is" —she giggled—"I'd get great satisfaction from it." The mirth left her eyes, and she looked at Drew. "You know, Drew, we are making light of this right now, and other times we avoid talking about it, but Joanna's attitude toward the children, especially toward Nathaniel, is very serious. We have always known that something might be said someday inadvertently, but Joanna will do all she can to make you miserable, and if she is able to use Nathaniel, she will do so without a thought to the child."

"I am hoping the fact of her own motherhood will temper her."

Gwynne looked bleakly at the water. "I once told you that you know little or nothing about women, Drew. You haven't improved. Joanna will never recognize the childhood of Nathaniel Dancer. He isn't and never will be a person to her. He is a weapon to use against you."

"She was quite civil to me this Christmas, and had been on other occasions. As other people forget what happened at our engagement, so shall she. What good would it do her to carry on a grudge for me? She doesn't care for me any more than I do for her."

Gwynne shook her head sadly. "She won't forget, Drew. I know my sister. Joanna has some sterling qualities, but she also has some terrible faults. You underestimate her—you always did."

"And you, my dearest one, have driven yourself into a blue, blue mood."

Gwynne mentally shrugged. Drew would never be aware of the potency of Joanna's hatred of him, and he would never understand how great a woman's power was if she chose to use it. She would have to keep a vigilant eye out for whatever it was Joanna would choose to do. She tore her gaze from the hypnotic movement of the water and looked at the tanned handsome face of her husband. In the world of men he was astute and canny, and he loved her very much. That was a great deal to have in anyone. She smiled at him, knowing that somehow she would see to the things that he would never comprehend or defend himself against. "I have," she said, and placed her hand on his. "I already miss the children, and truth to tell, I am afraid to return home. I don't want to see Daddy—ill—and perhaps dying. I don't want to think of it, and yet I can't help but think of it."

When they arrived at Charles Town, they went directly to Elizabeth's house, and found her packed and waiting anxiously for them.

"Gwynne, my dear," Elizabeth said after they were seated comfortably in the parlor and refreshments had been brought. "I had planned that we would spend a restful day here, and leave for Riverlea tomorrow morning, but I do think we must leave immediately. I have had messengers going between here and Riverlea two and three times a day for the past four days. Your father has had a series of strokes, and there is nothing the doctors can do for him. It is merely a matter of time. I am so sorry to have such terrible news to tell you, but you must know."

Gwynne put her face in her hands and sobbed. "Oh, Drew, I can't do this alone! I want you to be with me!"

Drew and his grandmother exchanged glances. Elizabeth shook her head, her eyes filled with knowledge and warning.

Drew put his arm around Gwynne and pulled her close to him. "I'll do whatever you want, my love. If you want me there, I shall go with you, but first I want you to consider what my presence would mean to your father."

"Daddy likes you! He wouldn't care!" she wailed.

"Your father has not been conscious for the last two days, Gwynne. I do not believe that is what Drew meant."

"No, I meant that my presence would cause tension among the other members of your family, and therefore affect your father. Joanna and your mother would—"

"Joanna! Joanna! It is always Joanna causing trouble. It has always been so!" Gwynne cried. "I hate her! I hate my sister! Why didn't she stay in England?"

Elizabeth got up and came to her young cousin. "Gwynne, please, dear, go upstairs for a while and lie down. Rest a bit and get hold of yourself, and then I am afraid we shall have to leave for Riverlea this afternoon."

Gwynne went to the bedroom suite she and Drew used whenever they visited Elizabeth. Pelagie came to her and gave her a hot tea of her own devising designed to calm her and allow her a short sleep. "Dis heah restoah you, Miss Gwynne. You shuts your eyes an' leab the worl' to Pelagie."

Gwynne opened her eyes and looked into the large dark face, and saw kindness and sorrow. "Pelagie, it is all so unfair . . . so horribly unfair. Why must it always be Joanna who has her way no matter how many it hurts?"

"Life don't very offen be fair. Don't seem like it care atall what comes to us. Looks like we got to see to that ourselfs. You sleep now an' get all your strength together. I be right heah 'side you."

Elizabeth waited until she was certain Gwynne was settled in her room, then motioned for Drew to follow her to her own suite of rooms. She closed the door behind them and indicated a seat for him. "I was not certain how much I should say to Gwynne, Drew. I thought it best to talk to you first; then you may tell her some or all of it—or I shall do it, if you prefer. Obviously she cannot travel now, but I believe we should make every effort to get to Riverlea this afternoon. William is not expected to live out the day."

"I gathered that just from the fact of your having been packed and ready to leave when we arrived."

"I have been packed and ready to leave for the last three days, my dear. I had no way of knowing exactly when you'd get here, and of course, I was hoping against good sense that it would have been sooner than it was."

"Why did you give me such a look when Gwynne said she wanted me to come with her? I am aware of Joanna's dictates, and Cousin Ruth's feelings, but under the circumstances—"

"No, my dear, you do not know how deep those feelings are right now," Elizabeth said, quickly interrupting him. "As soon as it was known how desperately ill William was, Joanna and Bert began to make inquiries about the will. That Bert Townshend is so anxious to get his hands on Riverlea, his palms are in a constant itch. But that is something else—the thing is that Mr. Kowler knows of no recent will. The last will he had knowledge of was one William wrote himself about six years ago."

"But—"

"Exactly! That will has named you the heir of Riverlea."

"Oh, my God," Drew breathed. "How did you hear of this? Surely Joanna would not have told you, of all people."

"Of course not! Joanna would choke to death before she'd breathe a word of it to me. Meg told me. Meg is a very unhappy young woman. After Gwynne ran off and married you, that left Meg as the dutiful youngest daughter destined to care for her aging parents, and as you know, Ruth and William both consider that their due. Now that this has come to light, Joanna is in a rage, and Meg is frightened to death. She is afraid you will put them all out on the street, and she came to me to ask if I thought you would forgive her and her mother."

"Lord! What a tangled mess this has all become. But, Grandma, if I went to Riverlea, couldn't I straighten this out? I don't want the plantation —even if I did, I would never take it away from Joanna. We all know William intended for her . . . and her husband to have it."

Elizabeth looked at him, her eyebrows raised. "Did he? There is a peculiar phrasing in that will, Drew. You are named, but Joanna is not. William has stated something to the effect that Riverlea shall be given to his son-in-law, Andrew Manning, and his wife, but the wife is not named. You see, that means Gwynne could as easily be the daughter named as could Joanna. You are his son-in-law, and Gwynne is his daughter."

"But he wrote it six years ago . . . he couldn't have known that Gwynne and I would marry."

"No. He could not have, but he did know after you and Joanna were not going to marry that Gwynne loved you. Perhaps William was not so much the old bumbler we all thought. We always assumed he was ignorant of what was going on with the plantation or his daughters, but one never knows. He had ample time to do something about that will and he did nothing."

Both of them were quiet for some time. Then Elizabeth went on, "This is a delicate time, Drew. Perhaps I am wrong, but I believe it is better if you are not directly involved. I ask you to remain here, and let Gwynne go to Riverlea alone with me. The will will be read, and it will be settled one way or another—either the daughter mentioned as your wife will be designated as Gwynne, as she is in fact, or it will be determined that William's intent was to name Joanna—or they may decide to have the entire thing heard in court. In any event, I think it is better if you leave it a battle within the immediate family. Even though I shall be at Riverlea, I intend to absent myself from the reading and keep out of the discussions."

Drew thought for a long time. He didn't know how he could best help Gwynne, and as he considered the situation, he wasn't at all sure what Gwynne would want to do in the circumstances, but he had a tight feeling in the pit of his stomach that Gwynne would take Riverlea from her sister if she could. Finally he looked at his grandmother. "What do you think of telling Gwynne everything you know?"

Elizabeth shrugged. "I have thought of little else, and am not decided. Had it not been for Meg's fright, I would have known nothing at all. I do not know what Joanna has done since, or if she has been able to do anything. I know she has been in Charles Town often these last ten days or so.

I believe that if there was any way at all to do so, Joanna has arranged to have the will interpreted as favorable to her. I believe that left to myself, I would tell Gwynne nothing about it, and allow the entire thing to unfold as it will. If Joanna has managed to manipulate the legalities, Gwynne shall never know that she might have inherited Riverlea, and if Joanna has failed, well, then . . . we shall see what happens."

Drew frowned, trying to imagine Gwynne's anger if she knew the will had been tampered with, and nodded. "I agree with you. Under normal circumstances you would have known nothing of this—and Meg may have been entirely mistaken in any case. There may be another will—or she may be in error about the wording of the old one. We'll say nothing."

"And you will remain here?" Elizabeth asked.

"I'll remain in Charles Town—on the condition that you will send for me at the slightest sign that Gwynne needs me."

Elizabeth took his hand. "You know you needn't ask that, Drew. I not only would call you at the slightest need, but I shall continue sending messengers between here and Riverlea twice daily. You shall be kept up to date on all that goes on there."

Drew smiled. "For many reasons, that will relieve both Gwynne and me. The children will be arriving sometime in the next four or five days, and she misses them already. By then she'll want news of them."

Elizabeth frowned and shook her head. "It is sinful! Joanna has become quite a little dictator. Of course, she has always had it in her—even as a young child she liked to boss her younger sisters around, and half the bondsmen's children were afraid of her. I am afraid your breaking the marriage contract was the last straw for Joanna. She is a cold, hard woman. God help her daughter. Rebecca is a pretty little thing—I can imagine what Joanna will make of her."

"This is becoming a weighty conversation, Grandma. Let's look on the brighter side of things. Should the will be so written and read, I shall do all I can to get Gwynne to agree to give it back to Joanna, or at least make some arrangement to satisfy her. And as to Rebecca, she has you and Meg and Gwynne to help her."

Elizabeth smiled and let him think she agreed with him. But she knew that what he said was just words, and knew that he knew it, too, but was not ready to face that. The rift that had begun when Drew and Joanna had not complied with the marriage contract made between Joseph Manning and William Templeton was about to widen, and it would never again be bridged. Never again would there be a Christmas season when the entire family would be together. Perhaps there would never be a time at all, not marriage nor funeral. Nothing. Elizabeth sighed and got up slowly, for once feeling the weight of her years and of all the events that had filled them.

"Drew, you had better awaken Gwynne. We must leave. There is little time left, I fear."

8

Elizabeth and Gwynne were both grim and quiet on the ride to Riverlea. Occasionally Elizabeth would reach across the seat and take her young cousin's hand and squeeze it reassuringly.

After a long time Gwynne smiled apologetically at Elizabeth. "I am sorry I am such poor company, Cousin Elizabeth. I don't believe I have ever made a trip home that I dreaded as I do this one. I do not want to part with my father. I do not want to see my sister. I don't want to be separated from my husband or my children, and all of these things are before me."

Elizabeth said nothing, but looked fixedly out the coach window, thinking. How strange, and ofttimes tragic, one seemingly small decision in a lifetime can be, she mused. Two men making a contract when their children were small children, thinking so little of it, thinking they were insuring the future for the benefit of all, and now twenty odd years later that same decision was tearing the fiber of the family apart.

As had become her custom, Elizabeth had sent a messenger ahead, announcing her and Gwynne's imminent arrival. The welcomer at the gate was not in his usual sleepy stance, so Elizabeth knew immediately that not only had her message been received and heeded, but most likely William was near death. There were few things that stirred the welcomer to alacrity.

At the sight of their carriage turning into the Riverlea gates, the man took off at a run, calling out news of their arrival to the house.

Jacob, William's man, was awaiting them at the front steps, but none of the Templeton women were about.

"Mastah bad off," Jacob said solemnly in response to Elizabeth's inquiry. "Mistress say I should take you direc'ly to his room. Ain't much time now."

Gwynne's face was paper white, and she looked anxiously at the Negroes who moved almost imperceptibly nearer to the house, their voices a low hum of mourning, their heads bowed. It felt like silence all around her, thick and heavy, but it was sound, low harmonized sound filling her mind and her heart. She moved to mount the steps, and had to reach out for Jacob's supporting arm as her knees were shaking too badly to trust.

She looked at the doorway, the entry hall, the curving main staircase, and tried to think of it as home, the home she had always loved and had grown up in, but it didn't welcome her. Afraid she would faint, Gwynne closed off all thought and stepped from one riser to the other, slowly and deliberately picturing Drew and each of the children in turn. She did not want to enter her father's room. She didn't want to see him die.

William Templeton lay in his bed motionless, his head held stiffly to one side. His face was ashen; gone was the ruddy look he had always had. Gwynne took her place beside her mother and next to her two sisters. She picked up her father's hand. It was dry and unyielding; the fingernails felt like pieces of wood, not at all her father's hand.

"They . . . the doctors say he can't last much longer," Meg explained, sobbing beside her. "I am so glad you got here in time, Gwynne. He asked for you before . . . before the last stroke."

Ruth kissed her daughter on the cheek. "Speak to him, Gwynne. He might hear you—one never knows. It will make him peaceful to know all his daughters are by his side—all his loved ones," she added, turning to include Elizabeth.

Gwynne leaned over and kissed her father's dry cheek. "I'm here, Daddy, I'm here . . . and I love you so much."

The women sat in the darkened room for the remainder of the evening, not talking, not moving, each of them with their eyes on the man lying unconscious in the bed. At dusk Jacob lit the candles, and the room jumped with long shadows and a golden glow. Near ten o'clock Elizabeth's head was nodding, her eyes closed, and the others were also battling sleep. It was too quiet, too warm, and too stuffy in the closed room. Occasionally one of them would get up and walk around the room, or go to William's bedside, touching his hand or face, then return to her seat.

At five o'clock the next morning the plantation bell rang, and the roosters began to crow, and the sounds of the animals could be heard in the close, airless bedroom. William Templeton opened his eyes and made a sharp convulsive movement, as though he were about to get up; then he fell back upon his pillows.

The women sat stunned and frightened, then one by one it came to them that he was dead. Meg wept loudly beside Gwynne. Joanna sat in stony, staring silence. Ruth slumped over in her chair, her shoulders shaking as she mourned the loss of her husband. Elizabeth folded her hands on her lap and prayed.

The doctor was sent for one last time, and then William's body was given over to the women to be prepared for burial. Dr. Reston gave Ruth laudanum and sent her to her bed. Meg, Gwynne, Joanna, and Elizabeth went downstairs for tea. "And then it is a long rest for you all, but especially you, Mrs. Manning. One of these days you are going to have to give in and recognize you are woman of admirable years."

Elizabeth did not cheer up at his words as she normally would; instead she said, "You need not remind me. I am feeling every moment of my life right now. It gives one no pleasure to outlive all one's loved ones, Doctor."

She drank her tea and left the others, going up to the room that had been prepared for her.

Joanna sighed. "We should all get some rest. As soon as it is known that Daddy has passed on, visitors will be coming, and we must be ready to greet them."

"Yes, of course," Meg said tensely, her eyes darting from Joanna to Gwynne. "You go on ahead, Joanna—I'll see that the tea tray is put away."

Joanna looked strangely at her sister. "Whatever are you babbling about, Meg? Flora or one of the other maids will see to the service. You must be very fatigued. You aren't thinking clearly."

Meg's eyes were large and staring. "I . . . I didn't mean that I would do it myself. . . . I meant that . . . that I wanted to give Flora instructions about sending tea up to Elizabeth a little later and . . . and I would . . . would see to her instructions, Joanna."

Joanna gave her another baleful look. "Do as you wish. You'll do it anyhow, I imagine." She looked then at Gwynne. "I suggest you get some rest while you may, too, Gwynne. You look very pale. I doubt you'll be well enough to see Daddy's friends and mourners as you are now."

"Yes, I'll go to my room now," she said, but before she could move, she felt Meg touching her side, just one quick thrust of her finger, and she settled back down. "I just want to collect my thoughts for a moment first, Joanna. I'll be right up."

As soon as Joanna had left the room, Gwynne turned to Meg. "What is wrong, Meggins? Even though I know you are grieved, I have never seen you as you are now."

Meg's face turned even paler. "I am so frightened, Gwynne. Do you hate me . . . and Mama?"

Gwynne blinked at her in bafflement, then took her cold hands. "How could you ever think that of me, Meg. I don't hate you or Mama. I love you both very much. What is wrong, Meg? Please tell me."

Meg looked apprehensively toward the door. "Do you think Joanna has truly gone up to her room? I didn't hear Bert . . . maybe she is in the sitting room, or—"

"If it worries you, we can take a walk outside. I'd like that, wouldn't you? We will both rest better."

"Yes, oh, yes." She jumped up from her chair and started to the door.

Meg was the middle sister in many ways. She was nearly three years younger than Joanna, and slightly more than a year older than Gwynne. She came between the two sisters in height, Gwynne being the smallest and Joanna the tallest. She had also, all her life, been the neutral ground in the battles that had raged between Joanna and Gwynne. Meg was quiet, rather shy, the most delicate of the girls, and longed only for peace. She hadn't Joanna's hardheaded and sometimes hardhearted determination, nor did she have Gwynne's courage or independence. She had wanted only a nice man to marry and a nice family to raise. It seemed she would get none of these, and once again she found herself caught between her two stronger sisters in a battle they would wage, but one that would affect her life.

Meg and Gwynne walked out onto the porch. Gwynne stopped, stretching, and breathing deeply. "It smells so good, and it feels so good to be outside in the air." She breathed and smiled. "Don't be so stiff, big sister. Come on, take a deep breath, and see if you don't feel better."

Meg started down the front steps, constantly glancing back at the door, her eyes scanning the candlelit windows. "Hurry, Gwynne, please! Don't say anything until we are well away from the house!"

Gwynne stood for a moment, not knowing what to make of Meg's behavior. She had never seen her sister like this. Surely her father's death had not affected her so strangely. She ran down the few steps and caught up with Meg. "We can talk now. No one will hear us."

"Joanna wouldn't like it if she knew I was talking with you," Meg whispered, and again looked back at the house.

Gwynne shrugged. "Meggins, you can't allow Joanna to rule you so. You don't have to do everything as Joanna likes. After all, she's not your keeper. . . ." Gwynne drew in her breath. "Oh, Meg! You can't be worried that Joanna won't allow you to live here after she inherits Riverlea."

"She won't!" Meg gasped. "She hasn't said anything directly yet, but she has made it very clear that she'd prefer Mama and me to live elsewhere— or, as she put it, travel extensively."

Gwynne stamped her foot. "What *has* come over Joanna! She gets worse every time I see her. I thought she had done her worst at Christmastime, but I see she has more depth than I gave her credit for. Well, you and Mama just stay where you are, and don't listen to her. She is not going to put you out, and as unpleasant as her tongue can be, it will do you no real harm."

Meg looked at Gwynne from the corner of her eye. "What would you do if you were in Joanna's place—supposing Riverlea was left to you. What would you do about Mama and me?"

Gwynne laughed. "Well, that is one thing we need not worry about. Riverlea is Joanna's . . . and Bert Townshend's. I really dislike the idea of Bert having this plantation. It doesn't even seem like home when I think of him as master of it."

"I feel the same way," Meg said, then went back to her original question. "You haven't answered me. What would you do about Mama and me if Riverlea were yours . . . and Drew's?"

"Nothing," Gwynne said lightly. "Your question is a silly one to begin with, Meg, but if it were so, what use would Drew and I have of Riverlea? We have Cherokee, and both of us love it in the Upcountry. Of course, I miss the city—and the Lowlands—but Drew is thinking of buying a house for us in or near Charles Town, so soon we'll have the best of both worlds. Perhaps we'll even see a bit more of you and Mama, if she gets over her dislike of Drew."

"You wouldn't put Mama and me out of Riverlea if it were yours? Even after all the terrible things we've said and done to you . . . and Drew?"

Gwynne stopped walking and took her sister by the shoulders. "Meg! You must stop this! You are very morbid, and all this is nonsense. Believe me, you will have a home here for as long as you want it. Believe me, Joanna would never dare put you and Mama out. Why, there wouldn't be a decent person in the neighborhood, or in Charles Town, who would have anything to do with her if she did that, and if there is anything you can count on, it is that Joanna will never mar her good standing with the people who count." She released Meg's arms, and with a little skip and a smile, she ran a few paces down the path. "Come on, Meggins! Cheer up! We have enough sorrow without looking for more."

Meg caught up with her, her demeanor a little less tense, but she walked for some time in silence, then said, "Riverlea will be yours, Gwynne."

"Hush! No more hypothetical talk. It is pointless. Let's go to the cemetery and say a prayer for Daddy at the shrine there."

Meg reached out and caught hold of her skirt. "I am not hypothesizing, Gwynne. I mean it. That is why I didn't want Joanna to know I was talking to you. It is all supposed to be a big secret from you."

Gwynne stopped again, a frown on her face. *"What* is a big secret, Meg? Stop beating around the bush and tell me what this is all about!"

"Daddy's will—he never changed it. Remember when you said you hated to think of Bert being master of Riverlea? Well, Daddy must have felt the same way. Of course, you wouldn't know, not having been here of late, but Daddy and Bert did not get along. Daddy wouldn't even socialize in the evenings with Bert and refused to have him help in the plantation office. So, when we knew there was little hope of Daddy recovering, Joanna went to see Mr. Kowler, saying that Daddy was unable to perform the plantation duties, and she needed the legal power to carry on for him."

"All right," Gwynne prodded. "And . . . ?"

"And he said he couldn't give it to her, that she was not the heir to Riverlea, and neither was Bert Townshend."

"But that's impossible! Daddy always made it clear that Riverlea would be left to Joanna because she was the eldest—unless, of course, she hadn't married."

"That's not exactly what Daddy said. He said Drew Manning."

"Yes, but . . ." Gwynne said, then didn't know what else to say. "Oh, poor Joanna! She must be—"

"Furious," Meg supplied. "She'd hang me from the live oak if she knew I told you about this, Gwynne. You won't say anything, will you, honey?"

"I won't say anything—I suppose it will all come out when the will is read."

"If it is read," Meg said cryptically, and gave her sister a sidelong glance. "Joanna will try to postpone or prevent it until she can do something about it." Meg laughed a bit, then grew serious again. "Now that you know all this, do you still think you'd bear no grudge to Mama and me for all the terrible things we've said about Drew . . . and how cold we've been to you?"

"Why were you, Meg?" Gwynne asked.

Meg shrugged. "I don't know exactly . . . you just ran off after the marriage contract was broken, and the next thing it seemed like you and

Drew were married—just like it had maybe been planned all along. I guess we all felt sorry for Joanna—then."

"It didn't happen overnight, you know," Gwynne said acidly. "I did not just run off and marry Drew. In case you've forgotten, Drew was married to Laurel and for a long time I was alone. I could have used a friendly word then. I was very lonely, Meg—and frightened. I didn't think I'd ever be married to Drew."

"That's why I asked you if you'd truly want us living at Riverlea if it were yours. We weren't kind to you, Gwynne. There is no reason why you should be kind to us now. We all thought Joanna was the one who'd have Riverlea, and should have our loyalty as well."

Gwynne let out a dry laugh. "Do you mean that if the will were as you thought, and Riverlea were going to Joanna, we would not be having this heartwarming talk, Meg? What am I to think? Your loyalty is mine as long as I control your home, and you'll be kind as long as it is advantageous to you?"

"Gwynne! That's an awful thing to say to your own sister!" Meg breathed.

"But is it true?"

"Of course not! I've always been fond of you, Gwynne—and Drew, too. After all, we all grew up together, but you've got to see I'm in a *very* dependent position now. What with Mama and Daddy needing one of us to see to them in their older years, I have to look out for myself. There won't be a Drew Manning or a Bert Townshend to be looking out for my interests. All I've got is whatever Daddy left me, and the goodwill of my family."

"Honestly, Meg! I've never heard such a caterwaulin' over nothing in my whole life," Gwynne said angrily. "You are just plain lazy and spend too much time feeling sorry for yourself. If you want to marry—go do it! Mama is not going to keep you in a box!"

"You don't understand my position at all, Gwynne," Meg said with some heat.

"I understand that you are allowing all this to happen to you. You are the one going around and telling half the county that you are going to spend your life seeing to your aging parents—not they, and now there's only Mama anyway. I'm sure she isn't going to want you hovering over her forever!"

"There's just no talking to you, is there? I'm sorry I told you Joanna's secret. Maybe I made a mistake—a bad mistake. Joanna never attacks my character the way you have."

"No, Joanna merely threatens to put you out on the road!" Gwynne said. Then she turned on her heel and marched back to the house with Meg hurrying after her.

"Gwynne! Gwynne, wait! I'm sorry. I didn't mean those awful things I said! Gwynne, forgive me."

"Oh, for heaven's sake, stop whining, Meg. You meant them—at least for tonight. Stand by what you say, and if you can't do that, then learn not to say things you don't mean! Good night. We'll talk tomorrow."

Drew was informed by messenger of William Templeton's death. He accepted the news with a mixture of deep sorrow and anger. He had lost a good friend in the man, and was barred from being with his wife. During the three days he waited for the children to arrive, and word from Gwynne or Elizabeth telling him he could come to Riverlea, he paid his personal, private respects to William Templeton's memory alone in St. Michael's Church and filled his waking hours with work. If he could not be at Gwynne's side, he could at least provide her with the home she wanted in Charles Town. He looked at every promising house and lot in the city. Because land was fairly inexpensive, and very plentiful, many of the artisans speculated in town lots, or sometimes tenements. Drew had quite a selection of lots to look at owned by men he knew among the Liberty Boys. He approached two men whose stores he patronized, Henry Timrod, the tailor, and Thomas Elfe, perhaps the best known and busiest cabinetmaker in town. Thomas Elfe made furniture for many people in Charles Town and was competent in the Hepplewhite, Adams, Sheraton, and Chippendale styles, as well as in a style he had developed on his own. Drew liked the man a great deal and trusted his judgment.

Drew told him of his wishes and asked advice.

"Advice," Elfe murmured. "That I got plenty of—a cheap commodity, when you're on the giving end." He winked at Drew, wiped his hands clean, and put away his tools and brushes. "It's been a long day, this day. What do you say we head on down to Dillon's have a long cold draft from the hands of sweet Polly, and then I'll show you a couple of pieces of land you might be interested in."

"That's the best offer I've had all day," Drew agreed.

"If you want my best piece of advice," Elfe said as they walked toward the tavern, "you'll invest in any city property you can lay hands on. I've got children like you, and every one of them is going to get a start from me, and I'll do it by means of property and these tenements I put up. A man just never knows when he won't be able to see to his family, and I'm making damned sure my Hannah will be taken care of."

"I don't spend enough time in Charles Town to make it worth my while, Tom. Maybe after Gwynne and I buy or build this house, I'll see it differently."

"A plantation's a fine thing—never be one to say it isn't—but the future is in the city, mark my words. You country folk get too isolated, especially those like you who are way the hell up in the hills. You ought to broaden your interests. You got too much money in human flesh. Those bondsmen are a burden, and they die off. Now, a good piece of land in a good port town—that goes on forever."

"I can't argue with that," Drew said, opening the door to the tavern and stepping aside for Tom to precede him.

They had a pleasant hour at Dillon's, then returned to get Drew's horse, and Thomas Elfe showed Drew several pieces of property, urging him incessantly to speculate in city property.

"I thank you for all your help, Tom. I'll be in touch with you as soon as my wife returns to Charles Town."

Penny Webb, the children, two wagons of trunks and baby supplies, and five men for escort arrived at Elizabeth's house the following afternoon. For once Drew saw Penny the worse for wear. She was bedraggled, and had Elizabeth in one arm and Susan in the other. "God bless us, Mr. Manning, I never thought to see you again!" Penny sighed.

Nathaniel stood at the edge of the coach, his arms out for his father to help him down. "Daddy! Daddy! I got to ride on the horse partway!" he squealed, then shifted his attention before Drew could say anything. "Where's Nonnie?"

Drew lifted him down, gave him a quick hug, and said, "You know Nonnie is with Mama at Riverlea. They'll both be home in a few days." Then he took Susan from Penny's arms. Mary burst into tears, having been left on the seat alone.

"It's been like this the whole way," Penny said. "They all have been crying for you and Mrs. Manning, and not a one of them wants to be left alone long enough for a body to take a deep breath. I've never been so fatigued in all my days, Mr. Manning."

"Well, we'll get them into the house, and everyone will get himself and herself in order. Come on now, Mary. I'll help you down, and then you can hold on to me, can't you? Aren't you the biggest girl of the whole family?" he asked the three-year-old, who looked up at him with startlingly blue eyes. Her hair was a fiery red aureole of curls around her face.

At the moment she was pouting, and Drew burst into laughter, which caused her to cry again. "Ah, Mary, my little Mary, how I've missed you. Come on, darlin', I want to get you inside, and I'll bet you'll find Nonnie has left you some cookies in her special jar."

"She fo'got," Mary pouted.

"Let's go see."

It took quite some time to get the two infants settled in cribs, and Mary and Nathaniel once more feeling secure and natural with their father. The children were rarely away from either of their parents, and had never before been away from both. Drew answered the same questions as to Gwynne's whereabouts innumerable times, and still neither Mary or Nathaniel was satisfied.

The day after the children arrived, Elizabeth's messenger arrived. "Mistress say I to wait fo' yo' answah, an' git right back to her, suh."

Drew read the note and went directly to the writing table. "Will leave for Riverlea in the morning. The children will come with me." He handed the man the note and pulled a coin from his pocket. "Go get yourself a cold drink. A few minutes won't hurt—just make certain it is a few minutes, though. If I get to Riverlea before you do, I'll skin you alive, hear?"

"Yes, suh. Thanky, suh," the man said, bowing and backing out the door, the note clutched in one hand, the coin in the other.

Drew returned to the sitting room and reread the note he had barely glanced at when the man had handed it to him. In one quick scan of the letter he had seen all he needed, and that was a request to come to Riverlea. Now he read it carefully and said aloud to himself, "The will won't be read until I have arrived? What the . . . ?"

"Bad news, Drew?" George asked as he came into the room and flopped down into a chair.

"I don't know—certainly peculiar. Grandma and Gwynne sent this message and say that Cousin William's will won't be read until I arrive."

"I wondered what all that smoke I saw on the horizon was," George said.

"What?"

"Joanna."

Drew laughed lightly. "Yes, I imagine Joanna is doing a bit of smoking. Before she left, Grandma said she had heard rumors that Cousin William's will had never been changed. If that is what this note is all about imagine you'll see a lot of smoke coming from over Riverlea way. No one will be happy about that."

"Not even you?"

"Not even me."

"You are a strange one, cousin. Not many men would turn their noses up at a plantation like Riverlea. I'll be glad to take your place."

"You're welcome to come with me. I'm taking the children. If we are going to upset Joanna's applecart, we might as well do it all the way."

"Dear God! Leave the little beasties here. Why would you burden yourself with such an entourage without necessity?"

"They just arrived yesterday, and all of them want to see their mother. I think it will be more peaceful to allow them to come with me, than to have to face them after another separation when we get back."

"You spoil every one of them," George said.

"I do indeed, and enjoy doing it," Drew said, and got up. "Now I have the thankless task of telling Penny that she must pack yet again, and get back into the carriage. She will not be happy. The trip down here nearly did her in."

"Penny?" George said mockingly. "Nothing could ever do Penny in."

Joanna Templeton Townshend was in high dudgeon. She moved through the house like a blast of March air, and most of the other occupants did what they could to stay out of her way. But that did not stop the quiet grumbling behind her back, coming mostly from Meg. "You would think she didn't care a bit for Daddy. All she can talk about is *her* property, and it doesn't look as if it is even hers!"

"It is mine!" Joanna said, appearing around the doorway. She marched up to stand in front of her two sisters and her mother, her hands on her hips. "Each of you knows in her heart that Daddy meant for me to have Riverlea! This plantation belongs to Bert and me, and we'll see that justice is served."

"Daddy . . ." Meg began, but Joanna cut across her words.

"While you're sitting here being so holy about honoring Daddy's memory, you might give some consideration to the dishonor you show by not serving his wishes. You and Mama are ready to sit here and see Riverlea handed over to Drew Manning, when you know perfectly well Daddy'd roll over in his grave if he knew."

"But there is no other will, Joanna," Ruth said, and blew her nose. She hadn't stopped weeping since William had been buried. "I can't imagine what William had in mind, but it seems he chose not to alter his last testament."

"Nonsense! And you know it," Joanna said sharply. "Either he has a will hidden away somewhere, or he was not competent to make the necessary changes. I shall ask that the reading be postponed until we can look into the matter. Mr. Kowler should arrive this afternoon or tomorrow. Bert and I will speak to him at that time. We'll see then what comes of this so-called will!"

Meg made a face behind Joanna's back as she breezed from the room.

"Well, I suppose this makes you happy, Gwynne," her mother said.

"No, Mama, it does not. But I don't see why Joanna is so upset about it —the will hasn't actually been read yet, and all this fuss is speculative. You know a bit about the will, Joanna does . . . everyone seems to have opinions, but has anyone actually seen the will?"

"William has spoken to me about it—the old will, I mean, and Mr. Kowler has indicated that the will was written over six years ago. What else could it be? And why else would he insist Drew be here for the reading?" Ruth's handkerchief went to her nose again, and great tears rolled down her cheeks. "Poor William. Poor Joanna. What will become of our whole family?"

Gwynne looked at her mother with a deep sadness. It was as though she did not even count as a family member. Why was it so terrible if she did inherit Riverlea? It was true she had married the man her sister had thought to marry, but Drew wouldn't have married Joanna even if Gwynne had done nothing. Just because Joanna had not had her way, did that mean that Gwynne had to remain unhappy, too, or lose her position in her family? She was exhausted from all the arguing and she was terribly lonely. Whatever the cause that brought him there, she could barely stand waiting for Drew to arrive. As she had so often that day, she got up and went to the windows, gazing wistfully down the plantation road.

"It won't be long now, dear," Elizabeth said reassuringly. "He'll waste no time in coming. I can tell from his note. When Drew writes in that clipped fashion, he is all business."

"I suppose he'll be angry with all of us," Ruth said. "There is already so much unpleasantness, and he will only bring more upon us."

"I rather doubt that is possible," Elizabeth said tartly. "You might make an effort to be hospitable, Ruth, and perhaps we need not all be talking behind each other's backs, and arguing face to face. Whatever William intended in his will, I am certain he would never have wished his family to be so contentious."

"I am always hospitable! Really, Elizabeth, I don't know what has come over you. You used to be much kinder."

"He's coming!" Gwynne cried from the window. "Cousin Elizabeth, I can see the coach. Oh! He's brought the babies! I can see Nathaniel hanging out the window! The little dickens." She lifted her skirts and ran from the room to greet her family.

Upstairs from her window Joanna looked down upon the arriving carriage. "He's here," she said to her husband in a monotone.

Bert, from his position on the bed, said lazily, "You knew he would come. There was no help for that, but it matters little. We'll talk to Kowler tomorrow and set it all straight."

Joanna looked uncertainly at him. "Supposing we can't, Bert. You don't know Andrew as I do. He is one of those who always end up having their own way. . . . He . . . he . . ." Her voice failed and she could say no more.

Bert patted the bed beside him. "Come lie beside me, and don't worry your head, love. Have I ever failed you? I told you it will be all right, and it shall."

Joanna moved to obey him, but said nothing. In his way Bert was a perfect husband for her. He enjoyed her entertaining and liked socializing with the important men and women of the neighborhood, but he did not like being burdened with her worries or her fears. He particularly did not like being reminded of Andrew Manning. The man's name came up entirely too often. The property rightfully belonged to him and Joanna, it had been as good as promised when he had married her, and that was the way it would be. Bert wanted to hear no more of it.

He stroked her breasts and hips, rolling over to kiss her. Joanna could not relax. "Bert," she whispered, and he sank back down on the bed.

"Bert, please . . . I am frightened. I don't think I could face being humiliated by Andrew again."

"For God's sake, woman, I don't want to hear about that damned fool! I am in bed with my wife. I want to undress you, and gaze upon you as no other man can. I do not want to be plagued with Manning!"

Joanna stared at him. He was a pleasant-looking man, but not handsome. His hazel eyes were too close set, his mouth a bit too thin, his nose a bit too long, but a nice-looking man nonetheless, and he asked so little of her. She loosened the fasteners around her skirt and helped him with the numerous small pearl buttons on her bodice. "I am sorry, my dear. It is just that I am frightened."

"And I shall make you forget that fright, my love. I shall make you forget."

Joanna lay back, and in a detached manner enjoyed her husband's efforts, but nothing was going to make her forget. She had learned too long ago, and too well, that trust was a risky virtue, and one usually regretted having it. Drew had broken her trust. Perhaps her father had. And Meg was already talking against her and trying to make it up with Gwynne because Riverlea might not be hers. She had no reason whatever to trust, and that was something she could not forget, even in moments when she wanted to.

Mr. Kowler arrived late in the afternoon, and William Templeton's last will and testament was read that evening in the front parlor of Riverlea plantation. Kowler had a deep, throaty voice, and he read slowly. He droned through a great deal of legal talk and finally got to the bequests. All of William's earthly goods were to be divided equally among his wife and three daughters, except Riverlea plantation. The plantation was bequeathed to Andrew Manning, and the daughter of William Templeton, his wife.

Joanna stood up and said, as calmly as she could. "I know that when my father wrote this will, he expected that I should be Mr. Manning's wife. As you know, that marriage never took place. I would like to request that this will be put aside so that a thorough search for a later will may be found, as I *know* one must exist."

Kowler gave her a smug smile. "I am afraid you are mistaken, Mrs. Townshend. The indication is that your father intended this will to stand. He has added a codicil, which unfortunately cannot be supported legally, but the date is one year ago."

Weak kneed, Joanna sat down and clutched at Bert's hand.

"Now, if I may be permitted to go on . . ." the lawyer said. He peered at each family member in turn over the rim of his spectacles. "In view of disappointments, and irregularities in family behavior and decisions made, I pass Riverlea Plantation to Andrew Manning for the span of his lifetime, and then to the first male child born in the Manning or Templeton family."

"Nathaniel!" Elizabeth burst out.

"No," came a strangled cry from Joanna. "He is not even a Manning! His name is Dancer . . . Nathaniel Dancer! You can't do this to me!" she cried, and Bert stood up and pulled her back into her seat.

"Hush, my dear, you are making a spectacle of yourself. . . . Do not humiliate yourself so."

"Please! You cannot do this! My father never intended it to be so. Mama! Tell them. Help me!"

Ruth spoke to the lawyer. "Are you certain this is the only existing testament, sir?"

"It is to my knowledge. Of course, it is possible that as Mrs. Townshend suggested, Mr. Templeton has hidden yet another will away, but he said

nothing to me about changing his will again after he added this codicil."
He turned then to Drew. "I doubt very much that any court would honor
this, as it contradicts the first part of the will. I tried my best to dissuade
him from adding it."

Drew sat in his seat, unmoving and silent. It was all true. All the rumors
his grandmother had heard and reported to him were true. And now he
would have to act upon William's wishes. If the old man had ever wanted
to punish Drew for running out on the marriage contract, he had certainly
succeeded with this piece of work. It mattered little what he said: Joanna
would hate him for his greed if he accepted Riverlea, and hate him for his
charity if he told her to remain here and leave things as they were. A
peacemaker William Templeton was not, and strangely enough he had
always seemed to be in life.

He said to Mr. Kowler, "Is that all? Is there any necessity for us to
remain here now?"

"No, sir, my duty has been performed. You do understand, of course,
that the Riverlea bondsmen are considered a part of the property?"

Drew nodded grimly, then took Gwynne's arm and walked from the
room.

Gwynne automatically turned to the staircase, but Drew pulled her
toward him and walked to the front door. "Shall we take some air? I'd
rather not see anyone just yet, and I do want to talk with you."

Gwynne nodded and walked with her head and shoulder against him.
"Drew, let's leave here as soon as we can. I want to go home."

"We'll have to say something to your sisters and your mother. And . . .
I'm at a loss, Gwynne. No matter what I do, I can't see a way of making
anyone comfortable with the situation."

"I don't care if you make Joanna comfortable or not. Did you hear what
she said about Nathaniel?"

"I heard."

"Why didn't you defend him?" she asked. "He is your son."

"I believe he is, but . . ."

"Oh, Drew, now she has made you unsure."

Drew took a deep breath and let it out slowly. "Joanna always reminds
me that Nathaniel's heritage will always be in question, and there is nothing I can do about it. To me he will always be my son, but to others he will
be Nathaniel Dancer and will always be questioned about his origins. If
only Laurel had come straight back to me when she was able, no one
would ever have known to doubt."

"Why didn't she?" Gwynne asked. She rarely asked anything about

Laurel, and did her best not to think of his first wife. Drew had given up so much to be with her; Gwynne imagined his love had to have been of heroic proportions, and the idea hurt her deeply. Though she knew he loved her, she could never forget that she had come second, and that Drew had married Laurel even after Gwynne had admitted her love for him.

He had answered her, and, lost in her own painful thoughts, she hadn't heard what he'd said, and now she was glad she didn't know. She supposed that with every couple there was one who loved more deeply than the other. With Laurel and Drew, apparently it had been Drew, and with her and Drew, it was she. Gwynne wasn't certain which thought gave her more pain. She hated thinking of Drew loving Laurel so much he was willing to give up everything for it, and then not having that deep trust returned fully, and yet she also ached that she might never know the kind of love that Laurel had had with him. Yes, she was glad she hadn't heard Drew's answer. She never wanted to know.

9

Penny Webb was not amused when Gwynne announced to her that the Manning family would be packing once more and leaving to return to Charles Town, although the packing and unpacking had reached comic proportions. She stood in the middle of the nursery, her hands full of infant clothing she had just taken out of one of the trunks. "But, Mrs. Manning, I haven't unpacked yet!"

Gwynne looked at her sympathetically. "I know this has been very hard on you, Penny, but please bear with us. Just this one last move and we will stay put for at least a week—I promise."

"We've only been here a day," Penny said wistfully.

"I know, Penny—but you will have the remainder of this day, and then tomorrow we'll leave. I'll send someone up to help you."

"No, thank you, ma'am. I can pack our children's belongings myself. I don't suppose it's my place to speak out, but I don't fancy having Mrs. Townshend's girl tell me all about Miss Rebecca, and how she's of real quality, while we're raggle-taggle white trash with quality clothes."

Gwynne produced a frown but barely stifled a giggle. "Did she truly say such a thing?"

"That and more. I guess I don't really mind packing up to leave here, but maybe next time Mr. Manning will just leave us behind. He never does stay here longer than it takes a ball to bounce off a wall."

"I believe Mr. Manning brought you all down here for my benefit. He knew how much I wanted to see the children, Penny."

"Yes, ma'am."

Gwynne went to her own sitting room and told Drew of her chat with

Penny, and the comment made to her about quality. "Can you imagine, Drew? I think Joanna has finally managed to outdo herself."

Drew sat back and watched his wife. There was still a great deal of little-girl rivalry that thrived between the two sisters, but he didn't think this was the time to give it expression and said, "Gwynne, I would like you to ask your mother and sisters to meet with us in the morning. We are going to have to tell them what we plan to do about Riverlea, and as much as I hate to spoil your enjoyment of Joanna's discomfort, this is no joking matter."

"Oh, Drew, don't be so serious. Joanna is sputtering around like an overheated teakettle. Why shouldn't I enjoy it when she has been thwarted? I didn't do anything to her—none of us did. If she has anyone to blame it would be Daddy."

"Listen to me for a moment, and allow me to give you my view of the future, then see what you have to say—and I shall listen carefully, as you know Joanna far better than I. But what I see is that if we allow Joanna to continue to live here, she is going to be resentful, and increase her criticism of you and me, and particularly of Nathaniel. After all, now it is to her advantage to have people think he is not my son. Providing she has a son, then once more she would have Riverlea, if Nathaniel is discredited. If we choose not to allow her to stay, not only will she have rather good grounds to complain of us, but that will also feed her fury regarding Nathaniel, and added to that, it would put your mother and Meg in a very awkward position. They would live here with Joanna more or less singled out and exiled, while she was the one everyone thought of as the heir to the plantation."

"Good heavens—when you spell it out like that, it is a sticky-pie, and not very funny. Daddy didn't do us much of a favor, did he? Could we just sell it and divide the profit from it equally?"

Drew shook his head. "At least not until that codicil has been declared invalid."

"Oh, yes, in a way this actually belongs to Nathaniel, doesn't it?"

"Perhaps."

"Why would Daddy ever have done such a thing? Surely he knew it would be an awful confusion." Gwynne shook her head in perplexity. "I don't understand—it's almost as if he didn't really give it to anyone."

Drew laughed dryly. "Perhaps there is your answer. All I ever heard William say was that he wanted Riverlea to remain in the family, and that he wanted a responsible man to run it. He seems to have accomplished his ends."

"But you won't be running Riverlea—will you?"

"No, but on the other hand, I won't see it mismanaged." Drew got up and walked to the windows that overlooked the back of the house and the road to the fields. "I couldn't bear to see this plantation go to ruin."

Gwynne just stared at his back. "And Daddy would know that. . . . Oh, Drew, what an old fox he was. And he knows Nathaniel . . . and at Christmas, once when we were talking alone, I confessed to him that I, too, wanted to give you a son."

"Well, well," Drew mused. "I don't think I ever gave your father full credit, either, but that does not ease our current dilemma, and that is what to tell your family."

"You have something in mind, or you would not be talking about it at all. What do you want to tell them?"

He walked quickly to Gwynne, took her hands, and moved to the sofa with her. "I'd like to tell Joanna and Bert that I think they have a perfect right to search for a newer will, and that I will accept it if it is found. In the meantime I think they should remain here and go on with life as it has always been for them."

Gwynne nodded, then said, "I agree, but, Drew, Joanna is capable of making up a will to suit herself and saying it was Daddy's, you know. You said I know my sister better than you, and that is true. I am not being catty when I say Joanna could do that."

"Would you rather we tell her and Bert to leave?"

"No. I agree with your decision, but I do want you to be aware that it may mean Riverlea is lost to us—and to Nathaniel."

"How much would that mean to you if it were? It has been your home, Gwynne. You grew up here."

"I think I would scratch Joanna's eyes out if she tried it," she said quickly, "but I still think we should do as you suggested."

The following morning Drew, Gwynne, Ruth Templeton, Meg, and Joanna and Bertrand Townshend gathered in the study that had been William's plantation office. With a good deal of pleasure Drew seated himself in William's oversized chair behind his well-used desk, and looked across at the Templeton women, and a petulant Bert Townshend. Briefly he told them of the decision he and Gwynne had made the night before, then asked if anyone disagreed, had questions or comments.

"Who will own the rice crop?" Bert asked. "Are you expecting us to do your labors and give you the proceeds?"

Drew's brown eyes hardened. He did not like this man and found it difficult to remain civil. "I'll expect a portion of it."

Bert gave Joanna a knowing glance, his hand going up to stroke his small, well-trimmed mustache. "And the darkies? They are your property, of course, but who shall make the decisions as to their handling? I have heard you have some very strange ideas regarding your bondsmen."

"I have some strange ideas regarding many men, Bert. What exactly is it you have in mind?"

"I mean the control of them!" the man spat out with a look of disgust. "Cousin Elizabeth is trying to educate them, for God's sake, and I've been told that is under your direction. I've also heard from Leo that you do not believe in the whip. I won't have my family living under the constant threat of insurrection among those savages. If I am to live here, then I want authority to maintain order in any manner I see fit. Have I got it?"

Drew sat for a moment, his hands folded. "Let's say you have it to a point, and that point is that if you damage one of my bondsmen—woman or child—you are responsible for that damage and I'll expect full restitution. That agreement shall be in writing, and the amount of that restitution shall be determined by me. You will match the sale price at which I would have been able to sell the slave before damage."

"That is nonsense! You could get any friend of yours to make a purchase offer for the slave at a ridiculous figure, and call that a market price."

"True."

"This is unheard of!"

"That is the bargain. You can accept it or lay down your whip," Drew said, and smiled. "Let me know your decision. Of course, there is one alternative. I could take all the Riverlea people and use them at Willowtree and Cherokee, in which case you would be free to buy and use your own people."

"Have you any idea of the cost of that?" Bert sputtered. "This place requires people working it immediately . . . we would have to purchase at least thirty blacks immediately—a fortune!"

"It would be," Drew agreed.

"Then you leave me no choice," he said.

"I have tried not to. You were absolutely correct in stating that I have some peculiar ideas regarding the bondsmen. One of them is that a cowed, resentful, whipped man is not a good worker. I prefer my people to be intelligent, content, occupied with their own interests as well as mine, and if at all possible willing workers."

"No darkie is a willing worker. It is in their natures to be lazy. You cannot change nature."

"Perhaps it is in their natures; perhaps it is in their condition. Whichever it is, we can do our best, and that is another peculiar notion of mine. Ruth, do you or Meg have anything you wish to say?"

Ruth put her head down, staring at the floor. "I believe you have been far more generous than any of us would have been, Drew. I also believe I owe you and my daughter an apology that is woefully weak in the face of the wrath we have all spent on you."

"Mama, there is no need to grovel," Joanna said. "Even Drew recognizes that this is a gross miscarriage of Daddy's wishes. Hasn't he said himself that Bert and I can and should try to disprove this will?"

"That is not what Drew said, Joanna," Gwynne said hotly. "He said you could search for another will. But one doesn't exist. This is Daddy's only will and testament, and I think he accomplished exactly what he wanted with it."

"I can't be surprised that you'd say that. You've lost sight of who you are, Gwynne. Everyone knows that. But we all know that Daddy would never put this plantation in the hands of a rebel—a traitor to his king and country—and that is what Drew Manning is!"

"Maybe Daddy was a rebel," Meg said meekly.

Joanna laughed. "Well, it hasn't taken much to make you all show your true colors, has it? A nice little speech, a roof over your heads, and you'll say anything to please the man with the keys. Come, Bert, I can't abide this any longer," she said, and marched from the room.

Drew looked at the others, his eyebrows raised; then he smiled, a brilliant flashing smile that made his eyes dance. "I think we have everything of importance settled, ladies. Ruth, you must get in touch with me if you should ever need anything, or if there is a problem of any kind."

"I am so very ashamed, Drew. I didn't want Joanna to hear me say it, for I love her a great deal, and she has been hurt, but I, too, believe William has accomplished what he wanted with his will. He hated what you did to Joanna, but he always said no one would ever take better care of Riverlea than you."

"I thank you for telling me that, Ruth. I have always been sorry I disappointed William."

They arrived back in Charles Town on March 23, 1774. As soon as they got to Elizabeth's house, Drew sent a messenger to Cherokee, with instructions that Ned was to give him a full report of the progress, and to tell him whether he was needed.

When Gwynne gave him a concerned look, and Penny looked at him in naked horror at the thought of packing the children for yet another trip, he laughed. "There is no need for either of you to worry. If I am needed back at Cherokee, you shall stay here."

Penny stopped holding her breath, and Gwynne smiled and said, "How long may we stay?"

Drew put one arm around his grandmother and the other around his wife. "Long enough for you two to shop for new clothes. Long enough for you to inspect three houses that might be suitable, and long enough for you to look at some lots if we decide to build our house to our own specifications."

"Drew! You didn't say a word about that at Riverlea. Why didn't you tell me? This is wonderful! When can we see them?"

"How marvelous it will be to have you living here part of the year," Elizabeth said, smiling as two other of her grandsons entered the room. "Leo, George, have you heard that Drew and Gwynne will be buying or building a house in the city?"

George bowed and smiled. "I not only have heard, Grandma, but I have had my hand in from the start. I have given my excellent advice as to which of many properties he should consider."

Leo was more subdued. He stood at the entry, his arms crossed over his chest. "You will be nearer to your liberal friends now, Drew—not that you need much more contact with them than you already have. I don't know if George told you or not, but there are several messages for you—mostly from mechanics—Liberty Boys."

"No, I hadn't been told. Thank you, Leo."

"How soon will you be coming here?"

"That depends. If we build, I don't imagine it will be much before autumn. Certainly by then. Gwynne will have a much easier time finding a tutor for Nathaniel here than she will in the Upcountry."

Elizabeth bit her lower lip and shook her head. "My, my, where does the time go? Imagine little Nathaniel already needing a tutor."

"Drew rushes everything," Gwynne said with a smile. "He was trying to convince me not too long ago that Nathaniel was old enough to ride the Cherokee fields with Drew."

Elizabeth laughed. "That may be rushing the child a bit, but I do think it is time he began his education. He is a very able little boy. May I have a hand in selecting his tutor with you, Gwynne? I do think the right teacher is so important."

"I would welcome the guidance—and I am sure you would do much better than I at asking the pertinent questions in an interview, and judging the character. There are qualities I think we must look for above all—"

"My dear," Drew interrupted, "I am going to leave you to your ponderings over Nathaniel's future and visit Dillon's for a time. You will excuse all of us useless men?"

During the next few days Gwynne and Elizabeth and Drew went around the city looking at the houses he had selected as suitable. None of them pleased Gwynne. The one she deemed the right size was too dark, the windows somehow allowing too little light in. "And I'm certain it would be unbearably hot in the warmer weather," she said.

The other two she declared too small. They went a little farther out of the main part of the city and looked at land. "Drew, I don't know anything about selecting land. You'll have to do that."

"We're not farming, Gwynne. All you need to do is select a place you like, and think will be beneficial to the children."

"Then I like the one we saw a few places back—the one with the stream and the hill. We could build the house on the hill overlooking the stream . . . there was plenty of space for a nice stable and a garden."

Drew put the heel of his hand to his head. "Why didn't you say something?"

"Because I know how you hate to plant on a hill when it can be avoided," she said apologetically.

"Oh! My thoughtful wife. Grandma, what am I to do with her?"

"Hush! You love everything she does. Buy her her land, and build her a fine house."

"Yes, ma'am!" Drew said, and saluted. "Well, Mrs. Manning, by this time tomorrow you should be on your way to being a property owner in Charles Town, South Carolina. How do you feel?"

Gwynne smiled, then twirled around, returning to Drew's arms. "I feel wonderful!" As his arms closed around her, Gwynne stiffened, glanced over at Elizabeth, then looked carefully at her husband. "What is it you are not saying? You have made me happy and have assured that I shall be busy and occupied for some time to come, so tell me what you are about?"

Drew laughed. "You think you know me that well?"

"I do indeed! And so does Cousin Elizabeth. When are you leaving and where are you going?" she asked with a kiss placed lightly on his cheek.

Drew turned and gave Elizabeth a look of helpless resignation. "She thinks she is a wizard . . . like you. I guess the only thing to do is make a clean breast of it. Now that I have the two of you happy and guaranteed busy, I am going first to Riverlea to relieve Joanna and Bert of three of their bondsmen, and then shall either send Amos with them to Cherokee, or if Riverlea cannot spare Amos, then I shall take them myself. Ned wrote in his last report that we are behind with the tobacco at Cherokee, and that he needs help. Three extra men should take care of his needs."

"How long will that take?" Gwynne asked, wide eyed.

Elizabeth stepped nearer and put her hand reassuringly on Gwynne's arm. How well she knew the feelings she was reading in Gwynne's eyes. When she had been young and so in love with her husband she could barely stand the normal separations of a day, it always seemed that more important and lengthy business took him from her just when she needed him most. So many thoughts of Gwynne's sorrow over her father's death, the division between her and her sister, the uncertainties of raising so many children, all flashed through her mind and she said gently, "Gwynne, my dear, don't worry yourself or Drew. He will be back as soon as possible, and you and I have much to keep us occupied. I was hoping that you and the children would come to Willowtree for the summer."

Gwynne swung dizzily from Drew to Elizabeth and back to Drew. "But . . . oh, Drew!"

He put his arm around her and led her back toward the carriage. "This is neither the time nor the place to worry ourselves."

"But I don't want you to leave me right now, Drew. I can't do all of this by myself."

"You won't be by yourself, dear," Elizabeth said kindly. "Drew will have a good architect working with you, and I am quite certain George will be more than delighted to act as our escort and aide. George has become quite an accomplished man."

Gwynne was just barely reassured during the next few days, but she fought no more. She knew Drew had to take care of the plantation, and need him or not, she was going to have to do without him. All that was left was for her to convince herself that she could handle the family in Charles Town with its attendant responsibilities while Drew tended to the two plantations.

When she said good-bye to him there were no tears in her eyes, and she managed a pretty smile. All of the children were dressed and ready to say good-bye to their father. After the family breakfast Drew kissed them all, held Gwynne for a long moment, then hurried to the stables without looking back, for he didn't want to leave her any more than she wanted him to go.

10

By the end of April Drew was beginning to feel the bone-jarring weariness he had felt the year he had ridden with the Regulators when they cleared the outlaw bands from the Upcountry. He slept on the trail most of the time, occasionally stopping in at a neighbor's plantation, and went back and forth between Cherokee, Riverlea, and Charles Town.

In little more than a month Gwynne, Elizabeth, his Manning cousins, and his children would all be at Willowtree, and he wanted to be with them.

Gwynne was faring little better than her husband. She went to bed at night exhausted, and awakened in the morning barely refreshed. The children, particularly Nathaniel and Mary, missed their father and wasted no opportunity to tell her so. His absence was always brought to the fore of her mind—not that she didn't miss him enough without reminders. Little Elizabeth, who was rapidly becoming "Sissy," a name Gwynne did not like, had not even recognized Drew the last time he had stopped in Charles Town. He had arrived for a brief visit and several meetings with the Liberty Boys, and then was off again to Cherokee because the tobacco plants had developed leaf spot. It was a malady which sounded not the least dire to Gwynne, but it sent Drew off at a run.

The young Manning family managed no appreciable time together until August of that year. In June, Drew returned to Charles Town to attend meetings designed to discuss and propose action regarding the Boston Port Act, the Intolerable Acts, and the Quebec Act that Parliament had passed.

Drew sat quietly talking with Thomas Elfe, William Hall, James Henderson, and some other men as they awaited latecomers. Though all were cheerful, and for the most part optimistic, none of them was taking the latest English action lightly. For a time there had been an element of bravado and daring to the actions of the radicals, but those years and months had passed, and there was little that could be taken lightly now.

"As far as I can read the times," Henderson said, "the biggest danger to any of the colonies is that one of us be caught in an action against Mother England alone. If we are to act, it must be as a unified group, not singly."

"These latest damned acts of Parliament are aimed at the people of Massachusetts. They always have been considered the real fomenters of trouble. Still, the strength of our protest has not been recognized. England is still hunting for a bogeyman in Massachusetts and a malcontent here or there in the rest of the colonies. Whatever we say, we still have not been taken seriously by England. I agree with James. If we are ever to be heard, we must all—all the colonies together—raise our voices, take action, and hold to it as one nation," William Hall said.

Elfe added, "Whatever we do, we'd better make up our minds soon. With Boston Port being closed, it is likely they will try to do anything they damned well please. Never mind if the Bostonians are fomentors of trouble or not. What is to prevent the British warships from closing Charles Town if we provoke His Majesty's disfavor?" He paused for a moment in thought, then went on, "It isn't just a matter of a port closing, men. The whole administration of justice in Massachusetts colony was reorganized. We've had our own problems with justice down here. None of us is immune from the meddling finger of old Mother England."

The men talked on for some time, with Drew doing more listening than talking. Those few times he did say something, it was most often to urge caution and a unified plan of action.

With others entering the room, the group broke up and each of the men joined other newcomers. The meeting was brief, for the subject matter was clear, and few men there failed to recognize that the time for action was at hand, and that it was essential for all of them that no one of the colonies should fail or betray its sister colonies by faintheartedness. It was decided that a meeting should be held on July 6, 1774, "to consider . . . such steps as are necessary to be pursued, in union with all the inhabitants of our Sister Colonies, on the Continent . . . in order to avert the dangers impending . . . and because of the late hostile acts of Parliament against Boston. . . ."

Murmurs of approval were heard as the resolution was read back to them. Caution was the word, and it was reflected in the quiet talk after the meeting. In earlier times the talk had been filled with boasts and urgings to greater action, but now all recognized that talk would give way to action. Slowly and ponderously, but nonetheless inexorably, England was moving against her colonies, pressuring them to behave as she wished, squeezing them with her might to comply to her trade wishes. Now all of the brave talk was so much wind, and either the colonies would forge a concerted, unified plan of action, or they would have to knuckle under and relinquish all their fine words of freedom and equality under law and citizen rights.

Because the July meeting was so near at hand, Drew remained in Charles Town and stayed at his grandmother's house. Though Elizabeth was not in residence, being with Gwynne and the children at Cherokee, Drew enjoyed the hospitality of his Uncle John and Aunt Eugenia.

The big dining-room table at the Mannings' was, as usual, lavishly set with china, candelabras gleaming with dozens of lit tapers, crystal goblets reflecting light, and the conversation was lively and occasionally heated.

Leo and Eloise Manning sat together and often talked with one another rather than the group as a whole, as if they were still newlyweds. The other reason Leo remained distant from the usual political wrangling was that he swayed with every political breeze. He had once been adamantly on the side of the radicals, then about two years ago had been just as adamantly Tory, and now he simply didn't know.

Rob Manning, just back from his education in London, and also newly married, had no such qualms. He was a Tory, both by conviction and because of a resentment of his cousin Drew which had developed over the years. Neither was he so tied to his new wife Velma as Leo was to Eloise. He leaned forward, his elbows planted ungracefully on the table. "If you were as all-fired interested in the welfare of South Carolina as you profess, Drew, you would stop all your agitating and beg people to give up this treason before there is no turning back. England is not a country to underestimate—believe me, I know whereof I speak. Their navy is beyond the ordinary man's imagination. Should she wish to, England could break the back of our trade in a matter of months and barely inconvenience herself."

Drew shook his head. "England shall not break our trade, nor shall she ever effectively enforce the sort of cruel policy she is attempting now. While you have been away, Rob, changes have taken place here."

Rob looked at him in utter frustration. "Don't you see how narrow a view of the world you have? My God, we are but one group of colonies belonging to the British Empire! We are almost insignificant in the greater scheme of things. We have nothing to win and everything to lose by defying England."

"Why should we be considered insignificant?" George asked his brother.

"You may not understand us, but, Rob, I no longer understand you. How can you offer such a statement as an argument? No matter how small we are compared to the rest of the British Empire, we have only ourselves. Are you telling us that we should not count—even to ourselves?"

Rob made a face of impatience. "Blast it all, George! You are always reducing my statements to philosophic drivel!"

"Robert! I shall thank you to discipline your language when there are ladies present."

Rob made a hasty apology to his mother, and then to his wife and Eloise.

Drew waited for a moment. "The next meeting will be held on the sixth of July. I suggest you be present, Rob, and present your opinions. Only a few of us have been to England recently, and we could all benefit from your information."

"Ha!" Rob said. "That's all you'd want, too—my information, hoping to glean some little tidbit that would help you and those artisans convince unsuspecting citizens that it is in their interest to rebel, when quite the opposite is true."

"I meant nothing of the sort. Tell them your feelings and reasons for it. It is not an actual rebellion the colonies want. We want justice, and recognition for ourselves. If there is a peaceful way of attaining that, I'm sure every man there would be interested."

"Is that what you actually want, Drew? I mean you personally?" Leo asked.

Drew laughed. "What do you think I am, Leo—a warmonger? One who wishes to fight for the sake of it?"

"I have questioned it. You were, after all, very active in the Regulator movement, and they certainly liked battling . . . even to the point of challenging established authority here."

"But for good and sound reason—and not too dissimilar from what is happening now. We wanted representation . . . justice . . . a chance to live well, and safely."

George ignored the petulant look on his brother's face. Rob wasn't nearly as much fun now as he had been before he had gone to London. "When will you go to Willowtree, Drew?"

"Sometime soon after the meeting. Are you going, too?"

"I think we shall all be going down at least for a while," John said. "It is unbearably hot in the city. I don't know how we've all tolerated it thus far."

"If you men don't give up these silly meetings, we'll all have yellow fever before the season is out. You, particularly, Leo, should be thinking about Eloise."

Leo frowned at his mother. "I asked you not to say anything! We wanted to tell everyone ourselves and in our own way."

"Tell us what?" George asked.

"You see, I didn't say a thing," Eugenia said indignantly. "You are the one who has raised everyone's curiosity. Oh, well, now that you've let it out, you might as well tell."

"I hate secrets!" Velma said in a surprisingly shrill voice. "Won't someone say what it is?"

"I suppose I'll have to be the one," Eugenia said. "Eloise is with child. Sometime around the end of the year we'll have another little Manning."

John beamed with pride at his son. "Well, now! This will be the first from our branch of the family." He motioned at the servant to fill everyone's wineglass, then held up his own. "I propose we drink to the good health and welcome of this child."

"Oh, John, you toast like that after the child has arrived," Eugenia said smugly. "Think of something else."

"I like my toast," John insisted. "If you don't wish to drink to the coming and welcome of this child, refrain, but I am going to!" He held his glass aloft, touched it to George's, who sat nearest him, then Bethany's on the other side, and drank deeply. "Ah! To a large and prosperous family."

George, waggling his head back and forth, smiled superciliously and said in a singsong voice, "But—! Shall it be an English family, or an American family? That is the question!"

After booing George's comment down, the family managed to think of several more toasts they could all agree upon, and then retired to the parlor to play games for a time before retiring for the night.

In the days immediately before the July sixth meeting, Drew saw friends from the Upcountry he hadn't seen in a long time. One hundred and four delegates from every region of the province, except Colleton, and Greenville counties, and Christ Church Parish, came. Along with the delegates others who were interested, or just wanted the excuse to come to Charles Town and be a part of the activities, also came. Charles Town was even more a beehive of activity than usual.

Among those who came to watch the doings was Ben Boggs, Drew's brother-in-law from his first marriage. Drew met him in Dillon's Tavern. As the young man walked toward him, Drew thought how old he looked. Ben was but nineteen years old, but his hair was graying at the temples and across the crown of his head, where he had been wounded in an outlaw raid some years ago. Ben's had not been an easy life, but only kindness and good cheer shone from his blue eyes. Now that Laurel's image had faded somewhat from his mind, Drew found that Ben reminded him of her. He took two quick steps and met Ben, his hand outstretched. "It's good to see you! Come, let's sit over here—tell me about the family."

If Ben had a favorite topic, it was his family. He grinned broadly. "I'm the damned luckiest man alive, Drew, that's how my family is. Star Dancer jes' made me the proud daddy of another boy not a month ago. Now Eli's got a little playmate."

"And Star Dancer recovered well?" Drew asked, concerned more than most men might be. After his experiences with Laurel it was something that always worried him, and he questioned constantly how a man was ever to know when a woman could no longer safely have more children, and what a man was to do about it.

Ben made a face. "Star Dancer jes' brings 'em out like there weren't anythin' to it. She ain't a-tall like Laurel was. You woulda thought God woulda made 'em all like Star Dancer, seein' they's the ones gotta carry on the race an' all."

"You would have thought," Drew agreed, but it didn't help much, for how well he knew it wasn't true. "What did you name the new boy?"

"Asher," Ben said proudly. "Asher Benjamin Boggs. The Benjamin's after me."

Drew smiled. "Where did Asher come from? That a family name, too?"

"Nope—at least not till now. None of my family's ever been called Asher an' that's the best reason for givin' the name to my son. How's li'l Harley doin' over to your place, or have you run him off yet?"

"No, I haven't run him off yet, but I'll tell you, Ben, I've been tempted. For a nine-year-old he's got the most larcenous mind I've ever come across."

"He shore takes after my old man," Ben said, shaking his head. "I'd give up on him, if I were you. I never did know where you got all the patience for the Boggses you have. You still feelin' guilty about Laurel?"

"No—not so much. For the most part that is behind me, but I still feel I should give her brothers and sisters a chance to make something of themselves when I'm able. I plan to apprentice him to a blacksmith or a carpenter when he's a few years older."

"Make sure he's a mean son of a bitch, or Harley'll rob him blind."

Drew laughed again. "There's no point in trying to talk seriously to you about Harley."

"Hell, Drew, I'm serious. He's my brother, man, I know him! My whole family ain't worth a turd—'ceptin' Laurel an' Mary, an' they're both dead."

"And yourself," Drew said, and caused Ben to smile broadly again.

"Yeah, I ain't done too badly, considerin'."

"Gwynne and the children are at my grandmother's plantation. If you can spare the time, I'd like you to visit a bit," Drew said. "Nathaniel misses you."

Drew got Ben's promise to visit and gave him the directions to Willowtree before taking his leave.

All the male Manning cousins went to the meeting together on the sixth. The hall was crowded, and men stood, or sat, in small clusters discussing alliances between the various groups so that they would each have some major say in the decisions made today. Unfortunately not enough alliances were forged before the meeting began, although nearly everyone at the meeting, whether he was of the planters' group, the mechanics', or the merchants', wanted action. Together they resolved against the latest British legislation and began proposing measures to secure repeal. It was agreed that delegates would be sent to a colonial congress in order to formulate a plan for nonintercourse against Great Britain. It was at this point that separate interests began to gain power. A heated debate flared up immediately.

Several men were on their feet at the same time, and it was difficult to hear who said what. One man whose voice was stronger than the others said, "Seventeen-seventy! Seventeen-seventy! Remember it! Hear me out! Quiet!" He shouted until he got attention, then spoke in a more normal voice. "We daren't rush into commercial nonintercourse against Great Britain. We must have concurrence on something so radical as this, and we have no guarantee that the northern colonies will follow our lead! In 1770 —with the Association—we were left alone. This time, should it happen, it could mean disaster to our economy!"

Others joined in agreement adding comments to the man's opinion; then one of the planters stood up and expressed their view. "We'll go along with the nonintercourse against Great Britain, but this year's rice must be shipped in November."

The room exploded in a babble of voices and shouted instructions, objections, and general confusion as everyone tried to gain support for his particular view. Several times the chair tried to impose order and bring the various resolutions to a vote. The planters, however, including Drew and his Uncle John, wanted the vote postponed until they could meet with other groups outside the meeting hall and make a compromise. Drew could imagine tons of Willowtree and Riverlea rice piling up and no market available to it. Many planters could be ruined with such a year.

Finally the meeting ended and was to begin again the next day. The Mannings straggled home the worse for wear, their voices hoarse, but for once they were all in agreement. John led the way to his study, where he fell into a chair and motioned for his son Rob to fix drinks for all the men. "We are agreed that we shall join with the merchants tomorrow and defeat the nonintercourse here, are we not?"

"Yes," said Drew. "I am, at least for now, or until someone wants to make the concession that the planters do not end up with a crop and no place to market it. It is to no one's advantage to destroy the economy, particularly now that we may very well need every bit of financing we can lay hands on for the years ahead."

"Oh, you give me a headache, and a toothache, and a backache, with all your doomsday talk of probable war, Drew," Rob groaned. "Why in the hell must you always think in terms of war! No one wants a damned war with Great Britain!"

"Want it or not, if things go as they have been for the last few years, Britain is going to retaliate with more than more laws. We'll begin to see ships as they have in Boston. If we continue down this road we've chosen, and I can not imagine anything that is going to deter us, then at some point we will be attacked."

"And you sit there like a hungry wolf with a freshly slaughtered sheep," Rob said. "If what you say is true, we should be voting against every damned proposal these radicals make, and not joining with anyone for compromise. Why are we agreeing to any of this?" he asked, looking directly at his father.

"Because we cannot stand alone, and presently the mood of the colonies, at least of the leaders of the colonies, is that we demonstrate our unwillingness to have control of our destinies in the hands of Great Britain. And there is something to be said for that, Rob. There is no guarantee that in the future Great Britain is not going to guard her home markets more severely than she is now, and then the American markets shall be bled white."

"There would be no point to that. Ruin us, and then what does she have?"

"It isn't a matter of ruin, Rob," his father said. "It is a matter of never being able to achieve what the colony is capable of achieving, and of always being dependent on the whim of a Parliament that does not essentially know our particular problems or put those problems first in priority."

The next day the meeting, and the newly formed alliances, went much as the Mannings hoped they would. The planters and the mechanics banded together and defeated the efforts of the radicals to enforce a nonintercourse against Great Britain immediately, and without the assurance that the other colonies would do the same. With that accomplished, the planters as a group shifted sides and voted with the radicals, enabling them to win a victory. It was agreed and voted that delegates from the colony of South Carolina would be sent to a congress which would meet in Philadelphia later in the year. Not only did this keep alive the issue of nonintercourse in trade at a later date, but it allowed the radicals to confer on the representatives' discretionary powers. One of their members said, "This was gaining a grand point!"

Grand as it might have been, it also left the entire outcome dependent upon who those delegates were, and how radical or conservative the overall mein of the Carolina delegation would be.

The election became a free-for-all of tactics. The merchants gathered themselves together, were joined by their clerks, and marched in a body to the polls. They were a powerful spectacle streaming through town on their way to vote. However, the tactic backfired. It so alarmed the radicals that they ran to the streets and went to every man who was a member of their group, and every man who leaned toward their politics, and urged him to vote.

Among the delegates elected, there was someone to please almost everyone, and a few who worried the more conservative Carolinians. Henry Middleton, Rawlins Lowndes, Charles Pinckney, Miles Brewton, and John Rutledge were delegates of the merchant planter group, while the mechanics elected Christopher Gadsden and Thomas Lynch, among others.

Once the momentum had begun, the meetings continued. On the following day there was a general meeting of the inhabitants of the province. They formed a standing committee to execute resolves and correspond with similar committees in the other provinces.

"This is getting to be very organized, and has the feel of something more serious than other attempts," George whispered to Drew. "Rob is not going to be a happy dinner companion tonight, I fear."

Drew listened as it was announced that the body would be designated the General Committee of the Province. It was composed of fifteen merchants, fifteen mechanics representing the town, and sixty-nine planters acting for the rest of the colony.

"Why aren't you going to be a delegate?" George buzzed in Drew's ear. Drew glanced at him in annoyance. "George, will you shut up? I want to hear how this is going to operate."

"Any twenty-two members of the General Committee may proceed on business," the man at the podium said.

"Why is that?" Drew asked. "The committee is going to be easily controlled by any minority who chooses to use it. The radicals are going to be jumping for joy over this one, for you can bet they will be keeping an eye on every opportunity to stir up sentiment."

"I'm surprised you are not screaming objection to this. It also means that the townsmen will have the greatest say."

Drew nodded. "I would object, but I doubt it would do me a bit of good today. Anyway, proximity is always going to win out. That is one of the distinct disadvantages to the Upcountry, and I see no way to solve it, unless we constantly send our own committee in to monitor the provincial committee." He chuckled. "It can all get a little ridiculous."

"I don't know about you, but I am filled to the throat with meetings. What are your feelings about leaving for Dillon's, or better still, just getting the horses and heading to Willowtree tonight?" George asked hopefully. "We could avoid Rob's tirade at dinner. . . ."

"I promised Gwynne I'd check on the progress of the new house before I left town. I've been meaning to do that, but haven't gotten round to it."

"If we leave now, couldn't we stop there on the way out of town?"

Without answering, Drew stood up and began to wend his way through the crowd of men. He, too, had had all he wanted of committees, and if his luck held, he would not be doing any traveling until the whole family returned to Cherokee for the harvest.

Two hours after they had left the meeting hall, Drew and George were on their way to Willowtree. Both of them felt good—relaxed and relieved. George Manning, in such a mood, was an irrepressible singer. He knew every bawdy barroom song ever written, so the two-hour ride to Willowtree was passed with George singing at top volume and Drew laughing at his cousin's lyrics and antics.

Part Two

Seth

11

Willowtree lay sleepy and elegant in the heat of the August sun. The land undulated in soft rolling hills, and the sweet breeze brushed against the rows of azaleas. In springtime it looked as though the land were covered with lush, slow-moving pink, red, and white clouds. Today all was a moving sea of green. On a lower level and far in the distance, observable only occasionally from high ground, lay the watery stretches of the rice paddies.

The live oaks along the plantation road stretched gracefully curved limbs to caress their neighbors across the road. Along the edge of the road was a border of brightly colored summer flowers, a hallmark of Elizabeth Manning. When she was in residence, the brilliant flash of color was everywhere to be seen and fragrance filled the air.

The house could not be seen, except for tantalizing glimpses, until the final bend in the road had been taken, and then before Drew's and George's gaze sprawled the huge plantation house Walter Manning had named for the willow trees that surrounded the pond on the front lawn. All the windows across the front of the house overlooked this pond.

The house was built of stone and stucco peculiar to the coast. Four Ionic columns stretched the full three stories. The ground-floor piazza was open and gently curved. Three steps graded the piazza to the level of the road, and again the brilliant spots of color brought by Elizabeth's flowers brightened the path from road to piazza.

Drew smiled. His grandfather had spared no expense, nor thought to making Willowtree both comfortable and beautiful. He had a moment's pang of guilt when he thought of how little time he had spent planning the house he and Gwynne were now building in Charles Town. "Think of the time and thought Grandpa put into this place," he said musingly to George.

"I barely remember Grandpa," George said. "I should, I suppose. I wasn't all that young."

"I wonder if our grandsons will ever ride up to a plantation and talk about the effort we put into it."

George made a face. "I'm not likely to have the grandsons to talk about anything. I think something is amiss with me, Drew. I've never met a single solitary girl I've really wanted to marry. Now, except for Arthur and Bethany, I'm about the only one in our generation unmarried. Arthur has his Leola, and they'll be marrying sometime soon probably, and . . . Beth, well, when she gets tired of having every man in a room beg to dance with her, she'll choose one and marry. I'll be the only one left."

"Meg," Drew said lightly.

"Yes, there's Meg. Funny—I always forget about Meg, and that, I think, is the saddest aspect of her plight. Everyone forgets about Meg now. I never thought Cousin Ruth would be the kind to hang on to one of her daughters."

"Meg is getting to be sour as an old lemon, too. She's given up, and now she clings to everything and everybody. When we were at Riverlea for the reading of the will, Meg shifted sides with every breeze."

"Waiting to see who was going to come out best," George said knowingly. "Are we changing because it is natural for a family to change, or is it the times, Drew? Ever think about that?"

"I think about it often, but I never come up with an answer. Maybe it's both. A lot of hurt and living takes place in any family, and then add to that the events of our times, and we have had many divisive pressures brought to bear on us. But I think we've only seen the beginning," Drew said, then smiled and waved. He dug his heels into his mount and pounded up the last few yards of the road. "Nathaniel!" he yelled, and whipped by the little boy, leaning from his saddle and pulling him up to sit in front of him.

Nathaniel gasped as his father wisked him through the air, but he didn't cry out. He had learned not to do that.

"Take the reins, boy," Drew said, and took the opportunity of having his son so close to hug him.

Nathaniel's small hands closed over the well-used, well-cared-for reins of his father's mount.

"Steady hands, Nat—keep them firm. He has to know who the boss is."

Nathaniel tried to do everything Drew said. His eyes were like saucers.

He loved riding, but he hadn't yet gotten over the feeling that the horse was more likely to do what he wanted than what Nathaniel wanted.

"Turn him around and bring him to a stop right at the steps, Nat," Drew said. They had passed the front of the house and were now on their way back down the drive.

Nathaniel tugged gently, and the horse turned. He laughed aloud and looked back over his shoulder at his father, his eyes dancing with happiness and pride. "He did it, Daddy! Look, he's going the right way!"

"Whoa!" Nathaniel cried a little frantically as they neared the piazza and the waiting groom.

Drew helped him down, and only then did he pay any attention to the black man waiting patiently to take the horse back to the stables. He stood with a relaxed athletic grace, holding George's horse with his left hand. Drew looked closely at the man for a moment. He saw none of the usual meekness or the laziness he often associated with the bondsmen. It was almost as if the man were considering himself an equal and wasn't afraid to let Drew know it. Then recognition dawned, and Drew managed a wry smile. "Seth," he said.

"Yes, sir," the man said, and enjoyed the look of surprise in Drew's eyes. His English the last time Drew had spoken to him was broken and barely understandable. Now it was good, nearly as good as most white men's, and Seth was aware of the effect that had on those same white men. It made them think about him, and consider him in a way nothing else did. He smiled at Drew, and wondered idly if he was going to get chastized for being insolent.

Drew said nothing, but gave the reins a smart flip into Seth's hand, and then vaulted up the steps to the piazza, with Nathaniel close at his heels.

Seth stood without moving until father and son had entered the house. Not many people puzzled Seth, but both Drew and Elizabeth did. He took both horses' leads in one hand and moved slowly toward the stables. It was a beautiful day with no need for haste. It was a day for considering. Considering was a word he had learned just recently in one of his lessons. It was a word he liked, and at least in the silence of his mind, he used it often. He enjoyed showing off his aptitude at pronunciation when talking to his superiors, but seldom if ever did he reveal to them what he knew, so more often than not his showing off was limited to simple statements, statements any bondsman might make, but said with the crisp purity of the whites.

He led the horses to the stables. He was good at his work, so said John Manning, but slow. Seth smiled to himself. John thought that he was slow in body and slower still in mind. John did not interest Seth. He could use John in his way, just as John could use Seth. For the most part Seth hadn't thought much one way or the other about his white masters. They weren't a whole lot different from those he had met in Africa. Most of them had an eye for money and power. If there was one single thing he had to learn from slavery, it was that in the white world power and money were king. Again he smiled as he thought of the words in the Koran, "How canst thou bear with that whereof thou canst not compass any knowledge?"

Seth slowly brushed the horse's coat, his mind moving easily over thoughts that came mostly from childhood. He thought of the wide open savannahs, the sparsely covered grassy plains, and the heat. There was no sun like the sun in Africa.

He was deep in thought, unaware of the slender young girl who lounged against the open door of the stall. Folly didn't make a sound. She liked just looking at him. Even before Seth had told her something about his life before he was brought here, she had known he'd be a king. She had heard tales of men like him, but she had never thought to meet one. She had just thought it to be quarter talk, but the minute she had seen him, she had known. He was different from the others. Finally she said, "How long you gonna brush dat one spot? Ol' horse ain't gonna have any hide lef', you keep it up."

Seth laughed easily. "Looks like I got lost in my thoughts, don't it? What're you doin' here, girl? Your mama's gonna be lookin' for you."

"I done all my chores." Folly pouted. "Don't see why I hafta hurry back so's she can give me more. I works more than the othah girls now."

Seth shook his head. "You shore can tell a story. Iffen you're gonna stand around eyeballin' me, pick up a brush and work on Mastah George's horse."

Folly made a face at the evil-smelling horse covered with dried lather. "Mastah John see you let the horse stan' like this an' he take a whip to yo' backside, Seth."

"Mastah John ain't gonna take nothin' to me. He know I do a good job. He ain't had a sick or lamed horse since I been here."

Folly giggled. "That's cause he don't know you know doctorin'. My mama say you gonna get foun' out one o' these days, an' then you gonna know what Mastah John's whip like." She looked closely at his face to see his reaction. As usual he showed nothing of what was going on inside him. She knew he was thinking. Seth was a thinking man. He was thinking all the time, and she didn't believe for a moment that Master John, or any of the others, would ever find out a thing Seth didn't choose to let them know. She'd just said that to see if she could get him to tell her what he was thinking. But he didn't. "Ain't you gonna say nothin'?" she prodded, then begged him to tell her.

"I ain't never tellin' you nothin', Folly, girl, y'hear? An' you wanta know why I ain't?"

"Why?"

" 'Cause you ignerrant, that's why. Don't tell no fool ignerrant girl nothin', 'cause she never know what to keep to herself an' what she kin tell without doin' harm. De Lawd said he make him strong in the land, and gave him unto everything a road."

"What dat mean? You jes' talkin' stuff so's you make me ignerrant. Don't mean nothin'."

"It mean we stron', 'cause the Lawd make us that way, and it mean there's a way for us to use that strength, but we got to fin' the way—that's our road. If you was to go to Miss Lizzbeff's school like you oughta, then maybe a man could talk to you when he ain't got nothin' better to do."

"That true? You talk to me 'bout Africa, an' the things you think iffen I was to go to Miss Lizzybeff's school?"

"Onliest way you ever know is to go an' fin' out." Seth smiled at her, his teeth flashing white in his dark, round face.

He was a tall man, straight of back and broad of shoulder. Most of the time Folly liked being a young girl. Her workload was light, and many of her transgressions were excused on that basis, but when she looked at Seth there wasn't an ounce's worth of little girl in her, and yet he made her feel like a child and treated her like one. Sometimes his presence made her say things she wished she could bite back. "I hates that ol' school. She won't let us in there lessen we take an' wash all ovah in the creek. What's that got to do with schoolin'? Bet she don't make you do that."

"You be right," Seth said proudly. "Ain't nobody got to tell me I got to wash, 'cause I knows that myseff, an' ain't never catch me dirty like y'all." He made an exaggerated shudder. "You come ovah here in one o' them ships, you don't evah wants to be crawlin' dirty again. I washes in the mawnin', an' I washes in the evenin' jes' as the sun go down."

Folly had never heard of such a thing. Most folks, even white folks, said washing would make a person sicken and die. What a strange and wonderful man! She stepped forward and without thinking touched the silky firmness of the flesh on his shoulder.

Seth stood still. Women had always liked him. He was used to it and enjoyed the attention. Folly's brown hand slid up and down the length of his upper arm. "You likes that, girl?"

Folly was too enchanted with him to hide her feelings. She looked up at him with liquid deep brown eyes. "I likes that, Seth. I likes you."

Seth laughed and took her hand. He held it for a moment, then deliberately placed it down by her side and stepped back away from her. " 'He said: Lo! ye are folk unknown to me.' "

"I ain't unknown to you! Why you all the time talkin' like that?"

"That come from the Koran—a holy, holy book, an' if you wasn't so ignerrant, you'd know that. See, girl, you wrong, you are folk unknown to me. You jes' a li'l girl playin' roun' with me, but I don't play, I needs to know what Miss Lizzybeff's school can teach me, an' then I let that holy book lead me to . . ." He paused thinking for a moment, assessing her, then he grinned and said, "The promised land."

Ignorant though she might have been, Folly was not stupid. She gave him a squint-eyed look and screwed up her mouth as she had seen her mother do when she was about to devastate her father with a bit of information, and said, "You gonna run?"

Seth laughed aloud and began to clean the stall with greater speed, but he said nothing.

"Well, are you?"

"Git on back to your mama, li'l girl. You ain't got no business aroun' here."

"What if I tell? What if I was to say you was tryin' to git us to rise up?"

"What if you was? Nothin' happen. Nobody believe you."

"They always thinkin' about that. Mama say so. My daddy hear all kin's o' things Mastah worries 'bout."

Seth straightened from his task quickly, spun, and jumped at Folly. "S'posin' I make it so you can't tell nobody nothin' ever!"

Folly leaped back, out of reach, but still near the stable.

Seth made another quick move, and Folly ran a few more steps. She wasn't sure what he might do. She couldn't tell when Seth was playing and when he wasn't. He let out a deep roar, and his face was a mask of rage, and Folly turned and ran all the way back to her cabin.

Seth threw his head back and laughed.

12

Drew entered the house and walked into the sight and sound of a heated quarrel. Elizabeth sat closed mouthed and angry, glaring from her son to two of her grandsons, Leo and Rob. George, too, was in the room, looking uncomfortable, and as though he wished he were anywhere but where he was.

"Is this a private battle, or may anyone join? You look as though you could use reinforcements, Grandma."

"This is not a matter for levity, Drew," she snapped uncharacteristically.

"You had no right to do this without consulting us, Mother," John repeated, a paper in his hand which seemed to be the object of their dissension.

"I had every right, and my pledge shall be honored. The amount I promised Mr. Gadsden is well under what would be my share of the crop. You may not tell me what I may and may not do with property that is mine to do with as I please."

"That is not the point, Mother! The rice you have pledged to Mr. Gadsden's committee will go to Massachusetts under the Willowtree name, not your own!" John straightened, sighed, and looked at Drew. "Will you try to make her see that the pledging of this rice from Willowtree to aid the people in Boston is going to make it appear that we—that I, too—support this radical cause. However we may disagree politically, Drew, I am sure you'll at least allow me the privilege of my own convictions, which is more than my dear mother is presently willing to do. Talk to her."

"I dislike it intensely when you speak of me as though I were not sitting right in front of you, John!"

"Grandma," Drew said, waiting for a moment to see if she was going to fire at him with a verbal barrage. "Uncle John is correct. The mechanics are lining up support wherever they can get it, and if you have the plantation pledging the rice rather than you personally, it is going to be thought that Uncle John and Leo and Rob are radicals—at least that they support them in aiding Boston against England's actions."

"They should! It is disgraceful to treat any city in the colonies as Boston Port has been treated. Imagine!"

"They don't feel that way, Grandma," Drew insisted gently.

"But I do," George said, speaking for the first time. "If Grandma's name is to go on that shipment of rice, I want my name on it as well."

John Manning groaned and turned away. He knew when he had read the subscription blank that Christopher Gadsden had sent round to nearly all the planters in the area, that there would be difficulty in his family. He had reached the point of avoiding any political talk whenever possible. It wasn't easy with Elizabeth and Drew in the household, and now it seemed that in his quieter way, George was joining them. Gadsden, in his subscription, called for relief of the "melancholy situation and distress" of the people of Boston. All John Manning wanted was the relief of the melancholy situation and distress in his own family. But Elizabeth, without saying a word to him, had pledged a considerable amount of rice, and some money. In all Gadsden was attempting to gather a thousand barrels of rice, two hundred to be sent immediately, with the remainder to follow.

John returned his attention to the argument that still went on among Leo, Rob, Elizabeth, George, and Drew. "Mother, all I ask is that you do not give your rice and your money in the name of Willowtree Plantation. Is that so much to ask of you? I am not trying to prevent you from doing as you wish, I simply do not want to be associated with it."

"Then don't be! You send your own missive disclaiming my pledge. I want Willowtree's name on it, because Willowtree was founded by your father, and I am certain Walter would have been right in the thick of things. The very idea of British ships closing down an American harbor to the detriment of English citizens would have sent him after his musket. He should be counted, at least by the use of his plantation's name." Her dark eyes flashed with conviction as she stared at her son.

John did not look away or back down as Elizabeth expected. He knew she would not give in or change her mind, and most likely not the pledge she had made, but for once he was as angry as she. "Mother," he said in a quiet voice, "you have gone too far. You have always been a headstrong woman, and out of respect for you we have allowed you your way. In these times, however, there shall have to be some curtailing of your independent, and often irresponsible, activities. We are not playing at gossip, or parlor games that will be over in the morning, Mother. Many of these men are talking about a complete break with the mother country, a very serious and treasonous act."

"Not if they win!" Elizabeth said.

"Whether they win or not is beside the point. There will be no victory, and it is time you, and my hotheaded youngest son—you, George—see that. If we should win and gain independence, all the subsidy of crops we now enjoy would be gone. Joseph would have difficulty finding a market for the Manning indigo. Some say indigo planting in this country would be gone forever. We would have a far greater difficulty getting good prices for our rice. And, of course, if we lose there will be retaliation of some form. A war is costly. Britain will not pay that price. By one means or another we shall. I do not want to be a part of any rebellion against my king and my country. Before you pursue this headstrong, ill-advised path of yours, Mother, you might give it some more thought."

"I have given it thought, John. And now that I have listened to you, I would like you to give me the same courtesy, and I shall try to tell you why I have taken what you call a headstrong and ill-advised path."

All five men sat down.

"When men feel as you have just described—that there is no way to win whatever the consequences—that is fear. Yes, we may live very well. We are wealthy in land, in money, in our social position, and in many other ways; but if we have reached the point that we feel we must abide by anything a tyrannical Parliament dictates to us in order to continue in such wealth, then we are not wealthy at all, we are captive. If a man is not able to feel the might and power of his own being, if he is unable truthfully to say that he is answerable only to His God, his own conscience, if his ethics and his judgment and his spirit are not free, then neither is he. Your father came here so that you and Joseph would have a place to begin, a place different from England. He wanted you to see life in a broader perspective, and to have a sense of your own innate value he thought you would not be so likely to have in England."

She paused and looked at John for a time, then went on. "I shall never alter from the course Walter set for us. We fought for this land, and we tilled it when there were trees and brush so thick and heavy you could not enter or even see through it. We cleared out the cypress swamps, standing in the murky water ourselves along with the darkies. And now you wish to bow to the wishes of a Parliament that wants to use the riches of this land for the benefit of English trade. While you do your own thinking, you might do well to think that what England is using this land for is not what your father intended when he came here. And part of what the English take when they ask us for taxes, and curtail our own industry, is the sweat of your father."

"You are exaggerating a bit, Mother, although I do concede you have some valid, if sentimental, points."

"I do not exaggerate. You have frequented Thomas Elfe's cabinet shop, have you not?"

"You know I have," John said perplexed.

"If men like Thomas Elfe are encouraged, they are capable of making furniture as fine as any in England, so they are not encouraged. The monetary system is made so that it is not easy for men like Elfe to compete. It has become clear to some of us, John, that England is not interested in the welfare and prosperity of the colonies beyond what insures the welfare and prosperity of Mother England. That is not sentimental, my son, that is truth." She stood up. "I am tired, John. I shall retire to take a little nap. I have said all I choose to, and I shall not change my pledge I have made to Mr. Gadsden on his subscription form. You may do as you wish about disclaiming it, John."

None of them had anything to say after Elizabeth left the room. For a time they all sat without moving, without talking, without even thinking. She had left them all empty of thought as if she had wiped clean a slate and each one of them had to begin his thinking all over again.

Finally Drew got up and excused himself. He went in search of Gwynne and found her in the pantry with Unity taking an inventory of supplies. As always she smiled as soon as she saw him.

"May I steal you away from Unity for a while? Grandma has just given me a headful of things to think about, and I'd like to walk for a while."

It wasn't often that Drew showed diffidence with her these days. When he did, she asked no questions. She turned to Unity and said, "We'll finish tomorrow, Unity. Why don't you make a little tea for yourself before you return to the quarters?"

Drew took her out the rear door of the house and down the path past the slave quarters.

"Where are we going?"

"To the paddies—down by the swamp."

Gwynne looked at him, worry in her eyes. "Why the swamp, Drew? Is something amiss? None of the slaves has run—or—"

"No, no, nothing like that. Grandma was talking about this land before it was Willowtree. She told us how she and Grandpa stood in the swamps alongside their bondsmen and cleared it out. I just feel like going there and looking and thinking. I know what it was like clearing Manning and Cherokee, but I've never really thought about Willowtree being anything but what it is now. I'd like to see."

Gwynne smiled and wrapped her arm around his. "I've never known anyone but you who would think of doing something like this. Even when we were children, growing up, caring about little but having a good time, even then you were likely to go off and do something like this."

"And you were likely to follow me," he added.

"It was like an adventure to me. Alone I could never see things as you seemed to, but when you were there, I got to take part in these dreams and adventures into the past and future with you." She looked up at him. "Did you know that was one of the first things I knew about you that made me realize that I love you?"

She waited for a time, but he said nothing. "Even now my confessions of affection for you make you uncomfortable. Why is that, Drew? I have loved you since I was a child. We have lived together out of wedlock, and now we are married and share a child together. Why is my loving you still capable of bringing you discomfort?"

"Perhaps because I know I do not deserve it."

"Perhaps, but I do not believe you truly think that," Gwynne said.

"No, I don't. But in a sense it is true. I have always managed to disappoint or do harm to those who love me. I shall undoubtedly do the same to you at some time."

"You may hurt me, Drew, that is possible, but I can't imagine that I would ever be disappointed in you."

"How is it possible to be hurt and not be disappointed?"

"It's possible. I think that was true of Laurel. I've never liked talking about her, you know. I have always been jealous of her—even after she died and you married me. But I don't think you ever disappointed her, and you should know that. Star Dancer has talked to me about Laurel a few times. She thinks I should confront my jealousy and be at peace with my idea of Laurel. And now I think that, if anything, I should feel sorry for her, for it was the outlaws and the hardships of the Upcountry that really harmed Laurel, never you. I don't think you should feel that you did."

"My mind was on everything except Laurel when she needed me. I was busy with the Regulators, and the politics in Charles Town, and then building the house at Cherokee, and then the crops. I never saw what was happening to Laurel while I was so occupied. And even though Ben and Ned both tried to tell me, I never realized how difficult being a Boggs was for her."

"Well, I can't argue. I know too little about all that, but I do know it will never happen to us."

Drew shrugged and looked away from her. "That is part of the reason I felt like walking down here. Grandma has said things this afternoon I have thought of on occasion, and some that I have never thought. What has stuck in my mind and given me a chill in my spine is that when she spoke of war, I could feel that. I don't know when it will happen, Gwynne, perhaps not for years yet, but we will eventually go to war. I must ask myself what I am going to do when it comes . . . if it comes in my lifetime."

"Good heavens, Drew, why must you find an answer now? Nothing may happen for years—you just said so yourself."

"If I wait, it will be too late. My father, my brother, my Uncle John, Leo, Rob, and Joanna and Bert will most likely remain Tories. Should there come an armed confrontation, Gwynne, I would stand with the rebels. How do I dare wait until I have a gun in my hand to ask myself if I am capable of shooting my own father—or brother . . . or your sister's husband?"

"Oh, dear God, Drew!" Gwynne breathed. "That can't happen! We would never let that happen."

"There may be no choice. Men are strange creatures, and not given to much intelligence, I think. We talk of politics as though it were the game of the day, and as though it were merely a matter of winning the point. It is only when we are facing each other in the heat of battle that it is realized that those clever maneuvers we have made have brought us to life and death, and have led us to take actions that alter the course of our lives and the lives of those we love. I became a Regulator without knowing that.

"Ned Hart once told me, on my first long ride, that I would have to learn not to feel when we hanged the outlaws we captured. He told me I had to learn not to hate or want revenge for the crimes they had committed, and that one day I would be able to look upon it as a task that had to be done to insure the safety of others. At first I couldn't do that, but then later I had seen so many die, and had fought so many battles, I just didn't care, and that was far worse than those days when I had hated and wept and agonized over every infraction and every death."

Gwynne leaned her head against his arm as they walked. "Why have you never told me of this before? There are so many things I might have understood."

"I haven't thought about them for a long time—not until Grandma reminded me of them again today. Now I feel I must think about it again. I must know within myself that I am prepared to fight for a nation and for principle against my own family, or I must know that I cannot do that."

They came to the edge of the rice paddies and stood facing the swamp. Drew looked around, and then moved a little deeper into the murky, soft-earth edge of the swamp. "There should be a punt tied here." He came back to where she waited, then walked down from her a bit, darting into and out along the edge of the swamp, hunting for the flat-bottomed boat without finding it.

He had gone about a hundred feet from her when she called to him. "Your boat has been found!"

He ran back to her, his eyes on the tall, slender black man who stood in the boat poling toward the higher ground where Gwynne stood. "You want to ride in the swamp?" the black man said.

"Seth, what the hell are you doing with that boat? Aren't you supposed to be at the stables? The bell hasn't rung yet."

Seth ignored Drew's question about the stables. "I come to look for the good herbs and the good peace of a quiet place. You want to ride in the swamp, I take you. I am good with the boat."

Drew stood undecided. By all rights, and by his Uncle John's authority, he should send Seth back to the stables, and to a good disciplining, but he really did not want to. He took Gwynne's arm and helped her into the punt.

"Where you like to go?" Seth asked, and pushed the boat away into the deeper water.

"No where in particular. I have never been in parts of this swamp. I want to see it."

Seth nodded his head, pushing the punt deeper into the swamp until the rice paddies couldn't be seen for the strange pyramidal shapes of the cypresses. The water was inky black and still between the trees, their long tentacles reaching into it. The knobby knees of the cypresses popped above the water, giving the trees an eerie animalistic quality.

"My people clear this," Seth said after a while.

"So did mine," Drew replied more sharply than he had intended.

Seth smiled. "Maybe be a lot o' bodies lyin' at the bottom of this ol'

swamp. Folks say they kin see their spirits floatin' aroun' in here on foggy
nights."

"That *is* fog they see," Drew said.

"Maybe so, maybe not," Seth said. "Lake just up ahead."

The punt moved smoothly, silkily, over the black tannic water, then it
grew lighter, and they came out of the swamp channel into a lake. It
glowed a bright green. Gwynne drew in her breath at the beauty of it. She
put her hand down along the side of the boat to touch the thick green
carpet of duckweed. Over to the side of them was a bed of tall rushes.

With a smile Seth took them all around the lake, pointing out wampee
and moving carefully around huge patches of lily pads.

"This is like another world," Gwynne said, and reached for Drew's
hand as an osprey let out a shrill scream. Birds abounded. She pointed at
wood ibises as large as turkeys with their white bodies and black-edged
pinions. "I am so glad we came here. Are you seeing here what you had
hoped, Drew?"

"I can see what my grandfather must have seen so many years ago."
Suddenly Drew looked up at Seth. "What do you see, Seth?"

"I see a swamp, a place where no people live, where no one knows what
happens. I see a place where there is only the man, and his own thoughts
and his own doings."

Drew's eyes narrowed a bit. "I trust that is not meant as a threat, Seth."

Seth looked at him; his gaze did not waver, and Drew sensed the power
of the black man. "It meant as answer," he said, and pushed the boat back
into the swamp channel leaving the bright green, duckweed-carpeted lake
behind.

Drew said no more, but he thought about Seth. He wasn't at all sure
Elizabeth's decision to educate him was a good one. Most uprisings and
insurrections were led by Negroes who had been educated. After the insurrection at Stono in 1739, men went even to church on the Sabbath armed
for fear of uprisings. Twenty-one white people had died at Stono. It was
not a thing to be ignored or to be taken lightly. He promised himself to
keep better tabs on Seth, but at the same time there was something about
this defiant, almost insolent black man Drew admired and liked.

Seth brought them back nearly to the spot from which they had started.
He held the punt steady as Drew and Gwynne got out, but made no move
to leave the boat himself. Drew looked at him, and Seth pushed away from
the paddy. "I have not gotten my herbs and roots," he said simply. He
quickly disappeared into the tangle of cypress.

Gwynne looked after him for a minute. "I don't think Seth would have difficulty deciding what he would fight for. I think his family would mean little to him if he wanted something they did not." She turned and walked away from the swamp. "John will have to deal with him sooner or later. I think he is a very frightening man. I don't like him or trust him."

Drew still had said nothing, but was staring into the swamp at the spot where Seth had last been seen.

"You don't think he is running away, do you?" Gwynne asked in sudden alarm.

"No, but I'd like to know what it is he's up to. The swamp is a good place for hidden meetings. He said himself there is nothing there but a man and the swamp and what he wants." He shook his head slowly in bemusement. "The man is intelligent. He contradicts almost everything we tell ourselves about the nature of the black people. Do we have any right to have slaves?"

"This is certainly your day for questioning," Gwynne said. "What I think is that you need a good supper and a long night's sleep. Perhaps then everything will look a little brighter to you in the morning."

Drew laughed, linked his arm in hers, and began walking at a brisk pace back through the rice paddies. "Thinking has always been my curse. I do too much of it with too little result. I never seem to find answers, only more questions."

13

Drew spent the remaining days of August overseeing the construction of their new home and then left for Cherokee to be at home for the harvest. The evening he had walked with Gwynne down to the rice paddies was the last quiet moment of thought he was to have in a long time.

Ned was overjoyed to see him. "I thought you had become a stranger for sure! Good to have you home, Drew. I got a few things to show you—hope you approve," he said, and wasted no time in getting Drew into the tobacco fields. "We tried a couple o' new things this season—experimental," he added with a wink.

"We put some Burley in this heavy clay soil over to the west, and been tryin' gatherin' the harvest a bit at a time. Every damn time one o' them leaves ripens we take it, and let the others be. Basil tol' me he'd been talkin' to a biology fella, and this is what he said. That way we don't take the whole plant before it all matures."

"It looks as if we have a greater yield this year than we've ever had before—or is that just the way it seems after having been away too long?"

"You're seein' right. That friend o' Basil's looks like he knows what he's talkin' about. We been suckerin' these plants heavily this year, too. That fella said it'd make 'em produce more, and by gummy, it did. 'Ceptin' for that leaf spot I wrote to you about, we haven't had a problem all season."

They walked slowly through the tobacco barns, and Drew took a deep satisfaction from the plantation. No matter how many houses he built in Charles Town, or how much he loved Willowtree, it was Cherokee that was his. He loved the land and the isolation of it. He had built it alone and for himself and his family.

The next morning he was in the fields with Ned and his bondsmen working under a clear blue sky with the sun beating down on his shoulders so fiercely it seemed it would burn a hole right through him.

By the time the harvest was ready, Drew was browned a deep bronze, and the red highlights in his hair shone with health. He moved along the rows of tobacco, cutting down the remaining plants. They were left in the field for a couple of days to wilt, the first step in the curing process. Then the leaves were gathered up to yellow and be dried, and packed for shipping.

It was work Drew loved, and the days flew by. He would have been completely unaware of the passage of time had it not been for the letters from Gwynne and his grandmother, and the occasional news bulletin from one or another of the radicals, who kept in close touch with him.

"They sure don't want to let you forget 'em, do they?" Ned said, chuckling. "Puts me in mind o' the time John Haynes an' Bart Cole thought you'd lost interest in the Regulators."

"It isn't a whole lot different. It's mostly the mechanics. The most radical men are in that party, and they sense this is the time to strike, so they're pushing with everything they have."

"Is this liberty and justice thing as widespread as it seems, Drew?"

"I'd say not. The ones who want it are the most vocal, and they're the most active. It's the age-old story, Ned—if you want something you have to work for it. These mechanics are out every day pushing and pushing for their point of view, and the Tories are sitting back counting their riches and counting on them being there next year."

"An' you? What will you do?"

Drew shrugged. "I think we're better off being an independent nation. It's going to be rough for a time, but in the long run I think we'll be better. This is a rich country. We'll find markets. It's just a matter of time."

"But while that time is passin' we may be smokin' a lot o' our own t'baccy, that it?"

"That's it," Drew agreed, tearing open the message that had come that afternoon from Charles Town. He read it quickly, then looked up at Ned. "Mostly it's news from Philadelphia. The first congress had representatives from every colony except Georgia," he said quietly; then, in a livelier voice, he said, "Well, well, Ned, we now have a Declaration of Rights and Grievances and a Nonimportation Agreement. The Continental Congress has resolved to suspend all trade with Great Britain after December first, 1774! Now we may see some real results from the damned English Parliament. They can't just ignore this appeal. We may avoid an all-out confrontation after all!"

"I didn't realize just how badly you wanted to avoid it, Drew. I think I'm finally beginnin' to get the picture. You'll go along with the radicals if it comes to fightin', but would rather not 'cause most likely your family ain't gonna be among those counted."

"That is it in a nutshell, Ned. I hope like hell we avoid the whole thing, and Britain starts to listen to the grievances and do something about them."

"Experience don't bear that out, Drew. You know how good the Charles Town Assembly listened to the Upcountry grievances. Couldn't prove by me that those fellas had any ears a-tall."

"Keep your fingers crossed."

"I s'pose this means you'll be headin' back to Charles Town again."

"I think it might be well for you to pay a visit to Charles Town, too, Ned, as soon as everything is taken care of here. The folks here in the Upcountry should be kept abreast of events. Gadsden's committees will be riding through from time to time informing people and drumming up support, but I think we ought to take it on ourselves to keep them informed."

"A man allus likes to know what's going on from one o' his own, someone he knows he can trust."

Drew didn't get back to Charles Town until the seventeenth of January, 1775. For the first time that he could remember he had missed the holiday season with his family. It brought back memories of last year's Christmas celebration. Elizabeth had said then that she wanted them all to be together one more time. He now knew that might very well be the last time. William Templeton had died this last year. And the coming year did not bode well for peace in the colonies, or in the family.

Charles Town was a hive of activity and talk when he arrived. George Manning grabbed hold of Drew before he had a chance to unpack the utility bag he had brought with him and wash up. "Drew!" George said breathlessly, "We've got to talk." He looked in all directions as if he feared someone was listening.

Drew looked skeptically at him, then smiled. "Are you harboring state secrets, or what? Why all the secretiveness?"

"You haven't been around here lately. Ever since the Council of Safety was formed to enforce nonimportation, you have to be careful."

"That is all public knowledge, George. There's no reason to keep mum."

"Well, damn it all, Drew, not everyone wants to adhere to that policy, and sides are drawing up real hard and fast. I told you we've got to talk. Let's go down to Dillon's." He looked cautiously about the room and doorway again. "At least we are free to say what we want down there. The whole place is swarming with mechanics and anyone else who advocates the radical cause. My God! You should have been at the Commons House last week! What a battle royal went on over there about the rice exemption from the nonimportation agreement."

"If you keep chattering on, there will be no secrets left to disclose at Dillon's."

"That's true. Daddy is up in arms over this, though. This is the first time the planters and the mechanics have really disagreed, and I think it is a serious split. If someone doesn't come up with a compromise solution, we're going to lose a lot of planters to our cause. They will go with the party that can assure them the sale of their crops."

Drew shook his head. "And you want to talk about it. You must like headaches, because that is all you're going to accomplish. There are no answers, George. For the time being, anyway, events are going to dictate what each of us decides to do with his life."

"You can't just eliminate a man's responsibility in this."

"No, but years back we did some thinking and some deciding that set off a chain of events, and now we are dealing with the consequences of them. Refuse the stamps back in 1765, and in 1775 you deal with nonimportation agreements. Observe nonimportation in 1775, and at a later date we'll deal with the consequences of that."

"You're making me tired," George moaned. "There will never be an end to it."

"Oh, there'll be an end. I just hope we like it when it comes," Drew said, going back to his unpacking. "On your way downstairs would you ask Pelagie to have hot water sent up for me, George?"

Drew bathed, shaved, and fell across the bed into a sound sleep. It wasn't until the following evening that George was able to convince him that they should go to Dillon's and catch up with all the talk of events that had happened since Drew had last been in Charles Town.

As soon as they had left Elizabeth's house, it was apparent that something major was going on down near the docks. Throngs of men, mostly mechanics, as judged by their clothing, were running toward the wharves. George and Drew looked at each other and joined with the hastening crowd. "What's going on?" Drew asked of a man who hurried near him.

"Ship from Bristol's in port with a cargo. A citizens' committee is going to make damn sure not a speck of goods gets off-loaded." He ran alongside

Drew and George for a bit longer, then darted into the crowd and was lost from view.

The ship bumped along the wharf in the Cooper River, her crew looking at the gathering mass of people with more than a little consternation.

"What's she carrying?" Drew asked, finding a familiar face.

Thomas Elfe stood a little back from the milling mob, trying to see over their heads. "Almost four thousand bushels of salt, coal, and some tiles, I believe. It's going to be a hurtful thing for some of our citizens to see this cargo lost. We're in sore need of some of those things."

"Umm," Drew said. "You forget the sacrifices that come when a principle must be upheld."

"Now, that's a fact," Elfe said cheerfully. "You going to join in the fun? Soon's the committee has made our position clear, that ship is going to be relieved of its cargo."

Drew stood stunned for a moment, then a loud roar came from the crowd, and men began to cheer and move closer to the ship. Excitement crackled in the air, and Drew found himself caught up in it. Before he realized what he was doing he was running into the thick of the crowd toward the ship. From the decks several men came to the side and looked over. "Are you ready?" one shouted and got a response of "We are ready!" from the crowd.

Drew managed to push his way through the milling, yelling mass of humanity and get aboard ship. With others of the committee he began to throw the cargo over the side of the ship into the Cooper River. Tiles, coal, and salt hit the surface of the water, splashed, then sank, leaving behind them the debris of broken barrels, crates, and other packings.

Sweating, and now exhilarated, Drew climbed down from the ship and went in search of George. He found his cousin being dragged onto the dock from out of the river. Several men stood around, their clothing wet from the river, their spirits high, and their need to continue their camaraderie great. Fifteen or twenty of them broke away from the mob and started down the street to Dillon's. Windows along their route opened as the yelling bunch laughed and horsed their way along. "By God! Did you see me? I must have thrown that salt clear to the other side of the river! Why I betcha we go over there tomorrow we find a pile o' salt tall as a two-story house," shouted a man known only as Tom.

"How tall?" George yelled, laughing.

"A damned two-story building!" Tom yelled back. "I was so strong, those crates was flying when they left my arms."

"Nobody's bringin' anything into port till we say so! We did it! We damned well did it!"

They hooted, hoorayed, and shadowboxed with each other all the way to Dillon's. Drew ran a few steps, turned and skipped backward, his fists flashing out within a hair's breadth of hitting George.

George yelped in pain as he tried to open the door to the tavern and five or so bodies pounded against his back. "Hey! Get back! I can't open the damned door!"

After a few well-aimed blows to George's vulnerable midsection, they moved back; then it became a race to see who could push his way in through the door first, closing it in the face of the man behind him. One by one they fell into Dillon's, hooting with laughter and shouting for ale. "Polly, my love, my own true love, set us up!" Tom shouted.

"He's a blackguard, Polly, serve me. I am the faithful kind," George said.

"You are that, Georgie, darlin'," Polly cooed, stroking her hand across his cheek.

"Ohhh nooo! Not George!" the others moaned.

They teased and played like small children, without a word of politics passing their lips, until the wee hours of the morning, when Robert Dillion finally begged them to go home and let him get some sleep.

"Just one more!" came the cries from all over.

"Home!" shouted Dillon. "My God, you've drunk everything I have in the place—even the water! Go home!"

Still laughing and fooling around, they stumbled out into the street. George and Drew, their arms slung around each other's neck for support, swayed down the middle of the road, aiming vaguely toward Legare Street and Elizabeth's house.

"Oh, how I wish Gwynne were waiting in my bed for me," Drew slurred.

"Ohhh, how I wish anyone were waiting in my bed for me," howled George. "Damn, Drew, sometimes I just feel like raping the bedpost."

14

In March of 1775 the first real threat to the Association arose. Robert Smythe, a citizen of Charles Town, returned from England and brought with him some furniture for his private use and a consignment of horses. The committee permitted the landing of the horses under the assumption that the prohibitions of the articles of nonimportation did not apply.

In a very short time the mechanics had heard of the decision and came en masse to argue the point, claiming the articles had been broken, and that the animals could not be landed.

Shortly there was a mob once again at the docks, milling about, shouting threats, and brandishing sticks, muskets, fists, or whatever else was available. The hue and cry was "We'll slaughter the animals if they are landed!"

An armed company was called in to guard the cargo as it was brought ashore. The mob backed away from the entourage, but the mood was nasty. From time to time one of the armed company merely dropped back and melted into the crowd, refusing to obey orders.

Other, calmer Charlestonians were alarmed and called for the committee to bring in more members of the body and reconsider the question. The meeting was held, but it did little to cool the boiling tempers. In some sense the battle with Great Britain had already been engaged, and every incident, no matter how insignificant in itself, was looked upon now as a breach of loyalty if the letter of the Articles of Nonimportation were not upheld.

"Much ill-blood will be occasioned by this night's work," the man next to Drew said bleakly.

And it was true. There was no restraint or tact in operation this night. Words of contempt were hurled back and forth. When Christopher Gadsden got up to plead with the body to reverse its decision, his powerful voice could barely be heard over the grumbling and name-calling.

John Rutledge argued in opposition to Gadsden's pleas, trying to make a case for the landing of the animals, but the debate was continually interrupted.

Edward Rutledge finally took the floor. Most responsible for the decision to land the cargo, he stood up and censured the mob. The sky and the walls of the buildings shook with the shouted accusations of "coward" and "traitor" and "disgrace." The clamor and din were so great that the man could not speak. Others left the hall insulted and angry. Some left it humiliated and embarrassed at the raw emotion that had come pouring out.

About seventy members of the committee remained, and a vote was taken.

By a ballot resulting in a vote of thirty-five to thirty-four the committee decided not to land the freight. There was not the cheering that might have been expected. The men who voted, and those who merely observed, still held within them anger and, to some extent, a newly fired suspicion of the good faith of their compatriots. The battle was heating up, and it was time to begin weeding out the hidden enemies who lived among their own ranks.

Talk was rampant in the next few days. Lieutenant Governor Bull, a South Carolinian himself, and always interested in the welfare of the colony, had his own opinions, and made them known to John Manning. Bull often visited the Manning house, and particularly when he wanted a welcoming, comfortable place to lay down the pressures and troubles of his office and talk freely. John gave him a large snifter of brandy and a huge footstool. "Come on, now, put your feet up," he said with a laugh. "We're all friends here—even Drew." He winked at his nephew. "Even though he is misguided and wrong-thinking, he is an honorable man. Just don't trust him around your womenfolk."

Bull chuckled lightly. "You have no idea what a pleasure it is to sit here and talk for the want of it, and not for the need. Decisions are burdensome things."

"You'll get no argument from any of us on that," Rob said, and got up. "I am glad I have had a chance to see you, but I must excuse myself. The Morgans are expecting Velma and me, and we will be late if I don't leave immediately. Good day to you all."

William Bull settled back in his chair, put his feet up, and sniffed at the

fine brandy John Manning had given him. Slowly, perceptibly, Drew and
the others could see the man relaxing. And then his troubles seemed to
come back to him. "If this question of the cargo had just been carried in
the affirmative, the merchants would have considered it a recession of the
Nonimportation Articles and immediately sent to England for goods as
usual. The likelihood is that the other colonies would have followed suit.
We were so close! One vote, and all the difference in the world."

Drew was seated comfortably in a wingback chair, his hands folded
across his flat stomach. "There were a lot of hot tempers flaring last night.
Some of the rifts that were created may not heal over."

Bull nodded his head slowly, his eyes on the deep amber of the brandy.
"It's true. The heat seems to have cooled a bit now that a decision has been
made, but there are some resentments remaining ready at hand to break
out on any future occasion." He swirled the brandy round in his glass, a
thoughtful smile on his face, as though amused by some private consideration of his own.

"It is a strange phenomenon, but in order for this cause to be fostered,
the people at large must be involved, and their voices must be heard. That
creates a many-headed power. It makes them difficult to lead, and on the
other hand makes it nearly impossible for us to return to conformity to our
former leaders."

John Manning couldn't hide his disappointment. "Then you think, in
your heart, that we have embarked upon a course we shall not be able to
turn back from?"

"I think it is entirely possible. We shall know better when the new royal
governor arrives, and when we have had time to see what comes of the
work done last night."

"It would help considerably if we could curtail the agitating behavior of
some of our citizens, most notably William Johnson, Daniel Cannon, and
that jokester Edward Weyman," John grumbled.

William Bull looked over at the two younger men in the room. "Neither
of you has had much to say. What are your feelings about the situation?"

"I do not want to see this come to the point of war," Drew said. "But I
am from the Upcountry, and I know from experience when there are true
grievances the authorities must listen, and act fairly, or change will be
brought about by force."

Bull's eyebrows shot up. "Manning—Drew Manning. Now I have you
placed." He chuckled a bit. "You were with that ragtag group that
marched to the Assembly with the list of grievances, and threatened to do

war on Charles Town itself. Well, well, so now you are agitating for the relief of grievances again with slightly larger stakes."

"The stakes are no higher for me now, sir, than they were in sixty-eight. Perhaps more people are involved, but each of us has only one life, and it doesn't matter much if it is over injustice in the Upcountry or injustice in all the colonies that our lives are injured."

"Surely you don't think Mother England is injuring your life?"

"What else does one call it when thirteen colonies are more or less held in bondage to service the mother country?" George asked hotly. "We pay our taxes, and heavy taxes they are, and yet our wishes are not heard and not heeded. Our mechanics are not encouraged to develop their own markets—those privileges are saved for English goods. We live on imports, and yet we have a vastly wealthy land. Given our liberty, we could develop our own markets and our own industries without interference from England. And we would not be having to quarter troops in our homes and cities."

"You've raised quite a young rebel, John," William Bull said.

"He does not fully realize what he is saying," John said quickly, casting a quick, warning glance to George.

George Manning was usually the mildest of men, but when his slow, easy temper was aroused, he was capable of being indiscreet. He now turned his nondescript brown eyes on Governor Bull, and asked, "Must I watch my words here in the privacy of my home? Shall I be labeled a traitor because I have opinions? Is this not in itself cause for grievance? Are we English subjects with the full rights of Englishmen, or are we merely pawns settled here to do service for a king who cares little for our happiness?"

"You are wrong, my friend," Bull said, looking at John. "He knows full well what he is saying." Bull got up and carefully placed his snifter on the table beside him. "I thank you for your kind hospitality, John. We shall talk again soon."

John Manning, now more than a little nervous both at his son's outburst, and the sudden departure of his friend, walked William Bull to the door.

Drew and George tactfully fled the room and went upstairs, thus avoiding the ire of John for the night.

But John was not to be held off forever, and on the following Sunday he demanded that both Drew and George accompany him and Eugenia to services at St. Michael's Anglican Church. The assistant rector waxed eloquent in his sermon on the evils of radicalism.

He told his parishioners, "We pry into our neighbors' secrets, oftimes misjudge them, hold them in contempt, ruin their reputations, and thereby sow the seeds of discord. Every idle projector, who cannot, perhaps, govern his own household, or pay debts of his own contracting, presumes he is qualified to dictate how the state should be governed, and to point out the means of paying the debts of a nation. Hence, too, it is that every silly clown and illiterate mechanic will take upon him to censure the conduct of his prince or governor, and contribute, as much as in him lies, to create and foment those understandings which, being brooded by discontent and indifference, come at last to end in schisms in the church and sedition and rebellion in the state."

George nudged Drew in the ribs and leaned close to whisper in his ear. "Do you believe you are hearing what you are hearing? 'Illiterate' and 'mechanic' used in the same sentence. A good deal of his congregation are artisans. Want to place a wager on how long it takes them to run him out of here? I give him a month."

"You are too generous," Drew whispered back.

Not having said enough, the minister went on, his chest puffed out, his face stern and righteous. "There is no greater instrument or ornament of peace than for every man to keep his own rank, and to do his own duty, in his own station, without usurping an undue authority over his neighbor or pretending to censure his superiors in matters wherein he is not himself immediately aggrieved."

Even John Manning groaned under his breath when the last was delivered. After services John put his hat back on his head, and took some time in adjusting it. George couldn't keep a straight face and finally laughed aloud. Jaw jutted out, John took long, purposeful strides, muttering, "The man is either a fool or he does not want to remain at St. Michael's and has taken this tack as expedient to his departure."

"He might have done better had he just come right out and named the men he was censuring. Did 'silly clown' make you think of anyone in particular?" Drew asked.

"Edward Weyman," George said instantly.

"He is hardly silly," John grumbled. "The man is filled with intent—rebellious and seditious intent."

In the days that followed, Edward Weyman, an upholsterer and a very active man in the rebel movement, proved almost everything either side wanted to say about him.

Soon after the disagreement about the off-loading of Robert Smythe's horses, activities in Charles Town heated up considerably. Some of these were humorous, and some were horrifyingly serious. Edward Weyman was a central figure in more than his share of them.

On April the seventeenth the Council of Safety intercepted some dispatches from England aboard the packet ship *Swallow.* Once the dispatches were opened and read, there was great consternation and a drive to make all the radical committees more active in gaining support for the Association. With the intelligence gleaned from the British missives, the council notified the other colonies that ten thousand British soldiers were being sent to suppress the colonial uprising, to blockade colonial ports, to restrict fishing off Newfoundland Banks, and to capture public stores of arms and powder.

Nothing was better designed to agitate people who were already in a state of agitation, or to drive men like Edward Weyman to immediate action. South Carolina's Secret Committee, of which Weyman was a member, and in whose activities Drew and George Manning occasionally participated, went into action, and raided the powder magazines in the area.

Dressed in dark clothing, Drew and George joined Edward and others of the town, including Henry Drayton, nephew of Lieutenant Governor Bull, and proceeded to the State House. Each man had an assignment. Both Drew and George were to bring their family carriages, as did several others. These were parked close by the State House, but not obviously in front of it. The men then moved toward the building.

George, always a bit nervous, couldn't help looking in all directions, until his head seemed to be swiveling on the pedestal of his neck.

"Stop checking everything out, George. You couldn't look more guilty if you wore a sign," Drew whispered.

They moved at a relatively normal pace through the darkness and slipped into the dubious shelter of the doorway. One of the men worked at the door, until they all sighed in relief at the telltale snap that told them they had broken into the State House.

"Hurry," Weyman urged. "The guard will be passing at any moment!"

All of them slipped inside the building and raced through the hall to the supplies.

As each of the men returned carrying a load of guns and ammunition, Drew stood near the door, watching for the guards. At his signal the men raced from the building to the waiting carriages.

Drew hurried from the State House last of all, only to encounter the guard. His heart pounded against his chest, but he tried to walk normally, his dark cape pulled tight around him. "Good evening," he said pleasantly, his head down, keeping his face in shadow. "It's a little cool tonight."

"An unpredictable time of year, sir." The guard moved on noticing nothing unusual in Drew's manner.

Drew waited for a moment, then bolted across the street into his carriage.

"We'll cover for you best we can," Weyman said from the dark depths of the carriage. "This will be discovered in the morning, and someone is going to have hell to pay. How clearly do you think he saw you? Enough to know who you are if he sees you again?"

"I don't think so. I kept my head down, and my cape around me. I'm not so well known in town as some of you."

"Is there someone you could trust who would claim to have been elsewhere with you?"

"There is always George. No one knows he was here tonight, so he might have been elsewhere—and me with him. Or my wife . . . she is arriving in town tomorrow morning. We're going to move into our new house. I might say that I had ridden to Willowtree tonight to fetch her and my grandmother and the children. Both Gwynne and my grandmother would support that story if it is necessary."

"My friend, it may be necessary. When you undertake these tasks for the cause of liberty, you do so with your neck in the shadow of a noose."

Drew hadn't taken Edward's words too seriously, until news arrived in Charleston several days later that on April nineteenth the colonials and the British had engaged in battle at Lexington. The shadow of the noose that Edward Weyman spoke of took on a more substantial aura than it had that night in the carriage.

The arms taken that night, and other nights that followed, were stored in the homes of men who were trusted patriots.

Gwynne Templeton discovered the day she moved into her new home that in a room off Andrew's study that had been intended as a supply room were secreted several dozen weapons. Appalled, she stared at the assortment of swords, sabers, muskets, and boxes filled with shot and gunpowder. She tried to speak, but couldn't. She turned and buried her face against Drew's chest.

Drew squeezed his eyes shut, then said, "I can't tell you not to be frightened, Gwynne. You have good cause."

"I am all right," she insisted. "I must . . . I simply must bring myself to accept this as part of . . . of our lives. It is just that it is so horrible when one is faced with it. It seemed like talk . . . something that would happen out of sight . . . until now, Drew. I wasn't prepared for what it would feel like when I actually saw the arms—in our house. They will be used, won't they?"

"They will, and, Gwynne, this is a part of our lives you may have to face sooner than you think. I am afraid I have blundered, and perhaps brought it to our doorstep. I was with the group who stole these arms, but I was seen by the guard as we left. I don't think he knew who I was, but I can't be sure."

"Drew!" she cried, clutching at his shirtfront. "They will hang you!"

Drew was pale, and try as he would to hide his own fear, she saw it.

"If someone should come here inquiring as to my whereabouts last night, you must tell them I was at Willowtree fetching you and the children. Are you able to do that? Can you bring yourself to lie for me, Gwynne?"

"I will lie for you, Drew. I will even kill for you if I must," she said, her eyes burning with love.

Drew gently touched the soft contours of her face, his fingers lingering on her cheekbones just below her vibrant blue eyes. He kissed her on the forehead, then touched her lips with his fingers.

"Drew, will you promise me something?" she asked softly, her lips kissing his fingertips. "Whatever happens, please promise that you will never try to protect me by keeping me out of that part of your life. I am strong enough to stand by your side through anything, my love, but I could not bear being made to stand alone in false security."

"Oh, Gwynne, my love, my darling love," he murmured. He kissed her deeply on the mouth, his tongue probing deep within the silky warmth. His hands moved swiftly, seeking out all the curves of her body, frantically fumbling with the intricate fastenings of her gown.

For a moment Gwynne luxuriated in the sensation of his hands once again caressing her body. It seemed so long since she had had him all to herself. It had been different then, and now he wanted her, and she could feel the heat and strength of his desire.

She shrugged her shoulders, aiding him in removing her gown, then deftly opened the front of his shirt. She ran her hands across the breadth of his chest, her fingertips memorizing the mound of every muscle, the feel of taut, smooth male skin.

His hand cupped the full roundness of her breast, his thumb moving slowly, provocatively across her nipple until it hardened into a rosy bud.

Together they sank to their knees onto the carpet and the velvet pool of Gwynne's discarded gown. He bent to kiss each breast, his hands cupped beneath her buttocks.

Gwynne's heart sang with the pleasure of being with him, and her song came forth in tiny moans of delight.

Before the open doors of the storage room exposing its clutter of swords and sabers and guns, Drew lay down with his wife and made love to her. Her skin was as white as new milk, and he feasted his eyes upon her before he covered that milky whiteness with his own sun-bronzed body.

Pliant and eager, Gwynne raised her hips to accept the lean hardness of her husband. As one they moved together, Drew driving deep within her as Gwynne undulated beneath him, bringing them both to ecstatic frenzy. She clutched at his back. They were one and yet Gwynne strove for even greater closeness. She breathed as he breathed, cried out with him, moved with him, clung to him.

Breathless and spent, they lay in each other's arms. Drew began to kiss her again, his lips touching each of the features of her face; then he said quietly, "I will promise you anything you ask."

In the days that followed, Gwynne was to think of that night many times. When the news of the battle of Lexington reached Charles Town, Drew found her in his study standing before the open door to the storage room staring at the assembly of arms. He walked up behind her and asked what she was doing there.

"I was just looking to see how they had changed. It is almost as if these things had a life of their own. When I saw muskets in the past, I thought of the turkey shoots we had at the holidays. When you brought them in here the other night, they no longer could be thought of that way. They became a threat, a question of my future. Now there is news of the fighting and they are things waiting to be picked up, taken from this room, and put in the hands of men I know and love so that they may kill one another. I hate these weapons, Drew."

"Without these weapons there would be no liberty for us. We would be helpless in the face of the British. We need them, Gwynne. They are only tools, and used properly they can bring about good."

Gwynne looked up at his earnest face. He wanted to reassure her, and she had no argument that would sway him. In any case it did no good for only one man to lay down his arms, and so in a sense he was correct. She smiled tentatively at him, but she couldn't forget the thoughts that someone she loved was going to lie dead as a result of American fire or British fire.

Though war brought fears and dreadful thoughts to the minds of the citizens of Charles Town, there was an excitement and sometimes a levity, too.

Edward Weyman was one of the most active and dangerous men in the patriot movement. He was fearless in the assignments he would undertake, and he was usually successful in accomplishing them. He was also a prankster.

Drew came rushing in the house one afternoon and insisted Gwynne accompany him immediately to see what the upholsterer had done this time. Weyman, using his professional talents, had made a demonstration directed toward royal officials, placemen, or other persons who were not in favor of the popular cause.

Drew hurried Gwynne along the street; then, as he neared Edward's demonstration, he slowed down, walking leisurely until the full effect was brought upon her.

A small crowd of people stood in the street and on the sidewalks looking up at a building on which was sitting an effigy of the pope. Whenever a known Tory or a royal official was in sight, the effigy moved its arms and made appropriate bows to those who "preferred royalty to liberty and social happiness."

Gwynne watched spellbound, until a petty official marched off down the street in a huff, followed by catcalls. Then she began to giggle. "He is so irreverent! Drew, how can he get away with it?"

"He has done nothing illegal—even Englishmen have a right to speak their opinions."

Gwynne laughed. "Edward certainly does that, and in very creative ways—look at the way he makes the hands move. It is most amusing."

"Some haven't seen the humor as clearly as you."

"I thought I might find you here," George said as he bounded up to fall in step with them. "I thought you might like to know that William Bull has been at the house talking with my father. Naturally the subject came round to you and me and our traitorous leanings. He is shaking the trees to find out who stole the arms from the State House."

"While he's checking up on traitorous leanings he'd better look within the ranks of his own family," Drew said. "Has he learned anything we should know about? For instance, did that guard happen to mention meeting a man well wrapped in a dark cape?"

George grinned. "That is the good news. Nary a word of any value has been dug out of anyone. The commander of the guard very glibly said that he had seen several persons about the State House, but could not say who they were."

"A good man if ever I heard of one."

"But that's not the best of it. Bull questioned Mrs. Pratt—you know, the woman who keeps the State House—and when she refused to say anything, he threatened her with the loss of her job, and still she refused to give him the names of the men. That was very brave of her, for from what I have heard, that job is the better part of her support. I can think of a goodly number of men who would not have the courage she displayed."

"But is there any danger remaining that Governor Bull will find out that you and Drew were involved in the break-in?" Gwynne asked.

"I suppose there is always some," George said cheerfully. "But I should think the greatest danger has passed. If he has not moved against Edward, I hardly think he's likely to move against us."

"I think we ought to visit Elizabeth at Willowtree for a bit, and let everyone forget about the two of you." She looked from one man to the other and saw the expressions of loss painted there as each of them considered the adventures they'd likely miss out on. For no matter what else could be said about waging war, it did produce a sense of danger and excitement that most men enjoyed, to a point. "This would only be a short visit," Gwynne prompted. "We could be back in time for the new royal governor to arrive. What can happen in so short a time?"

Drew and George exchanged glances over her head, but said nothing.

Then George said, "What would we do at Willowtree?"

"We could see how Grandma's educational plan is working. If you ask me, she is just paving the way for Seth to make a successful bolt. He soaks up every scrap of information she feeds him, and the man can speak better English than I can when he chooses to. He's got so many variations of language now, he is really quite a show to watch. He talks field-hand talk to the field hands, and house talk to the housemen, and the damnedest clearest English you ever heard to a select few whites."

"But what makes you think he's going to run?" George asked. "What do you mean by that? An uprising, or just running?"

"I'm not sure. He's a resentful man, and he doesn't take many pains to hide it, and at the same time he seems to like Grandma, and he's been pleasant to me."

"You said he was insolent," Gwynne said.

"In another bondsman I'd say that, but there is something different about Seth. What he wants is for me to look upon him as my equal, and damn it, George, I'm not sure he isn't."

"But what about an uprising? Will he stir the others up or do his disappearing quietly? I wouldn't mind a bit if we saw the last of Seth. You may think he's different, but I think he's a damned uppity nigger who doesn't know his place, and ought to be taught it."

"You may be right. The man caught my fascination, and that makes me a poor judge of him. I'd still think he's not likely to do harm to the people at Willowtree . . . but he may try to get some of the others to run with him."

"How do you know?" George asked with a little more heat in his voice.

"I don't really, it's just a feeling. Gwynne and I saw him in the swamps one night, and something about the way he acted, or looked, made me think that he would run, and that he didn't much care if I knew or not."

"I don't like the sounds of this at all. Soon as I get home, I think I'd better have a talk with Daddy about Seth. For one thing we better separate that whole bunch that just came over from Africa. Daddy has them all in one cabin, and everybody knows it's better to mix them in with the native-borns. If it were up to me, Willowtree would never purchase a single man, woman, or child fresh from Africa. They're always a pack of trouble. Can't speak the language, half the time they're sick from the voyage, and they don't want to do a lick o' work."

"Why did Uncle John buy the Africans, George?" Gwynne asked.

George shrugged. "He got a good price, and we needed more laborers— I don't know. Sometimes I wonder if Daddy thinks of that plantation at all. He never goes there unless he has to, and even then he stays only long enough to do what needs doing and comes back here. Most likely the Africans were the easiest solution to a request for additional people."

After a silence he added, "My father would have been happier to be a shopkeeper—but that wasn't to be the role of the Mannings."

"I cannot imagine Uncle John in a shop," Gwynne said. "Puttering in his garden, yes, frequenting his men's clubs, yes, but not in a shop."

George laughed. "Perhaps I exaggerate a bit. I often get quite angry when thinking about Willowtree, however. Being the youngest of three sons has many disadvantages, and no advantages that I have yet found. No one ever listens to my opinions. I'm either outvoted or considered to have no worthwhile opinion."

"Poor George," Gwynne cooed. "Now, what do the two of you say to a short visit to Willowtree? You can see what all this is about Seth, and if you want you can change the living arrangements of the Africans. If Uncle John cares as little as you say about the plantation, he won't care about that, and might not even know."

"He'd know. The change would have to be noted in the plantation book, and books are one thing my father cares passionately about. That's probably where I got the shopkeeper notion. What do you say, Drew? Shall we go?"

"If it was a short trip, we could keep abreast of what was happening here," Drew said.

"Yes," said George.

"And if anything was brewing, we are close enough that we could ride in in an afternoon."

"Yes," said George, then with a smile asked, "Are you going?"

"Yes!" said Gwynne.

15

Seth lay down in the little flat-bottomed boat and let it sway and glide as it would through the swamp channel. He had taken to using every spare moment he had to come here to the boat, putting it into the channel, and thinking. Seth got great pleasure from his thoughts, and the dreams he was in the process of changing into realities were the first bright hopeful thing he had had since he had been taken captive and sent to the colonies on that hellhole slave ship.

When he was in Africa free, he had had no need to consider the thoughts he thought of as a necessity here. He had never before questioned slavery. Perhaps he never would have had he not become a slave himself. African kings were no different from other kings in their attitudes toward their slaves. Slaves were property to be sold, bartered away, or given away, and Seth had never questioned this until now.

He hadn't questioned much of anything back then. His father had filled his head full of tales of the legendary and mysterious city of Timbuktu with all its learned men, and its magnificent mosques, and its busy market-places. As a child he had lain in the sparse grass, closed his eyes against the glaring hot sun, and dreamed of the promised day his father would send him there to learn, to study, and to begin a trade. Everything he was, and everything he had dreamed, had centered around his expectations of Timbuktu.

When the day had finally come and one of his father's brothers had taken him to the city, he could hardly believe his eyes. The city was built of mud, and there were houses everywhere. The dunes between the Tanezrouft Desert to the north and the swamps of the Niger River to the south held the shimmering city of Timbuktu. Some of the houses there had two stories to them, and wooden doors studded with iron bolts and small high windows. To a boy who had never seen anything but the small groupings of tribal shelters, Timbuktu was magnificent.

His uncle had hurried him through the crowded streets, and many times he had nearly been run down by rushing Arabs nearly hidden in their voluminous white robes. Fierce Tuareg nobles with veils covering most of their faces pushed among the throng clutching their traditional weapons, the lance, the shield, and the sword. Children ran through the streets in naked abandon, and at every turn a man or a woman had set up a stand to sell their wares.

At the edge of the confusion and trade bands of Arabs and Africans sheltered their camels as they rested from a long journey across the hot dry, Sahara, or awaited the start of another journey into those arid depths.

Seth had never seen anything like it, and immediately when he entered the city it struck a chord of home for him. He was not awed by the noise or the busyness, but enthralled by it. He liked the shouted calls for commerce and the haggling that went on over every sale. Before he had been taught anything, he recognized there was an art to this trading.

Seth was left in the care of an old man of the Malinke tribe who had come to the city years ago and had chosen to stay. He had provided a home for many young boys of Seth's tribe when it came time for them to be educated. Seth remained with the man for two years, and he worked harder in those two years than he had known it possible to work. He had learned to write in the Arabic language, to keep accounts, and to be proficient in the knowledge of the riches of his country. He learned about the foreign nations that had tried repeatedly to gain a foothold in Africa, and who were then succeeding. He learned of the many wars that had caused his people to move their kingdom time after time, always weakening the power of the Malinke, and he vowed that in some small way he would restore some of that power and respect in his lifetime.

He remained in Timbuktu for a little over two years, and when it was judged that he had mastered his studies, and knew the Koran as a true believer should, he was apprenticed to a *dyula,* a trader, who brought anything from salt to gold to woven fabrics from the city to the outlying tribes, and then brought goods back into the city to be sold at the market. It was during this time that Seth truly found his calling. He loved being a trader. There was no aspect of it he did not thrive on. The *dyulas* were not only traders, but they carried the news across their territory, and taught the message of the Koran to those who were not so fortunate as to be able to study in Timbuktu. Occasionally he and his mentor remained in one settlement long enough to see a mosque built. Seth had loved those few times, for eventually they were joined in prayer by the chiefs and people of the country.

It had been after one of these most wonderful of times that Seth had been taken captive. The people of the village had no more than stepped outside of their new mosque when a horde of warriors from a neighboring tribe had rushed upon them with spears from older years, and the guns supplied by the white slave traders that were so devastating. Seth had been among those men, women, and children who had been taken captive. His protests that he was not a tribesman, but a *dyula,* had been received with derisive laughter. He had been herded along with the others, thrust into a caravan, taken to the coast, and held in a pen until the next shipment of slaves was taken aboard a ship heading for the Americas.

It had all seemed so fast, and yet at the same time so painfully slow. His sense of insult and outrage had carried him through the first awful days, and there was the expectation that his mentor or his father would come rescue him. It had been a long time before he faced the reality that no one was going to come for him—not ever. Only then did he begin to look at the other captives as someone like himself. Most of his fellow slaves were from Angola, many were Bantu, and finally he discovered there were a few Malinke like himself, but from other tribes. These few clustered together, and vowed uncooperation with their fate. He would say anything, do anything, risk anything, to escape.

He began to think of his early days on Willowtree after John Manning had purchased him at auction in Charles Town, when he'd heard the sound of a bird repeated over and over again. He rose up from the bottom of the punt, resting his weight on one elbow, and peered out into the swamp. On one of the spits of higher land stood Rufus, Tom, Cuffee, and with them was Folly. He waved at the waiting group, got up, and began to pole to them. What to do about that Folly girl. She stuck to him like glue, and truth be told he liked her—liked her spirit—but an escape was no place for a woman. If it were, he would have Annie and his boy-child Isaiah out here planning to run with him. But it was no place, and he wasn't at all certain that he could make it with these men to aid him, but he would try, and later he'd return with money and power to buy the freedom of his woman and son.

As he pulled the boat near to the bank, the three men and Folly clambered aboard, nearly upsetting the steady little punt. With a good deal of squealing from Folly and laughter and advice from the men, they all settled down, and Seth began to pole them deep into the swamp, far away from ears and eyes of the overseers and white inhabitants of Willowtree.

Rufus, who was the son of Odo, and for a long time was not trusted by Seth because of that relationship, looked around him. "Sho nobuddy gwine fin' us in heah."

Seth gave him a cold look. "Feeling secure is the most dangerous of failings. We can be found in here, and must always be alert to the man who will come and see of what we do and hear of what we speak."

Rufus hung his head a bit, but his eyes were merry and he was grinning at Cuffee. "Ain't no whie man gwine come heah. He be afeered o' de snakes an' de suckin' mud o' de swamp."

Seth stopped poling. "I think you're not to be trusted, Rufe. I seen a white man back here myself. I talked to him, and he had no fear of snakes or mud or anything else, and I saw in his eyes that he could read what was in my heart."

"Who dat?" Rufus asked belligerently.

"Mastah Drew Manning," Seth said with supreme confidence.

"He ain't got nuthin' to do wiff Willowtree. What he doin' back heah?"

Seth said nothing, but gave a soft, menacing laugh. "Don't need an answer, Rufe, you need to have caution. It's enough to know he was here, and he is dangerous."

"Awww," Rufus muttered, adding words that no one understood.

Seth felt the sharp cold chill of misgiving race down his spine. He had known all along that Rufus was not a man he should include in his plans. He was too careless, and he seldom used his mind.

Seth pushed the punt deeper into the swamp, out onto the green-carpeted duckweed lake. He was heading for an island in that lake that he had not shown Drew and Gwynne. He had been tempted. Drew fascinated him, and his curiosity to see what Drew would have done on seeing the island had almost overcome his caution. Perhaps it had not been caution that had won out. It had been memory. Once captured as a slave, Seth never again wanted the horror of that experience repeated, and that was the only way he envisioned being caught. Being caught meant repeating the whole horrible nightmare-time again.

From his pen near the coast he could see the huge European ships coming toward the shore. They never came all the way in, but sat like huge fish some distance out from the shore. After a time the quiet, heated air would be split with gunfire from those black hulks sitting, bobbing hungrily in the water, and then there had been a flurry of activity in the compound. African traders in all manner of garb leaped into their canoes, racing across the surf to board those ships and bargain for the people caged in the pens.

Seth knew why the Europeans didn't come ashore. In his travels as a *dyula* he had learned much, and he knew about the salt mines, and the gold mines, and the ivory trade, and more than a little about the slave trade. He had even seen a few whites who had dared to live ashore become even paler when talk turned to the people of Africa who had sharpened their teeth to a point, and who had come in the deepest darkness of the night to steal a white sailor away unseen for a feast the following day. Seth knew these were not just stories; some were true. He knew of many occasions when a European had been taken in retaliation for the practice of disreputable Europeans of weighing anchor and enslaving chiefs or traders who had come aboard to bargain in good faith.

His memories were broad and deep, and haunted him like a bad dream that repeated itself night after night. They kept him ever vigilant, ever sensitive to the slightest breach of utmost caution. Rufus had been born here, and had no memories to match Seth's, and his father had taken the path of settling into the white man's way, and gaining respect and a position there for himself. There were others who had taken the same course at Willowtree, like Jehu, and that was the one misgiving he had.

Seth respected Jehu, and to a lesser degree Odo. He could not forget the time he had tried to talk to these older men, and Jehu had calmly and firmly said, "When ignorance is bliss, it is foolish to be wise."

Seth had been able to do nothing but blink in amazement at the man. "How can you want to stay here—to be a bonded man when the world is out there and you would be respected and able to do as you wish?"

"My world is no longer out there," Jehu said quietly. "My people are scattered, some are dead, I have no place that is mine to return to, and here I am respected. Never has the lash of a whip touched my body since I have come to Willowtree. I read my books, I do my work. I am an honored man."

Seth had not been able to argue. Had Jehu been younger, he would have done, but he had been taught well to venerate the aged, and he could not bring himself to argue merely to win his point. Finally he had said meekly, "All men must follow their own path. Yours is right for you, but it is not mine. My hope is on the open savannahs of Africa, and in the trading cities. I cannot rest here, for there is no place for me."

"You make your place," Jehu said firmly.

"My place has already been made," Seth had replied, and never again had the subject come up again between himself and Jehu, or Odo.

He brought the punt near to the island and helped Folly come ashore. Tom, Rufus, and Cuffee scurried about the small green island picking up wood dry enough to build a fire, and Folly unwrapped the kerchief she had tied around her waist, showing Seth proudly the scraps and bits of food she had managed to bring with her so that they would have something to eat later in the night.

Seth smiled down at the girl. Folly was fourteen, and he thought of her as a child, although he was himself only seventeen. He had grown tall and straight early, and he had been a man for a long time. He had felt the power of his being for a long time, and on occasions such as this he liked to show off a bit. He picked up a sharp rock that had been embedded in the spongy turf, then moved several feet away from Folly and stood motionless, listening, looking up into the trees. With a movement so quick that Folly hardly saw it, Seth's arm shot out and the rock hurtled through the air. Seconds later a bird, neck bloodied, fell to the ground.

Folly stared wide eyed.

Seth smiled, a regal expression on his face as though he were speaking to an underling. "The hunter has done his task. Prepare our supper, woman."

"How'd you do that?" Folly breathed.

"What does it matter to you? I have done it. Hurry, girl, we have business to discuss. The men will be hungry."

With Seth sitting at what he designated to be the head of the fire, Tom, Cuffee, and Rufus seated themselves at the other cardinal points. Seth waited for as long as it took for the others to come to attention, fall out of it, and then regain it, then he raised his hands, and bowed his head, and they prayed.

Seth would hold no meeting, nor would he eat before he had given honor to the gods and begged their protection for his endeavors. He always had a great deal to say to the gods, and Rufus and the others were tired of all the praying long before Seth was willing to stop.

Folly watched him from the corner of her eye as she worked over the fire they had built just for her to cook on. Now, and on other occasions, she had suspected that Seth's prayers lasted as long as it took for a meal to be prepared, but she hadn't been dumb enough to say so. But she had noticed that along with never beginning a meeting without prayer, Seth always managed to eat before he talked of their plans.

The bird was hot and juicy, the skin browned to a crisp, and Folly had managed to bring enough leftovers with her that they had roasted yams and warmed-up corn bread. Despite Unity's suspicions of Seth, she always came through for Folly, providing all sorts of delectables from the great-house kitchen.

Seth, satisfied with his meal, was finally ready to talk about business. He asked each of the other men if they had discussed their feelings about being enslaved on Willowtree.

Cuffee shrugged in a way so typical of him. Cuffee could say almost nothing without shrugging first. Sometimes the gesture was so extreme it gave the appearance of a nervous tic. "Ah ain't nevah seen such a bunch o' lazy niggers. Ain't nobuddy wants to do nuthin'. Dey all talkin' bout de rice an' de li'l patches Miss Lizzybeff gwine gib dem to work fo' demselves. Ain't nobuddy wants to run 'ceptin' us."

Seth nodded, his face grave. "That's Drew Manning again. That patch for the families was his idea."

"How you know?" Rufus asked. He questioned everything, jealous whenever Seth seemed to know something he did not.

"I use my ears," Seth said coldly. "I told you he is a dangerous man."

Rufus pouted but did not carry the disagreement any further. Sometimes he wondered if he ought to be putting his lot in with Seth. Once Seth was gone, or caught and hanged, Rufus would most likely be king of the young blacks in the quarters. Before Seth came, he had never thought of taking such a position for himself, but he was of the same build as Seth, and if no one looked too closely, he resembled him in feature—or at least he thought so. It would be mighty nice to have all the womens pantin' after him. He'd never seen the like of the loyalty Seth demanded of his women. Annie wouldn't cast her eyes in anyone's direction other than Seth's, and Folly was like a mangy ol' dog trottin' after her master. Maybe when Seth was caught, he and Folly could get together. He'd like that—or maybe better still, when Seth got them out of danger, maybe he and Folly could run off on their own.

Seth's voice pulled him back to the present. Seth was saying, "You all think that it is not likely that we can stir up an uprising against the Mannings on this plantation?"

All bowed their heads, shaking them back and forth with a low, hummed no in response. "Ain't nobuddy wanna harm Missy," Tom said, and then hesitantly added, "I don' wanna, neither. She be good to us."

Seth's eyes flickered a bit as he added Elizabeth Manning's name to his list of dangers. She and her grandson were powerful people. He recognized the power in them, for he had it in himself. Then quickly the face of a very young child crossed his mental vision, and he added the name of Nathaniel Dancer. He had thought often of that little boy, and always his curiosity was aroused. As scared as he had been the Christmas morning when he had first seen Seth, his eyes had been bold. It had only been his age and his size that had made him cower, not his spirit.

He went on with his information-gathering. "We got anybody who would make it look like there was trouble so's the plantation folk would be thinkin' there was trouble afoot?"

Rufus smiled. "I kin allus stirs up trouble. Don' take but a wink to gettin' Mule an' ol' Bill to fightin' over Bill's woman. We kin git them to kickin' up a storm in de qua'ters."

"Yes, and if the four of us could somehow steal a couple of pistols and a musket from the storehouse that would be enough to alarm the plantation."

"I be de bes' to git de pistols," Cuffee said, with such a tremendous shrug that Tom placed his hand on his shoulder and complained, "You gotta stop dat, Cuffee, you gibbin' me de jitters. Ah feels like I got somethin' crawlin' all ober me, when you does dat."

Seth put his hand up. "No more talk of that. Cuffee, you get the pistols and hide them here on the island."

"How'm Ah gwine git heah?"

"You know how to use the punt—pole out hea—here," Seth said.

"Ah don' like de swamp when Ah's alone."

"Ah go wiff you," Tom offered. "When we steals de pistols, Seth?"

"Not until I tell you. It must be very close to the time we are ready to leave. Best would be on the very day."

"When dat day comin'?" Rufus asked. "We been talkin' an' prayin' till we almos' too ol' to run. When da day comin'?"

"Cha's T'n be a busy place dese days," Cuffee said. He had a friend who worked in one of the Charles Town houses and gave him a report every Sunday night when they all went to the city for services. "He say won' be lon' til dey all fightin' de British right in de streets. He mighty upsot 'cause de guns an' stuff was stole from de public stores."

Seth smiled finally, a broad, pleased smile. "Then it will be soon. When attention is drawn to the city, that is the best time for us to run, for it will take them longer to organize. Even to gather neighbors, and their dogs, they will have to locate men who might be occupied elsewhere." Seth was particularly pleased with the idea of the English helping them in their bid for freedom, for he had since learned that it had been a British ship that had brought him to these shores and slavery. It was only just that they should help free him. He was certain now that he had the approval and the protection of the gods. In such omens as these small pieces of information came affirmation of the gods' intent.

They talked on well into the darkest part of the night, and they laughed over the happenings on the plantation, and then they put out their fire and got back into the punt. On silent feet they made their way back to the quarters and slipped into their respective cabins to sleep for the few hours remaining until the plantation bell rang at five o'clock in the morning.

16

As spring heated up into summer, the Mannings thought little about Seth and the possibility of an uprising. It was not a totally forgotten issue, for uprisings were always a concern for the inhabitants of South Carolina, but the swifter-moving events that were bringing the colony to the brink of war held their attention more closely.

In mid-June 1775 a series of events brought to light that there might be little difference between the Mannings' concern over an uprising and their worry over an approaching war. On June seventeenth a new royal governor arrived aboard the H.M.S. *Scorpion* to take over the leadership of the colony for the King of England. Charlestonians, fun loving and always pleased at the prospect of a celebration, displayed an unusual reticence and reluctance to celebrate the coming of the new royal governor in any joyful manner. Governor Lord William Campbell was greeted with near silence, at least by Charles Town standards. The new governor, and his wife, the former Sarah Izard of Charles Town, moved in with Sarah's relatives while they awaited the completion of their new home. His connection with the Izard family, known to have joined the ranks of the rebels, probably aided in making his arrival as pleasant as it was, but what was significant to the Mannings, no matter what their private leaning, was that it had not produced a festive welcome.

John Manning returned to his home after having greeted William Campbell. Eugenia chattered happily at his side, telling him unwanted details about Sarah's gown and the decor of the Campbell house. John listened distractedly, a frown creasing his brow.

As soon as the entire family had gathered, the Manning men headed of one accord to the study while the women set about preparing for dinner.

Rob, always at a loss when his father seemed to be, said, "It may not have any significance at all, Daddy. Many governors have come and gone —the populace is suspicious right now. Most likely it is a matter of testing the man's mettle, and then all will welcome him when he proves himself."

John touched his fingers together, making a steeple with his hands. "Is that how you see it, Drew? George?"

Drew and George exchanged quick glances. "No, sir," Drew said simply, not wishing fully to express his own opinion and end up in yet another of the increasingly heated arguments over politics that seemed to afflict his family these days.

John didn't press it. "I didn't think you would. I suppose you agree with him, George?"

George looked uncomfortable and shifted his weight. "I know you don't want to hear it, Daddy, but I do think today was significant, and I don't think William Campbell could prove himself and win his way into the hearts of the people if he turned out to be St. Peter himself. It's too late."

John looked at his son; dismay and pride both shone in his eyes. Tonight, after the house had quieted, and all others were asleep, he would rethink his whole position regarding the recent political events. He was a Tory, but his feelings were becoming muddled, or perhaps he was merely being caught up in the fervor of the patriots' zeal. Patriots, he mused to himself; patriots of what? England? A new nation? Suddenly he stood up and ended the possibility of any further conversation. "Well, gentlemen, let's find the ladies of the house. Our supper must be near ready, and I, for one, have quite an appetite for both food and some light conversation."

It was a quiet meal, with most of the conversational burden being carried by the women. Soon after they had quit the table, Drew and Gwynne and the children left to return to their own new home.

"You've been very quiet all evening, Drew," Gwynne said mildly as he concentrated on the road. "It is getting more serious all the time, isn't it? Uncle John is a different man—so quiet. He even looks old all of a sudden."

Drew took a deep breath and put his arm around his wife, drawing her close against him. "We're in for some hard times, Gwynne," he said in a low voice. "Uncle John is aware of it . . . we all are, even Rob, although he doesn't want to see it. We are all going to have to make our positions clear. The sides are drawing tight, and sooner or later each of us will have to declare our loyalties or we are going to be attacked from both sides."

"We shall be the enemy of the Tories because of those of us who are patriots, and we shall be enemies of the patriots because of those of us who are Tories. It is so awful, Drew. I think about it and I feel sick." She remained quiet for a moment, then added, "But, Drew, there is also something in me that is excited when I think of independence. Not only are my loyalties divided, but so are my emotions. Is that a terrible thing for me to admit?" she asked, looking up into his face.

Drew laughed lightly and gave her a one-armed hug. "If it is, then you have a good deal of company. I feel that way. George does, and I know Grandma does. I suspect Uncle John does in his own way, and perhaps Leo and Rob as well."

Gwynne snuggled closer to him, enjoying the scent and feel of him. "Then I won't worry about it. Except . . . it doesn't seem laudable to feel anticipation and excitement about the coming of a war. Why is it that human beings always seem to make their great forward movements by such devastating means?"

"Are you going to turn into a theorist on me . . . or a philosopher?"

"No," she said. "But I do wonder, don't you—ever?"

"Yes," he said slowly, and thought back to the time he had stood in a woods in the Carolina wilderness with a group of Regulators waiting for several outlaws to be hanged, and was unable to feel anything other than an impatience to get on with the job so the Regulators could be on their way again to search out more outlaws. "Perhaps it is because it takes too long for us to put our beliefs into practice. We wait until we can tolerate the violation of ourselves no more, and then we erupt into violence."

"But then what happens to us? How can we go back to living peacefully after we have wreaked havoc?"

"I don't think you would find more than a handful of people who would agree with me, and perhaps not even a handful, but I do not believe human beings are violent. I think we avoid a violent solution to the point that we exhaust all other options, and find ourselves with only that one outlet remaining. Look at this situation . . . we have been talking and petitioning England to change policies for over ten years. The Regulators petitioned the Assembly repeatedly asking for aid, a peaceful aid, for years before they actually took to the field to solve the outlaw problem themselves. We naturally resist change, and anything that might be disruptive to our survival, and then when the circumstances become so restrictive and harsh that we can bear it no longer, we erupt into violence."

Gwynne smiled in the darkness. "I do hope you are right, Drew. If you are, then perhaps someday we'll learn to listen to one another and we won't have wars," she said. "You make me very proud to be your wife. Have I told you that before? How very proud I am to be Mrs. Andrew Manning?"

Drew laughed appreciatively. "If you have, I like hearing it again."

Gwynne moved even closer to him, her head resting on his shoulder. "Have I also told you that I am proud of being the mother of your children?"

He kissed her forehead, tipped her chin up so that her eyes met his.

"You are going to be a father again, Drew," she said softly. "I think you are going to be having a child of the war . . . if there is one."

Drew just grinned at her. No words came to him. Then he let out a cry such as that used by the Regulators, and awakened Elizabeth, Susan, and Mary, and Nathaniel. The smaller children began to cry, and the two older ones brought forth a series of alarmed and sleepy questions as to what had happened.

Penny Webb tried to quiet them. Gwynne clucked at Andrew, and then began to laugh. "Your Daddy is a daft man, children. Pay him no mind and go back to sleep. He was merely baying at the moon like an old hound."

"Not so! You are going to have a little brother or sister in due time, children. We shall celebrate. Nathaniel, start a song!"

"Drew!" Gwynne protested. "It is very late! We can't be singing now."

"Why not? Sing, Nathaniel! Sing, all of you!" he cried happily, and began to sing in his deep rich voice.

Gwynne hid her face in her hands and laughed helplessly.

They drove up to their front door, something to be heard more than seen. The two younger children were still howling in dismay, and the rest were laughing and singing.

The air of festivity was shattered early the next morning when George Manning pounded at their front door. His face was pale, and he was panting in agitation. "Mornin', Gwynne. Drew, I've got to talk to you—privately."

Drew looked at Gwynne and shrugged. "Excuse us, darling," he said, kissing her quickly on the cheek. "Ask Millie to bring coffee to the study, please," he added. Then he hurried after George into his private room.

"What's happened, George?" he asked with concern. "Is everyone at Grandma's all right?"

"For the moment," George said. "Drew do you recall that conversation we had some time back about Seth?"

"Yes . . . has he run?"

"No, but by God, he may do worse than that. I came here to get your help in convincing Daddy and Leo that they had better keep a wary eye out on our slaves. I never did like that black bastard . . . we may be facing an uprising, Drew. Right out there on Willowtree!"

Drew shook his head. "George, drink this," he said, and handed him a cup of coffee from the tray Millie had brought in. "Now, begin at the beginning, and tell me what has caused your alarm."

George Manning ran a hand through his hair. "All right," he said with a concentrated effort to calm himself and begin in a logical fashion. "Late last night I was talking to some men after a meeting of the Liberty Boys. Secret British documents have been intercepted. The British have plans to incite the Indians and the blacks to rise against certain settlers. We are—"

"Now, wait a moment. Even if what you say is true and they succeed, Willowtree is owned by your father, a known and loyal Tory. The British are not going to incite anyone against their own people."

"It's Grandma, Drew! News of some of her innovations at Willowtree are widely known. You do realize, Drew, no matter how much we love her or admire her, our sweet little grandmother is a flaming radical. She makes most of the Liberty Boys look like innocent thumb-sucking toddlers."

"Surely the British are not out to make war on old women, George," Drew said. "I think we should look into the matter, but I think you are overly worried. Perhaps the papers of which you speak were mere suggestions, and not orders at all. The British are not fools, nor are they vicious. Everyone knows what could happen if an uprising of any size should occur. It would be a bloodbath. No one would want that."

"You have too much faith in human nature, and it isn't warranted in this case, Drew. This information is not the first we've had on such activities. The Council of Safety took the Superintendent of Indian Affairs into custody for supplying the Indians and Negroes with firearms. Well, Mr. Superintendent John Stuart has escaped. He is now safely aboard the H.M.S. *Saint John,* free to do his dirty work at leisure. I want your help, Drew. You've got to join your voice with mine and convince Daddy and Leo and Rob that a closer eye must be kept on the bondsmen at Willowtree, particularly Seth."

"Have you said anything to Uncle John about this?"

"Of course, I have, but as usual they listen politely to the youngest son, and do virtually nothing. Daddy said he'd look into it the next time he went to Willowtree—that's next week, if he goes in accordance with his usual schedule. Rob and Leo just looked at each other with knowing smiles, and said Jehu and Odo would keep everyone in line at Willowtree."

"They have a point. Jehu is part of the family, and he is the unquestioned head man among the bondsmen. None of them would make any kind of move without Jehu's approval and knowledge."

"Do you include Seth in that?" George asked, eyebrows raised.

"No," Drew admitted. "Seth acknowledges no man to be his better, including his white masters."

"And if we have an uprising at Willowtree, Seth will be the leader of it, and he has the capability for the kind of leadership required. And thanks to Grandma he is educated and prepared."

"I'll go with you to talk to your father and brothers. I still think you are most likely unduly alarmed, but Grandma and the family will be spending more time at Willowtree soon, and we'd better be safe than sorry. Let's have some breakfast, and assure Gwynne that you have not brought news of great illness or death with you. Then we shall ride to the city."

A serious group of men gathered in the study of John Manning late on the afternoon of June 19, 1775.

"George has already told of his concern, Drew—and Rob, Leo, and I have assured him we will look into the matter at the first opportunity. I am sorry you were made to take this journey this afternoon for something so unnecessary. I fear my youngest son has caught the alarmist fever of some of our more radical elements." He smiled suddenly, if a little patronizingly. "If he does not control his tendencies, he will make even you appear to be conservative, Drew."

"I am sorry, sir, but I believe you may be taking George's warning a bit too lightly. I am not at this point prepared to sound any kind of alarm, but I would suggest some prudent caution. As George has pointed out to both of us, John Stuart has been caught in the act of supplying arms to—"

John put his hand up. "No! He was not caught distributing arms to anyone, and it has not been proved. He has been accused."

"It is also known that he has spread inflammatory propaganda to the Indians and the Negroes. He is a dangerous man, and at Willowtree we do have a man fully capable of leading an uprising. All I am suggesting is that you quietly, without raising a hue and cry, look into the activities of some of the bondsmen at Willowtree and assure yourself that no unusual activity is going on, or that no group of bondsmen seem to be gathering too frequently. This may be accomplished, granted a little luck, without raising a question in anyone's mind. No one even need know it is being done."

"What would be the point of secrecy?" Leo asked.

"So as not to plant ideas where they may not already be," Drew said.

"I think the entire suggestion is twaddle," Rob said. "The British are not going to make any move against Willowtree or the Mannings—at least not our branch of the family. If you are worried about uprisings, Drew, perhaps you'd better look to Cherokee. I should think you'd be far more vulnerable to this kind of attack than we are. Not only are you known as a patriot, but your plantation is isolated, and the chances of success are increased."

"I have not overlooked the dangers to Cherokee, Rob. Before George and I rode back into town, I sent a messenger to Ned at Cherokee telling him of all the information I have regarding this matter, and suggesting he do the same as I am suggesting you do at Willowtree."

John took a deep breath. "Perhaps you are correct. Being cautious will do no harm. Leo, will you see to it? Ride to Willowtree tomorrow and see if there is anything unusual to report. Jehu can be trusted and will know what is being talked of among the slaves. See if he knows anything about the activities of Superintendent Stuart. I confess I will be amazed if he even recognizes the man's name.

"I think you ought to heed Drew's caution to keep your fact-finding quiet and secret. We should not give a man like Seth such an idea if, in fact, he does not already have it."

"My word! Why do you harp on this bondsman Seth?" Rob said in exasperation. "One would think he was some sort of super being. He can barely speak the language, and he is fit for nothing but work in the fields. We have tried to teach him more skillful tasks and he is hopeless."

"Then he is fooling you. Seth speaks very clear English, better than some white men I know," Drew said severely. "He is a bright, able man. If you have been unable to make him take a position of responsibility on that plantation, I assure you he is the one who has chosen the field."

"What makes you such an expert on Seth?" Rob said. "You do not know him nearly as well as we do."

"I know him well enough," Drew said. "And from what you say, better than you."

"Leo," John said, "You have not answered me. Can we count on you to go to Willowtree and look into this matter?"

Leo shrugged. "I'll go, but I don't feel as Drew and George do. I don't think we are a likely target for such activity by the British, and I doubt, even if Seth were capable, that there is another slave at Willowtree who would follow him."

"You have several Africans," Drew reminded him. "And the last time I was there, all of them were housed in one cabin. Africans are known to run, and cause trouble on plantations, especially when they are permitted to form close groups."

"They no longer live in one cabin," Rob said. "Leo and I changed the living arrangements several months ago."

"Well, there is no point in going on with this—we shall merely be arguing to no avail. Leo will look into it, and we shall await his findings. Drew, will you now stay to supper with us? It is a long ride back to your house, and we would enjoy the company."

"Thank you, Uncle John. I appreciate the offer, but Gwynne is waiting for me—she has several people coming for supper, and on the pain of death, I promised not to be late. I have time for a short visit with Grandmother, and then must be on my way."

When Drew came from Elizabeth's sitting room nearly an hour later, George caught up with him in the front hall and walked to the stables with him. "I will ride a way with you. I feel very strongly about this, Drew, and I know Leo. I could tell from the look on his face, he is going to do little or nothing about this."

"Give him a chance, George. If he does nothing, we'll talk to Uncle John again, and if that fails we'll go to Grandma. Let her do the talking and I'm sure Leo will move more swiftly if for no reason other than to quiet Grandma."

George managed to laugh. "You have a point. Has it ever occurred to you, Drew, that we Mannings seem to produce more strong females than males?"

"Watch what you say—my male pride will tolerate only so much of that kind of talk."

George laughed again. "Excepting yourself, and me, of course, it is true! This family has some formidable women in it. First there's Grandma—a monstrous force in anybody's book. Then there is Gwynne, and Joanna's no slouch when it comes to having her own way with nearly anyone, and I have a feeling that in years to come Bethany will be quite a woman, and God above—look to your own Mary! Tiny as she is, she turns those big blue eyes on you filled with indignation, and man—I don't stand a chance. I think it is the combination of the blue eyes and the red hair."

Now Drew laughed. "Yeah, she blinds you. Gwynne and I had hoped by now that the color of her hair would have faded a bit."

George was laughing harder, almost a belly laugh. "Not our Mary! I don't think she'll ever fade in any way. Hey! I caught up with you to talk of serious things, Drew."

"We'll take care of them—in their own time, George. For now, give Leo and Rob a chance."

"But supposing they do just what you warned them not to do and cause a problem where perhaps there was none?"

"And suppose the sky falls. We can't suppose. Right now all we can do is wait and see what happens."

"All right. All right, but I still say it is taking one hell of a chance. Both my brothers are so damned arrogant when it comes to the rights and wrongs of the patriots' cause they are likely to take this warning lightly, or make a mess of it just for spite."

Drew didn't dispute what George said, but short of ignoring his uncle's orders regarding his own property, there was nothing he could do right now. "I don't think either of them would do something foolish out of spite. Ignorance, perhaps—but our hands are tied for the moment. That's all there is to it, George. We must wait and give them a chance. Hope you and I are wrong in our worries."

"Well, I do," George said reluctantly. "But, damn, it smarts to think that our being wrong makes them right."

Drew clapped his cousin affectionately on the back. "Come with me to dinner. You won't be missed here tonight, and Gwynne and I would love the company."

"But you said you are having guests. . . ."

"And one more will be welcome, particularly when that one extra guest is you."

"Well, let's go! You're allus dawdlin' around, Drew," George said, laughing and running to the stables. "Hey! You in there! Saddle my horse!"

Part Three

Leo

17

Leo and Rob finally decided who would go to Willowtree to look into the problem of a possible slave uprising by tossing a coin.

"Damn!" Leo swore. "I don't know why I let you talk me into things like this. I always lose. I can't turn a card, and I never win a coin toss."

"When are you ever going to learn?" Rob said, grinning. "See you in a few days, big brother. Have fun with your spy duty."

"Eloise isn't going to like this. She doesn't like Willowtree—says there is nothing to do there, and she doesn't care much for the neighbors."

Rob shrugged. "Don't take her."

Leo looked aghast. "She'd never stand for it!"

Rob gave him a smirk. "Who wears the pants, Leo? Tell her to shut up, you've got business to tend to."

"You've gotten very crude of late, Rob. I don't speak to Eloise in that fashion."

Leo broached the subject of the trip to Willowtree with his wife late that evening after they had retired to their rooms for the night.

"It shouldn't require more than three or four days. The country air will do you good. We have been in the city too long."

Eloise Milton Manning looked at him with a cold, long stare. She came from a well-established Carolina family noted for its entertaining and its impeccable hospitality. Though she thought she had seen the same qualities in Leo that she admired in her father and brother, she was now convinced that she had been entirely mistaken. For one thing, the Mannings were anything but an orderly family. They were given to loud and volatile arguments among themselves, which seldom seemed to bring about any real hard feelings, but nonetheless kept the family on its toes at all times. "I see no reason to disrupt our routine simply because George and Drew have caused another uproar. I can understand George's troublemaking— after all he has nothing better to do than spend money and cause mischief. But Drew should be more responsible. Doesn't he have enough to do managing Cherokee and Riverlea and his new home to keep his nose out of your business?"

"He might be trying to help us," Leo said with little conviction.

"You said you do not agree with the information he and George gave you. I think it is ridiculous that you knuckle under to decisions you do not agree with. Stand up for yourself, Leo, and tell them *no,* that you are not going to be the errand boy on a task that is nonsense to begin with. As a matter of fact, I have been thinking for some time that we would be much better off living with, or near to, my family, Leo."

"Eloise," Leo said quickly before she could draw breath and go on. "I don't want to discuss our living arrangements at the moment. I just want you to tell the servants to pack our necessities for a short trip to Willow-tree. Perhaps I overdid my objections to what Drew and George have suggested. While I consider it no more than a remote possibility, I have sufficient respect for Drew's judgment to at least look into the matter. It would be a pity to awaken one night to find a shrieking, knife-wielding black at the foot of one's bed."

Eloise looked horrified. "And you'd dare suggest taking me into a situation so fraught with danger! Leo! I don't believe you care for me at all. You couldn't!"

Rob's parting words rang in his head. He took a deep breath. "Shut up, Eloise! I wear the pants in this family, and what I decide will become what we do. I shall go to Willowtree by myself. You will remain behind." He quickly got into bed and blew out the lamp on the nearby table before she could see the quiver of weakness in him or the look of triumph that flashed in his eyes. His only regret was that he hadn't an audience. No one would ever know how boldly he had told his wife to hold her tongue, and made his own decision. Perhaps this momentary strength would carry over to other things. Perhaps even so far as to aid him in deciding what uniform he was going to wear if war really came to South Carolina.

He shuddered and pulled the sheet higher up on his neck. He wished he could tell the patriots to shut up as easily as he had told Eloise. He had enjoyed being an English subject. It had never hampered him in the past, and even though there had been a few restrictive laws and taxes, overall he had led his life unimpeded. He had a beautiful city to call his own, a nice home, good society, money in his pockets, and the promise of more. Until the patriots had begun yelling over every tax, no one had seemed to mind a great deal what England had done. If he had his way, he'd awaken in the morning, and all the strife and the talk of liberty would be gone. A bad dream.

But it wouldn't be gone. He knew that. He had been wishing the same wish for over a year now, and it hadn't gone away. It had only gotten worse. There had been a time, which now seemed a long time ago, when he and Drew had been the best of friends. They had talked together about every imaginable subject, laughed together, fought together. Leo had thought then that it would always be like that. His cousin was his best friend and would remain so. But when Drew had gone to fight with the Regulators a change had taken place. Drew had returned from those long rides and hunts with the Regulators a different man. He had been rebellious, suspicious of authority—English authority. Drew had come out of the Regulator wars a man angry enough to challenge any authority that did not assure him of all his rights, and all his liberty. Leo hadn't understood that change and had reacted defensively. He still was defensive. He could no longer be Drew's friend, for Drew threatened Leo's security, and he couldn't stand that.

Leo rolled over, his eyes shut so his wife wouldn't talk to him, but he couldn't go to sleep. What really worried him, and what really separated him from Drew, was that he didn't think he could do what Drew had done. He hated the sight of blood. He dreaded the thought of killing anyone—he didn't really even like the Thanksgiving and Christmas turkey hunts. No one had ever noticed or commented that Leo had never brought down any of the holiday birds. He was a coward, but no one knew that except him. He did not want anybody to know—ever. All he wanted was peace. The English could do what they wanted with trade, with his rights, with his liberty as long as they let him live in peace and comfort. Under those circumstances the real Leo Manning who lived inside the public man would always remain private and hidden.

He didn't sleep all that night, and arose at first light to pack a small utilitarian bag to take with him to Willowtree. He was glad to be away from the house for a time and by himself. Perhaps by the time he returned, his errant thoughts would be under control again. He rode up to the front of Willowtree. No one was there to greet him, and though he had made no announcement that he was coming, and had sent no message, there was always to be a greeter at the gates of Willowtree to make any traveler who happened by privy to the Manning hospitality.

He jumped down from his horse, and ran to the front door. "Jehu! Odo! Where the hell is everybody!"

"I heah, suh," Jehu said, coming at a run from the direction of the quarters, wiping his mouth on a clean white kerchief. "I di'n't know you was comin, Mastah Leo."

"Obviously not. Are you aware that there is no welcomer stationed at the front gate?"

Jehu looked confused, then embarrassed. "Cuffee 'sposed to be out theah."

"He isn't," Leo said coldly.

Jehu looked around, as if hunting for someone, then glanced back to Leo. "I see to it, suh. I see to it right off. He maybe gone to take care o' his natural needs, suh." He spotted Folly walking quickly up the quarters road. "Folly! You come heah, girl. Hurry now, Jehu callin' you."

Folly smiled at Leo, her eyes dark and bold, without the old respect he had become accustomed to seeing in the children of Jehu and Unity. "Good mawnin', Mastah Leo. What you want, Daddy?"

"Run down to the gate an' see if that good-fer-nuthin' Cuffee is there. An' if he ain't you fin' out why he wasn't there when Mastah Leo done rode in, heah? Hurry, girl." Jehu watched after her for a moment. He twisted his hands nervously, then looked at Leo, a practiced, respectful smile on his face. "I sure am sorry we don' show you our good face this mawnin', Mastah Leo. I take your bag into the house an' get you settled an' comfortable in yo' room. Unity, she have a nice big breakfast ready when you comes downstairs."

"Jehu, this is a serious infraction of the rules of Willowtree. It makes me wonder if my father's policy of coming down here on a regular, preset day is a good idea. It makes me wonder what I might find if I were to come unexpectedly next week, or any day."

"You fin' things jes' like you likes 'em, Mastah Leo. Dat Cuffee a no-good nigger. I tell Odo to gib him a good whuppin' an' put him back in de fiel's where he belongs."

"Mnnn," Leo said, his lips in a tight line, his eyes resting speculatively on Jehu. "I shall have a bath, breakfast, then we shall meet in the office, Jehu. I think we need to talk, and I think you had better have some very good answers for me."

Leo climbed the stairs to his room and undressed slowly as he waited for steaming buckets of hot water to be carried to his bathing tub. He settled down into the hot water and rested his head against the back. Was he seeing bogeymen in what might have been an innocent error? Cuffee might merely have been off in the bushes relieving himself, or Jehu might simply have entrusted a man with a duty he was not yet ready for, and would have to be relieved of. It wouldn't be the first time a slave was moved from the fields to a more responsible position and found wanting. Perhaps he was being overly sensitive to any shift from the normal. On the other hand, perhaps this seemingly minor discrepancy was the sign of a far greater problem.

He put his head in his hands, his fists clenched tight and pressed into his eyes. He was the wrong man to send on this fact-finding mission. He didn't know what a break in normal routine meant and he didn't know what to do about it. How could anyone expect him to know? What would Drew do in his place?

Folly ran down the plantation until she was certain neither her father nor Master Manning could see her; then she veered off, and ran across the field and back to the quarters road, running as hard as she could for the swamp. She stood at the edge, her eyes straining to catch sight of Seth's boat. She saw nothing, so she whistled, the secret whistle they used to warn each other of danger, and prayed that he would be within hearing range. She wasn't very good at this, not able to send the sound so far as the men could, but she was persistent, and tried again and again, until finally she heard a response from a distance.

Impatiently she waited, knowing her father would be expecting her back at the house to tell him about Cuffee. She was going to end up with a good hickory-stick whipping from her father for this. She kicked a tuft of grass, then smiled slyly. Seth had better be appreciative of her efforts and the lengths to which she would go for him.

Seth poled the boat to the edge of the swamp where she stood. She began speaking immediately. "Mastah Leo come ridin' in, an' Cuffee wasn't at the gate. He be shoutin' his head off that there weren't no welcomer at the gate. He send me to see what Cuffee doin'." Finished, she turned to run back to the road.

Seth leaped from the boat, nearly upsetting Tom, Cuffee, and Rufe, and grabbed Folly's arm. "Whoa, little colt. Not so fast. Why did you come here with an alarm signal for this? You are not telling me all."

"That's all I know, 'cept if I don't git back, my daddy's gonna whip me good. Mastah Leo's fit to . . . to . . ." She stopped and looked blankly at Seth. "I don' know what Mastah Leo' fit to do. I ain't nevah seen him mad befo'."

"What has that to do with us?"

"Mebbe nuthin', 'ceptin' he want to know 'bout Cuffee. What you want me to tell him?"

"Tell him Cuffee was occupied with private business. Even slaves have a right to answer nature's call."

"Sure did take me a long time to fin' that out," Folly said with a saucy toss of her head.

"Then tell Jehu you ran into . . . uhh . . . Hedy and talked for a time."

"I gonna get whipped. What you gonna do about that?" she asked, and sidled up close to him, her hip thrust out, her breasts shown to good advantage.

Seth smiled appreciatively and ran his hand down the cool, smooth skin of her arm. "What you want me to do?"

"There's gonna be a nice moon out tonight. Bet the swamp be pretty in the moonlight."

"I bet you are right, my saucy little colt. Shall we find out?"

Folly smiled, puckered up her lips, and blew him a kiss. "Don' you forgit, or tell me they's some kin' o' fool meetin'. It jes' be me an' you tonight?"

"Until tonight," Seth said in a deep soft voice.

Jehu was nearly tearing his grizzled, graying hair out by the time Folly came sauntering back to the house. He might have doubted the leisure of her walk had he realized she was sweating and nearly breathless from her run from the swamp, but Jehu was too agitated to notice anything. "Did you find him?"

"He down by the gate jes' like he 'sposed to be."

"He wasn't there when Mastah Leo came in!" Jehu nearly yelled. "Why wasn't he?"

"He say he had to step into de bushes," she said, and managed a blush.

"Din't take you all that long to fin' that out an' run right back heah, girl. You lyin' to me? You knows what that's gonna git you."

"I seen Hedy. She got her mouth to runn' an' I forgot I was 'sposed to hurry back heah. Cuffee ain't done nuthin' bad noway, so's why I got to hurry? Mastah Leo allus teks a bath when he gits heah. Ain't no cause fer me to be runnin' when I ain't got to."

Jehu shook his fist at her. "You got a mighty fresh tongue, girl. I tek care o' you tonight."

"I ain't done nuthin'!" Folly howled. "Whyn't you gonna git Hedy? She allus talkin' an' gittin' me in trouble!"

Jehu made a sound in his throat and turned away from his daughter, walking back onto the piazza. "You jes' keep away from Cuffee, an' that Seth. You gittin' too uppity fer my likin', girl, an' iffen you make me, I'm gonna beat all that sassiness right outten yo' hide, y'heah?"

Folly looked after her father as he walked into the house. He was getting old in his body and in his mind. Seth was right. A new time had come. She had never considered the idea that she should think for herself, or that there might be more to her world than what was here at Willowtree. Before Seth had come to Willowtree, she had had the same ideas and expectations as her parents. She had been born on Willowtree, she would be taken care of by the masters of Willowtree, marry a Willowtree bondsman, raise her children here, die here, and be buried in the Willowtree plot for bondsmen. It was a safe, secure world. A small world. And Seth had torn away the limitations and left her considering a vastness of possibility and opportunity she was capable of imagining only in generalities. But even though she could not quite grasp what this broader world of which Seth spoke was, she wanted it. You had a yearning to experience it as she had never wanted anything before.

She skipped, then ran, back down the quarter road. Her daddy was going to be busy all afternoon with Master Leo and would not be on the lookout for her, and Seth was highly unlikely to be working. Perhaps if he was in a good mood, she wouldn't have to wait for the moonlight to get her reward. Seth might take her to the island in the swamp right now. Maybe they would just stay there on the secret island and watch the moon rise. Seth would hunt for their food and together they would prepare a succulent fowl over an open fire, and bake roots in the hot coals, and make love. Make love to the afternoon sun, to the rising moon, to the food they ate, to each other.

Seth proved difficult to find. Folly had assumed he'd be lounging outside his cabin. Seeing nothing but an empty chair and the remains of a jug of home brew, Folly stamped her foot in irritation. She stood, hands on hips, undecided for a moment, then walked briskly back toward the swamp, her dreams threatened, her temper rising.

Leo Manning emerged from his bath cleaner, but not relaxed, and certainly no braver, and wishing someone else had this task. Logic told him that there had been no major infraction of plantation order, but there was a nagging feeling that challenged logic. He couldn't really point to anything, but something was different at Willowtree. He hurried to the study and requested that Unity bring his meal in there to be eaten informally. The truth was he felt safer in there. He didn't want to sit alone and exposed in the huge Willowtree dining room.

Unity had outdone herself in a sincere effort to please—and pacify—him, but Leo simply looked at the smoked ham, oysters, eggs, and toast. His mouth was dry and he didn't seem able to taste anything. He waited impatiently for Jehu to make his appearance, shifting the food around the plate and occasionally trying a bite to establish some sense of normal behavior. Though he hadn't waited for more than five minutes, and he knew Jehu would courteously give him at least a half hour to eat and collect his thoughts, he rang the bell and brought the old black man into the study.

Jehu stood silent and self-conscious in front of Leo's desk, while Leo sat behind that same desk nervous and frightened to ask the right questions, and hear answers he didn't want to hear. The two men looked at each other for a while, each with his own regrets filling his eyes. Leo had grown up knowing and trusting Jehu. When he had been a toddler, and his grandfather was still alive, Jehu was nearly always in Walter Manning's company as he taught his young grandsons to hunt, and recognize the different grains of rice, and find their way around the plantation. Jehu was a part of all his fondest memories and a part of most of his life. Now, as he looked at the old man, it was almost as if his own mirror had turned traitor and made a part of his own familiar face subtly alien to him. He cleared his throat several times before he could trust his voice. "Did you find Cuffee?" he asked finally.

"Folly went to the gate," he said, paused for a moment, then added, "She say he was answerin' the call o' nature when you happened in the gate. She say Cuffee say he di'n't make no effort to hurry back to the gate . . . he a lazy no-good."

Leo played with a pencil, tapping it on the top of the desk. From under his eyebrows, he looked at Jehu. "Do you believe her?"

Jehu hadn't expected that question. He didn't know what to say, for he didn't know where his loyalty was owed. He didn't believe Folly, but she was his daughter, and once he admitted his doubts, Leo would be given the power to deal with her as he would. He had never known the Mannings to be violent or cruel in their treatment of the bondsmen, but never before had he experienced the feeling of distrust that now existed between himself and Leo. He wasn't sure why it existed. He had his secrets about some of the recent goings-on at Willowtree, but nothing very substantial, and he did not know if Leo was knowledgeable about these things, or if he was merely upset about not being greeted at the gate, and fishing for any kind of answer. Above all else Jehu did not want to cause trouble where there was none. For the moment he thought he could handle any unrest at

Willowtree. He had been the undisputed black male leader here for many years. He began to speak, began to say he believed Folly, but the words would not come out. He was still too much a Manning man to lie to any of the family. "I am not sure," he said finally, and with a rush of anger put the blame where he thought it belonged. "Folly's all bug-eyed over Seth. She . . . she don't always do right these days."

"Because of Seth?" Leo asked, his heart pounding harder than ever. If there was one name he did not want to hear brought up in this discussion, it was the name of Seth.

"He allus talkin' 'bout Africa an' how he be a big 'pohtant man ovah theah. Folly . . . she still a li'l girl. She get all big-eyed listenin' to his stories, and she don' allus want to lissen to her daddy no mo'."

"But why would Seth be interested in what Cuffee was doing at the gate? Why would he care one way or the other if Cuffee was doing his job?"

Jehu saw his mistake too late. He tried to evade by shrugging, but Leo was already alert and nearly trembling with the dread of it.

"Does Seth have a following, Jehu?"

"We all good people heah at Willowtree," Jehu said, his eyes watery and sad.

Leo felt his own eyes sting, but he managed to say clearly, "We do have the makings of trouble here at Willowtree, don't we, Jehu?"

"Yas, suh, we do, but ain't nuthin' happen yet, an' long's I draw breaf in an' outten mah body, nuthin' will happen."

"Ahh, Jehu, I never doubt your loyalty or your dedication. But I need some answers. When Daddy sent me down here, I didn't expect to find anything. And there hasn't been much to worry about—except for a feeling of something being wrong. The bondsmen aren't the same—their attitude is different."

"Yas, suh," Jehu said with bowed head, but didn't say anything more.

"Have you seen any strangers around Willowtree lately—white men?"

"No, suh."

"And, Seth . . . are there any particular men he seems to spend a good deal of time with?"

"He stay to himself mos'ly . . . 'ceptin' the darkies take to him, like to hear him talk an' tell stories 'bout Africa."

"But the man can hardly speak the language."

Jehu's dark eyes bored into Leo's. "He speak good, Mastah Leo. He be a smart man wiff lots o' book learnin'. He knows the ol' ways, an' he talk 'bout them to anyone who wants to lissen."

"What old ways? What do you mean?"

"He talk about the ol' gods an' the ol' knowledge."

Leo was speechless. He couldn't think of anything to say. He knew that these black savages were taken from the dark depths of a heathen land. They wore no clothes, were reputed to practice cannibalism, and lived like animals. What old ways was Jehu talking about? He felt sick. "I want Seth brought into the stableyard, Jehu. Tell Odo to find the old whip."

Jehu's eyes widened. "Mastah Leo . . ." he began hesitantly, sweating profusely. "You know I do anythin' you asts me, but kin I tell you . . ." He hesitated again, then forced himself to go on. "Ain't gonna he'p things you whup Seth, suh."

"What do you expect me to do? Allow him to do as he wishes to the point of causing an uprising right here? You tell Odo to get that whup, heah, an' I want all the bondsmen gathered in the stableyard to see him get what he deserves!"

Jehu reluctantly backed toward the door of the study. "I do what you asts, but I shore do hope you changes yo' min'. Gonna cause trouble, suh," he said, and turned and left the study and the house in search of Odo.

After another meeting with Jehu at which Odo was present, Leo designated that the time for the whipping would be after the slaves had come in from the fields and before they had had supper.

"Give them something to think about this evening," he said harshly.

"Suh," Odo said, "what we whuppin' Seth fo'? What he do?"

"He is a disruptive influence."

Odo looked at Jehu, then stared at the floor. "Uhh-huuh, dat mus' be mighty bad thing to do."

"It is indeed. It means Seth is not to talk to the other slaves in such a manner as to make them discontent."

Odo looked up with a smile. "Oh, he cain't do dat, Mastah Leo. We all likes Willowtree."

"You may know that, Odo, and Jehu might, but there are some new people here, and some young ones who might listen too carefully to what Seth tells them—and those things are lies! We cannot have Seth telling our people untruths and making them hope for something that will never happen. If they run away, they will be caught and punished severely. And that is if they are lucky!" Leo added with a vocal flourish. "Some of them will starve to death, and others will die in the swamp. Some will be torn to pieces by wild animals."

"Ain't nobody ever run from Willowtree, Mastah Leo."

"And there never will be a runaway at Willowtree. I want you to see to it that Seth and anyone who might be tempted to follow him understands that."

"Yash, suh," Odo said quietly.

The two black men walked off together after Leo had dismissed them.

Leo had a long afternoon of waiting. More than once he fought the impulse to call the whole slave community together and get the whole ordeal over immediately so that he could ride back to Charles Town and put this behind him. All the things Drew and George had said kept running through his mind. Jehu had said he knew of no strangers who had been at Willowtree agitating, but that didn't mean it hadn't happened. One thing he was beginning to see clearly was that Jehu's loyalty to the Mannings might be used against him and the Mannings. He would not be privy to many of the things that happened. Perhaps the English were going to use Willowtree slaves for an uprising. The plantation was in a good position for that. It was near enough to Charles Town that the news would spread like wildfire and cause rampant fear among the inhabitants, and it was distant enough to make it unlikely that the slaves would succeed in getting so far as Charles Town itself.

Leo wiped perspiration away from his brow and neck as he allowed his train of thought to run away with him. The Mannings were a prestigious enough family that their massacre would instill horror in others. They might well become sacrificial lambs for the British cause. And even if some of the family was known to be strongly Tory, what did the loss of a few men and women matter if a strong message was sent to the people of the colony by their terrible deaths?

He stood by the window looking out over the lush green lawn of Willowtree. It was beautiful. Brilliant splashes of bright-colored flowers glowed against the wide expanse of sun-washed grass. It looked so peaceful, not at all the place for such thoughts or realities to take place. Not for the first time he considered the idea that he might do well to join the ranks of the patriots. Even the possibility of an English-backed uprising made him feel betrayed and invaded. Perhaps it was as Drew said: he was not an Englishman, but an American.

But it didn't matter whether he called himself Englishman or American, he still wanted no part of contrived uprisings, and people being sacrificed cruelly for any cause. By the time the plantation's evening bell rang, Leo was more than ready, and had decided he would indeed make an example of Seth, and he would have his say. Except for an occasional greeting or word of praise, he had never spoken to the slaves. If any speechmaking was to be done, it had always been his father or his grandmother who did the talking.

Word of the impending meeting and the punishment of Seth that was to be the major part of it flew through the plantation like a brush fire. Heated, whispered words were blown from row to row, paddy to paddy, in the rice fields. The house servants worked with the low undertone of talk all day. The women in the plantation nursery speculated and worried as they cared for and fed the children of the bondsmen. There was fear and apprehension and hurt in all the talk. Nothing like this had ever happened before at Willowtree. Everyone knew there was a whip, but everyone knew the whip was never used. Willowtree people were good people. And no one knew or understood exactly what it was Seth had done that was so terrible as to bring this down upon them.

The bondsmen came to the stableyard in small clotted clusters, walking close to each other for comfort and protection. Occasionally there could be seen a sideways glance filled with anger directed toward Leo, who stood rigid-backed near the stable entrance. It took several minutes before the stragglers brought up the rear, standing in the back, almost hiding from what was about to happen.

When all were assembled, and quiet had fallen over the group, Leo stepped onto a wooden crate Jehu had placed in front of the stable for him. He stood for a moment and looked at the sea of dark faces. Then he said in a cool, businesslike voice, "I have called all of you together to witness the punishment of Seth. Some of you may not know why so unusual an occurrence is taking place here. I shall tell you. It has become known to me that Seth talks to many of you, tells you about what he calls the old ways, tells you tales of Africa, and speaks of freedom, and a life filled with leisure and pleasure. What he tells you is wrong. Your life here at Willowtree is your destiny. It is here that you will be happy. There is no promised land for any of you outside Willowtree. There is hunger and adversity. Seth has lied to you. He had misled you. He has betrayed the kindness of my family. He has dishonored the name and reputation of Willowtree. For that we shall enact and observe this unusual punishment. I pray that this will be the only time the whip must be used at Willowtree, but I warn y'all that it shall be used daily if I hear of or see any further evidence of disloyalty in any of you." He stepped down from the box and turned to Odo. "Odo, you may proceed."

Odo walked back into the stable and emerged with a bound Seth. As the two men stepped into the fading sunlight, Seth looked around the gathering, and impudently smiled, his teeth even and white in his dark face. A murmur of admiration from some, and shock from others, ran through the crowd. He was a bold one. Even Leo had to look at him with some degree of admiration.

Odo marched Seth into the yard, then stopped, looked around in confusion, then looked at Leo. "How we do this, Mastah Leo? He jes' stan' theah?"

"Secure him to something," Leo said.

Again Odo looked about him a little desperately.

"For God's sake, get on with this!" Leo growled. "If you can't think of anything else, bind him to the trunk of the oak over there."

With relief Odo nodded, and tugged at Seth to follow him. After some nervous false starts he managed to get Seth secured to the tree, then stood back, the whip in his hand. "How many times I got to hit him?"

"Thirty lashes," Leo said, then shouted for silence. With the bumbling attempt to secure Seth, and Odo's procrastination, the bondsmen had begun to mutter, and a low hum of noise sang in the air. It was a menacing sound, and Leo didn't like it.

Odo raised his arm and struck the first blow. Seth made no sound, but all could see the uncontrollable jerk of the muscles of his back. For a moment there was awed silence again. Odo struck the fourth and fifth blows, and the low hum of talk and muttering returned. Folly stepped about a foot nearer to Seth, looked defiantly at Leo, then turned her back on the scene.

Leo felt a sudden, unfamiliar rage rush through him, and he leaped forward, moving across the open yard to Folly, shouting, "Turn around! How dare you disobey me! Defy me to my face!" He grabbed hold of her shoulder, spinning her so hard that she twisted and fell to the ground. But even then Folly showed no fear. She looked up at him with burning dark brown eyes, her mouth curved down. "You gonna beat me, too, white man?"

"An' me?" a voice Leo couldn't identify called out.

Odo stopped in midstroke as he saw his son Rufus turn his back, then another man turned his back.

"Yes, all of you!" Leo screeched. "Every woman and child and man and boy on this plantation, if it is necessary." He grabbed Folly's thin arm and, without giving her a chance to get to her feet, dragged her to the tree near Odo. He yelled at Jehu to bring forward the others who had turned their backs. When there was a struggle between Jehu and Tom, Leo pulled his pistol out from under his coat. He fired once into the air, waited for a moment, then fired into the ground near Tom's feet. He reloaded his pistol in total silence. Every slave on Willowtree was now cowed and frightened. They still did not quite understand what Seth had done to warrant this. Most of them had never heard him talk of anything. But they clearly understood the defiance of Folly, Rufus, Tom, and three others.

"Ten lashes for the girl. Twenty for each of the men," Leo snapped, and stalked off toward the house. "Jehu! Come with me!"

As soon as he was inside the cool interior of the house, he leaned weakly against the wall and mopped at his brow and neck. His hands were trembling, and his knees were weak. "Jehu, I forbid any gathering of the slaves. No one may meet in a group without penalty. No one," he repeated weakly.

With a great effort of will Leo managed to force himself to remain at Willowtree until the punishments were over. However, as soon as the slaves had gone back to their cabins, he called Jehu. "Get my bag. I am returning to Charles Town tonight."

"It be near nine o'clock, suh. You bettah wait for mawnin'."

"I'll leave now," Leo insisted. He felt physically ill. He was terrified, actually afraid to sleep at Willowtree, and he wanted the aid and counsel of his father, and perhaps Drew.

Leo was uncomfortable and felt watched and in danger until he was well beyond the gates of Willowtree, and even then he could not remove from his mind the sight of Folly's hostile, hate-filled eyes. He wasn't really able to relax and feel safe until he was riding along the comfortably populated streets of Charles Town. Those who were still on the streets were promoting uprisings of their own design, but suddenly a rebellion against English rule seemed tame and civilized compared to the raw, primitive mystery of slave discontent.

18

Leo, in a state of agitation, rode toward the Mannings' Charles Town house, then turned away again as soon as he came to Legare Street. He spurred his horse to greater speed and headed back out of town, this time for Drew Manning's new home on the outskirts of Charles Town.

By the time he arrived there the house was dark and quiet. He hammered with his fist on the front door until he saw a light from within. A sleepy Drew came to the door himself. He pushed aside the window curtain and looked out at the porch and into the tense face of his cousin. He pulled the door open hastily. "Leo! What has happened to bring you here at this time of night?"

"I need to talk to you, Drew. George isn't here, by chance? I want him to hear what I have to say as well."

"It happens that George is here. He came home with me after you left for Willowtree. I take it all is not well there."

Leo shook his head. "Not at all, and I fear I have accomplished nothing except to make it worse. Would you mind getting George, Drew?"

"No . . . he's asleep," Drew said distractedly as he went around the room lighting lamps. "Come sit in here, Leo. Help yourself to a drink. I'll get George and assure Gwynne there is no immediate crisis . . . that is true, isn't it?"

Leo laughed bitterly. "I believe so, but even that I can't say with certainty."

Twenty minutes later Drew and George came downstairs to find Leo slumped on one of the easy chairs, his head in his hands. He looked up when they came in. "I should have listened to you, George. We all should have. You're the only one of us who understood the potential danger of the British Indian policy."

George sat down immediately with a plunk. "What is happening at Willowtree? Is it Seth who is the instigator? Or did you find worse? Had British agents been around?"

"I don't know about the agents. Jehu says there have been none, but I am not sure that is the case."

"Jehu would never lie to you, Leo. He is as devoted as a man can be," Drew said.

"It isn't that I think he is lying, Drew—I don't think he would necessarily know. Jehu has already been designated by some of the darkies as the enemy, the same as we are. I don't think Jehu is going to be a great help to us. Whatever plot is taking place on Willowtree, Jehu is not privy to. Secrets are being kept from him expressly in order that he should not be able to warn or inform us. Jehu's authority as leader of the bondsmen has been seriously eroded, and the most serious erosion has come from within his own family." Leo paused for a moment, gestured with his hands, and went on. "Odo is not in a much better position. Yesterday ended with Odo ordering his own son tied to a tree in the stableyard for a whipping."

"Rufus," Drew said quietly.

"Yes, Rufus. He always has been a sassy son of a bitch—he's very hostile now."

"But who is the traitor in Jehu's family? Surely Toby would never defy his father," George said.

"No, it's not Toby. Before I left, Toby came to apologize to me for his sister's behavior, and promised he would keep an eye on her for me. It's Folly, George. And though she is only a woman and a very young one, it was she who prompted the incident that may have made my visit more of a hindrance than a help." Leo sat back, his hands limply in his lap, his long, thin face solemn and sad. He told them emotionlessly of the outburst in the stableyard that had ended with his striking Folly.

Both Drew and George listened in complete silence. They sat attentively, making no comment, not interrupting. After Leo had finished, all three men sat for another moment, none of them knowing what to say.

Finally George said weakly, "We could sell off the troublemakers—if anyone would be fool enough to offer for them. But if they were split up, it isn't likely that they would cause trouble on their own—except Seth. Seth will cause trouble no matter where he is."

Leo nodded in agreement. "I should have listened to Grandma and

Drew a long time ago about Seth. He had me fooled completely. My God, I didn't even realize the man could speak English so as to be understood beyond a yes, sir, and a no, sir. What do we do with a darkie like Seth?" He looked to Drew for an answer, but none was forthcoming.

"Grandma recognized that Seth was different that Christmas morning she took Nathaniel to the quarters. She thought that if she educated him and prepared him for a more responsible task—perhaps even keeping the books—that Seth would settle in and become a valuable asset to Willowtree and to himself. Apparently he has merely taken advantage of the learning she has given him and used it to promote discontent at Willowtree. Did you talk to him at all, Leo? Do you have any idea what it is Seth is trying to accomplish?"

"I didn't talk to him at all, Drew. I told you, until this afternoon I didn't realize Seth could carry on a conversation."

"Lord, Leo!" George breathed. "What did you think Grandma was doing with her school? You had to realize that—"

"I didn't realize a thing!" Leo yelled back. "I never gave Grandma's project a thought. I've never seen any evidence of the effects of her education policy around Willowtree. Those darkies are just as ignorant now as they were before she started. How in the hell was I to know Seth is the exception? Everything I have ever seen led me to believe Seth was dumber than most. The black bastard has never done a decent job. He can't even hoe a cornfield without breaking every implement given him."

Drew took a deep breath. "That has nothing to do with his lack of intelligence, Leo. Most likely Seth has broken the implements deliberately, and for the purpose of making you believe he is incompetent. I haven't followed the work lists at Willowtree, but I would guess that Seth's load is a very light one."

"That's because he can't do a damn thing right!" Leo said in agitation. His breath was coming fast, and his voice rose again.

"Shut up, Leo," George said. "You're going to wake up the whole household."

"I'm sorry . . . I'm sorry, Drew . . . this is so unsettling. I don't understand how this could happen at Willowtree. It has always run so smoothly. What happened? What changed? Is it all because of one bad darkie?"

Drew looked at George. Obviously he had something on his mind and was hesitant to say it. George looked at him, then at his brother, and back to Drew. He knew what Drew was asking with the expression on his face, and agreed. "I think you ought to tell him."

"Tell me what?" Leo asked. "You know more about this than you have said? For God's sake, tell me!"

"No, Leo, it isn't anything directly connected with this particular problem—it has to do with Willowtree in general. Grandpa is the reason Willowtree is an almost ideal plantation. He trained Odo and Jehu, and many of the other old hands, and he did it so thoroughly that they have been able to carry on even though he's no longer there. Since Uncle John has been running Willowtree—mostly from his house in Charles Town—the whole burden of training the new men and women has fallen to Jehu and Odo. They are good men, capable men, but they are not the masters of Willowtree. Even if he is merely a presence, the darkies must know there is a strong hand in authority."

"But Daddy will never live at Willowtree . . . he likes the city."

"He doesn't have to live there, Leo. I no longer spend the whole year at Cherokee—but, by God, those darkies know I can be expected at any time, and I have Ned, who is there day in and day out. Even when I am not physically there, my presence and my wishes are felt and heeded."

"How?" Leo wailed. "You don't use a whip. I know you don't. How in the hell do you make them aware of your wishes?"

"Several ways, Leo. And before you start making hard-and-fast rules, I would use the whip if I thought it were necessary. The point is that I attempt to keep my people's interests closely aligned to my own, so that a serious infraction, should it happen, would be looked upon with as much disapproval by them as it would be by me."

"Fine words. Willowtree people are well taken care of. And some of them were appalled—but that hasn't stopped it from happening."

"Willowtree people do not have a personal stake in Willowtree—not any more."

"For God's sake, Drew, what are you talking about? Odo and Jehu and at least a dozen other of those old bucks had a chunk of Willowtree to call their own. Do you know what they did with it? They sold their produce at market and had the audacity to suggest they should buy their freedom and land of their own!"

"That's right, and your father refused the requests, and took back the Willowtree land, and since then none of the heads of household have had any plot of their own."

Leo looked blank. "What do you expect?"

"Grandpa intended for these darkies to be able to do exactly what you are so horrified at. He knew perfectly well that by the time Jehu and the others had earned enough to buy their freedom and their land, they would be well trained in a profession, they would have been established enough to be able to train their successor in their old job at Willowtree so the chain of command would never be broken, and they would be old enough that Willowtree itself would not need them and would be ready for a younger man to take over in that position. Had that policy been kept in force, right now Toby would be head houseman and Jehu would be living happily on his own small farm with Unity." Drew leaned forward and continued talking earnestly. "This whole plan was designed to ease the burden both on the bondsmen and on the plantation. Every planter knows the drain older slaves impose. Obviously if they can be made self-sufficient, it is an advantage to both. Grandma's attempt to educate some of the more capable slaves serves this same end. She must have talked to you before about this. I'm sure she's talked to Uncle John. It was something important both to her and Grandpa. Why haven't you and Rob and Uncle John continued the policy?"

"I'm not sure why Daddy didn't. I just thought it was another of Grandma's lenient ideas. She is a radical in her thinking, you know. Even you can't deny that. Some of her ideas are just plain irresponsible."

"I agree she is radical sometimes, but Grandma is never irresponsible."

"Oh, no? What about her interference in Gwynne's life? Look what happened before you married her. Maybe you and Gwynne and Grandma think the rest of the family didn't know what was going on in that apartment you kept in Charles Town while Laurel and you were still married. We knew. We all knew. It was shameful. You don't call that irresponsible?"

"Yes. On my part. On Gwynne's part, perhaps. But Grandma had nothing to do with that apartment."

"God, Drew, she encouraged Gwynne to leave home and stake her whole life on the chance that you loved her, because Grandma said you did!"

George put his hands up, calling the argument to a halt. "We can fight this out all night long and never reach agreement. Let's get back to the question of the plantation and Seth. What are we going to do?"

"We'll get back to it, George," Drew said. "But I am beginning to understand some of Leo's resentment of late years. Why didn't you tell me you knew these things? Why didn't you talk to me?"

"Why didn't you talk to me?"

"I couldn't very well, Leo. I didn't want anyone who didn't already know being told that Gwynne met me in that apartment . . . you can see why." Drew looked at his cousin and saw the hurt and the disgust in his eyes. It explained the animosity that had replaced their close comradeship.

Drew had assumed the hostilities were focused on their disagreement about loyalty to the king or the colony. He could easily see now that those loyalties had little to do with the whole. "I apologize, Leo. I wish I could change the past, and that we might have done things differently, but all I can say is I'm sorry."

"And that doesn't have a whole lot of meaning, does it, Drew?" Leo said acidly. "It doesn't put the family back together as a whole, and it doesn't erase from our minds that our cousin Gwynne threw herself, body and soul, after a man—her sister's man."

"I was never Joanna's man!" Drew said, his jaw set, his brown eyes glinting dangerously. "You can accuse me of being unfaithful to my wife, of dishonoring her and Gwynne, but Gwynne never threw herself at me, and I was never Joanna's man."

Leo's face crumpled, and he covered it with his hands. "Do you know what really sticks in my craw, Drew? After all you have done, and God, you have caused enough disruption in this family for a lifetime, after all that, it is still to your guidance we all end up turning when there is a crisis. I was on my way home to talk to Daddy and Rob about this situation at Willowtree, and turned back to come to you, because I knew neither one of them would know how to handle it. They are likely to do the same kind of thing I did, and make the whole thing worse. That isn't fair, damn it! They are good, decent men. You break every rule of decent living and always come out looking like the wise one."

Drew looked away from him when he spoke. "Maybe I am when it comes to things like war and slaves and running a plantation, Leo, but I haven't come out unscathed from the scandals I've caused. I have succeeded in developing Cherokee into my own plantation, and somehow or other I ended up with the responsibility of Riverlea, and, yes, you all come to me for advice at one time or another, but I also had a wife who died in melancholy and unhappiness, and I have a lifelong enemy in my cousin Joanna, and I am separated from my brother and my family. I live with these things daily, just as I live with the good things that have happened. I try to help when I'm given the chance, because it is the only way I can make up for some of the things I have done and cannot change."

George sat far back in his chair, trying to disassociate himself from the conversation. He didn't like seeing Drew so exposed, or hearing him talk like this. If he were ever to have a hero it would be Drew. He knew of Drew's failings, but that knowledge had never tarnished his opinion of his cousin. What he loved and admired about Drew was his courage to go on, the iron will that made him seek a positive direction even when all around him seemed wrong. He got up and filled everyone's glass with port, then sat down again. "Once more I suggest we get back to the problem at hand. We can talk about the various family disagreements and sins some other time. We would do well to address the problem at Willowtree, or we may visit there only to find ourselves attacked in our beds. I, for one, do not choose to die that way," George said.

"It's bad enough without going to dramatic exaggeration, George," Leo said.

"What makes you think I am exaggerating this time, brother? Those were the words or something similar you used when Drew and I first told you the British were going to try to stir up the blacks and the Indians against the white settlers."

"I apologize," Leo said contritely. "You are right, of course. I wouldn't listen before, but I am listening now. What can we do? What about you going to Willowtree, Drew? You could get everyone back in line and talk to the head men. They'll listen to you."

"I can go, Leo, providing Uncle John and Rob agree, but even if I can talk to Jehu, Odo, Seth, Rufus, and a few others and gain their cooperation, it is not the best solution. They all know I am not master of Willowtree and never will be. You or Rob, or best of all, Uncle John are going to have to spend some time there and establish an order and command there —one every man, woman, and child on that plantation recognizes and responds to."

"Daddy will never spend sufficient time there to accomplish what is needed. That means it will be left to you, Leo, because we both also know that Rob will not handle this well. He is too impatient with the bondsmen, and doesn't think that highly of them in the first place. You know Rob and his hunting dog," George said, and laughed.

"What hunting dog?" Drew asked.

"Rob thinks dogs and darkies were made to obey and serve. When one doesn't, he simply gets rid of him. It's his solution to everything. He was given a pup once, but it wasn't trained. Came from a long line of marvelous dogs, but the animal wouldn't do what Rob wanted, so he sold it for a pittance to John Bloom. About a year later Rob pitted his best hound against John's at a hunt with a fifty-pound wager on the results. John won, of course, and the hound was none other than Rob's worthless pup.

"But it didn't phase Rob a bit. He still said the hound was no good and would eventually turn sour on John," George added.

Leo laughed affectionately, thinking of his brother. "Rob is just a lazy so and so. He didn't want to be bothered working with the dog."

"Then, he will not be of any use at Willowtree in this circumstance," Drew said.

"No, as I said before. It is going to be you, Leo, or no one."

"What about you, Drew—why won't you take over?"

"Because Willowtree people are too intelligent not to realize that I am coming in as troubleshooter, and they will cooperate as long as I'm around, anticipating that they can go back to their plots and plans as soon as I leave. No, we must establish either your dominance or Uncle John's."

"I'll talk to Daddy later today. Out of respect I must tell him what has happened and what I suggest be done. I shall be sure he knows I'll be working under your guidance, Drew."

Drew laughed. "I'm not sure that will be an advantage, Leo, but I thank you for giving the credit. I do wish you would suggest to him that he reinstitute Grandpa's original plan."

"I will, but don't count on his agreement. I doubt we will get anywhere with that."

Drew stood up, and the other two men followed suit. "Well, let's get what rest we may. It looks as though the next few weeks are going to be busy ones for all of us. Leo, I'll show you to a guest room. It is far too late to ride home tonight."

"I don't want to be a bother."

"Not at all. Gwynne always keeps the rooms ready for guests, and none is more welcome than you." He paused and put his hand out for Leo to shake. "I am glad we talked tonight, Leo—I mean about things other than Willowtree. Nothing has changed, and I am aware now of how deeply you were hurt by some of the events that happened in the family because of me, but I feel we are closer again for having talked."

Leo nodded and took his cousin's hand. "I am glad, too, Drew, but I can't promise anything. We need to talk some more."

"Soon," Drew said, and smiled, then led the way upstairs.

19

As the heat of summer set in, more news came of the British plans to use various groups against the patriotic colonists. Lochlin Martin, a merchant, and James Daly, too often on the unpopular side of a question, found that they had something important to talk about. The two men talked to all who would listen. "Have you heard the good news?" Martin said with joviality. James Daly immediately came to stand near him so as to share in the credit for what was to be said. "The Liberty Boys and all the traitors hereabouts are soon to be taught a lesson not to their likin'. The niggers and the Papists along with the Indians are gettin' arms, an' while they're payin' back for their own, the British got a ready-made force jes' itchin' to quell this rebellion before it ever gets a start. What do you say to that?"

What they had to say was a roar of anger and outrage. Several citizens of Charles Town took the two men to the smithy's, tarred and feathered them, and marched them through the town.

The violence and swiftness of the reaction to two loudmouthed men caused a good deal of alarm in Charles Town. One of the questions most frequently asked was whether or not this heralded mob rule. John Manning was appalled and used the incident to prove his point. "Without the sanity of British rule we will have anarchy. This outrageous behavior will be the rule of the day. It must be stopped. We cannot tolerate such behavior."

"John, it was not an act of mob rule. If you would not insist on avoiding all patriots, you would know that they acted under an order," Elizabeth Manning said, sitting on the couch and looking deceptively demure.

"Mother," John said with some irritation, "this is no time for your unfounded opinions. This time the rabble has gone too far. Not even the more substantial patriots will countenance this."

"Would you call William Henry Drayton substantial?" Elizabeth asked pertly. "It was his order—his and Edward Weyman's."

John stared at her open mouthed for a moment, then denied the truth of what she said.

"It's true, Daddy," Leo told him, knowing his father would not believe George or Drew any more than he had believed his mother. "And perhaps it would be better for you to pay attention to what Martin and Daly were saying than to pay so much attention to what happened to them."

"Don't preach to me, young man! If nothing else, I've lived a lot longer than you have, and I give you warning that you young men had better take a good look at the words of these so-called patriots, and then look at their actions. The two don't match! They talk of liberty and then tar and feather a man for having his own opinion—for being loyal to the king of his country! What liberty is that?"

All of the Mannings were stunned into silence at John's outburst. His sons had seen such an expression of temper only a few times in their lives, and Drew Manning had never heard his Uncle John lose control of himself.

The older man glared at the young faces, then at his mother, and stormed from the room.

After he had left no one had much to say. More than at any other time when he had spoken calmly to them, he had struck home. As a family the Mannings were blessed with cool minds, and none of them liked irrational violence. John's comment about the discrepancy between the patriots' words and their actions of the day were disturbing.

Elizabeth excused herself and left the room. Drew, George, Rob, and Leo sat in uncomfortable silence. Finally George took a deep breath. "Well, we got some of the starch taken out of our sails, didn't we? What do you all say to going down to Dillon's and talking this out?"

Rob shook his head. "Count me out. I don't need to talk it over. I already know what I think."

"I don't. Shit, I don't know a damned thing, except that I'm mighty confused," Leo said. "Let's go."

Drew, George, and Leo went to Dillon's, and as soon as they walked into the popular tavern, they were immediately caught up in the fever and excitement of political argument. The long bar was crowded with men elbow to elbow, each shouting into the face of his neighbor, trying to be heard over the din in the smoke-filled room.

The three Manning men wended their way into the body of the tavern, their eyes searching for an empty table. Their names were called from many areas of the room. For the first hour and through several mugs of cold ale they greeted friends and talked.

When they finally came back together again and sat at a table with a couple of other men, their faces were flushed with the heat of the room, the ale, and the fever of the cause.

"Daddy has only a part of the question," Leo said with newfound confidence. "You know, I had it this afternoon, when I told him he ought to look to what the bloody bastards were saying and not so much to what had happened to them. By Jove! They deserved every drip of tar and every bloody feather pasted to them! If a man can't sleep in his bed at night without fear of the damned limeys turning the blacks loose on him, what is there to life?"

"Ha! That's my brother!" George yelled, and lifted his glass. "He finally has an opinion worth listening to. Cheers, fellows! We have among us a new patriot!"

A roar went up among the men near enough to their table to hear George, then it subsided into laughter and more talk.

"Damn it, George, you're a bloody embarrassment to be around. You're making a spectacle of me!" Leo rasped at his brother, his thin cheeks dotted with high color.

"Have another ale, Leo. There's no need to get all worked up. You're among friends. Now, that's one thing we can say about the patriots. We may be a rowdy bunch, but we are friends."

Drew gave him a wry smile. "Until we all get into a fight."

George was undaunted and grinned at his cousin. "But they are friendly fights."

One of the other men at the table, Wade Jenkins, took a deep swallow of ale, winked at George, and said, "We'll see how friendly it is after we've all been asked to take the oath of association."

"Oath of association?" Drew repeated, and leaned forward. "When has this come about?"

"Can't say exactly when," Wade said, "but the provincial Congress has ordered it, and all those loyal are to take an oath swearing to defend the colony in the event of a British attack."

"Does that include a British-inspired attack—like an uprising?" Leo asked.

"Mos' likely it will include anything that can be laid at the feet of the British. I haven't ever seen the feelin's runnin' so high as they are now.

Things is really heatin' up, and from where I sit, it don't seem likely that they'll cool down again, unless the British back down."

"I'll take that oath, and take it proudly," George said grandly.

"What about you, Upcountryman," Wade asked, his eyes squinted as he looked at Drew. "From what I hear there's an awful lot of quiet and fence-sittin' in the Upcountry."

"I'll take the oath," Drew said.

"There's gonna be a regiment goin' to the Upcountry to talk to some of your neighbors. Might be a good thing if you looked into that. Might be you could do some recruitin' among those backwoods folk," Wade said.

"It could be," Drew said. "But then, we Upcountrymen have a habit of making up our own minds and doing it for our own reasons. None of us are easily talked into anything, and in case you've forgotten, the Upcountry has very little reason to trust anything you Lowlanders claim as true. The only time we hear from you is when you want something from us."

"Now that's a hostile li'l speech, Manning," Wade said.

"And a well-founded one," Drew said.

Wade backed off a little. "Well, you said you would take the oath, so I jes' thought—"

"You told me what you thought—let's leave it at that."

Wade hesitated for a moment, then shrugged and smiled. "You still might be interested in doing some recruitin' for us—for your own reasons, I mean. It would be a big help."

"I'll look into it. I'd planned to talk with Edward Weyman this week and I'll mention it to him. He'll know if help is wanted and if I'm the right man to give it."

Wade Jenkins's information had been accurate. Members of the committee were busy the following day approaching citizens and asking that they take the oath. To begin with it merely caused a stir and some heated conversations regarding the patriots and the notion of citizens of England taking an oath to defend their colony if it were attacked by its own mother country. Though little else had been talked about for months, once again this issue brought to the fore of everyone's mind the peculiarities of the colonists' position. While loyalty seemed a simple matter in theory, it was proving to be elusive and confusing in practice.

Some of the confusion and disagreements burst into flame and regrettable incidents. The task of talking to John, Leo, Rob, and George Manning fell to Wade Jenkins. Jenkins was pleased with his task, and expected some good battling before he got all the Mannings to give in, but he didn't doubt his eventual success.

As Wade was ushered into the Manning parlor, John and his sons were listening attentively to Bert Townshend talking about the concern and determination of the British to end this nonsensical rash of rebellious spirit in the colonies. The men greeted Wade, with the exception of Bert, who already knew the reason for his visit. Bert Townshend sat even straighter than before, his red uniform jacket brilliant against the muted beige pattern of the chair. "If you intend to ask me to join in taking that supercilious oath of yours, I wouldn't advise it."

Wade Jenkins was not having as much fun as he expected. He wasn't used to such wealth as was obvious in the Manning house. Bert Townshend was obviously looking down on him, and speaking in both a patronizing and threatening manner. Wade had few resources with which to deal with this kind of attack. He knew how to fight his battles with his fists, with a musket, or on the back of a horse, but this polite verbal sparring with all the double meanings and the sly looks that passed from one man to another of whose meaning Wade was certain, made him uncomfortable, angry, and very nearly tongue-tied. "I come here to talk to the Mannings. You ain't a Manning."

"Captain Townshend is a cousin by marriage, Mr. Jenkins," John said coolly. "May I ask what your business with us is?"

"I come to tell you that all the Provincial Congress has asked the committee to tell all the citizens that's loyal to their homes to take an oath sayin' they'll defend South Carolina should it be necessary—that is, if it were to be attacked."

John laughed. "Surely this is not a serious request."

"Oh, yeah! It's serious all right, Mr. Manning. An' there ain't no middle ground no more. You're either gonna have to be with us, or you're our enemy."

John's face got red, and he stood up. "Young man, I'll ask you to leave my home immediately. You tell that committee of yours that I shall not be coerced nor threatened by anyone!"

Wade did not move. Insolently he glared at John, then turned his gaze to Rob, then to Leo, and finally to George.

Bert Townshend was on his feet and stood in front of Wade. "I believe you have been asked to leave by the master of this house. I suggest you do so."

"You're jes' all full of advising to, and suggesting, ain't you?"

"You are trying my patience, sir," Bert said stiffly, his hand at his waist, his fingers just touching the hilt of his saber.

Wade laughed. "You tryin' to scare me or somethin'. I come here to get these good folks to take an oath to defend their homes, an' I ain't leavin' till it gets done. Jes' las' night George there an' Leo tol' me they'd be more'n glad to swear loyalty to Carolina."

"Get on your feet, you ignorant ass!" Bert said through a tightly clenched jaw.

Wade sprang to his feet fast and hard, ramming his shoulder into Bert's stomach as he rose.

All three of the younger Manning men jumped to hold back the two combatants as they struggled with each other. Leo and Rob held Wade, each of them taking an arm, while George tried valiantly to hold on to an enraged Bert Townshend. "Let go of my arms!" Bert shouted. "You're interfering with one of His Majesty's men!"

"Daddy, just listen to Wade. He only tried to do what he was ordered to do by the committee. The oath is only effective if we're attacked," George panted to his father as he wrestled with Bert, and shouted over his shouts.

"We aren't the enemies of our own people!" Leo said.

Wade stopped struggling, shrugged his shoulders, and was released by Leo and Rob. Accordingly George released his hold on Bert. It was a mistake. Bert sprang forward immediately, drawing his saber in one quick, fluid motion. "The only oath you'll be giving will be from behind bars, sir," Bert said triumphantly. With stilted courtesy he excused himself from John's house and marched Wade out the front door.

Bert with Wade in tow had taken only a few steps when Wade began to shout to every man on the street that he recognized. "He's preventin' the oath! Jailin' me!"

With terrifying speed a crowd gathered. As they ran toward Wade, they stooped, picking up rocks and bits of debris in the street. Shouting and mocking, they ran at Bert and Wade.

The Manning men stood on the stoop of their home, watching in horror. Leo, the first to break free of paralyzing startlement, raced down the street. "Bert! For God's sake, run!"

Bert stood his ground, one hand on Wade Jenkins's coat sleeve, the other clutching his sword.

Before Leo could reach him, the crowd did. Rocks and pieces of brick and human bodies all pelted down on the British soldier. Leo flung himself into the melee, with George now following. Fists flew, and men screamed in hate-filled rage as they pounded on the red coat. Cries of pain rose and died off in a strangle.

The sound of horses intruded on the grunting, pain-wracked cries from the battle, and soon the struggling, pummeling men were surrounded by horsed soldiers.

Several of the patriots ran at the sight of the soldiers, others were dragged from the fight screaming expletives. Three were taken prisoner and shoved before swords on their way to the jail. George fought off another soldier, who was trying to pull him away from Bert. "He's my cousin, man! Let me see to him!"

Finally the remaining two soldiers were made to understand with the help of John's approach, and Bert was carried into the Manning house.

"Get the surgeon," Rob said, retching as he looked at the torn, bloody mess that had been Bert's face.

Eugenia and Beth came running down the stairs at the sound of the commotion, with Elizabeth coming at a more sedate pace. "John, what was all the shouting in the street?" Eugenia asked from the hall.

John ran to the door to prevent her entering the parlor. "Eugenia—there has been an . . . an accident. You do not want to see it."

Eugenia's face turned ashen, her eyes riveted on the front of his shirt.

"Daddy!" Beth cried, her hand quickly covering her mouth, and tears springing instantly to her eyes.

"Oh, no, my dear, nothing has happened to me. It is Bert—he was attacked by some rowdies in the street. Now, please, darling, take your mother upstairs to her room, while we see to Bert."

John supported Eugenia to the stairs, then handed her over to his daughter. Elizabeth stood to the side watching, her face pale. "Can I help, John? I am not afraid. I have seen blood before—and wounds."

John Manning stared at his mother without speaking for several seconds. "Yes, you can. The surgeon has been sent for, but his wounds should be cleansed. Perhaps Pelagie would help."

"I'll send for her. Thank you, John. I appreciate your not making an issue of my not seeing such things."

John gave a dry, unpleasant laugh. "Oh, no, Mother. I am afraid I think you very much deserve to see such unpleasantness. I think it is high time you saw what can result from your irresponsible encouraging of your young grandsons to fight for a cause that is traitorous, and which they do not fully understand."

Elizabeth's dark brown eyes snapped. "I might have known you were no more enlightened than before. This is just another of your shortsighted platitudes. Well, John, I am sorry for you, and perhaps you should awaken to the fact that very few things of value are gained in this life without a modicum of pain and loss attendant. We human beings are not graceful creatures in anything. We blunder and we hurt ourselves and others as we try to progress. I am sorry it had to be Bert who was injured, but I am not surprised; nor do I expect he shall be the last casualty we suffer in this family. Now, if you'll excuse me, I'll see to Bert. You can send for Pelagie. Tell her to bring plenty of water, and fresh rags—soft ones." She waved her son to one side and sailed past him.

By the time the surgeon arrived some half an hour later, Elizabeth had managed to dig most of the embedded gravel and dirt from the deep wounds on Bert's face while Pelagie worked on his badly damaged hand.

Dr. Rufus Atkins had a harried manner about him, which Elizabeth took exception to immediately. Sarcastically she said, "I do hope we didn't interrupt anything terribly important, Doctor."

Atkins's fingers went immediately to his neatly trimmed mustache. "I was having my midday meal," he said stiltedly. "It is difficult to find a moment's privacy when one is a surgeon—demands of the calling."

"Of course," Elizabeth said pertly. "Your inconvenience has been cleaned up as best we could. I think you might want to see to his right eye first. The lid seems to have been torn rather badly—I am not a doctor, so I am not certain as to the condition of the eye itself."

For a moment it looked as though the doctor were going to do nothing but pit his will against Elizabeth's, but then he moved closer to Bert and immediately had a change of manner. He asked for a chair and went to work, even taking a moment to compliment Elizabeth on her work.

"I thank you, Dr. Atkins, and I apologize for my too hasty judgment of you."

"It isn't the first time, madam, that I have been judged by my poor social presence."

"How badly damaged is his eye?"

The doctor shook his head. "It is scratched and bruised, but . . . we shall have to clean it, bandage it, and then it is in the hands of God."

"John, I think you had better send a messenger and a carriage to Riverlea at once. Joanna will want to be at his side. Also Bert's commanding officer shall have to be informed of his condition. Rob, can you see to that? George, have the west-wing guest-suite readied for Joanna and the family. And, Leo, I think you had better inform Drew and his family of what has happened."

Within minutes all the Manning men were out of the room, each of them seeing to his assigned tasks. Elizabeth stood where she was, deep in thought, trying to discover if there was anyone or anything she had forgotten. She started a little when she realized the doctor was laughing.

"You should be a general for His Majesty, Mrs. Manning. I am quite certain we would have no recalcitrant colonists with you in charge."

"Perhaps not, Dr. Atkins, but then, if I were in charge, we would not be a colony, but a nation."

"You realize that is a traitorous statement. I could report you."

"Yes, you could, and when you tried and hanged an old lady for treason, I would indeed contribute greatly to the cause of our becoming a nation. You would not do the British cause much good by such an act, but you would make me into a heroine—an American heroine. I should enjoy that position in history."

Dr. Atkins was silent for a moment, his attention divided between this fascinating woman and his unconscious patient. "You show little compassion for your cousin—he is your cousin, is he not?"

"He is my cousin by marriage. As to my compassion, sir, I am merely realistic. I do not feel that the King showed much compassion for his citizens when his soldiers fired into the crowd of people in Boston, or when he closed the harbor, or when he sent his troops to march against the citizens at Lexington. I don't believe that compassion has been shown in Parliament's dealing with the colonial requests for representation. And I do not believe that, in a dispute such as the one we are now in, compassion ever plays a great part."

"You shock me, madam. Your views are most unfeminine and unladylike."

"And your comments, sir, are most impolite and narrowminded. Perhaps my first impression of you was correct. You may be a . . . compassionate doctor, but you are a disagreeable man."

Doctor Atkins ran his hand through his graying hair and once more across his mustache. "I am sorry. It comes from living too long in barracks and being presented with the most unpleasant and horrifying aspects of war. I loathe the constant need to patch young men back together with balms and stitches only to have them come back to me torn apart again. In the end it seems to me the world changes very little. We have a new or a different king, or a different country lays claim to a territory, and the process is repeated. The farmers still farm the same land, and the people still live in the same houses in the same cities. Governments change and causes are fought for, but the people live much as they have always lived. Is that worth a young man's eye? His limbs?"

"If it were true, I would have to say no, but it is not true, Doctor. Men and women from all over Europe came here because so many of those interchangeable rulers you spoke of denied them freedoms they thought essential to life. They came here to worship freely, to work as they wished to, to build a good, safe home for themselves. These people have already left their homelands and suffered the hardships of wilderness, battled the Indians, the outlaws, and the vagaries of nature and fire. What we have here has come to us at great cost. We shall not hesitate to pay a bit more in order to keep it."

Dr. Atkins took a deep breath. "I do not doubt you, Mr. Manning. Though I would not want it widely known, I must confess I do not believe Great Britain should enter into an armed confrontation with the colonials. It is nearly an impossible task to bring a force here and cover the enormous territory that must be conquered. I am afraid we shall lose if our disagreements reach the point of armed conflict."

Elizabeth smiled. "I sincerely hope you are correct, Doctor, and I believe that you are. Now, if you will excuse me, I must see to the arrangement for Bert. He can be moved, can he not?"

"I doubt that it will do him much harm, provided, of course, that it is done carefully. I am a little concerned that he has not awakened. Usually I'd have expected him to come round by now."

Elizabeth looked at Bert, but said nothing. She took a deep breath and said a prayer to herself. There was little else to be done.

Bert was taken to the freshly prepared rooms, and the family sat vigil. In turns they waited for his return to consciousness and the arrival of his family from Riverlea.

Joanna arrived late that night and rushed into the house in a flurry of petticoats, servants, nurses, and baby equipment. "Where is he?" she demanded of Elizabeth before greeting her. "How badly has he been injured?"

"Dr. Atkins has seen him several times. He has regained consciousness, Joanna, and though he is badly bruised and looks terrible, we have been assured he is on the mend."

"But what of his eye? I was told that he may lose one of his eyes . . . and . . ."

Elizabeth put her arm around her young cousin. Seldom had she seen such emotion coming from her. Perhaps she did care deeply for Bert, after all, and that was something Elizabeth understood and had great compassion and empathy for. "Take heart, my dear. We do not yet know about his eye. The doctor said that will take time, and it will be a while before anything can be determined."

Joanna shuddered, and then Elizabeth understood the source of her emotion. With her face tear-stained and distorted, Joanna turned to Elizabeth and said, "Drew had something to do with this. Is he still here?"

Elizabeth let her hand drop from around Joanna's waist. "Drew is not here, nor was he here when this incident took place. We have sent word to him and Gwynne, so I imagine they will arrive tomorrow."

"I don't believe you!" Joanna sobbed. "Drew was here! He had to be here! This wouldn't have happened if it weren't for him. He is a vicious, evil man! You have no right to foist him on the rest of the family, Elizabeth. No right! These tragedies are on your head, as well as his. How does it feel to carry a weight like that, Elizabeth?"

Elizabeth's steady brown eyes met Joanna's anger-filled ones. "Wouldn't you like to see your husband, Joanna? He has been told you would be arriving at any time. He has been waiting for you."

Joanna laughed. "Oh, I know that ploy, Elizabeth. Take the notice for your responsibility from yourself by making someone else feel remiss for her actions. I have ridden through the night to be at my husband's side. You can't fault me on that."

"Did you ride through the night to be at your husband's side, or to confront Drew with his imagined part in this?"

"I haven't time to chatter nonsense with you, Elizabeth. I must go to Bert's side."

"Of course," Elizabeth said, and stepped aside so that Joanna could go up the stairs.

Joanna managed to turn the house upside down with her demands and complaints about the care taken of Bert. Early the next morning she was insisting upon taking him back to Riverlea. "He isn't safe here!" she shrilled at anyone who would listen. "You are madmen in this house. How could you allow something like this to happen?"

"My dear, you are hysterical," John said patronizingly. "Now, I suggest you take a tonic, go upstairs and lie down for a bit, and get hold of yourself. Later we shall gather the whole family and discuss how we can best take care of Bert, and arrange for your whole family to be together."

Joanna's eyes widened, her hand went to her throat dramatically. "You expect me to stay here and expose myself and my child to the dangers you have welcomed into your house? I don't understand you, Cousin John. Of all of you, I expected you to keep your wits about you . . . but . . . but I was mistaken. Bert has been attacked by the rabble right in your home, because you invited that rabble here. I will not remain in this house. I will not endanger my family. We shall be leaving this afternoon, and I ask only that you lend me the services of your household staff to assist me in accomplishing that. You shall feel more comfortable, I'm sure, once you are free to have your *associates* in treason free to return here, and Bert and Rebecca and I shall be out of harm's way."

John Manning's face grew red and his neck puffed above his collar. "Joanna," he said, exercising great control to keep himself temperate with her, "I have put up with your diatribe as long as I am going to. Bert was not attacked in this house. No treasonous rabble was invited in, and I have no treasonous associates. You will kindly refrain from blackening my character and that of my family, and remember that you are a guest in this house, as is your daughter and your husband. You might also keep in mind that were it not for me and my sons, your husband might be much worse off than he is now."

"Well . . . perhaps I have overlooked your kindness somewhat, Cousin John, but you must forgive me. You can see what a burden this is on me. I now have no man to guide me . . . Riverlea . . . the family . . . all the great burden of that is now on me. How shall I manage? I am terrified. We are unprotected. And you must admit that were it not for Drew and his constant involvement with outlaw activities, none of the Mannings or the Templetons would be so vulnerable to attack. We are simply not safe as long as that man is free to work his evil on us. Look what he has done to George! And my sister! Poor Gwynne, he has ruined her." She looked up at him, her eyes large and sad. "I am sorry, Cousin John, but my life is filled with sorrow and all of it can be laid at Drew Manning's feet. I cannot feel safe here. I must take my family back to Riverlea."

"I do not agree with you, Joanna, and I do not believe it is best for Bert to be moved right now. He should be nearer to the doctor than he will be in the country. But I will not prevent you from doing what you wish. If you are determined to leave, I shall assist you."

Joanna and her family left Charles Town and the Manning house early that afternoon. The Mannings stood as a group on the piazza watching the carriage that carried Joanna and Rebecca, and the wagon that carried Bert, move away down the street.

Eugenia shook her head. "I do not understand her, I'm afraid. Bert should not be taken on such a trip. Dr. Atkins said that he should remain as quiet and still as possible if he hoped to keep the sight in his right eye."

Elizabeth took a deep breath. "I am afraid all of us underestimated her hatred for Drew. There are times when I fear Joanna more than I do the entire British army. In many ways she has a cause far greater than they."

"As usual you overdramatize, Mother, but unfortunately this time I believe there's a kernel of truth in what you say," John observed, then turned, herding his family in front of him. "Come, let us go inside. For the moment there is nothing we can do. Let us be grateful for this brief time of peace."

John Manning was accurate in his assessment. It was a brief time of peace. As the hot, damp winds of summer blew in on Charles Town and heated the air until it was unbearable, the hot winds of unrest swirled within the hearts of the men who called themselves patriots. Every untoward look or remark was taken with great gravity, and too often acted upon. The British were not much different from the patriots. Remarks were thrown back and forth, fought over.

George Walker was the gunner at Fort Johnson, and in the spirit of rivalry and hostility he spoke loud and long about the patriots. Without hesitation a mob of men marched to capture him and correct his erroneous assessment of the patriots. George Walker had no more chance than did Bert Townshend to defend himself against the angry men. He was beaten soundly while a mob of citizens gathered to watch and then, one by one, to participate in what was now considered to be an exhilarating demonstration. Walter was tarred and feathered. A man standing near to the edge of the action yelled over his shoulder to those who stood behind and hadn't such a clear view. "He's got a new suit of clothing." Then he added with a roaring laugh, "Without the assistance of a single tailor!"

The word was passed back. Laughter was heard, shouts of encouragement to the main perpetrators rose, and the mob pushed closer to George Walker.

George, Leo, and Drew Manning were on their way to Elizabeth's house when they saw and heard the mob and went to see what was happening.

Bits and pieces of yelled information came to them, and the crowd began to move. The Mannings moved along with the surge, still not sure what was happening, but knowing that something having to do with the British authority was being executed. They had not even seen the tarred-and-feathered gunner yet.

The excitement caught them, and the three young men began to shout with the others that it was time that the British began to listen to their colony.

The crowd started up, then stopped in front of a known Tory's house. The roar went up, and George Walker was held aloft for the British sympathizers to see as they peered from their windows.

"Did you see that!" George gasped. "Look what they did to him. Boy! The fur will fly over this when word gets around."

"Who cares if it does?" Leo yelled, pushing into the mob.

The crowd moved noisily and slowly from one non–association member's house to another, showing what befell people who were not loyal to the American cause.

Boldly they stopped at William Bull's house. Several hundred people milled about the yard and in the street, shouting, "Grog! Bring us grog! A toast!"

A young man, prepared for all occasions, passed grog to those in front, holding fast to the unfortunate gunner.

With the grog in hand two of the men held Walker while a third forced the young man to drink the grog and make the toast. His voice strained and filled with fear and hate, Walker cried out, "Damn to Bull!" as ordered by his captors.

Others in the mob threw a bag of feathers onto the balcony of the Bull home. "Take care of this, Bull, until your turn comes!"

Laughter rippled through the noisy mob when another man yelled, "Charge the grog to the account of Lord North!"

"Yeah! Charge the grog to North's account!"

"Bull! Take heed, your turn will come! Keep the feathers for our return!"

Slowly, almost reluctantly, the mob moved away from ex-Governor Bull's house and moved on down the street. George Walker was finally left at the door of Dr. Milligan-Johnston, His Majesty's surgeon to the Carolina forces.

The depositing of Walker on the good doctor's doorstep was not the first time he had been visited by the patriots. Daniel Cannon and another carpenter named Fullerton, Johnson the blacksmith, and Edward Weyman had come before to warn him to sign the pledge of loyalty formed by the Association.

The Mannings left before the rest of the crowd did, and headed for home, without a thought of what impact today's actions might have on others.

The impact, however, was strong and immediate. Robert Welles, a mechanic who disagreed with the methods of his fellows, and a man who kept one of the finest bookstores in the colonies, closed the doors to his shop, never to open them again. Dissenters were too frightened to talk aloud about their views. Some royal officials left the city, and many ordinary citizens closed their homes, packed their belongings, and left as well.

"For the love of God, will you young men never understand that you cannot gain freedom by denying it to your own citizens! What kind of liberty do you call it that terrorizes its own?" John Manning ranted at a full gathering of his family.

"But no one meant for those people to leave the city, Daddy," George said. "The Congress wants them to stay—but to pledge loyalty to South Carolina if we are attacked. That is not a great demand—after all, it is their land."

"They choose not to be ruled by a bunch of witless rogues who enforce their views by violence and coercion! George is our king! England is our mother country. It is to her we owe allegiance, not to some group of mechanics!"

"Our loyalty is owed to ourselves," Drew said calmly. "This is our land, not King George's, not the mechanics'. We want the liberty to pursue our own best interests and to choose our own government."

"At what cost, Drew? What you suggest is a dream, you can see that. I shall not say that it is not an admirable dream. Men have been seeking Utopia for thousands of years, and to some degree that seeking is a strength of youth. Perhaps it is one of the hopes that enables us to face the disillusionments of later years, but it is a dream that has never been realized, for men are not capable of ruling themselves justly. Power in the hands of the many is the power of chaos, of mob rule, and we have all seen where that leads. This family must disassociate itself from the patriots before it is too late, and England ceases even to consider talking with us, before we have warships in our harbors and troops girded for war marching in our streets. The path you have chosen, Drew, and the one you and Leo are now taking, George, is a dangerous one."

Drew remained quiet and calm. He said, "Change is always looked upon as dangerous, Cousin John, but without it mankind never progresses. I don't deny that there have been excesses of zeal in some of the patriots' actions, but there are also noble ideas being spoken, and there is an honorable goal to be obtained. Either we shall win the attention and the respect of England, or we shall win our freedom and establish ourselves as a free and independent nation. It may be a dangerous course, but no more so than stagnation. Unrest acted upon may bring war to our cities and countryside, but unrest pressed into silence to fester in the breast of every man will truly cause chaos by reason of the meanness and rot that will seep into the daily habits of each of us. A nation eaten from within by discontent is a nation of petty hostility and crime and brutal personal violence. Were I given the choice, I would prefer to die by the hand of a man who was fighting for a cause he believed in, than to die by the hand of a malcontent desperate because he had no ear to hear his just complaints."

"Then you will not listen to reason and disassociate yourself from the patriots?" John said somberly.

"No, sir, I cannot. England has promised us the rights of British citizens, but those are merely promises. The laws and regulations of Parliament are for the benefit of Parliament, not the people of America. They place taxes upon us that we cannot amend nor argue—"

"That is not true!" John interrupted. "We have means of recourse."

"We have the means, not the reality. An ordinary man has not the finances nor the ear to have his case heard and considered fairly, and the final accounting will not be judged on the merits of the man's cause, but on the financial needs and interests of the mother country. I shall gladly fight to create a country in which a man may be his own master, a country which exists for its citizens and in which the labors and fruits of the citizens shall not be mere fodder for the government."

"That will never happen! Men are always dependent on their government."

"No," Drew said. "Men are not dependent on government—not until that government has become corrupted by its own power and size and wants its citizenry dependent on it. Any man living in a country such as this one can with his two hands feed himself, provide shelter, and work with his hands and mind to his own benefit. I believe in that. I will fight for it, if I must."

"And so will I, Daddy," George said. "I'm sorry. I wish you could see it as we do."

"Does that mean that you will follow the lead of these other two, Leo?" John asked his eldest son.

"I'm afraid it does, Daddy."

"You, Rob?" John asked again, turning to fully face his middle son.

"No. I have never had an argument with British rule. I see nothing oppressive in it, and I see nothing in the future of this rebellion but disaster. Battles will be fought on our soil, our lands will be ruined, and the well-being of Carolina retarded for many years to come, all on account of the wild and reckless ravings of some mechanics who are barely capable of spelling their own names, let alone of ruling a nation. I'll have nothing to do with it." He looked long at his cousin Drew, and then at his brothers. Then he turned his attention to the women in the room and said, "At the end of the week I shall be taking my family to Willowtree for the remainder of the summer. I would advise you to do the same, Daddy. We can wait out this latest spate of violence and madness there, and perhaps with the cooling of the weather and the change of seasons will come a cooling of overheated minds here, and a change of heart toward England."

Drew leaned forward in his chair. "Rob, if you and Velma are going to Willowtree, I do hope you will take into serious consideration the information Leo and George gave you about conditions there. Deplore the patriots' movement, if you wish, but please, do not underestimate the depth of it or the seriousness of the English retaliation."

"Just because I am not a patriot, Drew, does not mean I am a fool. I shall handle whatever problems may have developed at Willowtree."

"What has happened at Willowtree, Rob?" Velma asked.

Rob smiled at her and patted her hand. "It is nothing to worry about. One of the slaves has caused a bit of discontent, but he is merely a field hand and shall be taught to obey quickly enough. Nothing is wanted but a firm hand and some attention given to the plantation, all of which I shall provide as soon as we have settled in."

"Rob, I think—" Drew began, but was cut off by Rob's crisp voice.

"There is no need for your thoughts on the matters at Willowtree, Drew. As I hear it, you are planning to ride to the Upcountry to garner support for the patriot cause. I suggest you see to your business and leave me to tend to mine."

Drew looked at him for a time, then shrugged. "As you will, Rob."

20

Drew Manning was happy to be out of Charles Town for a time. The atmosphere of the port city, and of the Manning family, was tense and suspicious. Though Drew believed in the American cause and was fully prepared to fight for it, should it come to that, there was no question left that this would be a nasty battle from which no one would emerge without deep scars.

George Manning had decided to ride into the Upcountry with Drew and many other men to try to get support for the Association. He sat quietly, thinking in the sunlight that flowed through the windows of Drew's study. He was thinking about William Wragg, a man whose fate would not leave him in peace. William Wragg had been appointed chief justice by King George, and although Wragg had refused to accept the post, he was loyal to the King, and outspoken in that loyalty. As had become the way of things, the Association took exception to his disloyalty to their cause, and had tried to persuade him to change his allegiance. Wragg had stated that "he had a right to exercise his own judgment in the premises, although in doing so his sentiments might differ from the general voice." He had been banished to his plantation during the heat of the summer, leaving behind his wife, who was expecting their child. Though men like Wragg would harm the patriot cause, and George in no way disagreed with the feeling that the man had to be punished and made an example of lest others follow, it still left a bad taste in his mouth. Motionless, and deep in thought so long he felt cramped, George stirred and stretched, managing a smile as he said to Drew, "This may be the year we all come down with yellow fever. It looks like the whole family is leaving the city at the very time we should be racing to it. Is there some sort of divine message in that, Drew? Wragg is exiled to his plantation, and we go voluntarily to ours."

Drew laughed. "You've been thinking too much again, George. You know all that thought addles your brain. As soon as we have been on the road for a couple of weeks, you will be cured. I can guarantee you that the only thing that will worry you is the condition of your rear end."

"Ahh, it is always nice to have something to look forward to."

"Yes," Drew said a little more seriously. "I'm afraid it may be the only thing we have to look forward to. As usual the Lowlanders have very little idea of the Upcountryman, and will expect him to react as does the Charlestonian. That will not be the case. Most of those men in the Upcountry have little or no reason to trust the Lowlanders."

"Perhaps, at least, out of this will come a realization of what the Regulators were saying years ago."

"Of what value is that?" Drew asked, whirling to face George. "The suffering was done, the hardship endured. What does it matter now if our Lowland friends understand what we were telling them years back? Following that logic, we in the Upcountry should allow them to fight their battles with Britain alone, then in two or three years tell them we understand what it was they wanted now."

George's eyebrows went up, a wry smile on his lips. "Isn't that pretty much what you've been telling me they are going to say when our association approaches them?"

Drew had to smile. "I suppose it is."

"However," George continued, "I wonder if they will tell us with as much passivity as we are now discussing it?"

Drew stared at his cousin for a moment, his dark brown eyes dancing mischievously. "I wonder that myself. We may find ourselves in a donnybrook or two."

"Praise God, if it is just a donnybrook or two."

"Well," Drew said, "there is a lot of support in the Upcountry for the patriot cause in certain areas. If Drayton merely wants to rally that support, there will be no problem, but I have heard that there are pockets that are pure Tory, and they are not going to be convinced by any visit from me, or William Henry Drayton, or the Reverend William Tennent, or anyone else."

On July 23, 1775, Drew kissed Gwynne good-bye and loaded his gear onto the back of his horse.

"You needn't worry about us," she said, smiling. "I think I am finally resolved to be a soldier, too. We'll be fine, and Nathaniel shall be the man of the house until you return."

Drew bent and hugged the six-year-old standing at Gwynne's side. "Well, then, I shan't worry at all. You couldn't have a better defender than Nathaniel." The small boy grinned with pleasure. Manfully he shook Drew's hand. "If either you or your mother should want to reach me, send a message to Ned at Cherokee. He'll send it on."

Drew joined George, who was waiting for him at the stables, and the two men rode to meet William Drayton and Reverend William Tennant. The group of men started off in high spirits, and full of optimism. Their first foray was into the territories of Orangeburg, Saxe-Gotha and the Dutch Fork, all occupied by Germans who had never enjoyed what the English considered rights and liberty. Nor were these inhabitants of South Carolina American yet. Drayton's reasoning and persuasive abilities were almost entirely lost on these settlers. For the first time in their lives they were enjoying a bit of economic independence, and the king of England had been very generous to them by giving them land grants. They didn't understand at all the patriots' alarm over a tea tax.

"We do not wish to lose our grants because of a trifling tax on tea—we do not even use that tea!" one man said with a guffaw at the ludicrous suggestion that such a tax had importance. "What kind of man are you, that you should shoot at your king because he wants you to pay a bit for the tea he favors? You are a strange, imprudent man, Mister Drayton. I do not think I can trust what you say."

Later that night when Drayton, Drew, and George were alone, William Drayton threw up his hands in frustration. "I can't make them understand! What can I say to them . . . why can I not make them see we are fighting for the same cause that brought them out of their homeland in the first place? What am I doing wrong? Am I unclear in my statements?"

"No, no, not at all," Drew said, "But you must understand that what you see as oppression, they are still seeing as freedom in their terms. Perhaps if you sent one of their own, someone who has been here long enough to understand, they would listen better."

"Yes!" Drayton said enthusiastically. He was but thirty-two years old, and filled with the fervor of a just cause, and intoxicated with his own ambitions. "I know just the man—no, I know of two men. Together they would be undeniable! Drew, send a message to George Wagner, and the Swiss—what's his name—Felix Long, and tell them their services are needed here immediately. Give them all the background and information they will need to do a good job, and send it yet tonight."

Drew smiled and nodded, excusing himself to see to it. It was one thing to be dutiful to the cause, but quite another if that duty made him miss a beef barbecue. He could already smell the tempting aroma wafting through the open windows of the house, and he was going to be on hand when the festivities began. The Dutch settlement might not be in favor of the patriotic cause, but they did love good food. So did Drew Manning.

Well fed, but unsuccessful, Drew, George, William Drayton, and a few others pushed on in their quest for support for the cause, and to add to the list of names willing to sign the Association oath.

Finally, Drew convinced Drayton that there were areas far more likely to be favorable. "You'll find strong support here, if you go to the right places," Drew said.

"Well, perhaps it would be well to visit some of these men you assure me are supporters, but if they are as strong as you say, they will already have signed the Association, and what I need are new names."

"It wouldn't hurt just to give these men, who have been loyal all along, a little boost, and a reassurance that they are appreciated."

"I agree," Drayton said, and they set off to visit several of the men of the Upcountry who already represented their areas in the Provincial Congress. The recruiting group was wined and dined and encouraged by Benjamin Farrar, John Savage, William Wofford, and Thomas Woodward before Drayton grew impatient and anxious to invade less committed territory.

As soon as he entered the area most influenced by Moses Kirkland, an Upcountry leader, he again met with opposition. They stopped at the two-hundred-acre farm of Jacob Peters, and were welcomed in. Drayton arranged to have a religious service for Peters and his neighbors that evening with a meeting afterward during which he was to preach the benefits of rebellion against England.

He was greeted with hoots of laughter and derisive voices. Peters said, "Beggin' your pardon, Mr. Drayton, but we all know hereabouts that not one word that comes from the coast is likely to be truth. An' even if it were, we ain't no dummies up here. We all know this whole patriot cause ain't nothin' but Massachusetts lookin' out for her own interests to the detriment o' the res' o' us. As fer me, I don't give a damn what comes to Massachusetts. Let her look to her own."

Another man, a calmer one, said, "We shall gain no advantage, Mr. Drayton. I have no quarrel with your cause, but neither do I choose to place my assets at a risk for it. It will cost far more to raise troops to fight England than it will to pay any tax that might be placed on tea or any other commodity."

"The amount of the tax is not the question," Drayton said earnestly. "The question is that we are being taxed without being given representation. That is the real question and one we cannot tolerate—we will not tolerate!"

Drayton was stretching toward eloquence, and Drew scrunched down in his seat. He whispered to George, "He's walking right into a hornets' nest with this. Think of a way to shut him up."

George immediately stood up and stretched, and Drew made a slicing motion with his hand across his throat. Drayton looked at them, a puzzled look on his face, then went innocently on to take a question from the group.

The man, James Trent, stood, a smirk on his face. "You say taxation without representation is intolerable, Mister Drayton. It's also illegal to undermine the authority of the King, isn't it? But maybe that is to be set aside in the face of this intolerable lack of representation, is that right?"

"Essentially that is correct, but you must understand that we intend to do nothing violent, unless we are attacked. We are merely asking for support in the event that England attacks us and we are in need of defending the colony."

"What if they put you in jail?" Trent asked. Occasionally, he looked around at his fellow Upcountrymen and received amused, understanding looks.

"Why, we would release our men—by force, if necessary. We will not have our citizens abused."

Drew grimaced. It was getting worse and worse.

"Well, now, Mister Drayton, those are mighty fine sentiments," Trent said, and could go on no longer without letting his anger show. He turned to his friends and put up his hands, palms out. "I needn't say no more. Here is this fine fellow from the Lowlands asking us to fight for him in a cause that is identical to the one we fought for a few years back. This very same fellow and a lot of others like him were the same ones in the Charles Town Assembly who would not give us fair representation in those Lowland courts and government. Matter of fact, they didn't want to give us courts at all, nor schools. All they wanted from us was our tax money, which they were quick to collect, and our support in any cause that caught their fancy. Now they got a cause, and this fellow is here to sit at our tables and ask us to give him what he denied to us. I think we should bid him a quick farewell, and hope he has the good sense to go back to Charles Town, stay there, and leave us alone."

A roar of approval came from the men sitting in the room.

After a few more useless comments in an effort to rescue a lost cause, Drayton joined Drew and George.

Drew made a face and shrugged. "We tried to head you off."

Drayton's mouth was open. "That's what you were doing!"

"That's what we were doing," George said chuckling. "If you have to have a catastrophe, it might as well all be in one place."

"I'd advise you to stay off the subject of nonrepresentation with the Upcountrymen, unless you know they are already predisposed in your favor. And if it must be mentioned, I suggest you do so by informing them that you now understand their earlier plight much better now that you are experiencing it yourself," Drew said.

"I could have used that advice an hour or so earlier, Drew," Drayton complained. "Why didn't you tell me?"

"I have been telling you. You've been too damned enthusiastic to absorb the warnings."

"I'll be wiser now," he pledged, then added, "And if I'm not, get up out of your seat and muzzle me."

"A promise!" George said.

Travel in the Upcountry was slow and laborious, with long hours in the saddle, great distances between stops, and difficulties in gathering a sizable number of people to each meeting. On August seventeenth the group arrived at the Fetchall residence in Fairforest. The commissioners for the Association met Thomas Brown, Patrick Cunningham, and some others who had gathered to discuss the grievances of the Upcountry. Drew groaned and said, "You are a real glutton for punishment, Will. Do you know anything at all about Thomas Brown?"

"I know he is a leader, and that he is important in this area. That's all I need to know. If we can sway him, others will follow."

"You couldn't have picked a more difficult man to sway," Drew said.

Thomas Brown was a large man with even, pleasant features. Drew had known him for some time, and liked him. "Brown has not had the best of experiences with the Liberty Boys. He had a few choice things to say about them on one occasion, and they retaliated by tarring and feathering him. I doubt very much that you are going to convince him that the American cause for liberty is a better choice over the British."

"Drat!" Drayton said. "I keep running into all these inconveniences. How am I to make progress if everyone nurses every one of his old grudges?"

George Manning snickered, then laughed aloud. "A minor grudge that I think Mr. Brown is justified in remembering. Have you ever tried to remove tar and feathers?"

"No, but I saw Gunner Walker making the effort," Drayton said, and joined the laughter. "Do you remember that poor sod with all his feathers flying in the breeze trying to make a toast to damn Bull?"

They talked for a time longer about remembered sounds and sights of their cause, then went to face a group of disaffected men. No progress was made, but Drayton was not a man to give up easily. He met with a similar group of Tories on August twenty-third and was treated to strong hostility and objects hurled along with eloquent invective.

"We represent this colony, and I shall not be treated like this," he said in anger, still reeling from the insults that had been directed at him.

"It wasn't a complete waste," George said. "Seventy or so of that group signed the Association."

"It isn't enough! And it doesn't make amends for the audacity of some of these Tory leaders. We shall have to take action, and it must be strong and decisive."

Drayton sat down that evening and wrote to the committee asking permission to capture a dozen or so of the Tory leaders. He assured the Council that any insurrection which might result from this action could easily be put down. Satisfied, he looked up at his compatriots. "We need the Upcountry leaders to send their representatives to the Provincial Congress, and with these Tories running loose with even looser tongues, the elections will be postponed time after time. It has already happened twice, and that is twice too often. I have no doubt we shall be given leave to remove Mr. Kirkland, Mr. Brown, and several others from the arena of influence for a time."

Drayton's request caused a good deal of consternation in the Council in Charles Town. The question of the Upcountry and the loyalties of the independent men who lived there was always a touchy one, and many of those leaders in Charles Town had not forgotten the days when the Upcountrymen had threatened to march on Charles Town if their grievances weren't heard and acted upon. The greatest fear was that Drayton would arrest the wrong man at the wrong time and precipitate a civil war. At the same time they realized there was nothing to be gained by sending a representative to the Upcountry to garner support, then tying the man's hands when he ran into difficulty. With great doubt and trepidation the Council voted four to three to trust Drayton's judgment of the situation and give him permission to proceed.

Drayton received the news eagerly, though he had not truly doubted it would be forthcoming. At the beginning of September he gathered his patriot supporters and drove Kirkland out, arrested nine of the King's men, and set up headquarters at the town of Ninety Six. He sent his men out to enter the houses of known Tory leaders and to go through their papers looking for any information that would tell of British plans or be useful to the American cause. And he stirred up a good amount of hostility, and raised the spirit of retaliation.

On September the tenth Drayton and his men, who now were of sizable number, readied themselves for an expected attack. Drew and George repacked their belongings, saw to the horses, and prepared for what might be their first battle of the rebellion. Drayton and his two hundred and twenty-five men marched to the Ninety Six Courthouse and waited. Drayton set an ambush at Island Ford, where he expected the Loyalists to cross the Saluda River.

All the men were tense with excitement and anticipation. From various vantage points both sides could see the other assembling. Supporters of the American cause spread word of the impending battle and soon a thousand men were gathered on the south side of the Saluda. On the north the Loyalists gathered, nearly twelve hundred strong, but no battle ensued.

"Why don't they attack?" George asked, perspiration dotting his upper lip. "This waiting is making me jumpy."

Drew shifted and once again began cleaning and checking his musket. He was taut with tension, wishing for the very thing George had verbalized.

"Why don't we attack?" George continued. "Why in the hell doesn't someone do something?"

"Soon," Drew said tersely. "Drayton won't wait much longer. This is a battle of nerves."

"Well, I lost the damned thing," George burst out. "I'd rather fight ten battles than have to sit it out like this. You can't relax, the bleeders might just come at you, and you can't do a bloody other thing, either, till we get an order."

"They are in the same position we are, and I'm sure their men are just as jittery. They probably expect us to come pouring over the bridge any minute."

"But we're not doing a bloody thing!" George howled.

"They don't know that," Drew said.

George sat down and relaxed his hand on his gun, a smile finally crossing his face. "I just want to get into a foray with them, Drew. I guess we should all be hoping that this whole thing resolves itself without a shot ever being fired, but God forgive me, I want to fight."

The air of tension remained until September thirteenth, when William Drayton sent a proclamation to the Tory camp to be read before Fetchall's men. Drayton, in his proclamation, demanded that all the men disclaim all intention to use force against the Association, and warned of the armed vengeance that would follow should they try it.

In the Tory camp it was decided by the King's men that they would agree under the following terms; "We have as true and real regard for liberty established on constitutional principles as any men on the continent by whatever name distinguished and shall take every proper legal step in our power for its preservation and support." The conditions tacked on to that were that no person on account of his opinions be disturbed or deprived of his trading rights, that Governor Campbell be unmolested, and that Fort Charlotte be reequipped, as the forces of Congress had seized the munitions stored there.

Fetchall and several other men were designated to deliver the reply to Drayton's proclamation. Fetchall, not being a brave man, went into his enemy's camp and with alacrity signed Drayton's surrender resolution without ever mentioning the Tory terms of submission.

For several minutes after they had come together, both sides were pleased with the bargain struck. However, soon it was known that Fetchall had not given to Drayton any of the King's men's instructions, and they were furious. The courthouse lawn and interior rang with the harried talk of the Tories. Gallantly they honored the agreement.

George nudged Drew. "There is nothing else to be done for it if they are to remain men of their word, but it doesn't seem fair, does it? I think if Fetchall were on my side, I'd take him out back and hang the son of a bitch from the highest tree I could find."

"He's probably the reason we are not about to begin a battle, cousin. Drayton would never have agreed to those terms. We couldn't have anyway. We can't restore Fort Charlotte, and the Council would never authorize returning firearms to the Tories. It is just as well that Fetchall is a coward, and his leaders men of their word."

"I still say, I'd like to get into a little skirmish every now and then. All this waiting is enough to make a man mad."

"You'll get your chance. It's gone too far now to end without fighting," Drew said.

Before the Tories were permitted to leave, William Drayton extracted from Patrick Cunningham a letter stating he'd remain hostile. He took the letter with a great deal of satisfaction and put it into his waistcoat right over his heart. "I don't want any misunderstanding when I finally arrest you, Cunningham."

21

Gwynne Templeton Manning made a determined effort to be strong when she received a letter from Drew stating that he was going to remain in the Upcountry and add to the defense of Fort Charlotte until they were certain the Tories would remain quiet. It had been a long time since she had had to make her own way without Drew's strength and guidance, and her memories of that time were not pleasant ones. This time she was more cut off from her family than ever, because of the widening rift caused by old grudges and new disagreements over the conflict with the Crown.

She sat for a time mulling over her predicament and rereading Drew's letter, trying to divine some secret message in it that would tell her how long it would be before he returned home. No matter how many times she read the long informative letter, that one piece of all-important information was not there. She was sitting in an immobilized state of gloom when Nathaniel came into her room with Mary in tow.

Mary, seeing Gwynne's preoccupation, went immediately to her closet and began putting on her shoes and wrapping herself in the lovely silk, satin, and velvet gowns that she was permitted to play with on special occasions. Nathaniel stood quietly beside his stepmother, his great dark eyes studying her intently. "Why are you unhappy?" he asked.

Gwynne leaned forward and hugged the young boy. "I'm not exactly unhappy, Nathaniel, I am just a little disappointed. I just received a letter from Daddy, and he will not be coming home for some time yet. I miss him, and he misses us. Especially you. He told me to tell you he is very proud of you, and that you have done a good job of taking care of us."

Nathaniel tried to keep a serious face, but failed. He smiled broadly. "Did you tell him I have been looking after the house?"

Gwynne felt a wave of warmth for this child and restrained her impulse to hug him again. He wanted so much to do a man's work, and he tried endlessly, and usually with an amazing amount of success. "I did tell him, and now, my dear, I am afraid you will have to be brave and strong for a while longer."

"Why won't Daddy be coming home now?"

"There was some hostility at a place called Ninety Six, and though Daddy and his men think that it is all past, he is going to remain there for a time to be certain the Tories do not come back to cause trouble for the patriots who live in that area."

"You don't like it when Daddy isn't with you, do you, Gwynne?" he said, and took hold of her hand. "You should tell Nonnie to come here, and then you won't feel so bad."

Gwynne laughed, and this time did hug him. "You are absolutely right, Nathaniel. I shall ask Elizabeth to join us for a time, and she will make me feel much happier. Come with me—you and I shall write a letter to her right now, and then you may take it and select the messenger you think will be the fastest."

By noon Nathaniel had the letter on its way to Willowtree and Elizabeth. He stood outside the house watching Levi ride away with the letter. Gwynne found him nearly an hour later sitting on the steps still watching the road. She remained quiet and unseen for some time looking at the little boy with his mop of dark hair, his squared shoulders hunched over as he propped his head up with slightly dirty clenched fists, his eyes intently on the road waiting for the return of his messenger, and most likely expecting Elizabeth to appear momentarily. She stepped out of the doorway and sat down on the steps beside him. In many ways, as young as he was, he reminded her of Drew. From this six-year-old child emanated a power and a feeling of security. She looked over at him, but said nothing.

After a time he said, "How long does it take for Nonnie to come from Willowtree?"

"Well, when you ask something of Nonnie, she usually hurries as fast as she can, but Levi must get there, and Nonnie must pack, and then they must come all the way back here. She might not be able to get here until tomorrow."

Nathaniel thought for a moment, then shook his head. "No. Nonnie will hurry as fast as she can. She'll come today."

Gwynne ruffled his hair and laughed. "You're probably right. But you need not sit here on this step for the next couple of hours, because she could not get here that soon if she sprouted wings and flew. Why don't you take a ride on your pony now, and after dinner you and I will come back outside together and wait for her."

He hesitated, but only for a minute. He wanted to practice his riding so that he could show Drew, when he returned home, how good he had become.

Gwynne walked slowly back to the house after Nathaniel had run to the stables. How silly I am, she thought, realizing that she was sorry she had ended their vigil on the steps because she liked his company. "Penny," she called as she came into the foyer. As the girl appeared, she said, "Please send Mary and Susan to me in the morning room."

While she waited, Gwynne took from a cupboard a box of letters and numbers she often used to amuse and teach the children. The two little girls, both dressed in pink gingham pinafores and starched white dresses, curtsied as they came into the room.

Gwynne smiled approvingly at them, and with that broke the spell of good deportment. Both children ran to her, all but hurling themselves onto the sofa beside her. Mary's small four-year-old hands dug at the box, until Gwynne took her hands and stilled them. "A little order, please, Miss Mary."

"But I want the letters before Susan. I am very good at my letters."

"I want the letters," Susan said with her lower lip stuck out as far as she could manage.

Three-year-olds were barely more tolerable than two-year-olds, Gwynne thought, and sighed. "Susan shall have the letters, for she needs more practice, so she can become as good as you are at recognizing them, Mary." Gwynne put her hand up to forestall the protest that was in Mary's eyes and on the way to her lips. "And for you I have something very special. I have a primer, and I want to see how you do with making those letters into words."

Mary's bright blue eyes sparkled, and she took the book into her hands lovingly. Then quickly she turned to Susan and stuck out her tongue. "Ha ha! I have a book and you don't! You don't know your letters well enough."

Susan howled. Great tears spurted from her eyes, and her mouth was wide open in a scream of rage, sorrow, and frustration. "That's my book! Maaahhhmmy, I wanna book!"

Without a word Gwynne picked Susan up and sat her at a table with the box of letters in front of her. She picked out a dozen of them and placed them on the table. "If you are to hear me, Susan, you must stop crying. Place all the letters A in a pile. Tell me when you have found all the A's.

"Mary, you go sit in the chair near the window. Look at the book and the pictures in it, so you can tell me what you think the story is about."

Gwynne moved back and forth between the two girls, talking with them, showing them how to do each task she assigned them, for an hour. Neither child was able to go beyond an hour, for learning tired them as well as excited them, and Gwynne was quick to see and react to the first signs of fatigue. With a hug and several kisses she sent them to the kitchen for a glass of milk, freshly baked bread, and homemade marmalade that was still warm.

Alone again, she gathered up the letters, numbers, drawings, and the book and replaced them all in her box, and sat down staring out the window. The girls learned as fast as Nathaniel did. He was already stretching beyond her ability to teach, and it would not be long before Mary was, too. She and Drew had spoken of it often, but nothing had been done about the children's education. Perhaps with Elizabeth there she would see to hiring a tutor for Nathaniel and perhaps Mary. It would be a pleasant surprise for Drew, and it would give her something to feel proud of.

After dinner she went back to the front steps with Nathaniel and watched for Elizabeth's carriage. They sat until it was dark, and Nathaniel was getting very sleepy despite his desire to see Elizabeth.

"I don't think she will be here until morning, Nathaniel," Gwynne said, her own disappointment coming through her voice. "You had better go to bed, and get up early in the morning. She is sure to be here before noon tomorrow."

"I thought she'd come," he said sadly. He kissed Gwynne and walked listlessly into the house.

Gwynne walked around the grounds of the house several times until she, too, was tired, then went inside. Though she criticized herself severely, she was still restless and unable to sleep. She sat in the parlor, then went to her writing table, began a letter, but could not concentrate on it. She gave that up and went to the library to find a book. She took a novel and returned to the parlor determined to read if for no reason other than to make herself sleepy. She read no more than two lines before her mind wandered back to Drew. She thought of how he looked when working at his desk in the study, she thought of him in the fields at Cherokee. The more she thought, the more miserable and lonely she became. She had just given in to tears, her head resting against the chairback, daydreaming about the moment he would come home, when she heard the sound of a carriage in front of the house. She leaped out of her chair, mopping at her streaming eyes with her handkerchief, and smoothing her dress and hair as she ran for the front door.

It was midnight, but Elizabeth Manning stepped spryly from her carriage, a smile on her face as she walked toward Gwynne. "I'm a bit later than usual," she said with an impish smile. "I hope you'll forgive me, but I knew Nathaniel would be expecting me today."

Gwynne threw her arms around Elizabeth. "It wasn't just Nathaniel! I have been hoping and hoping you would arrive today, too! Oh, Elizabeth, what a comfort you are. Thank you for coming so quickly."

"Why, my dear, there is nothing amiss, is there? Your letter did not indicate—"

"Oh, no! Nothing. We . . ." Gwynne blew her nose and dabbed again at her eyes. "I feel silly saying it aloud. We were all just lonely."

Elizabeth patted her shoulder. "Well, my dear, we shall put that to rights. In a few days you will be so tired of my meddling you will be glad to have me leave." Quickly Elizabeth gave orders for her considerable luggage, far more than would be needed for a few days, to be taken to the room she regularly used on visits to Drew's house. "Would you mind awfully if I crept upstairs and awakened Nathaniel long enough to let him know I am here? I promise I shall not make a sound to awaken the little girls."

"Yes, it will make him very happy. I am afraid he went to bed very disappointed."

"It is difficult to accept, when we are young, that reality does not occur with the speed of wishes. It will give me pleasure to have this one come true, even if it's a little delayed."

Elizabeth tiptoed into the children's room. It was a long wide room that went the entire length of the third floor, and was divided into three sections. Toward the front of the house the three little girls slept; the central section was a playroom and the third section at the rear of the house was Nathaniel's sleeping area. Elizabeth sat on the edge of Nathaniel's bed, looking down at the sleeping child. His dark lashes sprayed out on his rounded rosy cheek. Asleep, he still had some of the look of a baby. She brushed his moist, curling hair from his forehead and gently called his name.

He opened sleep-filled, enormous brown eyes. He stared unseeing, half-asleep, then he smiled. "Nonnie?"

"Yes, my angel, I am here." She bent down and kissed him.

Nathaniel felt the rice powder on her skin and smelled the tangy odor of lavender on her skin and clothing. Arms robbed of strength by sleep went around her neck. He laughed softly once, and then was asleep again.

Elizabeth felt a fierce, protective love course through her as she tucked him beneath his light sheet. Despite, or perhaps because of, the manner of his birth, and how he had come to her, this child was her Manning of the future. She sat on the side of his bed for a time watching the sleeping child and thinking about herself, her family, and Nathaniel Dancer Manning . . . and the coming war. Once the war had come, nothing would ever be the same again, and for all her experience, and all her accumulated wisdom, she could not foresee or predict what would come of her family.

When she came downstairs again, Gwynne had tea and sandwiches waiting for her. "I thought you might be hungry."

"Considering how unladylike it is to admit to hunger, I shall simply say I am famished." Elizabeth took a sandwich and began to nibble on it. "I was in such a hurry to get here, I missed supper. Eugenia will nurse that breach of etiquette for months to come, and bring it up everytime I mention anything regarding her family's behavior. It does her good to have ammunition every now and then. Just so it doesn't happen too often."

"I think you are actually very fond of Eugenia," Gwynne said smiling.

"I am. She is a terrible ninny about some things, and I could positively pinch her when she feigns ill health if things get too much for her, but most of the time Eugenia is a very good wife to my son, and a good mother to my grandchildren."

"Well, she ought to be—she's lived with a marvelous example in you." Gwynne looked up at Elizabeth and said sincerely, "Have you ever thought about how much all of us rely on you, Cousin Elizabeth? Whenever Drew has a particularly difficult decision to make, it is always you he thinks of—in fact, I believe you are the only one whose judgment he values equally to his own. And I . . . well, I received a letter from Drew today saying he won't be returning home for some time yet, and I was feeling low and sorry for myself, and not being able to have Drew at my side, I immediately thought of you. Nathaniel put words to it for me, but I wanted your strength to help see me through."

"I hardly have any strength, Gwynne, but at my age it is a wonderful, blessed privilege to have one's friends and family desire one's companionship."

"I not only desire it, Cousin Elizabeth, I need it. I don't know what has happened to my independent spirit. I seem to have misplaced it when Drew and I married. I don't know what to do when he is not around. I find myself feeling frightened of the most ordinary things."

"But, my dear, that is nothing to worry about. When you and Drew married, all your goals and duties changed. When a woman learns to think of an entire family instead of merely herself, her burdens increase immeasurably. The only person unaware of this increased burden is the woman herself. Perhaps that alone is why God gave us marriage. One human being cannot battle the world and nurture the family as well. It requires both a man and a woman, and bless us all that this is so. Of course, you have not lost your spirit, Gwynne darling, you have merely increased its scope so far that you need a partner to aid you in assuming some of the duties your husband usually sees to."

Gwynne watched her with large intent blue eyes, then she smiled. "You always find cause for all human failings, don't you Elizabeth? It is no wonder we all need you."

"What I say to you is true, Gwynne. I am not soothing you falsely. It takes a great talent to be able to join ambitions and goals and energies to the life of another. It is no mean task, and rather than chastise yourself that you find it difficult to work without Drew, you should congratulate yourself that you have accomplished working with him. It is always easier to be alone—perhaps not so pleasant, but easier." She sipped her tea and took another sandwich. "Enough of this. What is it that you and Drew planned to do together that you are now reluctant to do alone?"

Gwynne lowered her head. On her lips was an embarrassed smile. "I feel a little silly even mentioning it now. It seems such a trivial thing. We were going to hire a tutor for Nathaniel and Mary . . . and to a lesser degree Susan."

"Then we shall get right to it. Tomorrow you and I shall speak to our friends and see if perchance someone knows of a qualified man or woman to serve in such a capacity, and we shall talk to the authorities—if we can discover who is now in charge of such things—and see whether any new bondsmen have come from England of late. Often a good woman can be indentured."

"Yes," Gwynne answered, but the doubt had returned to her voice.

"What is it, my dear? What makes you doubt yourself again?"

"I haven't the vision Drew has, Cousin Elizabeth. I don't doubt that I am capable of selecting an able teacher, but I am not so sure I am as able as he to select an able teacher who will also fortify and instill the values he knows are necessary to the children's education."

"I see. I should have known it was not a simple matter that has stopped you. Of course, you are correct. An able imparter of knowledge is not the same as an able selector. So much of teaching is in the selection of what material shall be taught. Not many realize that, Gwynne, but I still believe that you and I together will be able to select a teacher Drew would approve of."

"Perhaps," Gwynne said, unconvinced.

"Well, if we fail, he can always replace our choice with a teacher of his own choosing, when he returns."

Gwynne took a deep breath. "One thing is certain—no good can come of it if we do not even make the effort."

The two women gathered up the remains of their midnight repast still talking and laughing and planning their activities for the morrow.

"I fear neither of us shall awaken before the sun goes down again." Elizabeth giggled. "We have been very naughty sitting up and talking the night away."

"Tomorrow we may regret it, but I thank you tonight, Cousin Elizabeth. I am tired, but in my heart I feel ever so much better."

It took the two women several days to gather the information they needed, and then they began to interview tutors. At the end of an exhausting day of seeing and talking to six candidates, Elizabeth and Gwynne retired to her sitting room to discuss each of them and make a choice, or decide to talk with other candidates.

"I am so confused, I hardly know what to say, Cousin Elizabeth. Which of these do you think we should consider?"

"I do not know, Gwynne. Perhaps we should do better if we begin by deciding who we do not want. That one man—" she said, looking at her list, "Peter Burton. I would cross him off the list immediately. He is a very ill-tempered man, I think. I doubt the children would learn much from him, except perhaps rebellion. One rebellion in the colonies at a time, I think, is quite enough without starting one in one's own house."

Gwynne laughed. "General Nathaniel, I'm sure, would take up arms at the first opportunity."

"It is Mary I would fear. Lord protect us all from that fiery temper of hers," Elizabeth said.

"Mr. Peter Burton is crossed off the list. I imagine he shall be quite surprised. In his own opinion, in any case, he was certain he was the best qualified. I think we might consider crossing Alma Townes off, too. I do not believe she is astute enough. She would most likely find herself in the same position I am—not being able to guide the children far enough or fast enough."

"Agreed," said Elizabeth. "Mary Helms wants to be their mother. I think."

"Oh, we are doing well—we are down to three names. Jane Reston, Will Harp, and Winnie Jones."

"I liked Jane Reston very much," Elizabeth said thoughtfully. "She is very pretty, however. How do you feel about that?"

"I suppose I should worry about so attractive a woman being in the household, but I don't think it will be a detriment. Do you think otherwise?" Gwynne asked.

"Heavens, no! I don't, but I wasn't sure how you felt. So many women worry about that, but I don't see Miss Reston as being the kind who would seek her fortune by taking another woman's husband. She would be my pick if you had no objection."

"I have none. I liked her very much, too, and when she met the children I got the impression that they liked her. She seemed to like them."

"There may be one small problem," Elizabeth said, and at Gwynne's inquiring look, explained, "Well, Jane Reston thinks of herself as a governess, and what you are looking for is a tutor. We do not want to make Penny feel as though she is being pushed out of her rightful place with the children. When you speak to Jane about her employment again, and before you tell these others that they shall not be wanted, I think you had better make it clear to her that Penny is in charge of the children, and she shall be concerned only with their education. Unless, of course, it is time for Penny's duties to end."

"Oh, no! Penny is part of this family. Even if we could get along without her, none of us would want to. I shall make the delineation of duties perfectly clear to Miss Reston, and if she wants to accept the limitations, then she shall become the first indentured servant of the Andrew Manning family . . . if not, then we shall continue to look."

Jane Reston came happily to the Manning house to become a tutor to the three older children. All the things that Gwynne had mentioned apologetically to Jane as perhaps being drawbacks were pluses from Jane's point of view. The position at the Manning house was a blessing Jane had thought never again to see in her life. She had freshly come from England seeking a better life, but had had little hope of getting it. She had been poor all her life and had received little for the advantage of her hard-gotten education but hard work, and more hard work. Never before had she had an employer apologize to her for making her tasks limited. Previously it had always been "Jane, after you have finished your day with the children, you may help prepare the evening's meals in the kitchen with cook, and would you mind doing a bit of shopping for the missus on your day off? That's a good girl."

Jane was a small woman, standing no more than five feet and weighing no more than ninety pounds. She did her best to hide the curves of her body by wearing heavily gathered skirts with jackets, and oftentimes shawls tucked chastely around her shoulders and into her waist. She had learned repeatedly that her figure and the even, pleasant features of her face were a detriment to employment, and her poverty was a detriment to any other kind of life. So she wore unbecoming, dowdy clothes, and pulled her light brown hair severely back from her face. She kept her eyes downcast whenever she could remember to do so, and she tried to keep the lively intensity that flamed in her quiet so it would not show through her golden eyes. At first it had been very difficult to suppress her whole personality like that, but after she had lost two jobs, she had learned to make it a game. She lived two lives; one she showed to her employers and the other to her pupils.

In her classroom, with no employer to see, she would toss the shawl aside and allow her intelligent golden eyes to light up. And she thoroughly enjoyed learning and teaching about the world and all the people in it. She was considerably accomplished. She could play the piano, the violin, and was a fair hand at the flute. She could sew and do tapestry work, a little tatting, write poetry well, do a fair painting, and she loved to read.

Though she had done little more than meet them, she liked what she knew of this colonial family. The children were bright, and Gwynne was beautiful and kind. The elder Mrs. Manning seemed to be a very alert old woman, and something special—at least all the others of the family and the dark-skinned servants behaved as though she was. If nothing else, these seven years she would be in their employ would be interesting ones, and Mrs. Manning promised her that by the time her indenture had ended, she would be well enough off to start her life anew, and independent.

As she unpacked the few belongings she had and arranged her bedroom to suit herself, she discovered that the Mannings of America did not hold with the rigid rules and disciplines of some of the English families she had served. Nathaniel and Mary popped their heads in her door soon after she had entered. They had come to help her. The children had none of the air of wrongdoing. It was obvious that they were accustomed to socializing with the servants. She smiled at the two poppets. This was a bit strange, but she thought she liked this informality. Perhaps there was something to be said about this liberty and equality that the American rebels were fond of shouting about from every street corner.

During the ensuing weeks Jane Reston found it difficult almost to the point of impossibility to keep her demure, aloof demeanor. She put up an heroic effort, but Elizabeth swooped down on her one afternoon and ended all attempts. "Miss Reston, please see me in the study," Elizabeth ordered.

It was the first time Jane had heard an order spoken so authoritatively in this house, and she was shaking when she timidly presented herself to Elizabeth a few minutes later.

"Be seated, Miss Reston. I do not wish to get a crook in my neck trying to talk to you," Elizabeth snapped.

"Yes, ma'am," Jane said, and sat on the edge of a chair opposite Elizabeth.

"I have asked you in here to speak to you about . . ." Elizabeth paused, then forged ahead. "Well, to talk to you about a manner of behavior you employ. You never look directly at us, Miss Reston, and when you are present at supper with the whole family, it is as if you are pretending not to be really there. Mary is a great little imitator, and has taken the habit of averting her eyes and mewing about like a demented kitten. She has gotten this from you, Miss Reston, and I simply will not have it! If you cannot manage to be a bit more natural and livelier, then I am afraid I shall have to speak to Mrs. Manning and have you replaced."

Jane looked directly at Elizabeth dumbfounded, then as a matter of habit looked down again.

"There! You have done it again! What are you hiding, Miss Reston, that you do not want me to see your eyes?"

"Nothing, ma'am. I have nothing whatever to hide."

"Then what are you doing?" Elizabeth said in exasperation. "Surely you do not call it good manners not to look at the person to whom you are speaking?"

Jane glanced quickly at her, away, then at her again. "I don't understand . . . you would think me bold if I—"

"Do not presume to tell me what I think, Miss Reston, I shall tell you what I think! I think you are a ninny to hide yourself behind these ridiculous affectations, and I will not tolerate you teaching Mary, by example, a similar mode of behavior."

"Yes, ma'am," Jane said miserably, not knowing what was wanted of her.

"You shall be given one week to show yourself as you truly are, and if you cannot do that, then I am afraid your services shall not be needed here, and your contract shall be sold to someone else." Elizabeth stared at her for a moment, then said, "You may leave now, Miss Reston."

Jane stood up instantly. She walked to the door, stood there frightened, confused, and undecided, then, heart in throat, she turned and said, "Mrs. Manning . . . how do you want me to behave?"

"What I want is of no consequence, Miss Reston. You must behave as God created you. If that behavior is suitable for a tutor, we shall all be pleased. If it is not, then we shall do what must be done."

"You want me to behave as I would were I not in your employ?"

"That is correct," Elizabeth said briskly.

Jane stood at the door for a time longer, then again took all her courage in hand. "Mrs. Manning, naturally I tend to be somewhat gregarious . . . some even say boisterous."

"The Mannings do not tend toward reticence, Miss Reston. Until you have tried, none of us will ever know whether you fit in here or not."

"Yes, ma'am," Jane said, her eyes sparkling. She nearly ran from the room and took the steps to the children's room two at a time.

Elizabeth sat at her desk, nibbling at the tip of her quill, a smile on her face. "Things should liven up around here considerably," she thought aloud.

Jane didn't know whether to trust Elizabeth's words or not, but she reasoned that she had no choice, for if she did not show her true colors, Elizabeth was going to dismiss her. She stopped by her own room on her way to the children's nursery. Standing before her mirror, she loosened the severe hairstyle, brushed it out, then put it atop her head again, but this time the natural waviness of her hair showed, and Jane Reston was no longer staring at the image of the retiring tutor the Mannings had hired, but at the image of a pretty twenty-year-old girl who happened to have intelligence to match her comeliness. She felt a thrill of apprehension, then shrugged. She had no choice. Elizabeth Manning had taken that from her. Mrs. Manning wanted to see Jane Reston . . . well, here she was!

As the days passed, Jane found herself becoming more and more a part of the family. None of the dire consequences of her liveliness had come about. Even the young Mrs. Manning seemed pleased with her.

"The children have been very good and attentive to their lessons, Jane. I think we all need a reward. Tomorrow we shall take a long ride to the country and have an outdoor meal. Perhaps if we can persuade my cousin, we will go clamming. Please have some nature lesson prepared for the children, and we shall expect you to go with us," Gwynne said, and hurried off before Jane had a chance to say anything.

In Drew and George's absence Leo Manning had become the chief male companion and protector of the household. Leo had never before in his life had such demands put on his time. It seemed to him that he was constantly astride a horse, going to or coming from his home in Charles Town, Willowtree, or Drew's house. He was exhausted much of the time, but he had never been happier or felt more important. Once he had made the decision to be a rebel against the Crown, his entire life had changed. Even the attitude of his wife Eloise had altered. There were no more demands made on him as there had once been. He was the head of his own family—finally.

On the morning of the planned outing Leo was at Willowtree urging his reluctant and pregnant wife to hurry.

She gave him an acid look. "You have become very demanding of me, Leo. I am sure Gwynne will not be going. She will sit in the cool comfort of her home while you force me to tramp across fields and dunes and no doubt even into the water."

"I will make a bargain with you. If Gwynne remains at home, you may visit with her in the cool comfort. But if she comes with us, no more will be said about the delicacy of your condition. Hers is just as delicate, and if I am not mistaken, her child is due to be born sooner than ours . . . so she is even more delicate."

Eloise tried not to, but she giggled. She liked this new man Leo Manning had become. If truth were known she had always envied Gwynne a little being married to Drew. She certainly would not want Leo to become like Drew—Drew would frighten the wits out of her—but a little of his strength, masculinity, and adventurousness was very nice, and that is what she now had in Leo. She primped with her hair, enjoying the admiring look she was getting from him. Brush in midair, she paused and looked at him in the mirror.

"Have you ever noticed that nearly all Drew's children have been born in winter?"

"Susan wasn't," Leo said.

"I said *nearly*. This child shall be. Nathaniel was, and Mary, and little Elizabeth. Perhaps this child will be another boy."

"Perhaps ours will be a boy. I would like to have a son. Except for Grandmother and Grandfather, all the Mannings have been born on American soil, but these children of ours and Drew's and my brother's shall be the first to be born under the flag of an independent America."

"You are counting on something that hasn't happened yet," Eloise said. "We may be no more than a conquered colony in disfavor with the King."

"No," he said firmly, then looked dreamily out the window. With a sudden movement he said, "Hurry up! We are going to be dreadfully late, and we still have quite a drive before we get there."

Eloise made a face at him, and began to hurry.

The Drew Mannings were ready and anxious to be on their way when Leo and Eloise arrived.

"Oh, you didn't bring Miranda with you!" Gwynne moaned, when she saw her cousin walk toward the house empty armed.

Eloise shook her head. "I don't know how you do it, Gwynne. I suppose you have Elizabeth ready to go with us, and all the other children as well."

"I do, but Penny will look after them . . . and Jane. I have a lot of help."

"I still don't know how you manage. I get so tired when I am with child. The thought of having to watch after a little one just does me in, especially when she is so young that she does not truly understand what is going on."

"Perhaps she can come the next outing, or after this child is born."

Elizabeth came to join the two women, and they chatted happily about babies, clothing, and other necessities that would soon be wanted for the new arrivals while Leo, with Nathaniel's help, loaded the Manning dray and readied the coach. It was quite an undertaking to move the two families, even on something so simple as a picnic.

Soon Leo stuck his head into the parlor and, smiling, said, "We're ready, ladies, and I have an impatient crew waiting outside."

As one the women stood up and scurried quickly to find shawls for later, and Gwynne rang the bell for Jane and Penny to join them. As both of the hired women had learned, the Mannings' outings might be delayed over and over, and a scheduled eleven o'clock departure might not occur until two o'clock in the afternoon, but once the bell was rung that signaled their leave-taking, it was accomplished in a flash, and there was no place for a laggard.

Jane, with her newfound freedom, came racing down the stairs, her cheeks already highly colored with excitement. "Do you have your collecting box, Nathaniel?" she called as she caught sight of the boy coming into the house.

"Forgot 'em!" he replied, and pounded back up the stairs Jane had just come down.

"Good heavens!" Eloise breathed. "What was that? A whirlwind?"

"That," Elizabeth said with a satisfied laugh, "is the new tutor for Nathaniel and Mary. She is to be a homecoming surprise for Drew."

"I am sure she shall be!" Eloise said—then, with a grin added, "Although considering it is Drew who is to be surprised, she may seem a bit reserved."

At that moment Nathaniel came bolting back down the steps, and almost ran past his great-grandmother. She was quicker than he thought, and she caught him by the collar and whirled him around. "Exuberance is a good thing, young man, but not when it trespasses on good manners. You are not to push your way through. Now, if you please, walk calmly, and see your mother, your cousin, and me to the coach like a gentleman."

"But I have to give Jane my—"

"You shall do that after you have performed your duties as man of this house."

He gave her a cross look, but his spirits were never dampened for long, and he smiled and took the hand of his mother and his great-grandmother. "I'm sorry, Cousin Eloise, I don't have another hand," he said, laughing.

Leo selected a spot near the shore that had plenty of marsh grasses, dunes, and trees to please the hearts of everyone. The ladies sought the shade, the children the sunbaked open spaces.

It was a hot late August day, but the breeze coming off the ocean and the shade provided by the trees made it pleasant.

Eloise leaned back against the sand chair Leo had made and brought for her. "I am so glad I came." She sighed. "Leo practically had to twist my arm before I agreed. I really thought I'd be hot and uncomfortable, but this is heavenly." She closed her eyes and turned her face to the sun that dappled through the foliage. "I have been in the house too much of late."

"How is the situation at Willowtree, Eloise?" Gwynne asked. "Or was there ever anything to be worried about?"

There had been indeed, and still was a great deal to be worried about at Willowtree, but few were aware of it. Seth had been startled at the strength of Leo Manning's reaction to the subtle differences in the plantation when he had visited at the beginning of the summer. He had underestimated this Manning, and that disturbed him greatly. But he had also learned a good deal from Leo's visit: primary was that the Americans and the British might soon be adversaries, and the British might look favorably upon a man, even a black man, who would help their cause.

As soon as Leo had departed, and the round of punishments was over, Seth had gathered his small band and warned them that they must keep the atmosphere and work habits at Willowtree completely normal.

"Until the time is right, no one must know what we are planning," he said in his most severe tones.

"When dat gonna happen?" Rufus asked.

"I don't know yet," Seth said honestly. "I been learning some things from the masters, an' it will all work to our favor. We'll wait until it is the right time."

"You ain't nevah gonna do nuthin'," Rufus complained, throwing a handful of dirt onto the earth. "Jehu right. He say that whuppin' took all de sass right outten you."

"It is good that Jehu thinks that. We will help him and all the others to think it. That way we are free to plan without any interference from our masters."

"What that intafrance stuff?" Cuffee asked.

"That means they cannot stop us," Seth said. "I have heard that the British have use for folks like us, and they do not mind that we go free. I want to learn more about this freedom the British hold, so I must become trusted by Mastah Manning, suh"—he grinned—"so that I may go to Charles Town and talk to those who might help us."

"I cain't fool them into thinkin' I be a good girl no moah," Folly said. "I hates ever' one o' 'em. Ain't nevah gonna fergit that Mastah Leo had me whupped."

"You are going to go to your father and beg his forgiveness, Folly," Seth said. "You tell Jehu that you now know that my influence is a bad thing for you, and you don't want to have anything to do with me no more."

"I ain't gonna say that!" Folly cried. "Ain't true, an' nuthin', not even you, Seth, is gonna keep me from seein' you."

"'Course not, pretty girl, but that's what you're going to tell your papa, so's he won't bother us."

Folly gave him a dirty look. "When you talk to me like that, I knows you're makin' fun and sweet-talkin' me so's I'll do what you want."

"What else you gonna do for your man but please him?"

"I know you talks right when you want to, Seth. You talks jes' like a white man. Why you talkin' to me like a black man?"

"'Cause I is one," he said, making his accent heavier still. He leaned closer to her as if he were going to kiss her, then did a little dance-step forward and back, keeping his lips inches from hers. "You gonna do what I asts you, pretty girl? Huh? You gonna please yo' man?"

Folly put her hands behind her back, thrusting her breasts forward, "I would iffen you meant what you say."

"What do I got to do to make you believe me?"

"First you gotta stop talkin' like that to me, and then maybe walk me to my cabin—the long way round. Maybe then I tries to please my man. First I gotta know he mine."

"Ain't she somethin'?" Seth said, grinning, and looking at Rufus and Cuffee. "I thinks I gonna walk a girl home." Then, to Folly, he said in clear tones, "I will be glad to walk you the long way round, Folly."

After they had left the company of the others, Folly, leaning against him, asked, "Why you do that? I don't like you makin' fun o' me talkin' to me like a fiel' han', Seth. I knows I don' talk as good as you, but that don' mean you gotta make me a fool."

"I do not make a fool of you, I honor you. You know many sides of my being; they—those others—know but one. I am as an actor, playing to one audience at a time. You must never again interfere with me, Folly. Rufus and Cuffee understand little. They are small men with small visions. I speak to them in their language. I am a man with a wide vision, and my tongue must be large enough to accommodate all I must say to all I must speak to."

She looked at him with admiration, but she could not follow all that he said. Perhaps he was making fun of her again, but when he did it this way, she didn't mind. She just liked to listen to him talk, she liked to watch the burning look that came into his eyes.

"We shall succeed, Folly, but each of us must do our task. You, too, must learn to act—to pretend to feel what you do not, to pretend to be ignorant of what you are not, so you can gather information, and do what must be done to gain our freedom."

"I gotta tell my daddy I'm sorry, an' I wanna be a good house nigger," she said with a sigh.

"Yes, you must, and what you learn inside that house, you will tell me. Our masters believe that they have the right and the duty to fight the red-coated soldiers for their freedom. They will talk, and we will listen, for we, too, fight for our freedom. While our captors fight for their freedom, we will fight for ours. It is a bit funny, isn't it? Shadows hiding from shadows, each trying to flee the other. Amusing . . ." he said with a faraway smile on his face.

Folly's resistance to Seth's demands of her was only token. She knew that Seth did not really want to be close to any woman on the plantation. He didn't want the ties of family to bind his heart to a place he intended to leave. He was always trying to strengthen his memories of Africa and the life and family he had left behind there. This was not his home, because he did not want it to be. It left her at a terrible disadvantage, and one she could only hope to conquer by displaying her own independence and determination. Only by a show of strength and independent dependability could she extract the respect from him she needed to be close to him. He had to need her.

She held his arm as they walked toward her cabin. As they neared it, she danced a bit, circling him as they walked, showing herself off, knowing he wanted her, but fearing he'd have the power to walk away from her. At the door she took both his hands, her head tilted to the side, her eyes warm and flirtatious. "You been feedin' yourself with bitter seeds, Seth, now you let me sweeten you up with honey," she cooed.

Seth didn't pull his hands free of hers, but she could feel his resistance. She stepped closer and put her hands on his shoulders, her breasts touching his chest. Her face close to his, she ran her hands over the broad smooth muscles of his chest. "Honey, honey, honey," she whispered. "All warriors gotta know how to pleasure their women . . . pleasure me, Seth."

Seth's hands moved around to her back, then slipped down until his hands were under her buttocks. Holding her fast against him, he lifted her, pressing her hips into his, and took her into the cabin.

22

By late September Seth had convinced most of the other bondsmen at Willowtree that his plans for escape or an uprising had been squelched by the punishment meted out by Leo Manning and by the continued presence of the Manning family at Willowtree. He had not completely stopped talking of philosophy and of freedom, or telling his stories of Africa, but it was all very mild, and no one saw it as a threat. The men he had chosen to trust, Cuffee, Tom, and Rufus, still met with him in the swamp, and they alone knew that he was still planning to run away.

Seth's new plans required a great deal of patience, and some understanding of the political situation that was existent in the colonies. For Cuffee and Tom, this was agreeable. They understood nothing of politics, but didn't care, and they were in no hurry to do anything, so patience was an easy thing. They were entranced and entertained by the meetings and the prominence they had gained with the other field hands by being Seth's special friends. Rufus was a different matter. He did not understand the importance of the colony's disagreement with England, nor did he thoroughly believe Seth. Being a proud man, he saw an opportunity to challenge Seth's dominance of his friends.

"You jes' talk," Rufus sneered, stalking around the group of men sitting outside their cabins enjoying the cool breeze that had come in with the twilight. "Mastah Leo, he put de fear o' de Lawd in you, Seth. You ain't gonna do nuthin'. Gonna take a man to fin' de way to de promised lan'."

"Who dat man?" a field hand called Opie called with a grin.

Rufus strutted over to Opie, bent over so his face was level with the man's. He stuck his thumbs into the suspenders of his work pants. "You

knows who de man is, Opie. You be lookin' at him. Gonna git me a place
o' my own, an' hab a milch cow, an' mebbe a mule or two—ain't gonna
plough no fiel' wid mah han's agin. I gonna fin' mah own promised lan'."

"You gonna fin' yo'seff de en' o' a rope," Seth said, falling into the
heavily accented speech of the other men.

"Ah ain't scairt! Mastah Leo don' mek me be shakin' in mah shoes."
Rufus gave Seth another hostile look. "You gonna be heah talkin' 'bout
Affica when Ah be plantin' mah corn."

"I shore do hope that Christian God o' yours got corn fiel's up there,
cause you ain't gonna be plantin' on dis earth," Seth said. "You better get
smart, an' stop all this talk before you ain't given the choice."

"What kin' o' place you gonna hab, Rufe?" Opie asked.

Seth got up and left the group. Rufus liked to talk, but there was little
substance to what he said. Inadvertently he may have stumbled into the
one circumstance that might make him do something foolish. He had
caught the imagination of his fellows. Their questions, and their expectations and hopes that Rufus could accomplish what they only dreamed of,
might push Rufus into something foolish.

Seth walked for a long time. He couldn't see how any action, successful
or not, that Rufus could take would adversely affect his plans. Satisfied, he
returned to his own cabin. He would use Rufus, as he would use anyone or
anything.

Annie was there, as she always was, sitting in the corner, her head
bowed, her face sad. The infant Isaiah slept in his basket at her side. She
didn't look up or speak to him when he walked over to the basket and
looked down at his son. The infant was a strong, large child. If he'd have
permitted himself, Seth would have been proud that this was his son, but
he allowed himself no such feelings. He merely watched the child's progress. Since the birth of Isaiah he had never gone near Annie again. She was
known as his woman, and he would tolerate no other man coming near
her, because she had birthed his son, but he would have nothing to do with
her. When the day came for him to leave, he would have to be free to go
without feeling the need to look back. Even with his precautions he already had too much care for Isaiah. The memory would linger, and he
wanted it to grow no stronger than it already was.

Annie slowly got up, a resentful look cast at him from the corner of her
eye. She fixed him something to eat, smoothed out his pallet, then retired
silently back to her own corner of the small room.

With deliberate grace he lay down on his pallet. He knew Annie was
watching him and enjoyed the power he had over her.

Rufus continued his bragging. Being cock of the walk around the quarters was heady stuff for him. He had really had no plan to run away, or do anything else without Seth's leadership, but as he continued boasting, and others began to look up to him, he began to believe he was able to do what he pleased. With only rudimentary plans, he waited for an opportune time to run from Willowtree.

He found his chance in mid-October. The greatest part of the harvest was finished, and the discipline at Willowtree was a little easier. John Manning, Rob, and even Leo were very pleased with the bondsmen at Willowtree. After Seth's punishment the air of rebelliousness had vanished. Tools that had been broken, gates that had been left open, chores that had been sloppily done or neglected, were once more being done properly. The harvest was a good one, and even though Elizabeth was keeping to her promise to withhold one third of her rice for the patriot cause, the Mannings still had a bumper crop to sell at market. As a reward for the good work, and the acceptable attitude and work habits the slaves had resumed, the Mannings had taken to having barbecues in the quarters on Sunday evenings and occasionally on Saturday nights.

Many of the plantation masters allowed their slaves to make their way into Charles Town on Sundays to visit and go to services. The Mannings were no different, except that the number of slaves who could go on any given Sunday was limited. While Folly busied herself in getting a trusted house assignment from her father, Cuffee, Tom, Rufus, and Seth worked on Jehu's good graces to gain his permission to be among those who were allowed to go to Charles Town. Seth had managed to gain his second permission on the Sunday that Rufus decided to prove his own determination and superiority.

It was a dry, hot October day with the sun setting late and gently in the evening. There had been a service performed by an itinerant preacher earlier in the day, and now the smoke from the big barbecue pits hung heavy over Willowtree. Already some of the men were strumming homemade banjos, fiddles, and the slow, easy beat of drums was pleasant.

The Mannings were sitting on the piazza of the big, white plantation house listening to the sounds of talk and laughter mingle with the muted music that drifted toward the big house on the evening breeze. In the lulls that would come occasionally, they heard the sounds of nesting birds and the chorus of insects and frogs. It was a night for pleasure and enjoyment.

Rob Manning leaned far back in his chair. "I have to admit, Leo, I thought you had brought upon us more trouble than we could handle when you had Odo bring out Grandpa's old whip. Even now I hate to admit that I was wrong," he said, and gave his brother a lazy smile. "But this is the most peaceful time we've ever had here."

"And profitable in more ways than one. There has been far less breakage of farm implements this year," John Manning added.

"It doesn't seemed to have done any harm at all." Eugenia said. "Just listen . . . they have begun to sing. Isn't it beautiful?"

The sky was now a blaze of heated color, and the air was filled with the sounds of the Negro spirituals.

"I wish we could just go down and join them," Eloise said.

Rob laughed. "Somehow I don't think you would go unnoticed, my dear."

Eloise giggled. "Oh! You know that is not what I meant. It is so nice . . . I would like to be a part of it."

"Are we not enough for you?" Rob said with feigned hurt.

"Can you sing, Rob?" Eloise asked.

Leo sat back in his chair, taking great pleasure in the easy, silly pointless banter. It was easy to imagine that the family was as united now as it had once been. Ideas of liberty, representation, and war seemed remote and completely out of place on an evening like this. What more could they possibly want than they already had? Yet, somewhere, quiet within him tonight, but nonetheless in him, there was a restlessness, an eagerness to get on the battle. Perhaps it was that restlessness that put the edge of pleasure on gatherings such as this one. Perhaps it was only when a man was aware of loss that he was able to keenly enjoy. He lazily accepted another drink from the tray brought around by Jehu, then leaned back again, resting his head on the back of his chair, eyes closed.

At the quarters Rufus was dancing on the sharp edge of anxious anticipation. Always a clown, he pranced about the barbecue making his usual jokes, flirting with all the young women. Darting from one group of blacks to another, he found it an easy matter to steal a few potatoes here, a bit of meat there, and hide it in the cloth bag he had fashioned to take with him.

It was fully dark, and the slaves were sated with food and were dancing by the light of the fire. The fiddles had grown bolder and louder as the night progressed. The first of those who had gone into Charles Town were beginning to return; most had carried back with them some token of friendship sent from Negroes on other plantations.

As the crowd gathered to see what small treasures had been brought back from the city nestled between two rivers and the sea, Rufus moved stealthily at the perimeter, seeking the shadows, and then the darkness.

The plantation was slow to quiet down that night. The music played softly long beyond midnight. The Mannings could hear the soft strains coming in through their windows as they lay half asleep in their beds.

No one missed Rufus until the plantation bell rang at five o'clock Monday morning. Odo came to the big house at nine o'clock, his head hung low, a pained look upon his expressive face. "Rufus done runned away las' night, Mastah John," he said baldly. "I done look fo' him all ober dis plantation. He gone."

For a moment John Manning did not know what to say. He sat at the plantation desk, the ledgers spread out before him as though it were a day like any other day. This was the beginning of a new week. He had orders that had to be filled. He had lists of things that had to be bought for the plantation, things that were to be made in the smithy of the plantation, or in the carpenter's shop. These were the things of his world, not bondsmen who ran away. Not Rufus. Not Odo's own son. He had been willing to accept Seth as a troublemaker, but to discover it was Rufus was another matter.

Miserable and ashamed, Odo stood before him, his hat in his hand, head still bowed. "I be mighty sorry, Mastah John. He ain't no son o' mine. Cain't be. No blood o' mine would bring shame like this to us."

John shook his head and cleared his throat. "You're sure . . . he isn't ill, or just sleeping off too merry a night?"

"No, suh."

"How can this be?" John said in wonderment. "We must fetch him back immediately. Do the others know he has run?"

"I spec' they do. I been rootin' out every cabin."

"I . . . I must tell Rob and Leo. Tell them to come here immediately, Odo, then find five or six men you can trust and send them here. You see to saddling the horses . . . and have our muskets ready."

By noon the Mannings had gathered the neighboring planters, some of the regular patrollers, and several hunting dogs, and were in pursuit of Rufus. One group, under the leadership of Rob, patrolled the roads and pathways leading to Charles Town. It wasn't the most likely place to find Rufus, but the roads had to be checked. "The one time we don't watch these roads will be the one time one of the black beggars will choose to walk right down the middle of one," Rob complained, mopping at his brow.

"This is a first for Willowtree, isn't it?" John Davis asked as he trotted along side Rob's horse. "Far back as I can remember no Willowtree man has ever run."

"I guess there is always a first for everything. But I'll tell you, John, if

I'd have picked a nigger to run, it wouldn't have been Rufus. We got a couple of them I'd believe anything of, but not this one."

"Well, let's speed this up a bit—check the roads and get onto something more productive."

John and Leo Manning took another group of men and searched the slave quarters again, then went to the neighboring quarters, searching there. All known free negroes were visited, threatened, and their houses searched.

Meeting at the edge of the swamp, the two groups joined, then fanned out, the dogs baying ahead of them. "I say, John, it's a bad thing for you, but a little hunt like this sure does give us old fellows a bit of excitement," Troy Sloan said, laughing. "Makes a man old if he doesn't have a bit of a chase now and then."

"All you need is a greater distance from your supper table, Troy," Drake Peters said.

"A portly man is a prosperous man, Drake old boy. Your skin-and-bones speaks ill of that wretched strip of swamp you call a plantation."

"Pass that jug over here. I'm about to die of thirst . . . an' I can't abide hearing you two old coots nipping at each other," Michael Jones said, and took a long pull from the earthenware flask passed to him. "How much of a start do you figure this darkie has?"

"We don't know for sure. No more than twelve hours, though," Leo said. "They were having a barbecue last night and—"

"That always has been your trouble up at Willowtree. You Mannings always have been too soft with your blacks. Teach them who's master, and you can trust them. Treat them like people and they'll turn on you every time," Troy said.

"Hey! I hear a hound baying! Let's go, boys, I think we got us a nigger!" Drake yelled, and put his spurs to his horse.

The sounds of the dogs increased, and all the men spurred their horses. With whoops of anticipated victory men astride horses splashed through the spongy, wet swamp-muck.

Rufus had been frightened once he had left the warm light of the campfire, and as the lonely hours of the night outside the protective perimeters of Willowtree stretched out, he had been too scared to go on. He had wandered through the swamp, moving back and forth from one meeting place that Seth had designated to another. In the morning he had been certain that Cuffee or Tom, or even Seth himself, would have come and found him. He would have allowed them to talk him into sneaking back onto the plantation and begging illness because of the feast the night before. But the light had come, his friends had not. Now he was alone in the swamp, too frightened to go on, and ignorant of where to go, and too frightened and too proud to go back to Willowtree.

He had sat down under a tree on the small island in the middle of the swamp to eat the food he had taken away with him, when he had heard the first hound. Almost paralyzed, he stared as the dog came toward him; then, scattering his food, he ran.

The cry of the dog alerted the others. Dogs seemed to appear out of nowhere. Rufus ran harder, forgetting he was on the island. Soon he was back in the marshy water, the slimy mud sucking at his feet. The dogs stood at the shore of the island, their noses to the ground, circling in confusion, then backtracking, picking up his scent again, then losing it.

Rufus wasn't even aware that they were no longer at his heels. He ran blindly, blundering into deeper water, into parts of the swamp he had never before seen.

John and his men caught up with the hounds at the edge of the island. "Son of a bitch! He's in the water again." Troy cried. "We're going to be out here till Christmas."

"You know the way home, Troy," John said coldly.

"Now, don't go gettin' your dander up, John. I didn't mean anything like that. The dogs'll get him, but it's going to take time."

John wasn't mollified. He ignored his neighbor and rode over to Drake, who was trying to get the hounds organized and tracking again.

Rufus would have stayed in the water until his pursuers had given up had he been able to, but the swamp was full of snakes, and he had found a whole patch of them. He felt the sharp sting of one bite, then had to reach into the blackish water to release his ankle from another. His breath coming in ragged gasps, he tried to keep from crying out, but he was so frightened he had no control. He could hear the voices of the men and the baying of an occasional hound behind him. He looked up, trying to figure his directions by the sun, then charged across a long spit of land in the swamp. With luck he could get across it, find water again that wasn't too deep or too wide, and once again gain land. If he could only keep moving, he might be able to confuse the hounds badly enough so that he could get help from a freed Negro family that lived a few miles away in the north side of the swamp.

He had to hurry, for those snake bites needed attention, and soon. He plunged on through the thick, tangled growth that tore at his clothing and flesh. He had lost his satchel of food and precious water. He wasn't certain he was going in the right direction, and he was exhausted, his leg swollen and painful. Crying, holding his side, he stumbled onward, his eyes always searching for the opening in the junglelike growth that would tell him he had finally broken through the far side of the swamp.

John and his posse of men were surprised when they came upon him less than an hour later. He lay sprawled on the ground, his legs spread and bent as though he were still running.

"I'll be damned. I thought he'd be clear into the next parish by now," John Davis said.

"Most likely he's been running in circles. It's easy to do in a swamp like this." Troy said.

Rob dismounted and went over to Rufus, poking at him with the handle of his crop.

"He dead?" Drake called.

Rob bent over him.

"Careful, now!" Drake cautioned. "Once a darkie's gone bad, you can't trust him. He may be playing possum."

Taking heed, Rob gingerly prodded Rufus again, finally rolling him on to his back. "He's not dead . . . I don't think." He started to lean over him, then thought better of it and placed his hand flat against Rufus's mud-caked chest. "He's breathing."

"That's a blessing. I'd sure hate to have ridden all this way and then not had a chance to punish the damned rogue," Drake said. "What do you want to do with him? String him up to a tree here and take him back a dead example, or put him on the back of your horse and make him an example at Willowtree?"

"We'll take him to Willowtree," John said.

"If you'd allow it, John, I'd like to be present when you handle this with your people," John Davis said. "I've never had this happen at Oakhill, but if any of the rumors that are going around are true, I most likely will. I'd like to see what you do and how it is received by the other bondsmen."

John Manning gave a dour, short laugh. "You're more than welcome, John. Maybe we'll both learn something. I'm not much of a hand at this, either. Matter of fact, I don't know what to do with him."

"First thing is to bind him up good, so he doesn't awaken on the ride back and take your horse to finish his run," Drake said. He tossed a rope from his saddlehorn to Leo. "Bind him good, boy."

Leo, with Rob's help, tied Rufus hand and foot. "You sure he's alive?" Leo said in a low voice to his brother.

"He's breathing. I don't know what's wrong with him . . . I don't see a mark on him except these scratches."

"Maybe he hit his head on something," Leo offered, then stood as their task was finished. "Take his legs, I've got his shoulders."

They put him across the rump of John's saddle and secured him there by means of another rope. Slowly, and a lot more jovially, the men began the ride home.

There was no punishment for Rufus. He was dead by the time the half-dozen men rode into Willowtree. His body was given to his parents, Odo and Unity.

Odo, with a grim face, stared unblinking at John. "I ain't got no son named Rufus, Mastah. I don't know dis man."

Unity, with tears and muttered apologies, took Rufus's body. With the help of Seth and two other bondsmen she took him to her cabin to prepare him for burial in the slave cemetery. Seth's face was grim, but inside he was content. The worry of uprising had died with Rufus. Now he was free to make his own plans.

John invited the men into the house for something to eat and drink. Leo waited until the others had gone inside, then he followed after Unity. Catching up with her, he said, "Unity, I want you to know that we found Rufus lying on the ground. Daddy will let the others think what they will about his death, but I want you to know that we did nothing to him. I don't know what happened."

Unity wiped the back of her hand across her eyes. "It be bettah dis way," she said. "Rufus turned bad . . . he wiff de Lawd now."

Leo was uncomfortable with the unbending acceptance Unity displayed. He didn't know what he wanted from her. "I don't know what is happening to all of us Unity, but I hate it. Last night we were all enjoying the evening and the music and tonight you are preparing Rufus for burial. It is all wrong! What is happening?"

"It's a time of long miseries, Mastah Leo. I read my tea leaves every night. Ain't nuthin' good to see. That's all I knows. You takes care o' yo'seff, Mastah Leo. Now, I go sees to Rufe. He need me now. I brung him inter dis worl', I guess I gonna see him out."

Leo stopped walking and watched Unity cloaked in her private grief go on and disappear into the cabin.

Rob was standing in front of the house when he came back. "Did you tell Unity?"

Leo shrugged, not sure what response his brother wanted. "I thought she ought to know. Unity won't tell the others."

"Most likely it was the snakes that got him—that or a tree limb." Rob took a deep breath. "I know it because I saw him, I hunted him down, and

I brought him back, but I just can't believe Rufus would have turned and run. Why? I don't understand it, Leo."

"That's pretty much what I was telling Unity," Leo confessed. "I don't even know what is happening to me. Sometimes I get a wild, almost hungry urge to fight—to put on my uniform and go join the militia—and then other times, times like this, it is as if there is a great sickness in all of us, and I hate being a part of it."

"Do you ever think of the old time when we all had nothing better than to fight among ourselves? All the cousins in our great battles."

Leo rocked back on his heels. "We weren't afraid to mention politics then. Don't you think it strange that this war that we may all find ourselves fighting about is liberty, and we no longer have the liberty to talk about it among ourselves anymore?"

"As you said, things have changed," Rob remarked. He stretched and turned to go back into the house. "You coming? We may get a heady dose of politics tonight. Daddy and the boys are all talking about Drayton's trip to the Upcountry. As usual we are embroiled in that, too."

Leo shook his head. "No, thanks. I don't think I want to get into a discussion of that, or of Parliamentary policy or colonial representation, or anything else." He walked off toward the willow pond and its grove of trees.

Part Four

Drew

23

Drayton left Major Andrew Williamson in charge of Fort Charlotte to keep order in the section of the Upcountry around Ninety Six after he had left to return to Charles Town. In mid-November, Williamson heard that a large number of Tories were planning to cross the Saluda River near Ninety Six. Though not certain what the Tories had in mind, Williamson decided to intercept the force of approximately fifteen hundred Tories and prevent any major activity in the area he had been left to guard.

With a force of about five hundred men Williamson began the march to the little Upcountry town with the strange name. Ninety Six began as a trading post in the 1730s. There the English and the Cherokee traded, and because of that trade it was given its peculiar name. The post was located ninety-six miles from Keowee, an important Cherokee community in the foothills. At the time it was the nethermost post existing inland, and it was located on the path that led to the Cherokee lands, and in the other direction to Charles Town. It was a crossroads of those early days and as such, prospered. When the new courts for the Upcountry were established in 1769, it became the courthouse town for the Ninety Six district.

Drew, George, and James Mayson, a Regulator who had ridden with Drew in other campaigns, rode with Major Williamson, gathering supporters as they went.

Once the march had begun, there was no rest nor respite from the preparations for battle. Williamson chose his site outside the town proper in a field at the edge of John Savage's plantation. The men were immediately put to work building breastworks in the field. Using a couple of old buildings as one side, the men set to gathering old fence rails. George was one of those sent about the field and adjoining land collecting any piece of wood that could be fixed to the barn to serve as the breastworks. In about two hours the men had enclosed an area roughly in the shape of a square and comprising about one hundred and eighty-five square yards.

This would be their fort and the only protection they would have from Tory muskets. As soon as they had erected the rough framework they covered it with straw, hides, and anything else they could lay hands on that would afford them some protection.

On November the nineteenth the Tories made their appearance. They crossed the Saluda and marched into Ninety Six, taking over the town. The eighteen hundred to two thousand Tories selected the jailhouse as the position they would fortify.

George Manning, with Drew at his side, peered over the side of their hastily constructed breastworks, his eyes wide as he watched the activities in the town. "My God, Drew, I think we are really in it this time." He moved down the way a bit, seeking a better view. "Is that Patrick Cunningham?"

"That's him, and Joseph Robinson is with him," Drew said, and unconsciously moved nearer to one of the big guns the Whigs had mounted on the breastworks. "We may be in for a long siege."

George smiled over at him. "We can withstand that. We've got plenty of food."

Drew nodded. "That we have, but have you considered what we're going to drink? We may have made an error we'll regret. We don't have a water supply here." Drew patted the swivel gun he was standing next to. "Maybe I'm jumping at shadows. These may make it a shorter battle than I think."

Williamson stationed his men around his makeshift fort, then went out to parlay with the Tory leaders, hoping he could persuade them to retreat once again to the other side of the river. Several of his men went with him; the others peered out from behind the breastworks, imagining what was being said, arguing among themselves about whether it was better to remain peaceful and watchful, or to fight. All knew the answer when Williamson turned away and the Tories took advantage of the moment to seize two of Major Williamson's men. As soon as Williamson and the others were safe inside the breastworks, the Whigs began to fire. During a lull in the firing, Drew found himself next to Major Williamson.

"There was no talking to them, sir?"

"They ordered us to disperse," Williamson said with a taut laugh. "The thing is they seem to have no idea of the strength of the Continental

Congress. Perhaps we shall be able to educate Major Robinson and Captain Cunningham. I see that more men have arrived to aid us even in this short time. I am sure there will be more."

"We may have an unforeseen difficulty, Major. We have no water source. More men will merely make the problem more acute."

The Major looked at him for a moment, then said, "Can you see to it that we find a water supply, Manning? I turn the problem over to your capable hands." His eyes went back to the smoke-hazed view of the jailhouse across the field from them. "Take as many men as you need, but get us water."

The exchange of fire continued sporadically throughout the day and into the evening. It wasn't until dark that the men had a chance to think of eating or drawing a relaxed breath. With the fall of darkness the men lit a fire and gathered round to talk of the day's doings and await their meal.

"George," Drew said. "I've been ordered to find a way to supply the camp with water."

George bit into a piece of charred chicken, looking at Drew from the corner of his eye. "Good luck, and that wasn't meant to be sarcastic. I'm so thirsty I'm ready to raid the Tories camp single-handedly."

"Then you'll be glad to be a part of the crew who digs the well," Drew said with a grin as he got to his feet.

"Well? Are you soft in the head? We can't dig a well!"

"Why not?"

"We're in the midst of a battle and . . . I don't know why not."

"Then you'll help?"

George shook his head. "It was probably predictable. Here I am in the midst of the first shooting battle of my life, and what will I be doing? Digging a big hole in the ground."

Drew laughed. "You always look on the gloomy side of things. If you dig fast enough, you'll be underground and less likely to get shot."

"Thanks, cousin. I'll keep that in mind. By future generations I may be known as the water hero of Ninety Six. Go find the rest of your men, and, please, Drew, make sure they are strong husky fellows."

George had no idea that Drew would be back almost instantly with his men, and intending to begin the digging right then, but he was. The men with pick and shovel began the task of digging a forty-foot well, which would solve their problems at least on that score.

The Tories, however, were determined to cause them trouble on other grounds. The patriots were well protected by their makeshift breastworks, and the Tories were suffering too many wounded. They tried to burn the patriots out by firing the straw and hides that covered the breastworks. Smoke was thick, making it difficult to see or breathe. Behind a rolling battery the Tories had built they tried to approach the barn side of the breastworks. Both sides shot almost blindly in the haze and confusion. Drew could hear screams coming from the thick cloud, but he had no idea of who was hit or which side the men belonged to. As the Tories neared with their battery machine, the handmade vehicle burst into flame and sent them fleeing. A cheer went up from within the patriots' camp, and the musket fire and the boom of the swivel guns went on.

That night when relative quiet reigned, the patriots tended the twelve men who had been wounded, and mourned the loss of James Birmingham, who had been shot through the head.

Drew slumped to the ground, propped up by the breastworks. George lay on the ground near him. "George! George, are you all right?"

Slowly George opened his eyes. "I've got a bruised hand, but I'm all right. You?"

Drew nodded, then let his head drop wearily to his chest.

"You know, Drew, I hurt all over, and I'm tired to the bone. I watched men get shot today, and I was thinking about the things we've talked about from time to time. I was asking myself what I was doing here shooting men that I might very well know and like. But, you know what? I realize I also felt good. The Tories are wrong. I knew that today for the first time."

Drew looked at him with some surprise. "But you've fostered the patriot cause for quite a long time."

George smiled. "No, not fostered, more that I tagged along after. I would never have done anything if it hadn't been for you. I can never see into the future or read the signs of the times like you can. I've just learned to trust your judgment. . . . I don't always like it, mind you, but I do trust it."

"I believe I'll not question you too closely, and accept that as a compliment."

"You may. It was meant as one." They were both quiet for a moment, then George asked gently, "Those men who died today . . . how many of them do you think you knew personally, Drew?"

Drew took a deep breath and let it out slowly. "I don't know . . . at least two or three, I imagine. I haven't talked for some time to many of the men I used to ride with. I don't honestly know if they are Tory or Whig. Even as we were fighting, I was wondering if perhaps Jack Kimble or Jason Frobish were among those on the other side."

"What would you have done if you knew for a certainty that someone like Jason or Jack were on the other side? Suppose you could even see one of them. Would you shoot?"

"I don't know . . . if I could see Jack facing me on the other side of a line, I'm not certain I could shoot him. . . . God, George, what a question!"

"I'm coming round to something I've been thinking about for some time, Drew. The question I just asked you is something you may have to face, especially since we've moved into the Upcountry. You may not see Jack Kimble on the other side of the line, but you might very well see Arthur."

"Go to sleep, George, we're both very tired."

"Drew, you must give it some thought. Leo has come round to thinking as we do, and I still have hopes that Rob will, and also I think there is less likelihood that we would find ourselves fighting a trenched battle in Charles Town, but your brother lives up here, and it is not so unlikely. You can't ignore it, Drew. It could cost you your life if you're not prepared."

"I do think about it, George. I've spent many a sleepless night thinking about both my father and brother, but I can't answer it. I believe in the cause, but to do harm to my own flesh and blood—how can I answer that, or be prepared? I just pray to God that it never happens."

"I won't say any more. I don't know what I would do, either. But I can't help thinking of it."

"I know. Go to sleep now. The Tories will give us precious little time as it is."

On Tuesday, November 21, 1775, both sides agreed to call off the battle. Major Williamson appeared gracious to the Tories, but in fact he was greatly relieved to have the opportunity to end the fighting. The patriots were down to the last of their powder, having only forty pounds left.

The Tories agreed to move back across the Saluda, and as a gesture of good faith, the patriots' swivel guns were given up.

As soon as the word was given that an agreement had been made, orders were given to level the breastworks that they called Fort Williamson.

"First you put 'em up, and then you take 'em down," George said in a singsong as he worked at a section of the wall. "I don't mind taking this down, but I tell you, Drew, I'm going to howl so loud they'll hear me in Charles Town if I have to fill that damned well in."

The Tories had given up their post and abandoned their battle after they learned that Colonel Richardson was on his way to reinforce the Whig patriots. For the first time the Upcountry Tories began to understand the strength of the patriot movement.

The retreating Tories scattered to various fates and designs. Some were taken captive by Richardson's men, others fled to the Indian lands deeper in the Upcountry, and about one hundred and thirty of them formed a camp at the Great Cane Break on the Reedy River. There they tried to gain support from the Indians.

The patriots, knowing the band of Tories were not going to give up, and would try one means or another to mount a fighting force, marched after them. Under the command of Colonel Richardson, the patriots headed toward the Reedy River in December with a large force.

The failed Tory offensive was disposed of quickly, with some men killed and others captured. However, the patriots met with a new adversary, one far more powerful, and against whom they had no defenses. The day after the capture of the Tory prisoners it began to snow. For thirty hours the cold, windy wetness pelted down on them, covered them, chilled them to the bone.

Richardson's army were dressed in light clothing, had no tents, and were in no way prepared to protect themselves from the rain, sleet, and snow that nature hurled at them. Heads down, their teeth clenched against the cold and the penetrating pain the wet coldness caused, they marched raggedly across the open land and through the deep forests, reaching Granby on January 1, 1776.

The prisoners they brought with them included almost every important Tory leader in the area. For all intents and purposes the immediate threat of severe Tory opposition in the area around Ninety Six had ended. Colonel Richardson dismissed his troops.

Drew wrote a letter to Gwynne and sent it back to Charles Town with a messenger; then he and George made their slow and painful way to Cherokee to be nursed through terrible colds by a solicitous Ned Hart.

"By Jove, even if you are half dead, it's good to have you home for a time. I've got some home-brewed peach brandy that will stand the hair on your head straight up and cure anything you got," he said with great enthusiasm. All he received for a response was a chorus of coughing from his two patients.

Ned was disappointed in his desire for companionship, for George and Drew slept for the next two days, waking only long enough to eat and drink great quantities of water. Three days after he had arrived, Drew got up and took the first look around his plantation that he had had in months.

"Well, it's good to see you on your feet," Ned said as he caught up with him. "Takin' a look around, are you? You'll find everything fit. We've had a good year."

"I feel like a stranger here," Drew said wistfully.

"You damned near are, but all that will change after we get the King set straight."

"I hope it is we who set him straight and not the other way round."

"Couldn't happen—could it?"

"Well, there's rumor that he's going to send his army and navy over here to quell the rebellion, not to mention setting the Indians and the blacks against us."

"You don't remember it too clearly, I don't imagine, but I got a snootful during the Cherokee War. I wouldn't want to go through that again."

"It probably won't happen. So far the Tories have had little success tempting the Indians into the fracas. I suppose they figure that if they help defeat the patriots there will just be another group of settlers to contend with and one is no better than another. And as for his troops, I was reminded that this continent poses some problems that the King's men have not encountered in other wars. We are a large land, and our population is not concentrated. This is not going to be a contained European war, should it come. It is going to be an almost impossible task for any army to guard the expanses necessary to defeat us. Our greatest foe is from within. Should we not be able to see to the future, to the time the King's men can no longer supply the armies, and to the time they can no longer afford to be here, then we will give up and lose for ourselves."

"We've got good men. They aren't likely to give up. Now, I'm not so sure that same thing can be said about those cold fish up North. They've backed out before and left us holding the bag."

"Right now they seem hot enough for the cause," Drew said, then changed the subject. "What do you hear about my daddy and Arthur?"

Ned looked away and rubbed his beard in a gesture he habitually made when he was uncomfortable. "I was hoping you wouldn't ask."

"Is someone ill?"

"No. Not like you mean."

"What then?" Drew asked, stopping in his stride and bringing Ned to face him. "Ned, if something is wrong at Manning, I want to know about it now."

"Arthur got married," Ned said flatly. "Happened a couple of months ago. You were over at Ninety Six, or I would have written to you."

Drew just stared at him, making no attempt to hide the shock or hurt that he felt. "He didn't even tell me," he said in an almost inaudible voice.

Ned said nothing, keeping his eyes carefully on the horizon, and not on his friend.

Drew asked, "Who did he marry?"

"Just the kind you'd expect—snooty little loving English lady."

Drew looked at him, but did not ask again.

"Leola Kincaid," Ned said.

Drew envisioned the woman as he remembered her when he had last seen her. She had been seventeen then, and very beautiful. Her skin had the milky whiteness of fresh cream. Her blond hair was silky and always coiffed in the latest British style. She affected British mannerisms, and if one did not know, one would assume that she had come recently from England. He took a deep breath. "The last time I saw Arthur, I thought we had gotten along quite well," Drew said.

"It wouldn't matter to him now. He's a Tory through and through, Drew. No matter what his heart told him, he would not violate his loyalty to the King by inviting you to his wedding."

"But I'm his brother! No matter how we've disagreed in the past, and the Lord knows we've disagreed, we've always been there to help each other out when it was needed."

Ned looked sadly at him. "You got that just a little bit wrong, Drew. You've always been there to help Arthur out when he needed you. I can't say as I recall he ever come to your aid unless it suited his own wants, too."

"That's not true," Drew said and began to walk again.

"I'm not going to argue with you," Ned said. "You know I think of you as though you were my own son, and I wouldn't say anything to do you hurt, but it's time you looked clearly at your family, Drew. If you don't, you could make some bad mistakes in this fracas that's coming. When you broke that contract to marry Joanna, you lost your birthright as far as Joseph was concerned. He loves you, there's no question about that, but he's never going back on his decision to disown you. He's a man of his word. He'd cut his own legs off before he'd break his word, and he's done something as painful by cutting you out of the family, but, by God, Drew, he's done it, and he'll go to his grave with it."

Drew was angry with Ned. He wanted to argue with him, beat the man down with the strength of his argument and conviction, but he couldn't. He retreated into silence, and continued his inspection of the plantation. The next day he announced that he and George would be leaving on the morrow to return to Charles Town.

24

When Drew Manning arrived in Charles Town in mid-March, he gave only a cursory greeting to the other members of his family and closeted himself with Gwynne. It had been a long time since he had needed the presence and comfort of another human being as he did now. As soon as the bedroom door closed behind them, Drew took her in his arms, holding her but saying nothing. Though they were his arms encircling her and pressing her against him, he knew that truly it was she who was holding him.

She ran her cool, soft hands along the back of his neck, then gently raised his head and kissed him. "I am so happy, Drew. When you are with me, I am completely whole." He smiled at her, and she stood on tiptoe to kiss each of his cheeks; then, with the light touch of a butterfly wing, she kissed his lips. "But that wholeness I feel also tells me that you are troubled. You have not come back to me free, Drew. What has happened?"

Drew took a step back from her, giving her a tight smile. "Sometimes I think I married a witch."

Gwynne gave him an impishly mysterious look. "Sometimes I am a witch. And right now this witch wants to know what is troubling you. Come to the bed and talk to me."

Now he laughed and shook his head. "You want me to come to the bed, and talk about what's troubling me? My dear, nothing will be further from my mind if I go to that bed with you."

She sat on the bed and patted the place beside her. "A small respite from the worries that pressure you will do no harm, darling." She put her arms out to him. "Come to me, Drew. I have been without you for a very long time."

He stood for a moment, the lines of strain around his eyes easing as his desire for her mounted. He shrugged out of his waistcoat, then moved slowly toward her.

She got up from the bed, stilling his fingers as they worked at his shirtfront. "Let me. I am a shameless woman, Drew Manning. I want to touch you and remember all the other times we have been together."

"And so do I," he murmured, and as she undressed him, he undressed her.

He laid her on the bed gently; then the weeks of being without her, and the overwhelming feeling of loneliness that the news of his brother's wedding had produced in him took over. He covered her body with the long sinewy length of his own, his hard muscle meeting the soft pliancy of her. Drew drove hard against her, easing the desires and needs that had been building within him. His breathing was ragged. "I love you," he breathed, his mouth seeking hers again.

Gwynne moaned beneath him, and with a suddenness that alarmed her, he pulled away from her, propping himself on one elbow. "I'm sorry, Gwynne . . . I don't know what to say. Did I hurt you?" He ran his hand gently across the swollen mound of her belly. "I wasn't thinking."

She smiled at him and placed her hand on his. "You haven't hurt me, my love. I wouldn't allow that. There is no need to worry. Your little son is quite well."

"My son? How would you know if that is my son?"

"You said that I was a witch—sometimes. I know this is our son." She ran her hands along his arms, her eyes caressing him as well. "Come back to me, Drew."

More carefully he covered her again, slowly, easily, making love to her.

Satisfied and happy, Gwynne lay back against the pillows, a smile on her face, her hands on the child that kicked within her. Next to her Drew lay, his eyes closed, his arm around her, his other hand with hers on the child. "I love you very much," he said softly. "I don't think I've ever known how much until I was gone this time."

"I suppose I should say that I am glad you were gone, but I can't, Drew. I miss you so much when you aren't here. Elizabeth is not here by accident, you know. Nathaniel and I asked her to come. Actually, if Nathaniel hadn't asked permission to invite Elizabeth to come, I would have done it myself. I didn't seem able to do anything here alone, Drew. I am ashamed to tell you that, but it is true."

"I left you with a great deal of responsibility and very little help. If anyone is at fault, it is I."

"Well, all is well now. With the help of your very strong grandmother I have managed to take care of a few things we have discussed but never have gotten around to."

He raised his eyebrows, an amused smile on his face. "What have you done?"

"We have a tutor for the children!" she said with great pride. "You shall meet her a little later. She is very good with them, Drew. Nathaniel is eager to show you how well he reads, and Mary knows her alphabet and can recognize most of the words in her primer. Jane—her name is Jane Reston—is even working a bit with Susan. Though she is too young to make much headway, she is having a wonderful time."

"I'll have to meet this paragon. And I'm hungry . . . shall we make our appearance to the rest of the family?" he said, and began to get up.

Gwynne put out a restraining hand. "Not yet. You still haven't told me what is bothering you."

"It's nothing," Drew said quickly. "I warned you that if I got near that bed, it would vanish from my mind."

Gwynne smiled, but remained firm. "It has not vanished from mine."

He avoided her gaze. "It really is nothing. I feel more than a little foolish that I allowed it to bother me . . . it is something I should have anticipated. I don't know why I didn't."

"Drew, tell me what you are talking about, please. Put a name to it for me."

He shrugged and came to sit beside her on the bed again. "Arthur married Leola Kincaid recently. He didn't even tell me about it."

Gwynne lowered her head. "I wondered if you knew about that."

"You did? Did he write to me here?"

Gwynne barely glanced at him. She hated seeing the flame of hope leap up in his eyes. "No. Elizabeth told me about it. She went to the wedding. She had been back only a few days when Nathaniel and I asked her to come here."

"Why didn't you tell me? You wrote several letters after that?"

"I knew it would hurt you, and . . . I just couldn't bring myself to do it, Drew. I was so angry at Arthur. I don't know what has happened to him. He could never have been so cold or cruel before. When we were growing up, Arthur was always serious and quiet, even a bit stuffy, but he was always considerate. He would never have excluded any of us from an event of such importance. He has not only not invited us to his wedding, but were it not for your grandmother, we would not know it had taken place."

Drew sat silently, his head bowed. Finally he said, "I have been foolish. Because there have been times when he and I have helped each other in the past, I have always held the hope that one day we would be friends and brothers again in the full sense."

Gwynne took a deep breath. "It is frightening how seemingly small decisions of the past come back to haunt us later, isn't it? If your father and mine had not written a seemingly harmless wedding agreement between you and my sister—if you and Joanna had cared for each other—if you had not met Laurel—if, if, if . . . all such matters of the moment, and all so devastating."

"But, on the other hand, if many of those small matters had not happened, I would not now be sitting here with you, and above all, Gwynne, I am thankful that I am here, and that you are mine."

"Oh, my darling," Gwynne said, and turned into his arms.

Drew hugged her, then said, laughing, "Come on, get dressed, my love. If we do not join the others soon, we may never do it."

Gwynne got up and began to dress. Before they left the bedroom, she stood before him, her hands on his arms. "Drew, I know there is no way to undo the disappointment that Arthur has done, but it is he who will regret it in years to come. You are the stronger man, the more compassionate man, the more loving man. Surely that will be rewarded."

"It already has been," he said, kissing her quickly on the nose. "Introduce me to our new tutor. If she has passed the approval of both you and Grandma, she must really be something."

Gwynne laughed. "Oh, I must tell you about Elizabeth and Jane. For a time we didn't think she was going to work out, and then Elizabeth had a talk with her, and we now have a completely different woman, and a very satisfactory one."

"What did Grandma do?"

"I'll tell you about that later. I am anxious for you to meet her now, and I know Elizabeth and Nathaniel are eager to see you, not to mention your young daughters. The girls are nearly as enamored of you as I am."

"I wish it were so," he said more seriously. "I am afraid little Elizabeth won't even know me. I've been gone so much."

"Ah, you have. She is no longer little Elizabeth, but Betsy—thanks to Mary."

"Betsy?" Drew said in surprise. "Mary called her Betsy? What did Nathaniel and Grandma think of that?"

"You know Elizabeth. She rolled her eyes skyward, then shrugged and said, 'Isn't Betsy a beautiful little sister, Mary?' "

"So! My youngest daughter is now Betsy. Shall we go visit her?"

Drew spent the next couple of days reacquainting himself with the younger children and reestablishing the closeness that had been between himself and Nathaniel. He took the family on outings, played ball with Nathaniel and Mary on the beach, and went riding with his son early each morning.

At the end of the week he said, "How are you feeling, Gwynne? Are you up to some houseguests?"

Gwynne and Elizabeth exchanged knowing glances. "Let me guess. Could it be that you and George want to talk with Leo, perchance?"

"You know us too well," Drew admitted. "We have been gone so long, we are unaware of all events that have taken place on the coast. This is no time to be uninformed. Events are changing our situation with much too great a haste to allow us to remain ignorant."

"My dear, you have no need to justify your desire to see Leo. I would like very much to have Eloise and Leo here. I have become quite fond of Eloise, and so has Cousin Elizabeth. We shall send an invitation yet today."

"How does that sound to you, George?" Drew asked.

George was staring into space, a dreamy look on his face. He blinked at those in the room. "I'm sorry, my mind was . . . on other things. What did you say?"

A chorus of laughter greeted him. "What could it be that you were thinking about, George?" Gwynne said mischievously. "Or should I say who?"

George's face turned bright pink.

George Manning was smitten for the first time in his life. For the last few years he had been resigned to the idea that he would be the Manning who never married. There had been a time when he had considered courting Meg Templeton, since she seemed to be the spinster of the family, but he could never care enough for Meg. But now that he had met Jane Reston, he knew he would never again accept the idea of living alone. His feelings for Jane were strange and bemusing, especially to a man who had never before felt that compelling attraction to just one person. It was not entirely a pleasant experience for George. He found it difficult to concentrate, and no matter what his original destination, he somehow found himself gravitating to Jane Reston's schoolroom. Even when he was a child himself, he had never spent so much time in a schoolroom. It was as though he were a man dying of hunger, and that hunger could be assuaged only by the sight and presence of her.

Still embarrassed, he managed to meet the eyes of his family and smile. "I have been trying to be casual, but I'm not doing very well, am I?"

"No, George, you're not doing very well, so you might as well give up." He looked down. "I don't know what to do about it," he said.

Drew laughed. "I could give you a quick lecture on the courting of a young woman, George, if your education has truly been that lacking."

"I'm serious, Drew. Mama and Daddy are not going to take well to my courting an indentured woman."

"George, perhaps what I am going to say may be construed as disloyal to the family, and a detriment to you," Gwynne told him, "but I feel I must say it. Both Drew and I have suffered greatly to be together, and our match was one that was outlawed also. I can speak for both of us when I say that all the pain and the fright and the loneliness have been worth it. I am a strong woman, but I am completely myself when I am with Drew. Together we are more than either of us is alone. No matter what is said today, love is a great power. If you can find it with Jane, don't hesitate for fear the world will condemn you."

Elizabeth Manning got up and went to her youngest grandson. "I believe what Gwynne has said, George. You are probably correct in thinking that Eugenia and John will be displeased, but, my dear, one thing you can count on is the deep abiding affection your parents have for you. It may take time, but eventually they will accept your decision."

George couldn't help himself. His eyes went to Drew. The two men looked at each other, and George understood how deeply Drew felt the pain of separation from his family.

Elizabeth saw the exchange between the two men. "Other things were involved with Drew's situation, and that, too, may change."

George took a deep breath and shrugged. "Oh, well, this may all be academic anyway. Jane may not feel the same way about me, or even be interested in being courted. I have said little to her."

"Well, my dear, know that we shall be with you whatever your decision."

George took his grandmother's hand. "We are becoming quite a group —allies in all manner of things. I wonder if Leo will join us in this latest conspiracy?"

It didn't take Leo Manning long to have the opportunity to make up his own mind about his brother's romance. As he and his wife and child drove up the road to Drew and Gwynne's house the following week, George and

Jane were in plain view from the road. The two walking hand in hand across the wide, green front lawn, their attention closely focused on each other.

"Is that George?" Eloise asked peering from the window of the covered carriage.

Trying to be dignified, and failing, Leo squeezed into the small space with his wife and peered out as well. "George!" he said happily. "Who do you suppose she is? You don't suppose the reason we've been invited is to meet this young woman?"

"Oh, my!" Eloise gasped as Jane broke into a run, and was chased by George.

Not given to half measures, Jane Reston took her skirts in hand, raising them high enough to give George a good chase. Laughing loudly, the two of them raced across the lawn going back toward the house. They were standing, out of breath, on the front piazza when Leo and Eloise drove up.

"Leo!" George said, opening the door to the coach. "I thought this was our old buggy. Welcome, it's good to see you. Eloise, how's my favorite sister-in-law?" He gave her his hand to help her dismount.

"I think I ought to be asking that of you, George. That was quite a display you and this young woman put on."

George grinned. "She can really run, can't she? May I present Miss Jane Reston, Eloise, Leo."

Quickly the introductions were completed. Leo took Jane's hand. Always an appreciator of beauty, Leo looked at the pert young girl with the devil sparkling in her eye and sized the situation up quickly and accurately.

As the two women entered the house, Leo and George brought up the rear. "You've been holding out on me, little brother. Who is she, and when did you meet her?"

George hesitated, then said boldly. "She is the children's tutor—indentured. But she is a fine person. Ill fortune drove her family into poverty, and Jane has had the courage to come here and seek a new beginning." He looked at Leo, trying to assess his reaction. Seeing nothing he could identify, he plunged on, wanting to have this conversation behind him forever. "I have a great affection for her, Leo."

"How great?" Leo asked.

"I don't know—we've only known each other for a little over a month. She is different from anyone else I've known."

Leo suddenly laughed. "I didn't think you had it in you, George. I had begun to think you'd just always be Uncle George to all the children."

"You aren't sour on the idea, then?"

"George, it's your life. I think I'm beginning to learn that interference among nations or individuals is seldom, if ever, a good policy. With all the talk and devotion to liberty, would I dare deny you yours?"

George clapped him on the back. "I'll have to keep my eye on you, Leo. You're becoming quite the statesman."

As the men scurried away to Drew's study for brandy and talk, the women went to settle Eloise and the baby Miranda into their rooms. Gwynne and Eloise compared notes on the progress of their pregnancies. Elizabeth cooed and played with her great-granddaughter.

Leo, George, and Drew ran into an immediate problem in their talk. Leo was as eager to hear what had happened in the Upcountry as George and Drew were to hear about the doings in Charles Town and the northern colonies. After a raucous disagreement that rivaled some of their teen-age battles, Drew and George gave in and told Leo what had happened at Ninety Six and the Great Cane Break. "And then we limped into Granby and were dismissed to go home and nurse fevers," George concluded. "Now, what has taken place here?"

Leo threw his hands up. "What hasn't! It is unrelenting now. Every day brings a new threat. It's like watching two roosters ready to fight. In my letter I told you Lord Campbell escaped and boarded the *Tamer*. Since then the British keep threatening with that fleet, but nothing too serious has happened—yet. We all think it is merely a matter of time."

"What have the northern leaders been saying? Are they prepared to take the final step that will bring about war: severing our relationship with Britain?"

Leo shrugged. "It may already have gone so far that there is no choice left. Of course, they are all saying that no one really wanted this. Of course, at the same time, it was recommended and accomplished that we establish a new constitution, and in effect, declare Carolinian independence."

"And have we?"

"What choice did we have? Aside from the fact that events are pushing us in that direction, with Campbell gone, we have no government. The colony cannot prosper without leadership," Leo said. "Now I think it merely a matter of waiting for an attack on Fort Johnson."

"Are we prepared?"

"Are we prepared!" Leo said expansively. "I'm honored to tell you that three regiments were planned. When the call for volunteers went out, we had sufficient men to fill six regiments. Two of those are proudly serving with Mr. Washington's Continental Army."

"That still doesn't answer the question of meeting with the British." Drew said.

"Well, it's rumored that Washington is sending General Lee down here to help. On the other side of that rumor is the opinion that we don't want or need Lee to help us. If anyone can defend our city, it's us. We have the manpower, and, by God, we have the will."

George and Drew exchanged glances.

"What does that look mean?" Leo asked.

"Not much, except that we've just come from a battle in which blood was drawn, and there's a certain attitude a man can't help but sense once the battle lines have truly been drawn and men are ready to fight. I hear it in your voice, and I see it in your face," Drew said. "Like it or not, I think these American colonies are at war with the mother country."

"A toast, then," Leo said. "No wise man every fights destiny once it's been made apparent, no matter how much he might have desired a different circumstance."

The three men poured bourbon into their glasses, clinked them together, and drank deeply, their eyes on each other.

When Royal Governor Lord Campbell made the decision to flee the colony of South Carolina, he closed and sealed the halls the legislature had used in Charles Town, leaving the colony with no official government or place of legislative gathering. Christopher Gadsden hired Hallam's Theater, which the patriots used to form the new government.

Even with such momentous events taking place, there were still many who did not want to take the final step that would put them in irrevocable rebellion against England. However, no one denied that there had to be some form of government, if for no reason other than to keep order. On March 21, 1776, the citizens of Charles Town met and began debate on what kind of government would best serve the colony. During that debate a courier arrived from Savannah. He brought into the meeting a copy of the Parliamentary Act of December 21, 1775, which declared the colonies in rebellion. The act authorized the capture of American vessels and legalized all seizures of persons and properties, and of damage done to the colonies before the passing of the act.

The reading of the document stilled all remaining resistance to the formation of an American legislature for South Carolina.

John Rutledge was elected the first president of the Legislative Council. The assembly also elected a vice-president to replace the royal lieutenant-governor and a Legislative Council of thirteen members to replace the former King's Privy Council.

Five days later the new Assembly elected William Henry Drayton chairman of the General Assembly, and Henry Laurens as vice-president of the Legislative Council.

Four days later, almost before anyone had dared draw breath, the H.M.S. *Scorpion* captured the American sloop *Hetty* and used the ship as a tender for the H.M.S. *Falcon.* Outraged, the Americans took immediate action, and Captain Turpin in the *Comet* took the *Hetty* back and returned it triumphantly to port.

Along with hundreds of other citizens, the Mannings were at the dock when the ship was brought in. A hugh roar of approval was sounded as soon as the *Hetty* and the *Comet* were safely docked. Nathaniel sat atop his father's shoulders, his eyes bright with excitement, shouting his own approval.

George, with Jane at his side, nudged Drew and smiled at his young cousin. "We're making a patriot, Drew. He's becoming ferocious. He told me the other day that he hated all those men in the red uniforms."

"He's heard far too much talk. We shall all have to watch our tongues around the young ones. As this situation progresses, I am afraid there will be many unpleasant incidents between patriots and British soldiers. We can't risk one of the children saying something unfortunate."

"Well, you'd better inform Nathaniel right away," George said, and indicated with eye direction that Drew should look to his right.

Her gaze steadily on him, Joanna Templeton Townshend walked toward the family group, her arm securely held by her husband. Bert Townshend looked rakish and hard with the patch he now wore on his damaged eye.

"It isn't surprising to find you here, Drew, but I am a bit surprised to see you, Leo . . . and George."

"What is even more surprising is to find you here, Joanna. I didn't know you were in Charles Town, nor would I expect to meet you at a patriot triumph."

Joanna laughed. "A triumph! Oh, Drew, really. This is merely another rabble gathering. These people have nothing else in their life to cheer about, so nearly anything will do."

"Then, why are you here?" Drew asked.

"Why, so Bert can take note of who else has come to gawk, and who has made the same mistake that you have, and has chosen to see it as a triumph. It is rather foolish to look upon treason as triumph, wouldn't you say, Drew? You used to be more astute."

"Hello, Joanna," Gwynne said, stepping directly in front of her sister, so that she could not turn away.

Joanna looked with disgust at Gwynne's protruding belly. "I thought you had more taste than to make a display of yourself, Gwynne. If you'll excuse us, we shall be on our way. Good day." With her head high she took Bert's arm again and pulled him away from a conversation he was having with Leo.

"Goodness, she is cold!" Eloise breathed. "I don't know your sister well, Gwynne, but she is certainly nothing like you or Meg."

Gwynne still watched after Joanna. "No, I'm afraid Joanna has become very bitter. I feel sorry for her whenever she is gone, but I feel sorry for myself, or whoever else is nearby, when Joanna is present."

"I'm so sorry, Gwynne. It must be very difficult for you," Eloise said sympathetically, her hand on Gwynne's.

"I am going to have to come to terms with her attitudes, Eloise. I know my sister, and I am going to have to recognize that she is capable of causing terrible trouble for those I love, and she'll do it whenever she gets the chance."

"But what can you do? You are nothing like her."

Gwynne's deep blue eyes glittered. "Oh, I can be. Remember, we are of the same blood. If I must, I can be just as hard and as calculating as Joanna is. Perhaps it is time I paid my sister a visit and informed her she had best leave my family alone and unharmed."

Once her mind was made up, Gwynne wasted no time. She told no one what she intended doing, not even Elizabeth, and waited for the first time she knew Drew would be gone for the day and would not have the opportunity to question her visit.

She arrived at the house Joanna and Bert leased for their Charles Town home shortly after the midday meal, a time when she was reasonably certain that Bert would not be present and she could see her sister alone. She was let into the house by a smartly uniformed young black girl. If Joanna had nothing else, she had impeccable taste, and Gwynne walked around the parlor admiring the paintings and tapestries while she waited for Joanna.

"Gwynne, this is quite a surprise," Joanna said as she came into the room.

Gwynne managed a cold laugh. "I believe the phrase usually goes, 'This is a pleasant surprise,' Joanna, but never let it be said you are usual. This will make this visit easier anyway. There will be no pretense of sisterly love or concern, no hindrances like family ties or loyalty."

"Oh, do spare me your speeches. What is it you want, Gwynne? If you have not come for my help, get to the point of what you have come for."

"Your help? What kind of help could you possibly offer me?"

"It's pointless if that's not why you're here."

"Do tell me, please, Joanna. I would like to hear what it is you had in mind."

"Any sensible woman would be coming home with her tail between her legs and begging shelter after this amount of time. You have lived virtually alone while Drew trots around the countryside on his illegal maneuvers, and have been left to nurse and care for his . . . well, I don't know what one calls a child like Nathaniel. He's not Drew's bastard because he's not Drew's child, but it is you who have been saddled with him along with all those other little Upcountry brats."

"Is that what you really believe?" Gwynne asked with sincere curiosity. "You don't see the obvious resemblance between Drew and Nathaniel? If you could set aside your own disappointment and bitterness for just a moment, Joanna, you would see that Nathaniel is a wonderful child—very bright, and so very much like his father."

Joanna smirked. "But, I do see how *very* much like his father he is. You and I have no disagreement on that. What we disagree about is who his father is, my dear."

Gwynne closed her eyes in disgust. "I can see there is no purpose to talking, so I won't try. I came here this afternoon to offer a sisterly warning to you, Joanna. Soon we will be at war—actively, I mean—and the divisions between us will become more severe. For several years you have intimated that, given the chance, you would do Drew harm. I am warning you now that when and if this opportunity should come to you because of the war, do not take advantage of it."

"You came here to tell me that, Gwynne? Then I shall tell you, you have wasted your time. Britain will crush this ridiculous rebellion. Already there are warships amassing off the coast, and soon their guns will be pointed right here. It will all be over quite soon, and when it is over, Drew Manning will be a ruined man, and I shall do all I can to facilitate that happening, and Bert will use all of his influence and that of his family to aid me to that end."

"We are sisters, Joanna. You have chosen to bare your claws; I have not as yet, but I shall. I will protect my family and those I love. I will do you harm if I must to accomplish that."

"What a vicious little thing you've become. Why, my dear, you're nearly as common and crude as your husband. Betty will see you out, Gwynne. If not pleasant, this visit has been interesting." She left the room, and Gwynne remained gaping after her.

Gwynne was trembling with anger when she left her sister's house. She went directly to her bedroom when she returned home, and tried to calm down, tried to forget the superior look on Joanna's face. Joanna had always, even as a small child, liked to give the impression that she knew something that no one else knew, and that was the feeling Gwynne had left the house with. Whatever she was willing to do to protect Drew and Nathaniel and her other children from Joanna's constant gossip and plotting, she wasn't at all sure she could succeed. Joanna had planted doubt.

She complained of backache, and asked that her dinner be sent to her room. Adrian William Manning was born at eleven o'clock that night of March 28, 1776.

$$\underline{} \; 25 \; \underline{}$$

In May, General George Washington's attacks drove Sir Henry Clinton from Boston. Clinton turned his attention to the South and the upstart city of Charles Town. He joined his forces with those of General Howe and Admiral Parker, and sailed south.

In Charles Town, Daniel Cannon, an avid Liberty Boy and patriot, had been supervising the construction of the embattlement at Sullivan's Island. He had been given four thousand pounds for materials and workmen and a guarantee for compensation for any boats destroyed or Negroes killed or maimed by the enemy. James Brown undertook the repair and fortification of Fort Johnson, and another group of men under the leadership of Tunis Tebout were sent to see to the defenses of Fort Lyttleton.

So often the workmen would see British ships come near, tease, then move away. The men worked steadily with the certainty that one day soon the British ships would move in near the fort and the attack would be real.

General Charles Lee, sent by George Washington to take charge of the defense of Charles Town, arrived before the fortifications were complete. Upon his arrival he inspected the fort. It was small, square, and gave the appearance of being unsubstantial. The walls of the fort were comprised of two rows of palmetto tree trunks about sixteen feet apart with beach sand in between. It boasted only thirty-one cannon. Lee was appalled. "Why, this is a slaughter pen," he announced. "When those ships come alongside your fort, they will knock it down in half an hour."

Colonel William Moultrie, who was showing the general around his fort, said, "Then, we will lie behind the ruins and prevent their men from landing."

Lee looked at him as though he were a raving maniac and immediately advised that they abandon plans to defend Charles Town from this partially completed fort.

But he hadn't reckoned with the South Carolina spirit. Charles Town was their city, and this was their fort. No one would take it from them. The carpenters who had built the fort had worked for fifteen shillings a day and a measure of rum, far below their usual wage at a time when prices were soaring.

General Lee gave his recommendation of abandonment of the fort to John Rutledge, and received essentially the same answer he had gotten from Colonel Moultrie. The South Carolinians would defend the city from the fort when the British arrived.

Lee gave in, for he had no other choice, but he hadn't changed his mind. The western curtain of the fort was unfinished; it offered no protection against an enfilade from that side. Believing that Rutledge's refusal to order the abandonment of the fort was poor judgment, Lee removed a large number of his troops, and about half the powder, to Charles Town and Haddrell's Point.

The citizens of Charles Town were in a fever of activity. All manpower and supplies that could be gathered or given were put to use. Thousands of citizens and slaves built earthworks along the river frontage. Other people gathered sash weights and anything else that could be melted down and used as musket balls. Warehouses and stores along the waterfront were torn down so there would be clearance for guns and musket fire. However unprepared the citizens of Charles Town were in their fortifications, in spirit they were waiting and ready for the British. The rumored size and power of the impending attack did not dampen their spirit in any way.

The expected British fleet made its appearance off Dewee's Island, about twenty miles north of Charles Town bar, on May 31, 1776. It was the largest force the British had ever sent against the colonies. Admiral Sir Peter Parker moved toward Charles Town with nine warships, thirty transports, and an amphibious force under Sir Henry Clinton, aided by General Vaughan and General Cornwallis.

As did most of the curious, the Manning men rode along the shore assessing the might of the British fleet. Having found a good vantage point, Drew, Leo, and George watched the ships, trying to identify them and judge how many guns each carried.

"My God," Leo breathed as his eyes scanned the ships.

Off Dewee's Island rested the *Bristol*, Admiral Sir Peter Parker's flagship, carrying fifty guns. The *Experiment*, under the command of Captain

Williams, carrying fifty guns. The *Active* with twenty-eight guns, the *Solebay* with twenty-eight guns, the *Syren, Actaeon,* and *Sphynx,* each with twenty-eight guns, and the *Friendship* with twenty-six guns.

George scratched at the new beard he was growing because he thought it added dignity to his plain face. "There isn't a single ship there, unless you count the bomb ship *Thunder,* that doesn't have more guns aboard than the fort does. How many men do you suppose those transports are carrying, Drew?"

Drew just shook his head. "Too many."

"Maybe Rutledge should have taken General Lee's advice and abandoned the fort. What can we do with twenty-five guns in an unfinished fort against a fleet like this? They have near three hundred guns they are going to aim—and fire—at us."

Again Drew shook his head. "I think Moultrie is right. We can and we will stop them here and now, and if they destroy the fort, we'll do as he says, and lie behind the ruins and stop them as they land."

"Those are big words for someone who isn't in that fort," Leo said.

"I've been thinking about that, too, Leo," Drew said, and looked from one cousin to the other. "I am going to be in that fort. I don't want to miss out on this battle. I intend to tell Colonel Moultrie I am going to volunteer —even if it's only as water boy that he will take me."

George let out a war cry and tossed his hat high into the air.

Leo looked perplexed and bemused. "You two don't have a brain or a bone of caution between you."

"We can't all be heroes, Leo. You stay home and take care of the families." George laughed and poked his brother's arm.

"Like hell I will! If you're going to be damned idiots, I am, too."

The British were in no hurry. The little fort was almost laughable, and all that was wanting was a clear-cut plan that would assure success, and as little strain as possible. On June first the fleet dropped anchor in Bull's Bay. By June fourth they lay off Charles Town bar and had a clear view of the land and water areas they would be dealing with.

The confluence of the Ashley and Cooper rivers formed the peninsula on which Charles Town was built. Between the end of the peninsula and the sea lay eight miles of harbor. Two islands flanked either side of the harbor's mouth. On the west side of the peninsula lay James Island, and to the east was Sullivan's Island. To the northeast lay Long Island, separated by an inlet known as the Breach.

The British decided to land Clinton's troops on Long Island. The attacks could be coordinated, and the small fort would fall to the attack from the sea and be overrun by the land forces, which would be ferried across the Breach.

On June fifteenth Clinton's troops landed on Long Island. Drew and George joined the patriots at Fort Sullivan, and began the long, tense wait for the British attack. By the time the Mannings joined the American forces the firepower of the fort had been increased to thirty-one guns, and there was great jubilation about that, and more merrymaking about it than was warranted. A man standing with Drew and George said, "Well, the odds are a bit better now—fair, you might say. It's only nine to one. One big gun and one Carolina man equals nine big guns and any number of red-coated men the British want to throw at us."

"What I want to know is when they're going to come at us," George said. "I hate the damned waiting. When we were at Ninety Six a few months back, I thought I'd go daft waiting for something to happen. It was much worse than the battle."

"That's because you weren't one of those hit by a musket ball. You might feel differently if you had been."

George looked insulted. "Well, maybe I wasn't hit with a musket ball, but I did get my hand crushed under one of those swivel guns."

The soldier laughed, and Drew clapped his cousin on the back. "You're right, George, the waiting is a bad time."

Clinton had landed most of his men on Long Island in preparation for the two-pronged attack that had been set by the British for June twenty-third. At first examination Clinton was well pleased with the position the island gave to his men. Long Island lay to the north of Sullivan's Island, separated from it only by the narrow inlet called the Breach. Once he had accomplished the landing, he quickly lost some of his enthusiasm. Clinton had been told that he would be able to ford the Breach at low tide, giving him the opportunity to reach Fort Sullivan from the north. Once on the island, he discovered that the Breach was seven feet deep with deep holes, and treacherous sand shoals which prevented either a ferry operation for his men or the possibility of fording the water. To make matters bleaker and all the more frustrating, across the water inlet were seven hundred rebels behind breastworks pointing two guns and a great number of muskets at him. All of them looked more than eager to fire those weapons, and Clinton now found himself in a position of near helplessness. Certainly he was going to be of no value to the fleet. His men were as safely incapacitated on Long Island as they would have been had they been captured by the Americans and put in the jail. The entire operation to take the city of Charles Town rested on Admiral Sir Peter Parker and his fleet.

Clinton was frustrated, and not pleased with the current happenings in the war. He had had to leave Boston, and now he was stuck on a sandy island populated thickly with mosquitoes, while the two hundred and seventy guns of the British fleet would have to accomplish the entire mission as he watched. He sighed. There was nothing for it. At best he could be of minimal help, but in that he would do the best he could.

On the morning of the twenty-third, the date fixed for the attack, the wind shifted in the morning. As Clinton watched, the signals were lowered, and the fleet continued to rock in its anchorage in Five Fathoms Hole. On the twenty-seventh the signals, riding high for a time, were lowered as the wind whipped around to the northward. Each time the patriots tensed and manned their guns, then once more returned to the nerve-wearing waiting.

Leo Manning arrived and took his position in the fort with the others on the afternoon of the twenty-seventh. His face was grim when he approached his cousins.

"What is wrong?" George asked as soon as he saw his brother. "You look awful."

"Is the family all right . . . nothing is wrong with the baby?" Drew said.

"No. The family is fine . . . everyone is well, and the baby is thriving, Drew. But I do have some very bad news. We sent a peace council to the Esseneca Indians. No one expected trouble, and by damn if the British weren't stirring everything up and promising the Indians and the darkies things that will never happen, we wouldn't have had trouble this time."

"What did happen?" George asked.

"They suddenly turned on our emissaries. I don't know all the details, it just happened yesterday, but I do know that James McCall, James Baskin, and Patrick Calhoun are prisoners, and some of the military escorts were massacred as they slept. I don't know how many or who yet, but it is bad, and is indicative of how careful we are going to have to be. I still find it difficult to believe that Rufus decided all on his own to run away, and that he was the one behind the mischief at Willowtree. I just can't believe that a man like Rufus would think of it and carry it out."

"Neither can I," Drew said. "I still think the rat at the bottom of the woodpile is Seth."

George started to say something, then made a face and observed, "I wish you wouldn't talk about Seth and what he may do at Willowtree. Here we are on Sullivan's Island, unable to do anything if there is trouble, but when we're all at Willowtree no one does anything. If we all think Seth is a troublemaker, for God's sake let's do something about it. I don't want to find us talking about it another time when we're helpless. One of these times it will be too late."

"He's got a point," Leo said.

"Don't look at me," Drew said, "I've been telling you for months to keep an eye on Seth, but Willowtree isn't mine. I haven't a scrap of authority there. You and Rob and George will have to do something about him. If you want my help, you've got it, but that's the only way I can do anything."

At about ten o'clock the morning of the twenty-eighth Colonel William Moultrie watched the British signals hoisted once again, and this day the wind did not shift and the British fleet came for the rebels.

One line of four ships fired on the palmetto fort from sprung anchor cables off the harbor mouth, while a second line of three ships sailed past the harbor. The three sailing ships fired broadsides at the fort as they passed. The three fire-belching ships looked impregnable and awesome as they moved across the face of the fort. Then the rebels, protected only by the palmetto walls, watched as the three ships ran afoul of each other. In their efforts to right matters they ran aground in the shoal water.

As the ships met their fate, the men in the fort fired back at a steady rate, and the fort itself passed its first critical test. The spongy palmetto logs absorbed shot without splintering as might have been expected. Many of the shots that managed to land inside the fort landed in sand or marshy ground where they did little or no damage, for a good number of the shells did not explode.

Underestimating the fort, several of Admiral Parker's ships took heavy damage from the surprising defense put up by the colonials. One of the hardest hit, in the most devastating and embarrassing of British misfortunes that day, was the flagship. Captain Morris had his arm shot off and his other hand shattered. Forty-four men were killed and thirty wounded, but perhaps the most notable incident of the attack on the *Bristol* was the injury inflicted on Admiral Sir Peter Parker himself. His breeches were blown off and he was wounded. Lord Campbell, lately the last royal governor of South Carolina, was also aboard the *Bristol* and was mortally wounded.

It took very little time for the talented wags among the patriots to come up with a verse to commemorate Admiral Parker's wound. As so often happens with something that is better forgotten, the verse was singsonged by nearly all South Carolina children for years afterward.

The inside of the fort was hazy with smoke from the firing, and the air rattled with the ear-bursting din of the guns. Drew and the group of men standing nearby saw a shell coming at them and knew it would be a close one. They moved to protect themselves as the shell exploded on the fort's parapet and knocked down the flag Moultrie had designed. Sergeant William Jasper, who was standing next to Drew, leaped to the ground outside the fort, grabbed up the flag, and had it flying again from the fort. The men in the fort could hear, barely audible over the roar of the guns, and over the great distance separating them, the cheers of the thousands of citizens lined up along the Charles Town earthworks watching the battle.

The battle raged throughout the morning and had not let up by afternoon; however, Colonel Moultrie had a concern. He was defending the fort with only a portion of the powder that had originally been expected. The rest of it had been moved to Charles Town and Haddrell's Point by General Lee, who had been convinced that the fort would be destroyed by the bombardment of the British fleet within the first half hour or so. Despite his handicaps Moultrie and his men crippled the British fleet. The twenty-eight-gun *Actaeon* burned and exploded. Both the *Bristol* and the *Experiment* suffered considerable damage to their hulls and rigging. The bomb-ship *Thunder* and her escort the *Friendship* had to retire early in the battle with serious damage. The *Syren* and the *Sphynx* collided and were forced to retire.

While the fleet was taking serious damage, Clinton and his beached men were doing little better. Unwilling to accept defeat though his plans had been ruined, Sir Henry Clinton, with the aid of two armed ships, attempted to get his three thousand soldiers and marines across the Breach. Frustration continued to dog him. Across the inlet Colonel William Thomson and a force of about seven hundred and eighty men and two small field pieces stopped him. Each time the flotilla came within range of grapeshot, Colonel Thomson's gunners cleared the decks of the boats. Small in number but tenacious, Colonel Thomson's men finally dispersed the flotilla and ended the threat of a rear attack on Fort Sullivan.

As the day wore on, and the attack continued, Colonel Moultrie kept his men's spirits and energies high by serving rum in fire buckets along the gun platform.

About five in the afternoon President John Rutledge sent to the fort five hundred pounds of powder that had been stored at Haddrell's Point. With the additional ammunition Fort Sullivan's guns continued to blast at the British ships. The fleet took seventy hits from the fort. Until nine thirty that night the battle raged. In the dark the two sides aimed for the fire belches, unable to see anything else.

By ten o'clock that night the men in Fort Sullivan were exhausted but elated. After the battle John Rutledge presented Sergeant Jasper with a sword for his gallantry in raising the Carolina flag after it had been shot down.

Mr. William Logan, a citizen of Charles Town, showed his appreciation by sending a hogshead of rum to the fort with the following card:

> Mr. William Logan, presents his compliments to Colonel Moultrie and his officers and soldiers on Sullivan's Island, and begs their acceptance of a hogshead of old Antigua rum, which being scarce in town at this time, will be acceptable.

"I'll say it's acceptable," George said, savoring the odor and taste of his measure. His face was blackened and shiny from sweat. The day had been sultry, made bearable only by a breeze that the men had barely been aware of amid the continuous fighting.

Drew and Leo were no less tired, or any cleaner. All three men sat on the ground, leaning wearily against the palmetto logs. Leo sipped at his rum, then turned his head slowly toward Drew and George. "Both of you are unharmed aren't you?" he asked, his voice thick with fatigue and the almost instant effects of the rum taken at rest.

"Oh, God, I am tired," George said.

It sounded like a prayer, and Leo laughed. "What do you want him to do, George, come down and tuck you in?"

"I sure wouldn't object."

"The British took quite a beating," Drew said. "I heard Colonel Moultrie talking to John Rutledge. He said they judge that there were at least two hundred casualties aboard the British ships."

"How'd we do?" Leo asked, then gave an involuntary shudder as he recalled the sight of Sergeant McDaniel mangled by a cannonball. The man had fallen to the ground and with his dying breath said, "Fight on, my brave boys, don't let liberty expire with me today." He couldn't erase the sight of the man's destroyed leg, nor the sound of his voice speaking encouragement to his men as he died.

"Colonel Moultrie said we have twelve dead and about twenty wounded. Not too bad for a half-finished fort, too little powder, and fewer men than the enemy," Drew said.

"I hope the men up north feel the same way. Sometimes I wonder if they know there's a war going on down here, too. We sent a rider—Daniel Latham—just before dark to tell the news of our victory to Congress.

Maybe that'll get the Declaration of Independence signed. Something is going to have to get everyone off the mark. We can't be part of England and not part of England at the same time."

"Do you think the fleet is going to attack again tomorrow?" Leo asked, too tired to join in an argument with George.

Drew shook his head. "Maybe, but I don't expect it. Someone said that they thought Admiral Parker had been wounded, and that will slow them down a bit if it's true. That, and they don't have a ship out there that isn't damaged. The *Actaeon* is still sitting on the sand out there. Hey! Did you hear that Thomson and his men from Orangeburg held General Clinton on Long Island? He didn't get a man over here."

"That was not just because they were Upcountrymen, Drew," Leo said.

"Don't be too sure," Drew said, and grinned.

In the morning there was no return of the British fleet, but the fort, sporting its blue flag with the word *liberty* boldly emblazoned on it, opened fire on the only British ship within range, the grounded *Actaeon*. Captain Christopher Atkins, in order to keep his ship from falling into American hands, set her afire, leaving her colors flying and his guns loaded as he removed his crew to safety with small boats.

Quickly a volunteer party was assembled, and Lieutenant Jacob Milligan of the *Carolina* ship of war and his men boarded the blazing British ship. They stripped the *Actaeon* of her colors, the ship's bell, and as many stores as they were able to remove. Milligan and his men barely got clear of the flaming ship before she exploded.

Later that day military fever was heightened when word came that a plot instigated by the British in Florida had resulted in Cherokee attacks in the Upcountry. Several towns were burned and about sixty people were killed. Even men and women who had been loyalists throughout were now willing to fight with the rebels. Among those was Rob Manning, who came to the fort to tell his brothers and cousins the news of the Cherokee attack and of his own decision.

"As soon as we leave the fort, we're all going to Dillon's to celebrate!" George said. "By God! We will all be together again," he said, and then looked shamefacedly at Drew. "All except Arthur, that is."

"There's always hope," Drew said. "This may have influenced Arthur as well. We just don't know."

"Of course we don't," Leo said too heartily. "Anything could happen."

"But as to a celebration, I don't think this is one we should exclude the Manning women and children from. These events are going to be among those that become part of our family heritage. We should all be together."

In early August news of the signing of the Declaration of Independence came by packet boat about the same time that the British ships had been repaired sufficiently to limp away from Charles Town.

"It's time we went home!" Drew said, with a cough as he received another back-thumping from a joyful, war-whooping George.

"We did it! We did it, Drew! We ran off the British!"

"We ran them off the sea! And the Congress! By God, boys, we're an independent nation!" Leo cried.

26

"Daddy! Daddy, Mama took me to see you fighting!" Nathaniel yelled as he ran down the road to meet his returning father and cousins. "And Jane taught me a rhyme!"

"Whoa!" Drew said, with a laugh as he pulled up his mount long enough to lift Nathaniel up onto the horse with him. "You're going too fast."

"You made the British run, Daddy!" Nathaniel shrilled, his enthusiasm not in the least dampened. "I saw the ship burn!"

"You sure did see a lot, didn't you, pardner?" Leo said. "A few more years on you, and you would have been right there with us."

"Do you think we'll still be fighting the British when I'm old enough, Cousin Leo?"

"I sure hope not, Nathaniel. That'd make it a mighty long war. I don't think any of us would like that."

"I would," Nathaniel said, his eyes wide.

Gwynne and his little daughters stood at the front of the house, no less excited than Nathaniel. Drew helped his son down, then ran to his wife. With a quick smile to his grandmother, he enfolded Gwynne in his arms and let out a deep sigh of contentment. "I'm home now," he murmured, and breathed deeply of the sweet flowery scent of her perfume. Her skin was as soft as rose petals.

Leo was similarly engaged in the greeting of his own wife, and meeting for the first time the son who had been born in his absence. John Andrew Manning was still a small pink bundle with little to distinguish him from any other baby, but Leo insisted he was the spitting image of himself.

"Look at that square jaw!" he exclaimed, carrying his new son from one family member to another asking for agreement. Each of them smiled and gave him a laughing agreement as they looked down upon the round, softly jowled face of the infant son.

They had a large family dinner that night, and tales of the battle of Fort Sullivan grew to heroic proportions as the evening went on, and the Mannings found more and more to toast. They were still sitting at the dinner table at nine thirty that evening, and Nathaniel was still determinedly trying to keep his eyes and ears open so that he would miss nothing.

Gwynne watched him for a few moments, then said, "Nathaniel, it is long past time for you to be in bed."

"I don't want to go to bed," he protested. "I'm not sleepy."

Drew smothered a chuckle. "Even when you are not sleepy, you must obey your mother. Come on, I'll go up with you. We'll have a little man-to-man talk."

All smiles, Nathaniel got up from his chair, went dutifully to all his relatives, and wished them good-night and hugged them. He had a special hug for Nonnie. "He said we'd have a man-to-man talk, Nonnie. You told me when I grew up Daddy and me would have things to talk about. Is it now?"

Elizabeth held him close. "It is beginning," she whispered back to him.

Nathaniel ran off with his father, taking the steps two at a time as they raced for the top. Elizabeth's eyes were teary when she looked back to the others at the table.

George filled the awkward silence. "He's quite a boy. It's no wonder Drew dotes on him. He'd take on the whole British army alone, given the chance." Aside from murmurs of agreement, no one said anything, and George's eyes sought those of Jane Reston. "I hope one day, maybe not too distant a day, I'll have a son like Nathaniel."

"Or John Walter," Leo said.

"Or Adrian," Gwynne added laughing. "Shall we all get into a huge argument as to which is the best son?"

The Mannings stayed together at Drew's house for the next couple of weeks giving Eloise time to grow stronger, and the baby to establish a schedule, but mostly because they wanted to be together. This was a time each of them recognized as a special time of closeness and love among them.

However, they also knew it was coming to an end. Drew and Gwynne, in the privacy of their bedroom, talked about the options open to them.

"If we return to Cherokee, we'd be there in time for harvest," Gwynne said quietly.

"I know you'd rather stay here in Charles Town, but we have not tended to business at Cherokee for a long while," Drew said. "The neighbors need to see us—talk with us—and we must know which of those near us support the American cause and which do not."

"But I thought you said you believed the British would not bother us for some time, if ever again. We defeated them soundly. I saw the fleet myself —it took them days and days to make repairs sufficient even to sail away."

"I know what I said, and I believe it, but, my darling, the British fleet is not the only Crown support involved in this war, and it is a war now in every sense of the word. We shall have to guard against uprisings within the ranks of our own bondsmen, the Indians, and as much as I hate to say it, our own neighbors—perhaps even our own family." He was quiet for a moment, then went on. "And that is perhaps my most driving reason for returning to the Upcountry for a time. If there is the slightest chance that Arthur and . . . and my parents and I can reconcile our differences, it is now. This may be the last chance I have to . . . to unite us again, and if I can do nothing else, at least I can have my mother and father meet Adrian for one time, and the other children will get to see their grandparents and uncle one more time."

"I am so sorry, Drew. I know how much your family means to you. I wish there were something I could do to help."

Drew laughed and hugged her. "We're quite a pair. Neither one of us can lay claim to the hospitality of our families. Maybe we shouldn't try so hard—maybe we should be accepting the situation as a *fait accompli,* and worry no more about it."

"Maybe we should, but we won't. Of course, if we keep on the way we are going, we will have quite a large family of our own making to contend with. Do you ever look far into the future and see all the husbands and wives and grandchildren that will one day be a part of our immediate family?"

"Yes, I have, but I think my thoughts take a different turn from yours. I see a great base from which we Mannings will reach far into the making of this country."

"Ohh," Gwynne said in mock disgust as she patted his chest. "You are just like Elizabeth. She is always dreaming of the future of this country. I don't know how either of you keep your feet on the ground. I find it quite enough to run the house and manage the family and guests."

"Which is why I am free to dream my dreams."

"And part of that is returning to Cherokee. Both George and Jane will be disappointed. Have you watched them at all lately?" she asked, her deep blue eyes twinkling. "I think they are falling in love."

"And you love that, my favorite little romantic."

"I do. And George needs someone. He will be a kind and gentle husband."

"You seem to know a good deal about George."

Gwynne smiled, warmth filling her eyes. "I do. You must remember, it was George who discovered I was secretly seeing you in Charles Town and befriended me at a time I desperately needed a friend. He never once criticized me, Drew—or you, either—and he never passed judgment, though he certainly might have. I would like very much to see George married to a good woman."

"And you think Jane is a good woman for him?" he asked, looking at her. "I don't know her very well. Perhaps I should pay more attention."

Gwynne frowned at him. "Not too much. She is very comely."

Drew grinned. "I did notice that." Before she could say anything, he picked her up and carried her to the bed. "She isn't the only comely lady hereabouts I've noticed," he said as he placed her on the bed and rolled on top of her.

As they had done as young children, they began to tumble over each another, wrestling and laughing, until both of them fell off the bed with a thump.

Downstairs Jane looked up with alarm and moved to get out of her seat. George, sharing the sofa with her, took her hand and pulled her down beside him. "There is nothing to be alarmed about," he said placidly.

"But that was a terrible noise . . . someone has fallen. . . ."

George laughed. "Indeed, someone has fallen, but that took place a long time ago. What you heard just now was Drew and Gwynne engaging in one of their favorite activities. When we were all children, we all joined in, but Drew doesn't like additional participants now."

Jane frowned at him. "You are making no sense, and enjoying it at my expense. I don't care for that, Mr. Manning."

"Would you like me to demonstrate?" George asked with twinkling eyes.

"No," Jane said sedately, and got up from the couch. When she had taken a few steps toward the door, she turned back, eyes dancing, her mouth twitching with suppressed laughter. "Yes!" she said, and ran for the front door with George in hot pursuit.

The next week the various branches of the Manning family made preparations to move to different destinations. Elizabeth, Eloise, Leo, and the children were going to Willowtree. "We have the time now, and I think we'd better settle whatever plot is going on there," Leo said. "Better now, than to be sorry later."

"And I want to be there," Elizabeth said. "There is some feeling that Seth is behind all this, and if he is, the blame for his rise to power can be laid directly at my feet, and my liberal ideas that seem to backfire more often than hit the mark."

"Spoken like a true unrepentant, Grandma," Drew said, and winked at her.

Elizabeth made a face, but said nothing in her own defense.

George had stood in the background, listening to everyone else's plans. He shifted his weight from one foot to the other. "Are you going to need me at Willowtree, Leo?"

Leo just stared at him. "What has needing you got to do with anything? You're the one who has been complaining that you never have a say in the decisions made at Willowtree. Are you telling me now that you don't want to see this through?"

"Well, no, I want to . . . oh, shoot, yes, I'm saying I'd rather go to Cherokee with Drew and Gwynne."

"Oh, come now, George, if you're going to be that honest, why not be completely honest?" Gwynne said with a twinkle. "I don't really think Drew and I are the attraction—are we?"

George could still be made to blush with relative ease, and now, to his chagrin, he performed for all in the room.

"Leo, let us consider George's part in the problem at Willowtree accomplished, by means of his timely and persistent warnings," Elizabeth said.

George only managed a muttered "Thank you, Grandma."

When the farm wagons and carriages were finally loaded and ready to go to Willowtree and the Upcountry, there was a last warm round of hugs and kisses for all.

As the two sets of travelers parted at a fork in the road, Nathaniel and Mary were hanging out of the carriage still waving at Nonnie, Mary throwing kisses. "Mama, when will Nonnie come visit us?" Mary asked.

"She was just with us for a long visit, honey," Gwynne said.

"But not at Cherokee," Mary insisted.

"Well, it will probably be soon," Gwynne said, but she sounded distracted, and George noticed.

"What's wrong, Gwynne?"

She shook her head and smiled. "Nothing. I just don't like good-byes."

George considered for a moment. "No, it's something else. What is bothering you?"

"George, really, it's nothing—at least nothing important. I just have a strange feeling, that's all."

"What kind of a strange feeling, honey?" Drew asked.

"I don't know exactly how to describe it, Drew. George, do you remember that one time in Charles Town, when Laurel was still alive? I knew Drew had to go home, but I just didn't want to let him go? I had this same feeling then. I just knew something was going to happen, and that I wasn't going to see him for a long, long time. I almost lost him then."

George and Drew exchanged glances, then George asked her, "Who is it you feel that way about—or is it all of them?"

"I didn't feel it when we parted . . . it was when Mary asked me when Nonnie would visit us at Cherokee. I had this sudden feeling of awful loneliness."

For a time all of them were silent, then slowly they began to talk about Elizabeth, and the logical causes for Gwynne's feeling, along with the more alarming possibility that truth often did not lie within the realm of prescribed logic.

Their talk and musings was brought to a halt by the necessity of making a camp for the night. "Pretty poor planning, if you ask me," George grumbled to Drew, as he gathered wood and began building a pen for the animals.

"No need to remind me," Drew said, and looked to the woods that seemed to be all around them, and moving forward as darkness fell. "I don't like this one bit—not with things as they are. I think we'd better take turns with a watch, George. You go tell the drivers we'll set up four one-hour watches. Impress the importance of it on them. I don't want any fool sleeping." Drew turned to take over the job George was leaving, then called after his cousin. "Don't say anything to the women. We'll have a sing around the fire after supper."

"Keep 'em happy, while we keep an eye out for Indians, renegades, Redcoats, and God knows what else," George said. "You have the greatest confidence in yourself to control any unforeseen event of any man I have ever known—or heard about, Drew." He laughed. "I think it's called balls."

The night passed uneventfully, and Drew made certain they were near a plantation before stopping each night after that. The only problem remaining to them then was discerning which of the families whose hospitality they accepted were Tory and which were Whig. To insure their safety in this, Drew and Nathaniel had their second man-to-man talk.

Drew hunkered down with his son, plucking a long strand of grass, showing him how to make the blade whistle. "Now, a little serious talk, Nathaniel," he said. "There's an old saying that goes 'All's fair in love and war.' " He paused for a moment while Nathaniel absorbed the information. Then he went on, "You know we are at war with Britain, fighting for our liberty and our independence. We are fighting to build a new nation that will stand all by itself. Some of the people that live here don't want that to happen, and they are at war with us, the same way we are with them."

"Then we'll have to shoot them first!" Nathaniel said staunchly.

"No—not always, Nathaniel. We don't always know who they are, so we must sometimes keep what we believe in, a secret. Like tonight. The people we'll be staying with tonight are strangers to us, so we don't know if they are on the British side or on ours. If they are British and find out that we are not, they could do us harm, so . . ."

"So—we could beat them. I'd help you, Daddy, and Uncle George. . . ."

"No, Nathaniel. Our job is to protect your mama and the young children. You and Cousin George and I might be able to take care of ourselves, but what would happen to Mary and Susan and Elizabeth and little Adrian?"

Nathaniel just looked at him, his mind working fast, but coming up with no solution. "What do we do?"

"We listen so we can find out as much about these people as we can, and we say *nothing* about what we believe or think. And no matter what they say, we do not lose our tempers. Can you do that? This is a man's job, Nathaniel. Are you up to it?"

"Yes, sir," the boy said in total dedication to his father's request. "You told me a good man is one you can count on. I'm going to be that kind of man."

Drew tousled his hair. "Good. Here, take that carpetbag, while I carry in the crib. We've got to make it look like we were out here for good cause."

Until this evening Drew had never considered what a wildly patriotic little boy could mean. He said nothing to Gwynne, but he remained by Nathaniel's side as much as possible and found himself holding his breath whenever the child showed any sign of playing with the Miller children.

The real test, however, did not come until dinner, and then it was a test for all of them.

With the serving of the main dish, the Miller's serving boy poured wine, and Miller, at the head of the table, raised his glass, "God save the King!"

A stunned silence fell over the entire table. Drew looked quickly at his family, then smiled and raised his glass. He said nothing, but raised it. One by one the others followed.

Nathaniel looked confusedly from Mr. Miller to his father. "I don't have any wine."

Miller laughed. "Well, young man, you're a bit young, but your heart is in the right place."

Drew let out his held breath.

They managed to get through the remainder of the dinner in good order, but as soon as he could do so courteously, he begged they retire, claiming fatigue from the long day's travel.

"I thought I'd choke on that damned wine," George grumbled as they went to the guest house. "Why'd you do it? None of the rest of us would have, if you hadn't."

"Because we don't know the circumstances hereabouts. If he's an active Tory, we could be slaughtered in our beds tonight. We couldn't protect the children. Use your head, George."

George thought for a moment. "It's a whole different way of life, isn't it, Drew? Nothing will ever be the same again, I don't suppose. I'm not so sure I didn't prefer it when you could trust your neighbor's hospitality." Drew said nothing, and George continued. "We are doing the right thing, aren't we—breaking away from England, I mean?"

"I hope to God we are," Drew said. "An independent nation is going to have to be worth a lot. The cost is going to be high."

"It's just beginning," George said, wondering if he dared go on and confess his fright.

"Stop talking about it. You're going to spook us both," Drew said. "You'll forget all about this the minute you hear there's another British fleet or regiment to chase off."

George doubled his fist in a gesture of bravado. "Let me at 'em!" Then he punched Drew. "And there'll be no more toasts like tonight!"

It was early September when they arrived at Cherokee. Drew's first sight of the long rambling house made his heart beat faster. Of all the Manning homes this one was possibly the least imposing. It had grown in stages, and though Drew had built what was to have been the main house, it had never been completed to his plan. There always seemed to be necessities to be taken care of, so Cherokee had a main house, with wings on either side, and quite nearby there was a bunkhouse for the hired help. The quarters were within view of the house, as were most of the outbuildings. It was as much a fort as it was a home.

The distinct embattled, siege-ready look of Cherokee had been something Drew had intended to change. Now it gave him a feeling of security and pride.

Ned came out and rode back with them the last few hundred yards to the house. "Howdy, there, Nathaniel!" he called in response to the loud, joyous greeting he had gotten. "Come to help your old friend with the harvest!"

As usual Drew's family tumbled out of the carriages with their confusion and rambunctious members going in all directions. Within minutes of the carriage's stopping, Penny Webb's voice could be heard calling order and yelling at escaping children.

Only a bit calmer, Jane organized the unpacking of the children's equipment, giving special attention to all that would go into her schoolroom.

And as usual Drew disappeared, leaving Gwynne stamping her foot in frustration. With fire in her eyes she heard Jane refusing to take George's offer of help, and ran over to the couple. "Don't refuse him now, Jane. Believe me, whenever he offers, take his help. Drew quit the minute we were married!" She rushed off again, leaving the two of them gaping after her.

"I think I know why Drew disappears. I used to think he was just lazy."

As Gwynne knew, Drew had gone off with Ned to see his tobacco barns and the condition of the fields. "We're in good shape this year, and I've got a little surprise for you. I been busy makin' some improvements of my own," Ned said.

The two men walked to a field no more than a hundred feet from the back of the house. It was lush and heavy with vegetables. Ned proudly pointed out the rows of corn and beans and squash and half a dozen other varieties, then turned to point to the rear of the house. Two bright, white wooden doors glared in the sunlight. "Our root cellar. This week I've got a group of girls, and we're gonna pull up vegetables and keep the roots cool down there. We may not get the news as fast as you do in the city, but we get it, an' I figgered it'd be smart for us to be ready for the shortages that are sure to come. Wouldn't hurt to smoke a li'l extra meat."

"No. We've no way of knowing how much time we'll be spending here, or how many of us there'll be," Drew said. "You're a wizard, Ned. I don't know what I'd do without you."

Ned chuckled. "I've wondered that a time or two myself."

Drew wasted little time after his homecoming to approach his brother. After having sent a messenger and received no answer from Arthur, Drew asked Ned if he would deliver his message personally.

"Why don't you go yourself? He's not likely to refuse you in your own family home."

"He probably wouldn't, but he would see me simply as a courtesy, and I don't want that. I want to meet with Arthur—to talk to him brother to brother one more time before I give up and resign myself to the fact that we will be enemies in all senses of the word."

Ned Hart used every ounce of influence he had with Arthur Manning, reminding him of his growing-up years and the labor they had all done shoulder to shoulder when Joseph set out to build the stately mansion called Manning.

Arthur finally agreed with a shrug. "Don't expect anything to come of this, Ned. Drew and I have gone too far, our beliefs and our loyalties are too far separated, for us to turn back now."

"When you needed him, Arthur, he has always come through for you, and you have done the same for him. It isn't right to turn your back on that. You're blood. That must count for something with honorable men."

"And it does, but not to the point of selling my soul. I believe he is wrong. He and those like him will ruin this country, Ned." Arthur shook hands with him. "But I'll meet with him. We'll talk. Maybe it's best that we say all there is to say between us."

Ned looked at Arthur. He could remember Arthur as a child just as he remembered Drew. He couldn't help but feel a certain pride and sharing in the manhood of both these men now that they were grown. Ned Hart had watched them grow and many times had been there to help Arthur or Drew through difficult times. Just as Drew had, Arthur Manning had grown up tall and straight, an honorable man, a man with deep convictions. Arthur's hair was lighter than Drew's, more of a sandy brown, but with the same warm red highlights that graced his brother's dark chestnut hair. "You're a fine man, Arthur. So is your brother. I'm asking you now to keep that in mind when you meet. You don't agree, and to you he's a traitor, and to him, you are."

Arthur shook his head. "I can't understand how Drew can still be an honorable man and follow the patriots' cause, Ned. He knows what disaster such a course will bring to us."

"The indigo?"

"Among other things, yes, the indigo. Manning is built on indigo, and

Drew was the finest indigo man in these parts. Now it's as if none of that ever happened, and it has no meaning for him."

"I think you'll find that not to be so, but you and Drew can talk it out. I'll tell him you'll meet with him a week Wednesday."

Ned mounted his horse. Arthur stood, a wistful look on his face. He put his hand on the horse's neck. "I wish it were not this way, Ned. You've always been good to both Drew and me. If I had my way . . . if things were different, I'd like nothing better than to have Drew a part of the family. I miss him, you know." He laughed lightly. "When we weren't fighting, we were pretty good friends."

"For something so natural, life sure is tough to get through," Ned said. Then he put his heels to his horse, waving to Arthur as he rode away.

After he had told Drew about his meeting with Arthur, and Arthur's agreement to meet with Drew, he was quizzed unmercifully. Drew extracted from him practically every word Arthur had uttered, then asked, "Do you think there is a chance that we can find grounds for agreement . . . anything that will keep us from facing each other in this war?"

Ned bit his lower lip, considering. "I can't say that, Drew. He doesn't like this any better than you, but, by damn, you two are the hardest-headed men in the parish. You don't know the meaning of the word compromise. I just don't know."

This was not what Drew had wanted to hear. It had been a long time since he had heard or thought anything encouraging about his family, and now more than ever he wanted to know there was a way for him to go back home. He looked at Ned for a time, saying nothing, then away. "Let's take a look at the tobacco. I want to see how carefully the men are selecting the leaves."

The week and a half Drew had to wait until he met Arthur in Camden seemed the longest stretch of time he had ever lived through. Gwynne, too, was anxious, for Drew was tense and irritable much of the time. Those times when he wasn't anxious, he was remorseful and apologetic for inflicting his tension on her. Even Nathaniel had the good sense to avoid his father as much as possible, and thus gave Ned a chance to know him better. Ned took Nathaniel under his wing, much as he had Drew many years ago, when Drew needed to be away from his father. Ned was happy. He might never be a Manning in name, but he was a part of that family nonetheless, and it meant more to him than anything else in the world.

Drew was nervous when the day finally arrived, and Ned brought his horse round to the front of the house. He said nothing, but Ned smiled and said, "No man should be faulted for trying to do good, Drew. Whatever the outcome, the trying is good."

"But perhaps useless."

Ned shook his head. "Naww. That's not true. I've lived a long time, an' I've been told a heap of reasons why I oughta tread the narrow path and believe in God, but most of those reasons always seemed to oil some other fella's wheels. The only one I ever knew that makes good sense to me is that a good man grows when he's trying to do good, even when those efforts don't look like they work out. Now, that tells me something. You can put a ton of seeds in good soil, but without the sun nothing is going to grow and thrive. It's that sun for the seeds, and I've come to think its God for us people, Drew. It's the trying that brings the sun out."

Drew couldn't help but smile. "You're quite a philosopher, aren't you, Ned? This time I hope you're right, but I also hope that sunshine lights both of us and we find a way out of this impasse of principles."

Arthur Manning was no less nervous than his brother. When Drew rode up to the tavern in Camden, Arthur was standing outside, pacing back and forth.

Drew walked up to him, extended his hand. The two brothers shook hands, their eyes meeting, and in a burst of affection they embraced. They went together into the tavern, ordered food and drink, then found themselves sitting across the table from one another not knowing how to begin talking.

"How's Daddy?" Drew asked finally.

"Curious about you, but otherwise, fine. I think he might have liked to have come with me today."

"Why didn't you bring him?" Drew asked.

"I said he'd like to, but you know Daddy, he'd rather cut off his left arm than admit that he regretted the estrangement. He's still harping on your disgrace, and the harm done to the family name, but at the same time I think deep down he regrets ever having made that contract with Cousin William. You know, it's the old story: if you want to resent someone, do them harm."

"I'm not innocent concerning Daddy, and I don't resent him . . . at least I'd like to make it up with him," Drew said.

"Well, Drew, you never did do anything the way the rest of the world does. Mama is well, but she misses you a good deal. She wants to see her grandchildren. She's always telling Daddy he's depriving her of the rewards of motherhood." Arthur laughed, thinking of Georgina at her best. "She really talks him into a corner with that."

"I've often wondered if Mama really wanted to live in the Upcountry. Daddy very often doesn't see anyone else's point of view. If he's happy about something, he thinks everyone else should be too," Drew said.

"She talks to him about that, too. Mama isn't as quiet about things as she used to be. She claims she is going to stay for a time in Charles Town from now on, and if Daddy won't lease a house for her, she'll stand on the street corner and beg hospitality from a stranger."

Drew laughed with him. "There are a few things that will always bring us together, aren't there?" Drew said.

Arthur became immediately serious. "Only in memory, Drew. And we're no longer children . . . these things you speak of all belong to a time past. There are other things you do and believe now that will never become memories we share."

"Why are you so certain I am wrong, Arthur? You will at least admit that we have no choice now—we must show Britain our mettle."

Arthur took some time in lighting a cigar, then he sat back in his chair puffing on it. "Maybe this is the heart of our disagreement, Drew. I don't think this little war is showing our mettle. That had already been shown and recognized by the Crown and all the Empire. We are British citizens, honored and favored by the King. We had nothing to prove. We were revered as British citizens with all the rights and honor that accompany that status. These men who parade about calling themselves patriots are nothing but ignorant rabble-rousers who see an opportunity to improve their station in life. Their cause is not liberty, Drew. These men haven't the knowledge or culture to recognize liberty—their aim is license."

Drew took a deep breath. "That's quite a condemnation, Arthur."

"I don't look upon it that way. As I see it those are the facts, the truth of the matter. The mechanics will take over, dress themselves in fine clothing, and impose their vulgar ways on the populace; all the finer things that the few of us have tried to fashion in these colonies will vanish. Should these men win in their cause, Drew, they will have created a nation of common men."

"What is so wrong about a nation of common men?" Drew asked.

"Nothing, if you have a fondness for mediocrity."

"You really are quite a snob, Arthur."

"No, I'm not a snob, Drew. I love learning and culture and art, good music and philosophy. Your patriots may produce good technicians, good carpenters, good tradesmen, but I'll be willing to bow to your better judgment the day they produce a philosopher to match Descartes or Plato, an artist the rank of Leonardo, a politician to sit with any of those in England. Those kinds of inspired heights do not come from mentalities whose main concern is to feed their own bellies," Arthur said. "Your Americans are a warlike people, Drew. They are men of the physical, and most likely will succeed there, but they have nothing to offer the spirit, and eventually everything withers if the spirit is not fed."

"You seem to overlook, Arthur, that you are one of those Americans you condemn to mediocrity. You were born here."

"I am not an American. I never have been, Drew, and I never shall be."

"We don't seem to have much ground of thought to move about on, do we?"

"I tried to warn you through Ned. When he brought your request, Drew, I told Ned I would come, but that there was no hope of our agreement."

"It's probably my tendency to mediocrity," Drew said acidly. He tossed some money down on the table and walked toward the door. Arthur caught up with him. "Wait, our food hasn't come yet. Surely we can finish a meal together."

"I don't think so, Arthur. We'd only begin to talk again, and this time I'd insult you. You're my brother, and the same blood flows through our veins. I'll always try to honor that, but you are also my enemy, and to feed my own spirit I must do my best to defeat you."

"Then, perhaps there is one more thing I should tell you. Please, sit down for a moment."

The two men walked back to their table.

"What is it, Arthur?" Drew asked impatiently.

"If we are at such a stalemate that we will quite literally be opponents . . . my Tory involvement is not merely lip support, Drew. There have been a few changes at Manning. Daddy and I discussed it, and decided that it was time we showed our colors. Manning is the headquarters for the Tory cause in this area. I suppose Cherokee serves the same purpose for your allies."

Drew found it difficult to talk for a moment. "No, Cherokee is my home —no more. I . . . can't believe that you and Daddy would use Manning as a headquarters. That means you have arms there . . . and meetings . . . what about Mama? This puts her in a good deal of danger. If this isn't already common knowledge, it soon will be, Arthur. You'll be open to attack."

"We're prepared."

Drew just shook his head. Deep in his stomach was a hard pit of dread. "God, Arthur . . ." he stood up, once again leaving his food on the table. "I'm sorry. God help us both."

27

The rebellion of the American colonies presented several problems to the British. With the power of their fleet the British would have little difficulty in eventually controlling the coastal areas, but the vast interior of America was a different matter. The British army was always in hostile territory, and the logistics of supplying the army were nightmarish. Many said that the American war was one impossible to win, and should not be attempted; however the British had two large blocks of the population from which to draw allies.

One source of manpower came from the pool of those citizens who had remained loyal to Britain and the Crown. The other was of greater concern to the colonists were the blacks. Few British questioned that given the opportunity and encouragement, the blacks would rise up against their masters and seek refuge with the British.

In most of the major southern communities the greater part of the population was black. The thought of an uprising sent waves of terror through the most stalwart planter. As soon as the rumors of British instigation became widespread, the planters increased the size and power of the regular patrols. When the war was in earnest, any runaway was killed. There were no questions asked nor exceptions made, for no chances could be taken.

The planters also had learned from experience that their greatest danger came from those slaves most recently brought from Africa, and there were many southerners who were calling and had been calling for the end of the slave trade for some time, Henry Laurens notable among them.

The situation at Willowtree was no different from that on other plantations. Leo had wasted no time in talking to John as soon as he returned from Drew's house, and the Mannings of Willowtree had dropped their attitude of superiority regarding the behavior of their slaves. For years the Mannings had had such unshakable confidence that none of their people would ever run, or cause trouble, that they had scoffed at those who imposed curfews on their people and rode the roads at night searching for runaways. Now it was different. Though it hurt his pride, John Manning looked at the facts squarely, and joined with his son in volunteering to ride with the patrollers, and encouraged the others to beef up the patrol. A new day had come to Willowtree plantation.

The increase in discipline and the patrolling were not the only changes to come to the plantation. Elizabeth, too, had had a long talk with her son. She had told him that to be true to herself and to his father's memory, she had to support the patriot cause. "Your father came here because he did not approve of some of the restrictive policies in Europe, including English policy. This continent has been called many things, among them a collection of ne'er-do-wells, thieves, and rogues. Your father thought of them as people who needed a new start, and freedom from the eye of government. I came here with him, and I agree with him."

"But, Mother, if we should succeed in the war, which is unlikely, we can never hope to succeed in the long run. We need the British markets, the order the King has always supplied. Though, perhaps, all men need a chance to succeed, that does not qualify them to run a country, to know how to make decisions that will carry us forward. We are a collection of colonies, Mother, and not a cohesive collection. We have the signs of great rifts between the North and the South already. We shall never be able to remain together. We will not become a united nation, even should we soundly defeat the British Army and Navy."

"You may be correct, John. Many others have said the colonies are too different, and have needs that do not indicate we can remain united, but we must try. If we fail—then we fail, but with honor, and with the knowledge that we made the effort. I am going to do all I can to aid the cause."

Though John Manning had not advanced so far as to want to admit he was no longer the staunch Tory he once was, he was not upset or alarmed at Elizabeth's statement. He looked at his diminutive mother and suppressed a grin. "What have you in mind, Mother?"

"I am going to turn the schoolhouse into a factory," Elizabeth said.

"A factory?" John asked, scratching his chin. This was not among the things he had considered. "What kind of a factory have you in mind?"

"The Continental Army is going to be in short supply of clothing, blankets, and such like. Our South Carolina men have made up six regiments to join that army, and this patriot is going to do all she can to be certain they are kept warm and clothed. I intend to set up spinning wheels and looms. Pelagie is quite good at that kind of thing, and she has told me that Hedy has a knack, too. I will probably need five or six more, which I shall select from the field hands."

"I notice you are not asking permission," John said wryly.

"I thought you might object. I am sorry, John, but I feel very strongly about this. I am surprised you don't. Two of your sons will be, and have already engaged in battles for the patriot cause. Your children are Americans."

"Tsk, tsk, Mother, you seldom slip up, but you forget, Joseph and I were also raised American."

Elizabeth looked at him for a moment, wondering if she was merely reading into his words what she wanted to hear. His eyes twinkled, and the smile lines around his mouth deepened. Elizabeth put her arms around him and held him close to her for a long time. "Praise God! I have been given my son back again."

John put his arms around his mother, a warm feeling that he hadn't felt for a long time running through him. Perhaps there would always remain some small part of the child who craves his mother's embrace throughout life. "I didn't know you thought you had lost me," he said.

"It has been a long time that you and Joseph and I have been close, John. What else could I feel? I am your mother. Part of me shall always be with you. I am sensitive to the slightest separation."

He kissed her cheek. "Well, you have me now. I still have my doubts about this rash American cause, but on the other hand, I do not want to find myself driven from the land I consider mine. With so many already leaving, I am afraid those of us who continue to pledge our loyalty to the King will find the atmosphere intolerable should the Crown lose."

Elizabeth's eyes twinkled. "Do I detect the hint of a conviction that the Crown is going to lose, John?"

He grinned at her. "A hint, Mother, just a hint."

Elizabeth was still a woman of enormous energy despite her seventy-odd years, and she set immediately to work with her factory. Nothing Elizabeth Manning undertook was without joy, and in her factory there was much laughter and talk and singing among the women. The spinning wheels were never stilled, and the piles of freshly spun wool mounted. Others carded cotton, and others worked looms of all sorts. In the beginning they were content to leave their newly loomed materials the natural color. But it wasn't long before Elizabeth began to fret that the cloth should be blue.

"I was thinking, John," she said on one of the occasions she had talked him into seeing her progress in the factory.

He groaned in good-natured dread.

"Before you make fun, you might listen to what I have to say. I think it is a very good idea, and perhaps we could please me, and tempt Joseph into joining the rest of us."

"Uh-oh, if it is to do all that, this one has to be a buster."

"I want to color the cloth. We could set up dying vats right here, and do the entire process ourselves. Blue. And that made me think of Joseph. Why not ask him to supply us with Manning indigo?"

"To dye the material for uniforms for Continentals," John finished for her. "I doubt that he'll do it, Mother, but it will do no harm to try."

"John, you really must curb the habit of always expecting the worst. We shall assume success until we find otherwise. I shall have the vats set up, and expect Joseph and Arthur to send me the first wagonload of indigo in —what is reasonable? A month?"

"If he agrees, it would be a month or perhaps six weeks."

She nodded her head in agreement, then left him standing in the factory alone, while she hurried off to the house to write her letter.

John looked at Pelagie and shrugged.

Elizabeth did many things well, and her courage seldom failed her, but in taking disappointment, she did not do well. About three weeks after she had sent her letter to Joseph in the Upcountry, John found his mother sitting in the sunny small parlor at Willowtree. Though she tried quickly to wipe away her tears and smile at him, he had already seen. He had also seen and recognized the handwriting on the letter she pushed into her sewing basket.

"He refused?" John asked, sitting down on the footstool before her chair. He took her hand into his, running his fingers over the soft old skin.

Elizabeth tried to speak, but couldn't at first. "I don't know him, John. He is more stranger to me now than son. I was just sitting here remembering that Christmas a few years ago when I insisted we all gather." She stopped talking again, dabbed at her eyes with her kerchief, then took a deep breath. "You know, Gwynne always claims that you can feel—sense —what is to come, because a part of it has already happened within the hearts of those people involved. Perhaps she is right, for I was afraid that Christmas might be the last time we were all together. It would seem that it was."

John was awkward in situations such as this. He hated seeing anyone unhappy, and would say nearly anything to ease the situation. "He will change his mind. You know Joseph is always saying things for which he is regretful later."

She patted his hand. "I know Joseph is prone to making some very foolish decisions, and saying some equally foolish things, and sticking to his word no matter how much it hurts him or others. Joseph is a King's man right or wrong. I do not think anything will change that, even alienation from his entire family."

"Now, wait a minute, Mother, we once thought Drew would never again be a part of the family. It appeared as though he was going off to the Upcountry with that girl, and we'd never have him again." He paused and looked a bit shame-faced, then said, "I admit, I didn't want him to come back, but I don't feel that way now. We all change—that's my point."

"Joseph hasn't changed. He had a part in Drew's leaving. Drew has changed and made many efforts to see his parents and brother. Joseph will have none of it."

"But . . . just the other day you told me I'd have to learn not always to expect the worst. You have to have some faith in Joseph, Mother. Trust him."

"I do have faith in him, and I do trust him. He will do just what he has said he will do. He will fight for the King, and he will consider all those who do not his enemy. I cannot change that, John, and neither can you. We shall have to accept it . . . but it is a bitter tonic to take." She pulled the letter from her basket and handed it to him. "Read the letter for yourself. It will make his position clearer to you."

He read the short letter quickly and let it fall to his lap. They both sat in silence until Bethany walked into the room.

"What's the matter with everyone? What are you watching?" she asked, peering out the window John and her great grandmother were staring through. "I don't see anything."

"That's because there is nothing to see. Your grandmother and I were talking—we just ran out of talk."

"Well, you are pretty gloomy."

Elizabeth looked at the piano. "A little music would go a long way toward cheering us up, wouldn't it, John?"

"I always love to hear my little Beth play."

Bethany made a face at him. "Daddy, I'm nearly twenty-two years old —I'm an old maid!"

"Bite your tongue!" Elizabeth said.

"I mean it. Cousin Meg is the spinster in the Templeton family, I guess I'm it in this one."

"You'll find the right man, Beth. Don't be so impatient."

She gave her great-grandmother an impish smile. "All right, I'll while away some of the time by playing for you. Maybe my prince will hear these clear tones and come and carry me off before I finish."

As Seth hoed the flowerbed near the house, he heard Bethany playing. He stopped his labors and leaned on the hoe, enjoying the soothing, beautiful sounds. These days he spent as much time near the house as he could. Even though the Mannings had taken what were for them unusual precautions at Willowtree, they were quite careless about talking among themselves. Seth had learned a great deal listening at the open windows of the house. Today, for instance, he felt sorry for the old lady. He liked Elizabeth Manning. Right now, however, his only interest in her was that she was an avid seeker of knowledge, astute when it came to politics, and very talkative.

He had already worked out a route to take on his escape, and he had established contact with a British soldier who had promised to aid him. He didn't much like Bert Townshend, and he didn't like the terms of his aid, but Seth wanted to return to Africa more than he wanted to remain alive here, or to preserve anyone else's life. If Bert Townshend wanted him to stage an uprising at Willowtree in exchange for a boat, then he would get his uprising.

There had been one other requirement for Bert's help, and that was that Drew Manning had to be at Willowtree at the time of the uprising. That had posed Seth more problems than anything else. Drew had been visiting with a fair amount of frequency last year, but this year he rarely came, and when he did it was only for an afternoon, which did not give Seth sufficient time to organize. One could not pull a bell rope and order an uprising. It took preparation, a building of passion. He needed days for that, not hours. In the meantime he lurked about the house and grounds waiting, hoping to hear the one bit of news that would tell him when Drew Manning would be coming to Willowtree for a visit with enough length to give Seth the time he needed.

It was a long wait, and Seth was edgy and irritable by the end of October, when the news finally came. He was planting the fall flowers around the house when he heard Elizabeth's laugh. He knew her ways and moods well enough by now to recognize that the tone of her voice meant she had had good news. He had seen the messenger come to the house and had quickly positioned himself near the windows of the room she was likely to be in at this time. Elizabeth liked to sit in the late afternoon sun, and that put her in the small parlor with the wall of windows overlooking the front lawn. On his hands and knees in the soil Seth was not seen, but he could hear easily.

"Pelagie, what wonderful news! I never realize how much I miss Drew until I hear he is coming to visit. Oh, we shall have to plan a day of shopping in town next week. I must have my new gowns and Marie promised they would be finished by the first of November! What a stroke of luck!"

"Good heavens, what is all the merriment?" Eugenia asked as she came in and sat down. "If it's good news, share it!"

"Drew is bringing the Cherokee harvest in himself, and will visit with us before he returns home."

"How nice! Will Gwynne and the children be coming with him? Perhaps we could have a fall festival. It has been a long time since we have had that celebration at Willowtree, and it has always been one of my favorites."

"What's this about a fall festival? What is that?" Eloise asked.

"Oh, my dear, you have never been at Willowtree for a fall festival," Eugenia said, and patted the sofa next to her to indicate a seat for her daughter-in-law. "You'll love it! We have horse races, and a ball—we'll all have to have new ball gowns! Oh, Elizabeth, let's do have the festival. We could all use some fun."

"It's a wonderful idea! If we plan for mid-November, we can be certain that Drew will be here. I imagine he sent this letter by messenger, the same day he left Cherokee for Charles Town. That is his usual procedure—he knows I hate to wait."

Eugenia stood up, her hands clasped. "Then I am going to find John and tell him and Rob and Leo to begin preparations. There is so much to be done . . . invitations . . . food . . ." She walked toward the door, talking to herself, checking off a list of things to be done. At the doorway she turned and asked, "He didn't happen to say if George would be coming home with him, did he?"

"I am assuming he is. Drew didn't say, but he kept using the pronoun 'we.' No doubt he assumes we know who 'we' is."

"I certainly hope he is. Why, my goodness, I hardly ever see that boy of mine anymore." She gave them a bright smile. "Well, I'm off to find John."

As the Mannings set their plans into operation, Seth did the same with his. The long time of waiting was over.

Drew arrived at Willowtree on November 9, 1777, and with him were

Nathaniel Dancer and George Manning. Nathaniel had been given his own horse to ride to Willowtree from Charles Town.

"Nonnie! Nonnie, I took the crop to market!" he announced proudly as soon as Elizabeth stepped outside the house.

George and Drew were loosening the packs from their saddles. Drew looked over his shoulder as his cousins all spilled out onto the lawn. "We thought you ladies might like a few play pretties with things getting so scarce. Show us to your parlor and a cold drink, and the Greek will unburden himself of gifts."

Elizabeth laughed. "I hope you're more trustworthy than the saying implies."

"Grandma! You cut me to the quick. Would I fool my favorite lady?"

"Come, you rogue, I shall give you a cool drink, and we shall have a good talk. I take it you had a good harvest this year?"

"One of our best," Drew said, giving a wry smile to George over his shoulder. "The problem is we have no place to sell it—or at least most of it. Most of the tobacco will sit in warehouses or be given to the army." He shrugged. "There will be another great crop year, and maybe that time we'll have a place to put it."

"Drew, I'm so sorry," Elizabeth said. "We are in much the same position here. Even with setting aside one third of our rice, we have a large crop, but many of our usual markets are closed to us, or too risky with the British fleet in the waters. We'd rather keep it, and perhaps use it ourselves or supply the army, than see it taken. We'll all get by."

"Ned had the foresight to build a large root cellar at Cherokee, and plant a new field in vegetables. With that and a supply of smoked meat, we are secure at Cherokee. I imagine John has done much the same here?"

"He has," Elizabeth said, then smiled up at Drew, her face shining. "Drew, the most wonderful thing has happened. John has finally seen . . ." She paused and shook her head. "No, that is not entirely true, he has not seen the cause as we do, but he has joined the ranks of the patriots for his own reasons."

Drew squeezed her arm and pecked lightly at her cheek. "I'm happy for you, Grandma . . . for all of us. I wish I could report a similar success with Arthur, but I can't. He is adamant."

"I know, Drew. I tried to persuade Joseph, and got in return a very cold, succinct letter stating his position. But I don't want to talk about that. I find it greatly dismaying, and we have decided to have a fall festival while you are here. This is a time of joy for us, so we shall not muddy it with talk of Joseph and Arthur."

"When will the festival take place?"

"It is planned for the fourteenth. We thought you and George might like a few days to rest up and perhaps to pick your horse for the race."

Drew looked at her in alarm. "A horse race! Grandma, my favorite mount is at Cherokee."

Elizabeth laughed. "Oh, Drew, you'll never completely grow up. Would it hurt to give the other men in the field a fighting chance this once?"

Drew grinned. "Not if I win," he said. "I'll raid your stables. John has a pretty good mount, and I doubt he'll be riding. He doesn't usually." Drew and Elizabeth kept talking as they walked across the lawn to the house, but Drew's eyes were on the black man who moved slowly, almost keeping pace with them. He seemed attentive to his work, but nonetheless Drew's attention was repeatedly drawn to him. "When did Seth begin to work near the house, Grandma?"

"Oh, Seth has turned out to be quite a wizard with the gardens. I don't think Willowtree has ever looked better at this time of year."

Drew raised his eyebrows. "A man of many parts, our Seth."

Drew and George went over the entirety of Willowtree in the next few days with Leo. "Everything seems calm and quiet again. Whatever was in the air, we seem to have stopped. We are keeping up the extra patrols, but aside from that we have eased a little on the curfews and have restored the bondsmen's privileges of Sunday barbecues, and an occasional Saturday-night gathering—of course, these are closely watched, and no spirits of any kind are allowed in the quarters or to be given to the bondsmen. The fall festival will be the first celebration we have had in nearly a year that we will allow the darkies to participate in," Leo said.

"What about the tool breakage?" George asked. "Has that stopped?"

"Not entirely, but it is far less of a problem than it was. For a time we couldn't turn our backs for an instant. The stall doors were left open—in the evening we'd find stiles down and the livestock wandering where they would. The carpenter and smithy shops were working round the clock trying to keep us in tools. I don't think we had a decent piece of tack anywhere on the plantation, then it stopped. Of course, that was after the curfews were put into effect, and quite a few punishments were meted out."

"And what about Seth? How much a part did he have in the careless-ness?" Drew asked.

"None at all. Seth was never one of those punished. If he was a partici-pant, we never caught him at it."

"That's very interesting," Drew said. "He's the one we'd all pick as a capable organizer and one of the most likely to want to run, and yet he is innocent. What do you think of that, George?" Drew asked, and gave George a knowing look.

"I think we have one mighty clever darky to deal with."

"Wait a minute," Leo said. "He might not be involved. After all, you two haven't been here, but I have. If Seth had wanted to run, he would have done so long before now."

"Seth will never run until he is as sure as he can be that he will succeed. You'll never find him snakebitten in the swamp like you found Rufus," Drew said.

"What do you suggest?" Leo said with some exasperation. "I can't just punish him or confine him because you and George think he is capable. The man gives me no cause to take action against him. He's become one of the most valued and reliable workers on Willowtree."

Drew shrugged. "He's damned smart. Just keep vigilant where he's concerned, Leo."

News of the festival had put everyone on the plantation in high spirits. The fall festival at Willowtree lasted three days, the first of the three being devoted to the family, and highlighted by a barbecue and a dance in the quarters. The second day the guests arrived, and would be feted with a large dinner, and contests the men participated in, and the final day was the day of the horse race and the ball in the evening.

Seth presented the picture of the happy man looking forward to a kind of celebration he had never before participated in. He was even bold enough to remind Leo that the last time there had been such a festival at Willowtree, he had not spoken the language well enough to understand what was happening, nor had he made friends or acquaintances with whom to share it.

"I surely am looking forward to this one. I'm thinkin' about it as my first."

"It's good to hear you are feeling a part of Willowtree, Seth," Leo said warmly. "I'm sure you'll enjoy yourself."

Seth smiled, showing beautiful white, even teeth. "I'm sure I will, sir. An' I'm gonna have these gardens lookin' so pretty all your guests is gonna want you to hire me out to them."

Leo laughed and went on about his business.

With the barbecue pit dug, and a roasting pig scenting the air with a delicious odor, the Manning women retired to Elizabeth's suite to dress for the evening.

Eloise watched closely as Pelagie laid out her gingham dress. "I never realized how attractive these coarser materials could be, Elizabeth. I am so pleased you suggested we try them."

"My dear, we are going to be lectured sternly enough. We were all told to economize. Even Drew, who is always open handed, is talking about economy." Elizabeth busily worked with the ruffle on her bodice.

"Everyone needs a bit of cheering up from time to time," Eugenia said. "I'm sure John will appreciate the way we look. Did you hear that the Remingtons are bringing Louise with them? I couldn't believe she would actually leave her Charles Town house. She must be anxious to see you, Elizabeth."

"Probably," Elizabeth said a little haughtily. "Louise is such an old woman, she—"

"Elizabeth Manning!" Eugenia cooed. "She is the same age as you!"

"Perhaps in years, but she is really far older than I. Why, that woman walks around in the gown she will be buried in. I think she expects to keel over at any moment and wants to be prepared."

Eloise giggled. "Grandma Manning, I never knew you were such a cat. I think it is wonderful."

"Dear Eloise, you will learn that a girl is born feline, and the best of us die feline."

Eloise gave her a quick hug, then smoothed her dress again and ran her hands over her hair to make sure all the curls were in place. With a bright smile to Elizabeth, who was engaged in the same sort of preening she said, "Shall these two li'l kittens go do a bit of hunting, Elizabeth?"

Eugenia joined them. "I do so wish Gwynne were here. She'd enjoy this. Gwynne just loves girl talk."

The women joined the men in the parlor for a glass of port, then went out onto the lawn. This was a time when the slaves had an opportunity to display talents to their white masters that were seldom seen. The bondsmen organized and put on their own show, displaying musical skills, mime, dancing, and singing for the pleasure of their masters.

Seth, Tom, and Cuffee stayed near the back of the mass of slaves who gathered round to watch their more talented members perform. About a half hour into the programming Seth tapped Cuffee on the shoulder. With a grin the man hurried off into the darkness in the direction of the quarters. He soon returned pushing a wheelbarrow loaded with jugs. He hid the wheelbarrow in the bushes and brought out two of the jugs, setting them on the ground near Seth. Tom, Cuffee, and Seth exchanged knowing smiles and waited until a group of men who had been dancing hurried off the lawn area that served as their stage.

"Bet you is thirsty," Cuffee said with a grin. "Too bad Master Leo won't let us hab a li'l libation, ain't it?"

"Law-wd, wouldn't I like a sip o' 'tato wine jes' now," Toby said as he mopped at his brow, his head thrown back, his dark skin glistening.

Cuffee giggled. "What you say iffen Cuffee say he kin get you a sip o' dat wine?"

Toby guffawed. "I say Cuffee a liar. Mastah Leo lock it all up."

Cuffee giggled again and motioned for Toby to follow him. They slipped off into the dark where Seth sat, the two jugs at his feet. "You keep yo' mouf shut, iffen we gib you some?"

Toby's eyes grew large. He looked at Cuffee and then Seth in disbelief. "Wheah you git dat?"

Seth smiled. "It doesn't matter where we got it, we've got it. Have some."

Toby took the jug and drank deeply. He wiped his hand across his mouth. "Dat's de bes' tastin' stuff I had! Whooo-eee!"

Seth encouraged him to drink again. When he had had his fill, and Seth was sure there would be the desired effect, "Tell the others to come get some refreshment," he said. "You tell them to come one at a time. We don't want Master Leo finding our secret, do we, Toby?"

Toby threw his head back. He was loose and limber, his graceful body now moving more fluidly than ever. "I tell 'em. Gonna dance me up a conjure. Gonna dance me up de spirits," he said in a singsong as he moved away doing a weaving dance-step.

One by one Seth got the men, and then some of the women, back into the shadows to partake of the homemade wine. As one jug would empty, Cuffee made certain there was another one to replace it. When his wheelbarrow was empty, he trotted back to the quarters and replenished the stock. For months he and Seth, Folly, and Tom had been making their brew, keeping it in the swamp until this night. There would be more than enough to accomplish their purposes.

When Seth had assured himself that a sufficient number of the men, among them a few easily antagonized types, had had enough to drink, he motioned to Tom and sent him to the swamps to retrieve other needed supplies.

Seth sent his best emissary for violence out into the crowd of tipsy slaves; Cuffee, always a bit of a clown, also had a malicious side to him. He was a busybody and knew the secrets and weaknesses of all of his fellow bondsmen. Now he darted about, in his hopping way, making a comment about Joe's woman being off in the bushes with Jeb, or Toby's saying that Ham was a fool.

As soon as tempers began to flare, Seth and his two helpers, and a man named Luck, who had recently joined them, raced off into the darkness in search of Jehu and Odo, the two men they knew they could not coerce, or force to join in tonight's activities. These two would be taken captive.

The Mannings did not realize for some time that anything was amiss. All noticed that the dancing had become more hypnotic, and much faster. The slaves seemed to be less aware of their white audience, and the rich voices singing the low, seductive songs became more enticing and intimate. But there was nothing obvious to alarm them or to warn them of the acts that were taking place in the darkness beyond the lighted torches on the lawn.

Eloise Manning shivered and rubbed her arms. "I think I'll go in, Leo . . . I'm not comfortable."

"Shall I get your shawl?" he asked. "You might want to stay. I believe Jehu is going to play the fiddle and Unity will sing. They are very good."

Eloise smiled at him. "Perhaps I'll come back out later. I'll listen for them from the house."

"I'm coming with you," Velma said.

Rob looked up at her from his seat. "It wouldn't hurt you to sit here a bit longer. This means a great deal to the Willowtree people."

"I don't like it," Velma said. "And I don't see why I have to be uncomfortable to please a bunch of darkies. I told you earlier I didn't want to come out here tonight, Rob." She took a few quick steps and caught up with Eloise.

Elizabeth was no more at ease than the two younger women had been. She leaned over toward John and whispered, "Did you give them anything to drink, John?"

"Good heavens, no! All spirits have been strictly forbidden and locked up. We have watched to be sure no home brew was made in the quarters."

"They are certainly acting strange—aren't they, or is it my imagination?"

"I think we're all a bit edgy. We've become so cautious we jump at anything. But, to be on the safe side, I'll ask Rob to have Jehu check on our star performers and ascertain their sobriety." He smiled. "Don't worry. If anything is out of order with them, Jehu will see to it."

He got up and went over to talk to Rob. Rob got up instantly and walked toward the lighted area looking for Jehu.

With a hummed chorus a line of women moved across the stage area, moving in unison, their bodies looking almost as if they were connected, forming the body of a huge sinuous snake.

Suddenly, in the darkness behind the lit area, a roar of angry voices went up, and two-hundred-pound Toby and an even larger man tumbled out onto the lawn, their struggling bodies under the feet of the sensuously moving women. Cries of rage were punctuated with cries of pain as the two men pummeled each other. In the darkness others could be heard fighting.

Seth was talking. No longer was he holding back any of his thoughts or powers of persuasion. With those slaves who were drunk but not fighting, he began to paint the picture of punishment and perhaps death the Mannings would inflict once order had been restored and they got help from the patrollers.

At his signal Tom began to hand out the weapons he had brought from the swamp earlier. During the time that the slaves were breaking farm implements, Tom had used his job in the smith to repair the tools and at the same time fashion weapons, mostly crude but sharp machetes. Now he placed them in the hands of aroused, inebriated, punishment-fearing men and sent them into the command of Seth. Seth, now the rabble-rousing general, pumped the fears of the men and told them where to go with their arms and the torches that Cuffee and Folly were busy lighting. A group of five shouting Negroes ran toward the house. Another group toward the stables and barns, and yet another group for the quarters. Those that were left—some of the men, most of the women and children—milled around in confusion for a time, and then the women gathered up their children and ran for the safety of the swamp. A few sought refuge in their cabins.

Rob had not even reached the performing area before Toby and his opponent slammed onto the ground among the dancers. He had taken a running step forward, shouting at Toby to stop, when he heard the other shouting and fighting beyond the lights. He turned for a moment and shouted at his father to get the women inside and call for help, then plunged into the darkness.

"Jehu!" he shouted as he pushed his way through the milling Negroes watching the melee. "Jehu!" He grabbed at the nearest writhing body and slapped the man across the face, hard, with the back of his hand. He could smell the alcohol now. It was everywhere, and the scent was strong. For the first time, looking into the angry, enraged black faces, he was frightened. "Get to quarters! You got one minute! Y'all gonna regret this."

Seth loomed out of nowhere to stand in front of him. The blacks around them stopped, breaths held, waiting to see what he would do. "What am I going to regret, white man?" Seth asked boldly, a sneer on his mouth.

Rob gasped in rage. He raised his fist and shook it in Seth's face. "You're going to hang! Your damned black carcass will rot in the sun, till there's nothing left but bones!" Rob screamed.

"We'll see who rots in the sun," Seth said, with a deep, throaty laugh. He raised his right hand and put the long eastern sword over his head. He placed his left hand on the hilt, stood with it raised over Rob's head.

Rob was too stunned to think or move.

Seth brought the sword down, cutting, crushing through Rob's skull. He pulled the sword free with difficulty and brought it down again, hacking deep into his shoulder. With a high-pitched cry of war Seth looked at those around him, then ran off to direct his minions to their destruction and the destruction of Willowtree.

Rob Manning lay dead in a pool of his own blood. The men and women who had served him, and some who had loved him, stared down in horror and revulsion. Then the enormity of the deed dawned on them, and they knew they had little choice. They joined Seth, or would die as Rob had.

John had stood near his seat stunned, seeming not to comprehend the situation; nor did he respond to his son's shouted demand for help. Drew jumped up, took John by the arms, and shook him. "Get the women into the house. Arm yourself! I'll go for the patrol." He ran two or three steps, then turned back. He had forgotten about Nathaniel. He searched for a moment, then saw the boy with his great-grandmother. "Nathaniel! This is the time you grow up, boy. Run as fast as you can with Nonnie for the house. Hide yourself in the root cellar, and don't come out no matter what happens! Go, Nathaniel! Run! Nonnie will come." He looked quickly at his grandmother and helped her toward the house. "Get Grandpa's pistols, Grandma, and for God's sake, if one of them gets in, don't hesitate to shoot."

Elizabeth was parchment white. She couldn't speak, but she nodded, and let go of Drew's hand, running toward the house. Pelagie was quickly at her side.

Eugenia had heard most of what Drew had said, and without being prompted, ran for the root cellar.

Elizabeth ran through the front door of the house and nearly fell as she saw Velma sprawled on the bottom stairs, a large stain running down the front of her dress. Horrified, Elizabeth looked up into the crazed eyes of Ham, his machete raised. He lunged for her. With an agility she didn't know she still had, Elizabeth darted to her left and into the room that had been her husband's plantation office.

But Pelagie hadn't Elizabeth's agility, and she wasn't thinking of her own protection. She wanted to stop Ham from harming Elizabeth. With no other thought in her mind, she ran at the man, her hands extended, clawing at his face. Ham shoved at Pelagie with one massive arm, and found her more formidable than expected. He hit the old woman, then drove the curved machete blade into the soft flesh below her breastbone. Pelagie collapsed at his feet, still trying to claw at him as she slumped down. She had given Elizabeth precious seconds, but still it was only seconds. Ham stepped over the body and ran into the office just steps behind Elizabeth.

Elizabeth was at the gun cabinet, her fingers stiff as they worked the latch. With him steps away, she opened the cabinet. On the lower shelf were Walter Manning's pearl-handled pistols. Elizabeth took one of the weapons in her hand, turned, and shot. She didn't think, or even aim, she just shot. Ham's hurtling body crashed into her. His blood was warm as it soaked into her gown. She stifled a scream, and as Ham fell to the ground, Elizabeth pushed his weight off her, got up, and once more ran for the root cellar.

"Nonnie!" Nathaniel cried when he saw his great-grandmother.

Elizabeth could no longer control her trembling or her voice. She took the child into her arms and said in a panting whisper, "I'm all right. I . . . I just . . ." She stopped, realizing she was about to tell a child not quite eight years old that she had just shot a man and that her best friend had been murdered. Her eyes sought Eugenia.

Eugenia cowered in the corner of the cool dank cellar, her arms wrapped around herself, her face a mask, her eyes huge and filled with terror.

Above them they could vaguely hear the sounds of running feet, the thudding of what they supposed to be crashing furniture. For the most part they were cut off, being able to hear little and see nothing.

Seth watched, perched on a rock, merely guiding what was happening, but doing nothing himself. He had seen Drew run into the barn, and with some surprise had watched him emerge. He had expected Drew to die in the stables, but it didn't matter. He would not bring the patrollers any sooner than they would have come themselves. He was not worried. He was merely waiting for the right time to leave.

He stood up when he saw a line of flame climb up the side of the livestock barn, then leap, licking its way across the roof. Within fifteen minutes Seth could see fire in the big house. Filmy curtains, blowing in the windows, were aflame; the interior of the house grew increasingly bright. In the quarters cabins small fires could be seen here and there. Soon the whole quarter row would be aflame. Seth stood and began to give a cry that was like an exaggerated owl hoot. He repeated it over and over, until from different directions, Tom, Cuffee, Luck, and Folly ran from the darkness to join him. The five of them ran down the quarter road, heading for the swamp.

With ease they found their flatboat, and with Seth sitting at the head, Tom poled them toward the island in the middle of the swamp. Even in darkness there was not a channel or pathway in the swamp that the men didn't know. They had practiced over and over, during the months of waiting, the various ways of escape from the murky, dangerous marshes. From the island they would split up, each of them taking one of the routes out of the swamp that they had learned and explored. They were to meet just outside of Charles Town at the house of a free Negro, who would hide them during the day, then at night they would go to the wharf on the Ashley River that Bert Townshend had shown them. The boat he had promised would be there. And if it were not, Bert Townshend would not be alive to know that they had stolen what he had not given.

Seth's patience had paid off. He was no longer worried. Deep within himself he knew he had succeeded. He had only to execute the necessary steps now. He sat back in the boat and enjoyed the dark ride in the swamp. The insects were singing with the chorus of frogs. It was peaceful in the swamp at night.

28

Billowing smoke and shards of flame could be seen in the night sky when Drew found the patrollers. They, too, had seen the smoke, and had been on their way. Drew wheeled his horse around, and he and the six patrollers rode back toward Willowtree. A seventh patroller rode alone to raise the neighbors.

George and Leo Manning had gone with their father to a storehouse they kept at the back of the house. The three men had taken muskets and pistols from the store of arms. They carried as many of the weapons with them as they could, knowing that sooner or later the slaves would break open the storehouse and have them in their hands.

"Shoot any you see," George said. "We can't differentiate, not even Jehu or Odo."

The men moved cautiously out of the storehouse, staying close to the house or taking cover near the house by the shrubbery that Seth had planted.

As they separated and spread out, they could see where the others were only by the occasional flash that came from one or another of their muskets. George was the only one of them who had ever been in a battle, and the two that he had been in had not prepared him for this. If he saw movement, he shot. He didn't know if it was friend or foe, man, woman, or child, not truly certain that he was not shooting at his own father or brother.

Elizabeth, Nathaniel, and Eugenia huddled in the root cellar. There were no more sounds coming from the house above them. They didn't know for a time if the uprising was under control, or if the house was still a danger to them.

Eugenia cried softly, unable to stop. Elizabeth was near to fainting. Her back hurt terribly where Ham had shoved her into the gun cabinet, but she said nothing.

"Elizabeth!" Eugenia suddenly cried. "I smell smoke! Oh, God, Elizabeth, smoke!"

"Nonnie," Nathaniel asked in a thin voice. "Are they going to burn us up?"

"No," Elizabeth said with effort. "The men will come for us. They'll stop this."

"They're dead!" shrilled Eugenia. "They won't come! No one will come!"

"Daddy's not dead. My daddy's not dead!"

Elizabeth held him. "No, of course he's not dead. Your daddy is bringing help. Eugenia, for heaven's sake get hold of yourself. You are going to have all of us hysterical with your ravings."

"I can't help it, Elizabeth. I don't want to die. I don't know where John is."

"Eugenia!" Elizabeth said forcefully. "You are not helping John or yourself! Be quiet, keep calm. We are not out of danger, and must be prepared should it come."

Nathaniel had been watching her closely. He had seen her hand go to her back, seen the look of pain on her face in the murky darkness, heard the quick intake of breath. "You're hurt, Nonnie. The man hurt you."

"It's all right, Nathaniel. He bumped me and hurt my back a little, but I'm all right." She pulled him nearer to her. "Sit close to me, my brave little one. Your Daddy will come for you."

When Drew and the patrollers rode into Willowtree, Leo and George already had a water line going. Most of the women and children of Willowtree, and a few of the bondsmen, were in the line, some of them passing buckets, gourds, anything that would hold water, to and from the well, others wetting blankets and sheets, trying to smother the fire that had long since been out of control.

"George! Where's Grandma? Did they get out of the house?"

"No one has seen them," George shouted.

"They're still in there! My God, George, they're in the root cellar!" As a man ran past, Drew grabbed hold of him and took the heavy horse blanket he was carrying.

George saw and realized what he had in mind. He grabbed Drew by his shoulders, knocking him off balance. "You can't go in there, Drew. No one can get through those flames!"

"My son is in there!"

"Drew! You can't help him! Help us put out the fire." George's voice broke. "Please, for God's sake, Drew, if they are still alive, we have a better chance of getting them out if we can get the flames under control. Even if you got them out of the cellar, you couldn't get back through the house. Please!"

"Drew! Have you seen Eloise? Or Velma?" Leo cried. "I can't find them."

Drew shook his head, moving constantly along the line passing the water containers along.

Soon men from all the neighboring plantations were streaming through Willowtree's front gates. Wagons rumbled along in the darkness, carrying food, buckets, clothing, blankets, and anything else they thought might be of use. Several women had come with them, and with the aid of some of the Willowtree slave women, they set up a campfire and began to brew hot water for tea, and some food.

When Jehu regained consciousness the plantation was already in flames. Dazed, and bound hand and foot, he rested against the tree Tom had tied him to, drifting in and out of consciousness. Snatches of frantic conversation came to his ears as he lay there. It was some time before Jehu's old brain was working well. Once sensible, however, the old man, right hand to Walter Manning, began to work to free himself. Seeing movement in the trees to his left, he shouted for help. His own daughter, Hedy, popped her head through the thick bush.

"Hedy! Free me, I am bound!" Jehu said urgently.

"Daddy, I gotta keep runnin'. I got Mastah Leo's baby an' Miranda wiff me. Dey fools back dere is like to kill'em. We mos' di'n't git outta de house."

"Free me, girl, so I can be of help!" he ordered.

Hedy pulled Miranda through the thicket and told the petrified little girl to sit on the ground. John Andrew Manning squalled in protest as he was placed on the pine-needle-strewn ground. She went to work on the knots that restrained Jehu.

"Where's Miss Elizabeth?" he asked. "She git out safe?"

Hedy shook her head. "She be down in de cellar. She be dead now," Hedy said ruefully. "De whole house is like a big bonfire. Ain't nobody gonna come outta dere, 'ceptin' as a ha'nt."

"No!" Jehu roared. "Miss Elizabeth ain't no ha'nt! I git her out. I git her!"

"Daddy, you git burned up like a crisp o' bacon," Hedy said.

"You git those chil'ren to de swamps. Hide, don't come out till you don't see no fire, an' you don't hear no shoutin'. Hear me, girl? You p'tec's those chil'ern wiff your life, girl."

"I p'tec's dem, Daddy."

Jehu stood up, weaved a bit, supporting himself, his hand on the tree trunks. Slowly the dizziness passed and he moved stealthily along the path until he got back to the bright, painfully heated quarters road. Most of the cabins were aflame. There was nearly no one around, no human sounds, only the roar and sharp cracking sounds of popping wood. Occasionally he saw a frightened, bewildered child wandering about, hunting its parents. "Run to de swamp," he ordered, and was obeyed. He had been the head man among the slaves for as long as any could remember. Except for Seth's group, all of them obeyed Jehu without question. Some he told, "Run to de rice paddies."

As he came to the end of the road, where it joined the courtyard of barns and stables, he could see there was no way he could get through the main part of the house.

Now, more cautious since he was highlighted by the light of the fire, he moved toward the back of the house. There was an entrance to the root cellar there, as well, and it was far closer to the outside of the house than the main entrance was. It was still engulfed in flame. He stood staring at the wall of fire that licked and curled across the beams of the house. He was frightened. There was no use trying to get into that root cellar. No one would be alive. The trap door was already burning at the edges. As he thought and argued with himself against trying to get into the root cellar, Toby, his face battered and bloody, staggered into the courtyard. His appearance made up Jehu's mind. "Toby, get me a blanket—wet it down."

Toby groaned and stared at his father through puffy, swollen eyes. He put his hands on either side of his head, as though trying to hold it together.

Jehu's brows drew together, and his mouth turned down into an expression his children had learned from infancy to fear. "I tell you to git me a blanket!" Jehu roared, and Toby, his hands still holding his head, stumbled off toward the front of the house. He took one of the blankets from the wagons of supplies that were still rolling into Willowtree from the surrounding plantations and had Etheline wet it down for him in the well.

Jehu took the blanket, put it over his head, and wrapped it around himself, then ran to the back of the house.

Toby yelled after his father, "Wheah you goin'? Daddy! You be burnt up!"

Jehu kept running. He plunged through the flames, expecting instant pain, and was surprised when it didn't come. Then he took a deep breath and felt the searing heat enter his throat and lungs. Wrapping the wet blanket around him, and staying as close to the ground as he could, he clawed at the catch of the root-cellar trap door.

Elizabeth, Eugenia, and Nathaniel could hear the scrabbling at the trap door. They moved so that their backs were against the wall farthest from it. Three sets of eyes were fixed on the square in the ceiling, and the wooden staircase leading up to it. Elizabeth felt along the shelf for the pistol she had set there. Her hand was trembling so badly she knocked the pistol to the floor. Nathaniel fell to his knees, feeling for the gun just as the door opened and let in a brilliant burst of light and heat. Nathaniel looked up and saw the body of what looked to him a black giant coming down the steps.

Eugenia put her hands over her ears, her eyes closed as she screamed with a high shrill cry.

"The pistol, Nathaniel! Give me the pistol!" Elizabeth said, but her voice was quaking.

Nathaniel picked up the gun, held it out before him with both hands as his father had taught him. The pistol barely shook at all. The little boy aimed the gun at the broadest part of the man, his chest, then squeezed the trigger.

Nathaniel Dancer fell as the burst of fire flared from the pistol. "Nonnie! He fell!" Nathaniel yelled.

The boy stood still, afraid to move, but wanting to know if his enemy was dead. He had been a man, and protected his great-grandmother, but he was terrified, and he felt sick.

The smoke grew thick in the airless room, and the flames from above began to lick down the wooden steps. Elizabeth tried to get to the stairs, but fell, lying on the floor not too far from the man's body. "Nathaniel, you must close the trap door, or we shall burn to death," Elizabeth gasped.

The little boy stared at the bright, hot light that was blazing in the opening. He moved to the steps, climbed a few, then backed down away from the heat. "It's hot, Nonnie. It hurts."

Elizabeth got to her knees and painfully crawled across the earthen floor to the steps. Her vision was coming and going, with bouts of secondary blackness overwhelming her, but Elizabeth Manning was not one to give up. By sheer willpower she continued on until she got her hands on the ladderlike rails of the steep steps. She pulled herself up; the heat was atrocious, but Elizabeth kept going. She could feel the drying and burning of her skin and hair. She reached up into the flames, her hands an agony as she pulled the door shut.

Eugenia managed to gain enough control of herself to grab the blanket from the dead man and run to Elizabeth's aid. Elizabeth's hair was aflame, and the old woman was strangling on the smoke and pain. Eugenia threw the blanket over her and patted desperately at her, and helped her to lie down on the cool earth. Elizabeth turned face down, where the air was a bit easier to breathe; then she lost consciousness.

Nathaniel was standing over the dead man, his eyes showing shock. Nathaniel Dancer had protected his great-grandmother. He had shot his enemy, but as he stood there staring, it was his friend Jehu who lay dead at his feet.

George and Drew and Leo also worked at the rear of the house, dousing the flames that were around the trap door. With the aid of a blanket, and George and Leo's continuously throwing water on the flames, Drew pried the door open with a wooden bar. "Grandma! Nathaniel! Are you there?" he called, and began to descend the steps.

"Drew!" Eugenia cried, and got up from Elizabeth's side. "Oh, Drew, thank God!" She fell to a spasm of coughing, choking on the smoke.

"Stay down, Eugenia!" Drew shouted, coughing himself.

Nathaniel was still staring at Jehu, tears streaming down his face, partly from the smoke, and partly because he couldn't understand what he had done.

Drew grabbed hold of his son gave him a quick hard hug as he swung him up to his shoulder. "Cousin George is up there, Nathaniel. I'm going to hand you up to him. Stay where he tells you." Drew mounted three steps, then shouted for George.

Hands came down the opening and Nathaniel felt himself being pulled upward away from his father's comforting arms.

Eugenia, with a little help, managed the steps by herself. Drew could hear her hysterical crying as she saw George and Leo. He knelt by Elizabeth, leaned down to see if she was still breathing, then scooped her up in his arms, his chest bursting with smoke and pain, and began awkwardly to clamber up the steps. "George! Leo!"

The two men positioned themselves on either side of the door, and as soon as they could reach her, took Elizabeth from Drew.

The wounded, maimed, and ill were taken to a makeshift camp the neighbors had set up on the lawn. A series of tents and campfires dotted the area around the willow pond. The women were making bandages and cleaning wounds and burns as fast as they could. Elizabeth was deathly pale in the early dawning light. Drew looked down at her, his face a mask of sadness and rage. Then he looked over at his young son, who sat unmoving and staring on the campstool he had been assigned. Drew went to him and knelt down. "You have been very brave, Nathaniel. Aunt Eugenia told me what you did."

Nathaniel burst into the tears he could no longer hold back and threw himself into Drew's arms. "It was Jehu," he wailed. "Daddy, it was Jehu!"

Though he didn't know if what he was going to say was in this particular instance true, for this terrible night it was a rule all of them had had to live by, he said, "Nathaniel, we don't know that Jehu was still our friend tonight. You did the right thing. I would have done as you did, and perhaps you saved Nonnie's life."

"Jehu wouldn't hurt us," Nathaniel cried.

"I didn't believe any of our people would hurt us, Nathaniel, but they have. Cousin George and I shot anyone we saw, just as you did. We could do nothing else. Jehu, if he could talk, would tell you the same thing."

Nathaniel dissolved into a spasm of hiccoughing sobs and trembling.

One of the women handed Drew a cup. "Here is a little diluted brandy. It will do him good."

Drew thanked her and put the cup to Nathaniel's lips. The boy sniffed at the pungent odor and turned away. "It is a man's drink, Nathaniel. It will make you feel better—clear away the smoke and some of the ache of shooting Jehu."

Nathaniel obediently took a sip, made a face, and sipped again.

It wasn't until late in the morning that one of the neighbors found John Manning lying face down at the edge of one of the rice paddies. A deep gash had laid open the muscle of his left upper arm. When he was brought back to the tents, Leo and George looked at him stone faced. "He's lost a lot of blood," George said tonelessly.

Leo looked at Drake Peters, who once again was helping the Mannings. "Has anyone seen Eloise?"

"Sorry, Leo. We're still lookin'. Troy and John Davis are searchin' the paddies. That's where we found your daddy, so we thought maybe Eloise was with him."

Leo's voice was barely audible, "The children?"

Drake merely shook his head. He stood there, awkward and uncomfortable, then said, "I'm goin' back out there. If there's a shred o' hope left, Leo. We'll keep on huntin' for 'em until they're found."

Some of the men were now moving through the smouldering remains of the house. Stark chimneys stood tall and blackened in the mass of charred wood and smoldering, stinking ash. Carefully they made their way through the debris, searching for bodies. Troy Sloan came back across the lawn bearing the remains of Rob's wife, Velma Manning, in a blanket. "I ain't sure who this is," Troy said, "but it's small enough to be a woman. Maybe a young boy." Troy kept up the façade of cool indifference, but he put down his grisly baggage as quickly as he could and disappeared behind the wagon, until his stomach had stopped roiling.

Eloise Manning was found naked, with her throat cut, at the far edge of the paddies late that afternoon. Hedy walked along behind the men carrying Eloise, bringing Leo's children back to him.

Leo stood crying unashamedly, not knowing whether to go to his dead wife or bear the pain of relief that would come with the embrace of his children.

Hedy stood before him frightened and uncertain. She didn't know what he would do, or if he would blame her for the carnage that had taken place. He might think she had taken the children for evil purposes, and not to protect them as her father had instructed her. "I kep' 'em in de swamp," she said hesitantly. "Dey was burnin' de house 'roun' our heads. . . . I was skeered, an' Jehu say, 'tek dem to de swamp, an' don' come out 'til I don' hear no shoutin', or see no fire.' "

Leo was too stunned to even understand what she was saying, but Drew got to his feet, took John Andrew, who was now screaming from hunger as well as discomfort, and gave Hedy a hug with one arm. "Hedy! Hedy! Bless you, girl!"

Hedy smiled tentatively. "I did right? You ain't mad I took dem to de swamp? I di'n' let nothin' hurt 'em."

"You did just right. Go over there to Mrs. Sloan. Tell her I told you to ask her for something to eat . . . and feed this little fellow. He's about to shout the sky down."

Leo had one arm around Miranda, who was falling asleep in his arm, and his other hand rested on the blanket-covered body of Eloise. "She's . . . look what they've done to her, Drew."

Drew pulled his cousin away. "I know how you feel, Leo . . . I remember the day I found Laurel in the woods, but you can't stay here looking at her, imagining what she went through, hating yourself and everyone else for letting it happen to her."

"I can't help it. Look what they did to her! She . . . she was such a little . . . she couldn't have defended herself."

"I know," Drew said. At the time of Laurel's death no one had been able to talk to him, not even to give him advice that he knew was good. He hadn't been capable of listening, but he tried with Leo again. "You can't dwell on it, Leo—not right now. Look at the child in your lap. She needs you. Help her. Think of her—she's all you have of Eloise now . . . her and John Andrew. Don't let them be hurt any more than they have already been."

Leo stroked his daughter's hair. It was matted and tangled, and tears again ran from Leo's eyes as he thought of the shining crown of clean hair he thought of as being Eloise's. Eloise had doted on her daughter. Young as she was, the little girl was much like her mother. Leo gathered her up and hugged her so tightly she awakened and cried out. "I am so sorry, my sweet," Leo told her sobbing. "I hurt you. Oh, God, will it never stop!"

"Leo!" Drew said with authority. "Take Miranda to Mrs. Sloan and see that she is fed. Take care of your daughter."

Leo moved slowly, almost like a man asleep, but he took Miranda and walked to Mrs. Sloan. Drew watched him, knowing the horror that was whirling around inside him, and knowing that there was nothing he could do to help.

"We have to get a doctor out here for Daddy," George said as he came up to Drew. "We've done all we can, but his arm looks very bad."

Drew nodded. "We can send one of the bondsmen into town."

"Bondsmen!" George shouted. "You'd trust one of those damned savages? My God, I think you're demented. Look around you!"

"Not all of them took part, George. If it weren't for Hedy, John Andrew and Miranda wouldn't be alive. They would have burned in that house."

George looked at him, his mouth taut, his eyes blazing. "You're right. I know you are, Drew, but by God, I can't help it. I hate the damned bastards—every one of them!"

Drew couldn't answer him. "I'll see to getting a doctor out here. If you don't want me to send one of the darkies, I think Michael Jones would be willing to go."

"Has anyone seen Seth?" George asked suddenly.

"No."

George doubled his fist up. "When he's found, Drew, I'm going to kill him with my own hands. I want him to beg for death before I finish with him."

"It won't bring them back, George."

George let out a bitter laugh. "What does that mean? Would you rather I do nothing? Eloise is dead, Drew, and Velma, and, my God, Rob was nearly hacked to pieces. Grandma may die and Daddy! What else can a man do but extract revenge when there is nothing else?"

"I don't know, George. I'd help you hang Seth, but . . . all I know is there is never an end if revenge is extracted. It is not a part of justice, it is a continuation of hatred. It is a lifeblood to evil."

"Bullshit!" George spat, and walked off.

Drew sent Michael Jones into Charles Town for a doctor, then went to the group of tents and asked what he could do to help.

It was nearly dark again before the doctor had finished with Elizabeth and John. He came to talk to the three Manning men, who sat together on campstools. He was shaking his head sadly. "I couldn't save his arm," he said, wiping his hands on a clean towel.

"You . . . you cut it off," Leo said dazedly.

"If he has a chance of surviving, this is the only way. There was too much damage . . . he had been cut to the bone, and the wound was full of dirt. I'm sorry."

"What about Grandma?" Drew asked.

"I feel helpless, Mr. Manning. I wish I could give you better news. . . ."

"Will she live?" Drew asked, raising his voice.

"I just don't know. They are both in the hands of God. She was badly burned about the head and hands, but the worst damage seems to have been done inside. The heat of the fire has caused difficulty in breathing. Her hair will grow back—I imagine there will be considerable scarring, but . . ."

"You just don't know," Drew said.

"Neither of them can be left out here in the open," the doctor said.

"We'll be taking them to my home," Drew said. "It is the closest place to Willowtree."

"Well, in the meantime keep them as warm as you can. I have given Mrs. Sloan an ointment for the burns and instructions as to their care. I will come to your place tomorrow to see how they are doing."

Drew nodded.

With the help of some of the other men Drew, Leo, and George built the fires higher and put extra blankets on Elizabeth and John. Then they lay on the ground, exhausted, but too overwrought to fall asleep. George lay with his arms folded behind his head, looking up at the star-studded sky. "Drew, I'm sorry I took my outrage out on you. It wasn't deserved. We couldn't have gotten along without you—not now or before. I guess if we had listened to you from the start, this might not have happened. Maybe it is us I should be hating."

"Think of tomorrow, George. Let the last couple of days die," Drew said, and his voice trailed off as his eyes closed in sleep.

John Davis, Troy Sloan, Drake Peters, and several other men of the area had organized a search party shortly before dark. "Most likely the black beggars went off through the swamp. We're not certain how many of them we're lookin' for, but that Seth is their leader."

"How many aren't accounted for?"

"Ten," Troy said, "but most likely they didn't all run. We'll be findin' bones for days yet. Best as George could figure, the runners would have been Seth and maybe two or three others."

They discussed plans and the possibility that they might be dealing with the British agents as well as the slaves, then set off on their search.

As night fell, Seth and Folly emerged from the cavelike cellar Ben Logan had dug under his house to use as storage, or to hide fellow Negroes when the occasion demanded. "When we gonna meet up with Cuffee an' Tom an' Luck?" Folly asked as they ate.

"Soon," Seth said. "I'll tell you when."

Long after nightfall Seth asked his host for a supply of lamp oil, and he and Folly left to meet first Tom, then Cuffee, and last of all Luck.

Without warning Seth walked up to Luck and threw the oil over him, then set him afire. The others watched and listened in horror as the man ran and writhed and screamed in his death throes.

Tom and Cuffee backed away from him, their eyes large, all their trust gone.

"You," Seth said, pointing from one of them to the other, "Have no place in Africa. You belong here."

The two men stood together, neither of them speaking. Folly looked at them, then her face twisted and she threw herself at Seth, fingers curled into claws. She raked at him. "You nevah gonna take us! You gonna leave us heah to die!"

Seth stayed her attack on him easily. When she had quieted somewhat, he held both her wrists with one large, strong hand. "I'm not leaving you here to die, Folly. The Mannings will not kill you."

Tom managed a bitter, sarcastic laugh.

"I said Folly, not you two. I will tell you what to do. You can trust me, or you can stay here and risk a halter round your neck. Go north into the wilderness, or south to Spanish lands. Either way you will find a new life."

The two men stood still for a moment, looking at him, then first Tom's head went down, and Cuffee's followed. They shuffled their feet, almost in a dance step, thinking. Tom and Cuffee glanced at each other, then away, back again and away, a conversation going on with their eyes. The two nodded at Seth, again almost in choreographed movement, then began to walk south without looking back again. In just a few seconds Seth and Folly heard them talking, then laughing.

"None o' you is no good," Folly said with disgust. "Y'all gonna leave me here alone. Don' care what happens t'me. Masta don' kill me, my daddy will."

"No one is going to kill you, Folly. Trust me. You will be welcomed back to Willowtree with great affection." He spread his fingers wide and gestured expansively.

Folly spat on the ground at his feet.

"Little Folly girl, you have slain your abductor, the—"

"A-ducker? What dat?"

Seth laughed, relishing the superiority Elizabeth had so graciously given him. "It means I stole you away from the plantation. You couldn't help coming with me, 'cause I made you do it. When we stopped for the night, you took some oil and threw it on me, and burned me alive, 'cause I was such a terrible, mean man to you. Understand, Folly? You tell them you knew what I was going to do at Willowtree and tried to stop me. I took you, and then you killed me."

"You ain' nothin' but talk. You right heah, 'live as me."

"I won't be here much longer, Folly. There will just be you—and Luck, except that no one could tell for sure that is Luck. It's just a burned-up body, and you're going to tell Master Leo that is me."

Folly's eyes widened as she began to understand, then she was angry again. "I don' wanna go back! You promise me I kin go wiff you. I wanna go to Africky."

Seth's head went up. "I'm going alone. Tell them what I told you, Folly." He began to walk away from her.

She stood for a moment, then ran after him, jumping onto his back and beating him with her fists. Seth whirled, throwing her to the ground. Folly righted herself and began to get up. "I'm leaving, girl. Come at me again, and you won't wake up for a long time. Wouldn't hurt for them to find you with a few marks on that pretty face anyway," he said, and brought his big, hard hand across her face. Folly's head snapped back, and he drove his hand into the muscle of her arm. She cried out. Seth kept slapping her face, and punching her arms, until her lips were torn and bleeding. Her eye was swelling and almost shut. He slapped her once more, knocking her to the ground. As she lay there, he stood over her. "Don't you come after me this time. If you're smart, you'll tell them that's me. I don't care for myself. I'll be on my way to Africa." He walked away toward Charles Town and the Ashley River. He didn't look back.

Folly crumpled on the ground and sobbed.

The patrollers found her there the next morning asleep in almost the same spot Seth had left her.

They awakened her, shaking her roughly by the shoulders. Unclear and disoriented, Folly put her hands up to defend her bruised face.

John Davis turned from the burned corpse when he heard Drake Peters exclaim, "Damn, girl, what happened to you?"

Folly scrambled to her feet and began to talk. Babbling, she told the story Seth had told her to tell. Though the men did not hit her, they pushed her around, shoving her from one to the other as they fired questions at her.

"If we'd a mind we could hang you right here," Sloan sneered. "What do you think about doing a dance in the air, Folly? It's gonna hurt a whole lot. Who was with you?"

Folly was shaking; her eyes wild. "Seth!" she screeched.

"Who else? It wasn't just you and Seth," Drake said.

"Tom! Cuffee! They make me come. I don' want to!" Her whole body was now twitching.

"That girl's about to have a fit," John Davis said. "You know those darkies—ain't got a real good hold on themselves. Let her alone or she's going to be squirmin' all over the ground and can't talk."

Drake nodded at the body, kicking it so it was face up. "That look like Seth to you?" he asked the others.

"Looks like a charred pig," Troy Sloan said.

"He's about the right size. That Seth is—was a big son of a bitch," John said. "I say we take the girl, the body, and go back to Willowtree. Leo will be able to tell if that's Seth."

"What about the other two?" Troy asked.

Drake said, "We all need some rest. We can send the word along to other communities to hold 'em when they pass through, then we can go out after 'em again. That Cuffee hasn't enough sense to find his way out of the barn without help. He won't go far."

"What about Tom?"

"What about him?" Troy said and spat in Drake's direction. "He'll turn up, and then we'll hang him. Niggers like them two don't go far."

They packed Luck's remains on the back of the spare horse they had brought, and made Folly sit with the body touching her. She was nearly crazed with fear, but she couldn't move, for they had her hands bound to the saddle horn, and her feet tied with a rope that went under the horse's belly like a second cinch. "He gonna git me." She threw her head back and wailed.

As Folly was being taken back along the plantation road leading to Willowtree, Seth was sailing away from Charles Town bar. No one paid any attention to the small boat, or the black fisherman who manned it.

News of the massacre at Willowtree plantation had spread rapidly, and people were frightened, mistrustful of their own servants, guarding their houses and plantations. Patrollers were everywhere. Bert and Joanna Townshend heard the news at a dinner party at the Smiths' house in Charles Town. Joanna put her hand to her throat. "What happened to the family? The Mannings are my cousins!"

Bert put his arm around the back of his wife's chair. "Do you know if anyone was harmed?" he asked.

Reuben Smith's head was almost touching his chest when he said, "I am sorry. I did not know your connection with the Mannings or I would not have broken the news to you so harshly."

"Was anyone hurt?" Joanna asked more shrilly. "Please, I must know."

"I fear one of the Manning men was killed, another seriously injured, and two of the women died, but I do not know which of them it was. I wasn't told the names. Old Elizabeth Manning was badly burned. They don't know if she will live, and several of the servants died."

"Who? Who was killed?" Joanna said in what was little more than a whisper to herself.

Bert excused himself and her, begging to take her home, and then be on his way to aid his relatives. "Of course, they are known patriots, but at a time like this . . ." He shrugged and left the sentence unfinished.

When they were in their carriage, Joanna sat up straight, her eyes sparkling. "How shall we know if it was Drew who died?"

"I'll find out for you, my dear. You have been able to count on me thus far, haven't you?"

Joanna put her head back against his shoulder. "Yes." She drew in a deep breath through her perfectly even teeth, and closed her eyes. "Oh, Bert, if only it is true! For the first time in my entire life I shall be free of him!"

Bert kissed her lightly on the forehead. He thought, once free of Drew, perhaps for the first time she would belong to him, her husband.

29

The Mannings decided that those who had died in the uprising at Willow-tree would be buried there in the family cemetery. Elizabeth and John were taken to Drew's home just outside of Charles Town, and after a day of rest, Drew, George, Leo, Eugenia, and Bethany, who had come to Drew's from Charles Town, went back to Willowtree for the funerals.

The funeral procession came from the Davis plantation, the closest to Willowtree. Marla Davis had offered to see to the preparation of the bodies, and the offer had been gratefully accepted. Three newly made coffins, smelling of fresh wood, rested on the flatbed of a big dray decorated with pine boughs and flowers. The Manning men rode their finest steeds, and the women rode with their neighbors in highly polished black carriages. Nearly a hundred neighbors, friends, slaves, and family stood at the open graves while their minister prayed for eternal life for the dead and forgiveness to come to those left behind.

The Mannings listened and tried to find forgiveness within their hearts, but it was not a matter of simple forgiveness. It was difficult to forgive when one did not know who had wronged them, or suspected that perhaps many had been involved. Drew Manning did not believe the slaves of Willowtree had joined in a plot to massacre their masters, yet they had been the instruments of death. Had it been Seth? Alone? Had it been the interference of the British agents? The Tories, their own friends and neighbors from a happier time? How did one forgive when one did not know whom to forgive, or if the deed were forgivable?

It was a quiet and sad group of men and women who returned the next day to Drew's house. Eugenia and Bethany went up to sit with Elizabeth and John as soon as they returned. Leo, as he did too frequently, went to his room, preferring to be alone. George and Drew went to Drew's study. Drew poured them whiskey, then sat down.

Staring out the window into the bright, cheerful sunlight, George asked, "Did you know it would be like this when you first espoused the patriot cause, Drew?"

"How could I know, George? If I had, I'd have been a madman to encourage us to reach this day."

"I wasn't thinking quite that specifically. What I meant was that you used to tell us of the outlaw raids, and the homes burned and looted, the women raped and murdered, and we all thought you exaggerated, but . . . you have already experienced what we are now experiencing, haven't you?"

"It is different when it is your own family," Drew said. "I have seen carnage, it's true. Some of those experiences I will take with me to my own grave, but I don't think the patriot cause is the only way this would have happened. We are too discontent under British rule. Another law, another tax, and the agitation would have begun again."

George nodded. "I can't argue. I suppose what I hate so much is that though we are fighting for freedom from Britain, we are killing our own. It is the blood of our fathers and brothers and sisters soaking into this soil, into this land we want to represent liberty."

"It is a small word that carries a heavy legacy. It has a far different meaning and import to us now than it did when you and Rob and Leo and I fought each other under the Liberty Tree. I wonder what greater import it will have ten years from now."

"Or a hundred," George added, and smiled. The whiskey was having a soothing effect, as was the talk. "Gwynne knows what has happened by now, I suppose. Will she and the children be coming here?"

"No. I think they are safer at Cherokee, and there is little Gwynne can do. She is very worried about Grandma. I had to promise to send her daily messages. That will last a couple of weeks, then my men are all going to rebel. That's a long trip to keep my wife posted on Grandma's progress."

"Will you really do that?"

"Not quite. I will keep her posted, but not daily. It is too strenuous a trip for that. Given a little time, she'll understand. It's just that she feels isolated up there . . . my mother used to complain about the same thing."

George shrugged. "Aunt Georgina got used to it. I don't remember hearing her complain. Gwynne will get used to it, too." He got up, stretched. "I'm going upstairs to see Daddy and Grandma. Join me?"

John Manning was sitting up in bed, the stump of his arm bandaged. His face was pale and gaunt, but in his eyes the light of life shone strongly. He smiled as George and Drew walked into the room.

Eugenia, still jittery and tending to hysteria, got up, and fussily rearranged the two straight-backed chairs in the room. "Sit down, Drew. George, are you feeling all right? No one has been seeing after you. . . . I know I should be, but . . ."

" 'Genia, dear, sit down and relax. The boys are all right," John said, and patted the side of his bed with his one hand. He looked to the boys. "I must say you two did come through it relatively unscathed—a few bruises and cuts. I congratulate you, and I thank you. In the last few days, 'Genia has been telling me that none of us would likely be alive were it not for you and Leo."

"All that counts now is that we are still here, you are on the mend, and there's a new day ahead for the Mannings."

John laughed. "It sounds to me, Drew, that you need an excuse to use that toast. 'Genia, surely we have brandy or port or something around here that we can drink."

"John, do you think you should?"

"You have given me liberal quantities of spirits to ease the pain, my dear. Am I not to be allowed a single drop for pleasure?"

Eugenia gave him a shy smile.

When Drew got to Elizabeth's room, she had just awakened from one of her frequent naps. It was difficult for him to look at this poor, damaged creature that lay on Elizabeth's bed, and think of her as his grandmother. Her hands were bandaged up to her elbows, and her scalp was an angry mass of burned flesh.

"Drew," she said in a whispered voice. The fire had left her with some difficulty in breathing.

He came to the bed, leaned over, and kissed her on the side of her face that had not been burned. "How are you feeling today, Grandma? Is the pain any less?"

"Yes, it is a little better—every time I awaken from sleep, it seems to be a little better." She paused, breathing rapidly, trying to catch her breath.

"Don't try to talk, Grandma. It tires you."

"I am not going to give in to this, Drew. You shall just have to be patient with me, and allow me time to catch my breath between sentences"

—she began to laugh—"sometimes between words." And then she dissolved into a fit of coughing.

Drew's impulse was to stop her again, but he sat back, trying not to allow her discomfort to bother him. He struggled to think of her and talk to her as he had always done in the past. "You're incorrigible, Grandma."

Elizabeth gasped and panted, her eyes steadily on him. "What I am is a frightful-looking old woman, Drew. But I am not going to add to that handicap by being a retreating frightful-looking old woman!"

"Bravo!" Drew said, and laughed. "I think perhaps you will mend quite well, after all."

"Were you in doubt, Drew?"

Drew hesitated for a moment, then again thought that before the fire, he would not have hesitated to tell her what he had been thinking. "Yes, for a time, I was. I wasn't so certain you'd have the will to heal this time, Grandma."

"Because I am an old woman?"

"No, no, because . . ." He stumbled over the words again.

Elizabeth's eyes lit up, and she smiled. "I see! You are astute . . . my vanity."

Drew managed to blush, which caused his grandmother to laugh, then cough again.

When the spasm had subsided, she said, "Of course, you are correct. When I am alone here, I give that a good deal of thought." She was quiet for a moment. "This time, I will not have my Pelagie around to keep my spirits up . . . I don't know how I shall manage."

"No one will ever take Pelagie's place with you, Grandma, but perhaps Hedy would be a good woman to have with you. She has shown considerable courage and loyalty through this," Drew said.

Elizabeth smiled, then dabbed gingerly at her eyes. "Hedy was the one Pelagie herself had selected to replace her when the time came. She . . . she was always certain I would outlive her, and that there would come a day someone else would be my companion and servant. It is nice that you should choose the same girl."

"Then you would be agreeable if I made arrangement for Hedy to serve you?" Drew asked, and with Elizabeth's affirmative answer he rose to leave. "I'll let you take another of your miraculous little naps, then."

"Drew, wait just one moment. There is something I want to say to you. I have been wanting to for days, but I haven't been able to stay awake long enough to manage it till today. I want you to go home."

Drew sat down and just looked at her in amazement.

Elizabeth lowered her eyes. "I know this is your home, but that isn't what I meant. Nathaniel comes in here every day and sits by my bedside watching and worrying. It is no good for him, Drew. I shall be well again, and that is the time when Nathaniel and I shall have to go over the details of that terrible night, and lay to rest all the ghosts and specters that haunt him. Right now, however, he belongs at Cherokee, where he can run, and will not dwell so heavily on this tragedy. And Gwynne needs you."

"But so do you."

"No, I don't. I have George and Leo. Of course, I am assuming that you would have no objection to leaving us totally in charge and possession of your house."

Drew waved his hand at her. "You know that you all are welcome—forever, if need be."

"I thought as much. Then you have no just cause for lingering."

"But it is such a burden, Grandma. There is only Eugenia and Bethany to care for you and Uncle John, and Leo, though he is not physically injured, is not at all himself. Leo is at Willowtree so often trying to see to the bondsmen that were left, and—"

"Leo is thinking of rebuilding Willowtree, but that is something we shall all have to discuss and decide upon. As for the rest, we will grieve together, and we will mend together. Your task is elsewhere now, Drew. Don't neglect it."

"I'll think about it, Grandma. You may be right, but I shall have to give it some thought. I do agree with you about Nathaniel, and no matter what I decide for myself, I will see to it that Nathaniel goes home to Cherokee and his sisters and brothers."

"I am going to sleep now, Drew. I am sorry, but I seem to have worn myself out," she said as her eyes were closing.

The week before Christmas, Drew visited Elizabeth's room with a letter in his hand. "I have come to say good-bye this time, Grandma. As usual you seem to have sensed what was about to happen. I received this letter from Ned this morning by messenger. There is a good deal of Tory activity in our area. He suggests I return. A suggestion from Ned is the equivalent of a strong request from anyone else."

"When will you leave?"

"I had planned to remain here until after Christmas, but in view of this I shall leave tomorrow. Nathaniel and I will spend Christmas on the road somewhere between here and Cherokee. It is not a good thing for Nathaniel, but I can't see anything else for it."

"It may be a very good thing for Nathaniel, Drew," Elizabeth said.

Since their last long talk ten days before, Elizabeth had made great progress. Although she was still occasionally breathless, and probably would be for the rest of her life, and her voice had taken on a throaty, soft quality, she was much easier in talking and was now able to sit in a chair and enjoy the view for short periods of time. The burns were beginning to heal, and she was talking about buying a wig, and having new gowns made for her that had high collars and would hide most of the scarring along the one side of her face. "We too often have a mistaken idea of what Christmas must be, Drew, and perhaps this is a very good opportunity for you to show Nathaniel that there is a good deal more to Christmas than the celebrations he is accustomed to. The Christ child was born in a time of difficulty for his family, Drew, just as we are now experiencing difficulty, and he was born into a world struggling for a freer spirit. The Holy Child was born to carry heavy burdens; His life from the beginning was one to be marred by the constant presence of strife and of obstacles to be overcome. If there is a valid message in Christmas which we repeatedly ignore with our merrymaking, it is that from birth each of us begins a quest. It is courage, faith, hope, and determination that will allow us to rise out of the primeval muck of commonness, and that we are given an example of in this Babe, whose birthday we celebrate, so that we know how, and can see that we can succeed. Take this Christmas with Nathaniel, Drew. You'll be on a road with no place to lay your head, unless someone offers you hospitality. Celebrate as you never have before, and learn."

Drew said nothing for a long time. He was remembering another Christmas when Elizabeth had given to Nathaniel Dancer a very special view of this holiday. He wasn't quite sure why, but he felt very humble in his grandmother's presence today, and merely said, "I will, Grandma."

As he went to his room to pack to leave for the Upcountry, Drew remembered Star Dancer telling him how she had let the Archer, a constellation of stars, guide her, that she had heard the voice of the Spirit within her and she had followed. Perhaps his grandmother was telling him the same thing. It was not always necessary, or even advantageous, for a man to celebrate by his own design. Perhaps there were times when to celebrate was to follow an unseen path and listen for the Spirit to speak within him.

The two set off for the Upcountry with Drew in somewhat of a bemused mood. He was very conscious of "listening" within himself without the slightest idea of what he might hear, or how he'd even know if some message were imparted to him. Drew had had little experience with this sort of thing. When he wanted something, he asked help of God, and when

his life was blessed, he thanked God, but Drew had never thought of
listening for his Maker's voice within.

Drew told Nathaniel what his Nonnie had said. "Now, I don't know
how to do some of the things your Nonnie does, Nathaniel, but we'll try.
Are you game?"

Nathaniel smiled happily, a sight Drew had seen all too infrequently
since the night of the uprising. "I know how to do it, Daddy," he said.

"You do?"

"Yes, and I'll show you. Nonnie has told me about this lots of times. We
read all about King Arthur and Jesus, and Moses and Abraham. Abraham
had to listen a whole lot."

Drew laughed to himself. "Hmmm, I have a feeling I'm one of those
who's going to have to listen a whole lot, and then maybe even have
someone else tell me what I heard."

The weather was cool and changeable, but each night they were able to
sleep in the open, Drew did. Nathaniel had already lost the forlorn look of
confusion and sorrow he had carried too long for a child. Whether Elizabeth had been speaking figuratively or literally to Drew about Christmas,
she was a wise old woman who had once again set both her grandson and
her great-grandson on a quest that renewed their spirits.

The last night before they would arrive at Cherokee, Nathaniel and
Drew slept in the open despite the bitter cold and a biting wind that kept
them close to their fire. Nathaniel lay snuggled in his father's bedroll,
looking up at the stars. "How do you tell when something is bad, Daddy?"
he asked.

"There is usually something that tells you. Maybe if you said something
it would hurt someone's feelings, and wouldn't do any good. Or if you take
something, you would be depriving someone of something that was rightfully his, so you don't steal. The commandments give us a pretty good
rule."

"Then it was bad when I shot Jehu," Nathaniel said.

"You didn't know you were shooting Jehu, Nathaniel. You thought you
were shooting a man who was going to hurt Grandma and Aunt Eugenia
and yourself."

"Then it isn't bad to shoot people I don't like?"

Drew made a face and expelled a held breath. "Not exactly. You have to
have a much better reason than that."

"Like what?"

"Well, take the uprising. It would be wrong to just go out and shoot one
of the bondsmen, even if we didn't like him, because he has not threatened

us in any way. But the night of the uprising a few very bad men, who wanted to cause trouble, got everyone hurting each other and burning the house. So we were either going to stop those men, or we were going to get killed. So we stopped them. It was still a bad thing, and we must never use extreme measures unless there are extreme causes, and it can't be just our opinion, it must be so extreme that anyone can see there is no choice but to defend yourself."

"What if you like the person who gives you no choice?"

"You hope that never happens," Drew said, wishing fervently his son would get sleepy and stop asking him questions he was hard pressed to answer.

"What if it does?"

"Then you must ask yourself which of your lives is worth more, and since God gave you only one to call your own, you must preserve it, for He knows better than you why He created it."

"Golly!" Nathaniel breathed. "That must be what the rebels think when they kill the Tories."

Drew said nothing. Nathaniel was moving closer and closer into an area he did not like to think about or examine. "Go to sleep. It's late."

"Don't you have to try out a lot of bad things before you can tell what the good ones are?"

"No."

"How can you tell if you don't try them—I mean the ones that the commandments don't tell you about?"

"Go to sleep, Nathaniel," Drew said, and rolled over with his back to the boy. "That is not something you need to worry about yet."

But it was something Nathaniel Dancer was worrying about. He would never forget seeing Jehu's face on the body of a man he had thought was an enemy. He had tried to do something good, and it had turned out to be something bad. How was he ever to be sure the reverse wasn't true, unless he tried that, too? Two feelings welled up in Nathaniel Dancer as he lay there and thought while his father slept. One was a nagging feeling somewhere in his vitals that didn't like what he was thinking, and the other was something that made his eyes shine and his heart beat a little faster, because he realized how powerful his decision could be. For the first time he knew what it was like to have a secret person living inside the one everyone saw and knew as Nathaniel Dancer. He should have felt very good, but he only felt restless, and he couldn't sleep.

Gwynne took one look at him when he and Drew came home, and began to scold at the same time she was hugging and kissing him. "You look like you haven't slept in weeks! Go tell Penny to have a bath drawn for you—and you climb right into bed, young man. I will be up to see you . . . and give you a very special dinner in bed. We have a lot to talk about."

"Where's Mary?"

"She is with Jane in the playroom. She has been watching for you every day since I told her you and Daddy were coming home. But, Nathaniel, you will have to be careful what you tell her. Daddy has told me what happened at Willowtree, and that is very frightening."

"I won't scare Mary. She isn't a man yet."

Gwynne smiled and suppressed a laugh. "No, she isn't. I'm glad to know you understand."

As soon as Nathaniel left the room, Gwynne moved into Drew's arms. "I am so relieved that you are home, and I can touch you and know you are all right."

"You didn't have to wait until the boy left," Drew said and kissed her.

"I knew I couldn't touch you without letting it show how terribly frightened I've been, and I got a letter from Elizabeth in which she said to say as little to Nathaniel as possible about the uprising until he talked to me. I trusted her, Drew, but I wasn't able to keep it inside unless I stayed away from you."

"That isn't very complimentary, love," he said teasingly.

"To me, it isn't. I have no control over mind or heart where you are concerned."

"For that I am thankful. While Penny is bathing our son, would you like to perform the same service for me?"

Gwynne made a face, "Poor baby, do you have a difficult time scrubbing your back?"

Drew grinned at her and pulled her close against him. "Among other things." He kissed her again. "For tonight, I want to think of no one but you, and nothing but being with you. Tomorrow is soon enough to talk about Willowtree, and about what is happening here. Before we go upstairs, I want to tell Ned that I won't meet with him until tomorrow."

Gwynne nodded and went upstairs to have his bath drawn while he went to see Ned. She trusted his intentions, but she wondered if he would actually be following her upstairs before many hours had passed. But she had underestimated the effect the events of the past months had had on Drew, and he was upstairs before she had even given the order for the bathwater to be warmed.

Gwynne stood for a moment in the hallway, a bemused look on her face.

The idea that Drew might want or need her as much as she needed him made her feel suddenly shy and bold at once. Quickly, before she had time to think of what she was doing, she asked the servants to bring the large copper tub to the room, then went to the bedroom.

She felt naked and exposed, all her emotions fully displayed, and Drew did nothing to help her. He stood near the bed, his eyes dark brown and warm on her. He smiled slightly and put his arms out to her.

Gwynne's dark blue eyes shone as she moved toward him. He had taken his shirt off, and Gwynne unconsciously reached out to run the tips of her fingers across the well-defined muscles of his upper arms and chest. Drew watched her with pleasurable amusement. Then he slowly, carefully, opened the buttons on her blouse. As he pulled the garment down over her shoulders, she swayed toward him, her eyes closed, her lips curved in a smile. He ran his fingers along the curve of her throat and bent to kiss her upturned mouth. Gwynne melted into his arms, the warmth of her flesh blending with his; then she pulled away from him, breathless, agitated. "The . . . the servants . . . the bath . . . I ordered the copper tub. They'll be bringing your bath. We can't let them find us . . . we . . ."

Drew smiled and hugged her to him. "You ordered the copper tub?"

Gwynne giggled.

Drew placed his hand beneath her chin and raised her head until she was looking into his eyes. "Should we disappear into the dressing room until the tub is in place? I don't believe I am in the mood to sit here with you in gentlemanly fashion for the benefit of the servants."

At her nod he picked her up and carried her to the dressing room, placing her gently on a chaise longue.

Nuzzling each other as they undressed, they heard the busy sounds of the servants setting up the bath, and then leaving with a definite click of the door latch.

"I think we can come out of hiding now." Drew laughed.

Gwynne quickly picked up her robe, but Drew stayed her hand. "No. I want to see you." He put his arm around her and led her to the large tub that stood in the middle of the room.

The water was warm and filled with soapy bubbles. With a twinkle in her eye Gwynne reached across the narrow space and took from her dressing table a bottle of scent. Before Drew could do anything she had poured several drops of the fluid into the bath water. "I want to smell good if I am to bathe, Drew," she said, laughing lightly.

"Must I?" Drew asked, and pulled her down into the water and on top of him. He scooped up a handful of soap and blew it at her. With bubbles on her forehead, nose, and chin, Gwynne came up with her hands cupped with water. She tossed it at him, laughing and squealing as he tickled her under the water. They laughed and played like two children. Gwynne had forgotten all shyness and self-consciousness, her hands roving over Drew as she wished, touching, caressing, fondling, until he deftly pulled her atop him, his hands cupped around her breasts. Gwynne eased herself down until she was astride his hips. They moved together, the warm soapy bath water making their skin feel silky and soft. Trembling, Gwynne leaned forward and lay against him until the water cooled. Drew reached for the heavy towels left for him, and wrapped her in them, and carried her to their bed. He lay down on the bed beside her, his hands running over her body, drying her off. He kissed her face, then followed the trail of his hands, kissing her neck and chest, each of her breasts, his tongue teasing her nipples into tight buds. He kissed her on the mouth, his tongue probing, darting, tantalizing. Gwynne moved beneath him, her legs wrapping around his narrow hips and drawing him closer.

Drew's fingers twined in her long dark hair. "Gwynne, Gwynne, I love you."

"Hold me, Drew. Hold me closer," she murmured.

He thrust deep within her. Each of them was breathless and lost in the wonder and magic of the other. With a shuddering burst of passion they finally lay still, entwined in one another's arms, quiet, warmed, and loved, unwilling to release each other. They fell asleep still embracing. When they awakened it was dark, and long past suppertime. Drew kissed her on the tip of the nose. "It's good to be home," he said. He got up out of bed, reached for a robe, and tossed hers to her. "I am hungry, Mrs. Manning. Would you accompany me to the pantry?"

In the darkened, quiet house, they tiptoed down the stairs, enjoying their midnight raid on the pantry. They ate cold fried chicken, and the remains of a salad, then went back upstairs to their bedroom to talk and laugh and make love long into the night.

Ned Hart was not happy about Drew's delay, but he understood it. Already this had become an ugly war, with friends and family taking the brunt of the fighting more so than Britain, and the news he had to tell would make it no better. He resigned himself to waiting until Drew was ready to listen.

Drew was ready the following morning.

"It looks like the activity is fairly simple, Drew. There isn't much in the way of real fighting, it is more attack and run. I've talked to a few of the Regulators, and it looks like a supply-gathering mission with two ends in mind. One, of course, is to accumulate as many arms and as much ammunition as they can, but the other is to assure that the known patriot houses have none, or as little as possible."

"So, you think it is only a matter of time before Cherokee is paid a visit by these marauding Tories, most likely one of whom is Arthur."

Ned shrugged. "It figures. Most of what they take goes right to the British outposts, but some of it is stored in homes like Manning. These little attacks that aren't a whole lot more, for the most part, than annoyances, come from the Tory supply houses. Now, I know you told Arthur that you don't store anything here for the cause, but he won't believe that —no one will. Even I wouldn't if I didn't know it first hand, Drew. You've been too active for too long."

With a dry laugh Drew said, "You sure do pay for a long time for each decision you make."

"Especially if what you do serves somebody else's needs."

"I don't really believe Arthur has any particular desire to see Cherokee attacked, Ned."

Ned shook his head. "Don't be too sure, Drew. This has become a nasty war. We've got some real highfalutin slogans, but that's mostly the doin' of those Yankees up north. We're at the throats of our neighbors an' friends. It's a mean little war, and the wrong people are getting hurt."

"The Yankees are fighting for the same things we are, Ned," Drew said tiredly.

"Like hell they are! That's one mistake you better never make, Drew. They are fighting for what they want, and couldn't give a spit in hell what goes on here unless it serves them. It's always been that way, an', by God, it always will be. When it suited them in seventy they left us with our drawers flappin' in the breeze, but, by God, when Boston Harbor was closed, then they were all friendly-like, tellin' us we're all in it together. Self-servers, Drew. Always was, and will be. We're different breeds."

"Maybe, but that doesn't solve our problems here. What's being done about the raids, and how serious are they?"

"For quite a while it was nothing to bother about—a few storerooms broken into, a few muskets here and there and some powder. Lately, however, the tenor has changed a little. The patriots are getting a little tired of having their fields all tramped up, and their possessions taken, so there have been a few skirmishes on individual farms and plantations. That led to a little barn-burning, and a little musket-shot. It's getting out of hand. Basil Robinson, your old friend John Haynes, Jack Kimble, and a few others are forming a group, and say they're going to teach the Tories a lesson."

"Basil and my father used to be good friends," Drew said.

"No more. Basil is hopping mad. He says Arthur is behind all these raids hereabouts." He shook his head. "For the life of me, I can't see Arthur out riding the roads with a band. Every time I think of him, it is in your Daddy's study with a book in his hand." Again Ned shook his head. "Just can't judge what'll make a man change his whole life. Anyway, your Daddy and Basil don't even speak these days, 'cept to call each other traitors."

"Where do the patriots meet?" Drew asked.

"Sometimes at Kimble's, sometimes over to Jasper Spikes's house. You remember Bart Cole's sister, Lisa? Well, she married Jasper. They got a fine family now."

"What about Ben Boggs? Is he with them?"

"Off and on. He lives a bit of a far piece, but you never know. Just when you think it's time to count Ben out, he shows up. Ben's got three kids of his own. Two little boys an' a girl," Ned said, and scratched at his chin. "Now Eli must be about Nathaniel's age, an' Asher is somewhere around six. Star Dancer got that far without an Indian name in the bunch, but then that little girl came along, and Star Dancer said that the babe was special, that she had the mark of the Spirit. She named her Onawa."

"Onawa . . . what does that mean?"

"The girl is supposed to be quick witted, an observer of life's dangers and joys. Hope Star Dancer's right. That ain't a bad way to be," Ned said cheerfully.

"Where's the next meeting being held, and when?"

Ned grinned. "Just happens it's tonight. That's why I was havin' fits when you said you didn't want to talk about this right away. It's over at Jack Kimble's house."

"We'll go," Drew said.

"You want me with you?" Ned asked.

"Yes. I want you to be aware of what is going on. You'll have to keep on handling Cherokee while I'm gone. You'll be able to plan better if you know what we'll be doing."

"Wheww," Ned said with an exaggerated swipe across his brow. "I thought for a minute you wanted to mount these old bones on the back of a horse and ride me across the countryside. I mean to tell you, boy, I'm too old! Just thinking about it makes my joints hurt!"

As a result of their attendance at the meeting, Drew was gone from

Cherokee at least two or three days and nights each week. He and his friends patrolled the roads and occasionally raided one of the Tory houses. Ostensibly their objective was to gain additional names for the list of those having taken the Oath of Loyalty. In the process of threatening and badgering men to take the Oath or soundly refuse it, they searched houses, confiscated arms, and caused general havoc on the farms wherever they went.

In less than two weeks after the start of the patrols, there was retaliatory action. Drew and half a dozen other men who had been at the meetings, including Jack Kimble, Jasper Spikes, John Haynes, who had married Basil Robinson's daughter Hope, and old Jed Blakely, rode together. On what had become a regular patrol of the Upcountry roads and byways, they came upon a group of Tories riding toward Basil Robinson's house. Both groups of men scattered into the cover of the trees as soon as they saw each other.

"That seals it!" Jasper whispered in the darkness. "They're up to no good. Let's get 'em!"

"Show 'em what a real American's made of," John said aloud.

War cries pierced the air. From out of cover the men wheeled their horses. Several shots were heard as they plunged into the darkness of the trees on the other side of the road where the Tories had gone.

Drew whipped his horse with the long end of his reins and charged after a man he could hear better than see. Behind him he heard another volley of musket fire and a scream, horses thrashing through the brush, and men shouting. He turned the horse sharply, then again, cutting his man off. At close quarters he saw the pale outline of the face of a young boy no more than sixteen or seventeen. "Damn!" he swore, and lunged for the boy, dropping his musket to the ground. He shoved the boy off his horse. The kid struggled, but Drew wrestled him to the ground and pinned him. "What's your name?"

"None of your affair!" the boy screeched.

"If you don't want a thrashing that'll leave you sore for a month, it's my affair. What's your name?"

"Tobin! Tobin Fisher."

"Jeremy Fisher's son?" Drew asked, surprised, and wasn't sure why he was. Jeremy Fisher was another of his father's friends. "You tell your daddy for me, that if I ever run into you on the roads at night again, I'll come to your house and take it out of his hide!" He released the boy slowly, guarding against the young man's jumping him. "Now, git!"

The boy scrambled to his feet, ran a few steps toward his horse, then stopped. "Who are you, mister?"

"Manning! Drew Manning."

"Oh, jeez, my Daddy told me about you," the boy said, and raced for his horse.

Drew fumbled around in the darkness trying to find his musket, then mounted his horse again and went in search of his companions. He found them back on the road.

"Hey! There he is," Jasper yelled. "We thought we lost you, boy."

"No. I was a little busy putting the fear of the Lord into Jeremy Fisher's kid."

"You shoulda blown his breeches off," Jack Kimble said. "That damned Jeremy's a yellow-bellied coward. Mighta taught him a lesson if his son came home with his skinny backside stickin' out."

"I think I got one of 'em. Couldn't see in the dark, but he sure did let out a holler," Jason Frobish, who was riding on this patrol, said, then accosted Drew. "How've you been, Drew? I haven't seen you in years, but I sure have heard about you. Ol' Ned keeps me up to date on your doings. Don't s'pose you've been to any country socials lately?"

Drew shook his head and shook Jason's hand. "How about the fiddle, do you still play?"

"Me an' Daddy still tune 'em up every chance we get. Whyn't you get us up there at Cherokee an' let us show you? You give the party, we'll give the music."

"You have a deal. I'll tell Gwynne. It's been a long while since we've had a get-together at Cherokee. It wouldn't hurt for us to keep these Upcountry families close, anyway."

"Whatever you say, Drew. I don't know what the rest of you fine fellows are going to do, but I'm heading home. See y'all," he said, and dug his heels into his horse.

Drew left shortly after. He took the horse to its stall and found Levi waiting for him. "What're you doing here, Levi? This is a nice surprise. I thought I was going to be rubbing this old horse myself."

Levi giggled. "No, suh, Missy Gwynne she been nudgin' Mistah Hart all night. He say if she cain't sleep, he cain't sleep, an' if he cain't sleep, Levi ain't gonna sleep, neither."

"Maybe now we can all get some sleep." Drew hurried to the house and found Gwynne standing near the front window peeking out into the darkness. He opened the door and she ran into his arms. "Drew, you're home. Thank God."

"Has something happened?" he asked, pulling her away from him so that he could see her face. "Are the children all right?"

"Nothing is wrong here, I was just so worried about you. You've been gone a long time."

He took her arm and led her to the parlor. "Come here, Gwynne, and sit with me. We need to talk. You can't do this every time I leave the house on a patrol."

"I'm so afraid you won't come back, Drew . . . or that something will happen to you. I couldn't stand it, Drew."

"And making yourself sick with fright isn't going to help, Gwynne."

"I can't help it," she cried, and buried her face in his jacket front.

"You can, and you will," Drew said sternly. "You can either accept that we are at war, and I will be doing my part, or you can live in Charles Town until it is over. What you cannot do, Gwynne, is wait at the door every night I am with the patrol, scaring yourself to death that I will not be coming back. No one can live every day in terror. It will destroy you, Gwynne, and I won't let that happen."

"You'd just send me away," Gwynne said, tears running down her face, her voice resentful.

"Yes. You can't worry about what you don't know."

"I don't know anything now! That's what's so frightening. I don't know what's going on out there in the dark. I imagine all kinds of terrible things!"

"The 'terrible' thing that happened tonight was that I tackled a young boy, knocked him off his horse, threatened him, and sent him running home with a message to his daddy not to send him out on a man's work again."

Gwynne blinked her eyes at him, then giggled. "You did that? That's what you were doing tonight?"

"That's what I did. I also rode through some bushes and a stand of trees."

She looked at him with disbelief. "Nothing else. There was no shooting or anything dangerous?"

"Nothing that I was a part of," he said.

"But there was, wasn't there?"

"There was some shooting. One of the Tories might have been hit, but none of us were."

"But it could have been one of you. It could have been you, Drew. How do you expect me not to worry, when that could happen at any time?"

Drew clasped his hands between his knees, his head down. "Gwynne, I believe in what we are fighting for. You are going to have to decide if you do—not because you're my wife and I believe, but because you do—or don't. If you do, then the risks that come with the fighting must be taken. The cause can't be yours because it is mine, Gwynne. Either you want to fight for independence—or you don't."

"I . . . I've never thought about it for myself, Drew. Whatever you wanted . . . wherever you are, then . . . that's where I will be . . . and what I want."

"It can't be that way this time. You may have to go on alone, and if you should come to that, you have to know that independence is worth whatever it costs."

Gwynne shook her head frantically, her face pale. "I can't say that, Drew. I couldn't . . . nothing is worth you to me. Nothing. No one, nothing at all!"

Drew nodded his head. "Then we had better go to bed and get some sleep. The children will be up calling for you in a few hours, and there isn't anything else for us to say about this."

"You're angry with me. Drew, please . . ."

"I'm not angry, Gwynne. I had hoped we were of one mind, but I am not angry."

The sorties continued, and grew more volatile. Jasper Spikes was slightly wounded one night early in March. As he was healing from his wound, a band of Tories rode onto his property and burned his barn and silo to the ground, destroying all the stored grain in his silo.

A meeting of the patriots was held the next day. As one they agreed that it was time to stop the little skirmishes along the roads.

"Damn, it's almost like a game. We send a few men out, and they do, and we dance around each other. Then, by God, they make a sneak attack like this on a helpless man and his family," Jason said. "We're damned fools if we take that."

John looked around the room at his fellow patrollers, then at Drew. "Sorry, Drew, but sooner or later somebody's got to say it. We all know who's the leader of these raids, and we all know from where they get their supplies."

"You mean my brother," Drew said, sighing. "I knew this would come sooner or later."

"Well, now, there ain't a one of us here that wouldn't understand if you were to just not show up the night we ride over to Manning," said Jed Blakely. "Can't very well ask a man to attack his own kin."

The others murmured agreement. Then Jack Kimble said, "With or without Drew's help, we're going to have to call in everyone we can. This won't be one of the ordinary patrols. I can't speak for the rest of you, but I'm not going to be comfortable if we go with less than twenty or more men, and plenty of powder."

"We can always call from a neighboring district. Ben Boggs will be with us on this, and he can bring near half a dozen from his area," John said.

"Put out the word, and we'll meet again. Once we get an idea of how many will be coming in, we'll need a place for them to stay." Jack pulled out a letter as he spoke. "The news is a bit long in getting to us, but Mr. Rutledge informs us that Savannah has fallen to the British, and he believes that there will be fierce activity aimed at the Upcountry, and then they will attempt to take Charles Town once they have separated the strength of the Upcountry from that of the Lowlands. All of this means that our Tory bands are going to be encouraged in their attacks, and we must stop them before the British decide to make better use of them."

The men continued to talk about the time of their attack, and the plan. Drew listened in silence. Before he left that meeting this night, he promised himself he would make his decision and tell his companions. Nearly an hour later Jack Kimble called for a bottle of whiskey. "We've worked enough for one night. Let's do a little celebrating."

Drew stood up, his hands clasped hard behind his back. His face was serious, and he felt as though the words were being pulled from his mouth. "I'll be with you when you mount the attack."

30

Gwynne was waiting for him when he came home with a letter from Elizabeth. "This came minutes after you left. I thought you would want the news, so I waited for you," she said with a coolness that was not usual in her.

Drew just looked at her. There was nothing to be said, and the coolness had been between them since the night she had waited for him by the door in fear and dread. "I thank you for your consideration, Gwynne," he said stiffly, taking the bulky letter from her.

"Shall I now retire to my room to prove to you that I waited for no other reason?"

As she passed him, he reached out and caught hold of her hand. "There is no need for sarcasm, Gwynne. I am sorry you have not understood what I was trying to tell you, but the coldness between us and the sarcastic remarks will do neither of us good."

"As usual you are right, Drew—you nearly always are—but I can't help what I say. It is not merely sarcasm, Drew. It is a reflection of what I feel inside. I know what you want of me, but you do not understand my espousal of the cause. Perhaps it is true that my loyalty is more to you than to any principle, but you have severed our unity by demanding that I espouse the cause for my own reasons. I do not have the fervor for politics in the same way you do. My politics are within the confines of this family, but don't ever mistake that there are politics and that my arena is a real one. I have taken the cause to my heart. My sin is that I have not taken it in the same manner you have."

Drew remained seated, holding on to her wrist. She waited for a moment, then said, "Have you nothing to say, Drew? I expected a lecture on the folly of my ways. Surely, in your view, what I have said must be terribly ignorant and naive."

"Gwynne, don't do this—to either of us. Come, sit down again, we'll read Grandma's letter."

She hesitated; then, with a trace of sullenness still remaining, she sat in a chair distant from him. "All right. I am listening."

Not knowing what to say to her to heal the rift between them, Drew opened the letter and began to read to himself. As soon as he had finished the first part of the letter, he said, "I am sorely tired of bad news."

"What has happened now? Is Elizabeth all right? Her recovery is still progressing?"

"The family is all right, and Grandma is doing quite well, she says. She has had a wig made and is pleased with it, but there was a terrible fire in Charles Town right after Nathaniel and I left. She says that an entire area around Church Street was destroyed . . . nearly two hundred and fifty houses were destroyed. It was arson. The British sailors who come ashore come to do more than gather supplies."

Gwynne closed her eyes. "There is nothing so foul, so low, they will not stoop to in order to conquer us."

"Arson seems to be the main form of attack at present. Uncle John and Grandma have decided that they would be safer in Charles Town despite the fire, for they would have help there they could not count on at our house outside the city. I suppose it is a good move—though I don't know how any move can be judged properly in these times."

"Does she say how the Continentals are managing?" Gwynne asked.

Drew laughed dryly. "There is little to say about the Continentals. The British, however, are doing quite handily. Georgia is subdued, and they are moving easily through South Carolina, trying to split the coastal area off from the Upcountry. I'd like to say they aren't succeeding, but it isn't true." Drew's head was down as he continued to read the letter. "The second part of this was written from Charles Town. Grandma doesn't waste any time once her mind is made up. She must be feeling more herself. She says that Leo is alarmed, as is George. Apparently the city's defenses have been allowed to fall into shocking disrepair, and they have had word that Clinton is mounting a new expedition. We must keep Charles Town, or the entire southern coast will be British."

"There must not be too great a danger, or Elizabeth and the family would not feel they are safer there than at our house," Gwynne said.

"Mmmm," was all she got out of Drew. The letter was resting in his lap, and his mind was miles away.

"Do you not agree with them?" she prompted.

Drew looked up. "I don't know. I don't think the Continentals take what is happening in the South seriously enough. Their attention is in the North, but they have not launched a campaign for months now. Perhaps Savannah or Charles Town does not mean as much to them as Boston or New York, but, by God, if the British run over us, they have a clear field to crush the North."

"And you think they are not aware of that?"

"I keep getting the feeling that they do not think of us at all. It is not merely a matter of being of less importance, it is as though we do not exist at all, except as we directly affect them. They need supplies, we are here to provide them, they need arms, they ask for ours, but do they see us as a part of this nation they are fighting to establish? I can't say I have much faith in that, Gwynne. More and more I agree with the notion attributed to Thomas Jefferson, that we are two separate nations, and shall never truly be one."

"That doesn't speak well for the future, if it is true, Drew. What is the point of fighting and dying and killing for a nation that will never really be a nation?"

"We don't know that, Gwynne. It is an opinion."

"But you just said—"

"I said, I keep wondering about it. That doesn't mean it won't change. We have not even freed ourselves from the yoke of English rule yet," he said with a film of irritation coating his tone.

Gwynne sat quietly, not knowing whether it was wise or even if she wanted to risk another no-win conversation with him. After a while she said, "I will probably regret this, but something is bothering you, Drew, and I wish you would let me be a part of it."

"It is nothing that concerns you," he said.

"I suppose that means it has to do with the war. The same one you want me to espouse for my own reasons. Since you say talk of it does not concern me, does that mean that you wish me to take up arms and go out and fight for myself in the field?"

"Don't be ridiculous!" he snapped.

"You are being ridiculous! I cannot fight, I cannot talk, and yet it is to be my cause independent of you! Nonsense! Utter, foolish nonsense!" She screamed, her hand tightened into small hard fists. "You must talk to me, Drew, you must!"

"You are becoming a shrew!"

"If I am, you have only yourself to thank!"

She sat angry and rigid for a few more minutes, staring to the left of his head, then got up and fled the room.

Drew remained where he was, the letter forgotten as it fell to the floor. He didn't know if Gwynne's outburst was warranted or not, for all he could think of was the upcoming attack on Manning, and what that would mean to him, and to his brother, father, and mother.

At the next meeting the patriots planned the attack for the thirteenth of April, but as so often happened in the country, other things interfered. Both Tory and patriot turned to their fields and crops. Tory activity dropped to almost nothing, and the patriots decided that feeding their families, and trying to produce a crop were more important than wiping out a Tory stronghold, particularly one that was not currently a problem.

Drew gratefully worked in his fields, basking in the sun and the freedom from constant worry. He and Gwynne were still cool with each other, unable to bridge the gulf between them. Though difficulties seemed to center around the war, Drew was not at all convinced that was the real problem. He wasn't sure what it was. The only way they could get along at all was to avoid any subject they disagreed about. Cherokee had become a well-ordered but stiltedly formal household. It made no one happy, but it kept peace.

As soon as the harvest was in, the activity of both Tory and patriot heated up again, and the attack on Manning was set for October 23, 1779. As soon as he heard the news, Drew's ill-temper returned and he and Gwynne began to fight again. This time, however, even if Drew did not realize the correlation, and if Gwynne did not know the cause, she recognized that something had happened, and simply began to avoid him. Once again a rather sullen peace reigned in the house.

The patriots met at Jasper Spikes's farm on the afternoon of the twenty-third at four o'clock. The foray would not take place until darkness had fallen, and in the intervening hours the men awaited their fellows, who were coming from as far as fifty miles' distance to join them. By the time Jasper Spikes's wife, Lisa, began to serve dinner with several of the other wives who had gathered, twenty-five ex-Regulators and farmers had come to increase the group to a little over thirty men.

About seven thirty the men mounted and began the ride across the fields and woods and marshes that would bring them to Manning. As usual, Arthur Manning was slow with his harvest. In a long line of vats the last of the Manning indigo crop stood in various stages of completion. Torches had been lit along the work area, and Drew could hear the familiar sound of the slaves' song as they worked. He no longer felt the fear he once had; now all that was left was a deep, unabating sickness in the pit of his stomach. From minute to minute he thought of turning back, letting the others go on without him, but each time he pushed down the urge. If he believed as he claimed, then he belonged here, and it was unlikely that anyone would be hurt. This was merely a foray to seize the arms stored at Manning, and to force Arthur and his father to take the loyalty oath to the colony. Of course, they would not do that, Drew knew, but he thought that a pledge of neutrality could be gotten from them.

The men lined up on a slight ridge overlooking the work area. One of them said in a pleased voice, "Now, isn't that a nice, peaceful picture." He turned to the man next to him. "This won't take but a few minutes. They aren't expecting a thing."

At a signal from Jack Kimble, they spurred their horses and rode down the hill. Spreading out, they rode through the work area, scattering the black workmen and overturning the blue-violet contents of the huge vats. Turning in formation, the horsemen rode toward Manning house. They had cleared the home farm field, and were coming up on the back lawn when they were greeted by a volley of musket fire coming from a low brick wall that enclosed the wash area of the yard. Nathan Parker's horse screamed as it plunged to the ground. Nathan rolled with the horse and painfully crawled on his belly to cover. For a few minutes there was confusion in the ranks of the patriots as they realized the peaceful picture was just that, a picture to deceive, and the Tories had been waiting for them.

Jack Kimble shouted orders above the din of musket fire, screams, and snorting horses. The men regrouped on the plantation road among the rows of crepe myrtle that Joseph and his sons had planted with their own hands.

Jack motioned for a group of men who had come from the western part of the colony to come forward. "Can you smoke 'em out of there?"

"We can burn 'em out," one man said.

Jack thought for a moment, conferred with several other men, then nodded. He spoke again to the group of men who were bowmen, then talked with several others, placing a leader at the head of each group of five men. He had a word with Drew just a moment before the attack began again. "You know you would almost always be my first choice to lead, Drew, but this is . . ."

"I understand, Jack, and I appreciate it."

"I didn't expect this. No one meant to do harm to Manning."

"I know." Drew took a deep breath. "Let's get on with it."

Jack began to walk away, then turned back for a moment. "You're sure you're all right?"

"I'm sure," Drew lied, and mounted his horse.

The men got into position, and at a signal from Jack, the bowmen and one group of musketeers rode, screaming war cries, past the barricaded wash-courtyard of Manning. The torched arrows flew through the night air, striking the roof of the wash barn and the rear porch of the house. Others fell harmlessly onto the brick courtyard. Jack's riders raced past and back to the safety of the trees. Another group took their place, and in relays the patriots kept up an endless barrage of grapeshot and flaming arrows sailing into the Manning yard.

Drew rode with a group, racing like demons, their bodies as flat against their horses as they could be, rising only to shoot their muskets; when one of the torches landed on the roof of a building Drew had never seen before. Carelessly curious, he peered over the wall, trying to see what the building was. He landed with a heavy thud on the ground as a burst of flame went up with the powder magazine. Chaos ensued, men pouring out of the Manning courtyard and the patriots dismounting and running to meet them.

Stunned, Drew lay on the ground for a moment at the periphery of the fighting. Then, gingerly, he got to his feet and stood staring as the flames burst and jumped in great gulping leaps toward the house. Skirting the main battle area, Drew headed for the house, approaching it from the side on which the dining room was situated. He pushed at the window, hoping to find it unlocked; but it wasn't. He smashed the glass in one of the French panes, reached round for the latch, and climbed in. The house was in darkness, and he moved cautiously and quietly through the silent rooms. The smell of beeswax was heavy and spicy as he remembered it from his childhood. He was looking for his mother, and in his mind's eye he pictured her putting the scents into the wax that she used for so many things.

He had reached the main hall, and was about to climb the stairs, when he heard glass breaking and the shouting of many voices from the study.

Joseph Manning stood in the near dark of his study, an old saber in his hand as he watched three smoke-blackened, enraged men burst through the double doors from the outside. He motioned threateningly with the sword.

"Step aside, old man," one man yelled with a laugh. "We're here in the name of the independent state of South Carolina. Put down your sword and raise your hand to swear allegiance and defense."

"Whoreson!" Joseph roared, his face purple with rage. He brought his sword down in a sweeping blow across the man's arm.

The man screamed and rolled to the floor in anguish as his compatriot leveled his musket at Joseph Manning's chest and fired.

Both Drew and Arthur heard the scream of rage from their father and the shot that followed. Drew ran from the front of the house, Arthur down the servants' stairs from the back. They met in front of the door to Joseph's study. Drew was intent on the door, his hand outstretched for the knob.

"Halt!" Arthur shouted.

Drew spun, his pistol cocked and ready to shoot. He was crouched, and with the slightest pressure on the trigger he would have killed his brother. Slowly he stood up, and his eyes went to the door. He jumped for the doorknob again, his hand firmly on it, when Arthur fired.

Drew staggered, his leg giving out under his weight, then buckling under him. He stared through a haze of pain at Arthur standing over him, wondering if he would shoot again. Arthur drew his arm back and hit Drew across the forehead with the butt of his pistol. As Drew lay unconscious on the hall floor, Arthur carefully opened the study door, and careful not to expose himself, fired into the murkily lit room.

Jack Kimble's foray had destroyed the magazine and the store of arms kept at Manning, and he wanted to risk losing no more men. He rode around the house shouting the retreat. There was only sporadic firing, and soon after, Manning was left in eerie silence, everyone's attention concentrated on putting out the spot fires that had started all over the property.

Drew awakened with pain in his head and in his leg, his arms bound tightly behind him, and his brother sitting stonelike in a chair about four feet from him. Drew tried to sit up, and with a groan fell back. Somewhere, in another part of the house, he could hear his mother crying. "Is Daddy all right?" Drew asked.

"Daddy is dead," Arthur said coldly.

Again he struggled against the red haziness of pain that came when he moved to sit up. "Let me see Mama."

Arthur got up, walked to the window, and looked out. Seeing what he was looking for, he hurried to the front door and admitted three uniformed British soldiers. Without a word he turned Drew over to them. Kinder than his brother had been, one of the soldiers stemmed the flow of blood from his leg before putting him on the back of a horse for the long ride to the Camden jail.

Vague thoughts of Gwynne, his children, his mother, his father, and Arthur drifted through his mind, but none of them stuck. He could barely remain seated on the horse. By the time they arrived in Camden, he was barely aware of anything that happened. The following morning he awakened with a bandage on his leg and another on his head, lying in a cell of which he had no recollection. Again he tried to think of Gwynne and the other important people in his life, and what this would mean to them. He tried to stir himself up so that he could do something about his situation, but he didn't care. All that would come to his mind was the final look on Arthur's face, the sound of his mother crying, and the cold information that his father was dead. He didn't think anything about it, it was merely a scene that played over and over in his mind without offering relief, understanding, punishment, or enlightenment. There were only two things for him. That repeating memory, and himself. He no longer cared about either one.

When Drew had been brought into the jail at Camden, there had been a good deal of talk and gossip about him, because he was Arthur Manning's brother, and because of the circumstances of his capture. There had also been a good deal of resentment and even hatred directed at a man who some said had killed his own father.

The mad dog, as some called him, showed no interest in anything they said to him or did to him. Bugs, dirt, and vermin were often added to his food. Drew did nothing. He seldom ate anything they brought him, and when he did eat, he didn't seem to care what the food was. He made no response to anything or anyone. He sat in his cell, his eyes blank of emotion, his body always still. If one did not look carefully, it was difficult to tell if he was breathing.

The doctor had told them it was the fever, and that he would change soon enough, but rumor said otherwise. Those masters of truth claimed that he was a deranged killer, always quiet and uncaring until provoked, then instantly turning into a madman of heroic strength, wild like an animal charging until sated by the shedding of blood.

The rumors and the stories that grew about Drew kept everyone in the outpost interested and entertained for quite some time, but as the days turned into weeks, and the weeks began to add up, Drew did not change. No one could provoke him, and many had tried. By the beginning of December no one talked about or paid much attention to Drew Manning.

31

Jack Kimble came to Cherokee to tell Gwynne and Ned Hart of Drew's imprisonment. Gwynne sat down with a weak-kneed thump. She began to cry and laugh at once. "I thought he was dead! Oh, Jack, I don't know what to say! He's alive! Ned . . . Drew is alive."

"Gwynne," Jack began hesitantly, "of course you are relieved he is alive, but . . . this is not good news. We were told he was wounded, and the British are not likely to think kindly of Drew Manning. To them he is the worst kind of traitor. I don't want to frighten you, but you must see this for what it is."

"We can have him released, can't we?"

Jack and Ned exchanged looks. Gwynne watched the two of them, then understanding dawned in her eyes. "It may be no different than if he had died that night . . . that is what you are telling me?"

"I hope it is nowhere near that extreme, but I don't want you thinking this is nothing."

Gwynne sat unmoving after Jack had left. Ned came back and sat down across from her. He said nothing until she was ready to talk.

"What can I do, Ned?"

"Gwynne, that is what I think Jack wanted you to realize. This is going to be very difficult, for there is nothing you can do. I'll see if I can locate someone in Camden who can get news of him, but other than that we are going to have to sit on our hands, hope for the best . . . and it wouldn't hurt to do a little hard prayin'."

"I'll write to Elizabeth," Gwynne said, as always reaching for her second mainstay of support when the first was missing. "If she is well enough, perhaps she'll come. She'll know what to do."

"Well, I'm sure not going to tell you to keep this from her. Miss Elizabeth should be told, but she isn't going to be able to do anything, Mrs. Manning."

Gwynne looked up quickly. Ned never called her Mrs. Manning. He was too much like family, and called her by her given name.

Ned leaned forward. "You heard me right, I said Mrs. Manning. That's who you are now, and you've got to start thinking of yourself that way. Cherokee is now your responsibility, and so is that house over near Charles Town. You're going to have to do for Drew what he would do if he were here."

"But you're here . . . you'll take care of—"

"Uh-uh. I ain't young enough for you to be counting on me like that. And there's another thing you've got to think about. Nobody, not even an old man like me, has got a sure lease on tomorrow. Those Tories could come down on this place anytime."

Gwynne sat open mouthed, frightened into muteness.

"I'm going to teach you all I can. You're going to learn how to run this place and so is Nathaniel. He's going to have to do some fast growing up, too."

"How . . . how can you talk like this? It's as if you don't care about Drew at all—as if he'll never come back. I . . . I thought you loved him."

Ned's eyes crinkled about the edges, and his mouth turned down. "He's as close to a son as I'll ever have. I'd give my life for the boy, but I can't do that. All's I can do is try my best to see that his family can go on if . . . if he don't come back."

"But you must believe . . . have faith that he will, Ned! We can't give up!"

Ned took a deep breath, then let it out slowly. "There's more than one way to look at faith, Gwynne. I remember a conversation I had with Drew when he wasn't but nineteen or twenty years old. He was going on his first real hard ride with the Regulators. They knew they were going to get those outlaws. There was going to be hangings and killings, and it was his first time. I told him then, he'd have to learn to think of it like business. Something that had to be done, so he'd do it, but he couldn't let himself feel it. He thought I was being cold and hard then, just like you think I am now. Maybe I am, but that's not the way I see it, Gwynne. Faith sometimes means you go on without the person. It means you keep on building just like he would. A friend steppin' into another man's shoes till he comes back to fill them himself. If he doesn't come back, at least what he spent his life building goes on. If he does come back, you've kept him current, so he can move on without any catching up to do. That's faith to me."

Gwynne put her head in her hands and sobbed.

Ned sat and waited patiently until she quieted.

"I'll tell Nathaniel in the morning. I . . . I can't do it tonight, Ned. And then I'll write to Elizabeth. I'll listen to you and I'll try, but I think you are counting on me more than you can, or than I can." She sat for a moment looking at the floor, then said, "I think, if you don't mind, Ned, that I'd like to be alone. I don't want to think anymore. Not tonight."

"It's been a hard day. I'll see you in the morning, Gwynne."

She wrote her letter to Elizabeth and tried not to think of anything but the duties of the plantation and the family. Ned was patient and insistent. She didn't give him the letter for three days. Somehow telling Elizabeth and Leo and George gave it a reality that she didn't want yet to admit. In some ways, she knew, she had just been pretending that Drew was gone on business for a time—to Charles Town with the crop, or Cheraw or Ninety Six. Once she had let go of the letter, there would be no more pretending.

The news that Drew had been taken prisoner, and the circumstances of his capture, were as great a blow to Elizabeth Manning as the uprising at Willowtree had been. Quite suddenly it seemed to her that nothing was as it should be and that no one could be trusted. Joseph was dead. Her youngest son was no more. For the first time she could ever recall thinking it, Elizabeth Manning thanked God that her husband was dead, that he had been spared these terrible days.

She was also thankful her husband was not with her to know the thoughts and feelings she was having. Not only was she saddened beyond words at her son's death, she was angry at him. For too long Joseph had held himself away from the family, had been too righteous, too proper. How much tragedy could have been avoided!

When she had sufficiently calmed herself, she got up and went to John Manning's room. He had acquired the habit of taking an afternoon nap, and she knew he wouldn't really be asleep. She knocked at the door and entered at his invitation. "I am afraid we have more bad news."

"I don't think I want to know what it is, Mother. I sometimes think it is a pity that black beggar missed my neck and hit my arm."

"That is foolish, sinful talk! Read this. Your brother is dead, and your nephew is in prison, put there by his own brother."

John winced, but maintained his indifferent attitude. "Why should we not have traitors within the family? We have them in the new nation." He looked at her with raised eyebrows. "You haven't heard? Our dear General Charles Lee was dismissed last month. Remember General Lee, Mother— the man who suggested we yield Fort Sullivan to the British without a fight? Yes, well, it seems General Lee was also impertinent, disobedient, and had a penchant for taking money from the British."

"Are you truly as cynical as you seem, John?"

The air seemed to go out of him. He lay back against the pillows, his hand unconsciously rubbing the stump of his lost arm. "Mother, I am tired. I don't know if that is cynical, I just know it is tired. There are just too many disappointments and too few rewards to life these days. I may not have had liberty, but I was a far happier man when I was under the thumb of British rule."

She handed him the letter. "Read it when you feel up to it."

"What will you do, Mother? About Drew, I mean."

She shrugged. "What can I do? I shall pray, I suppose."

John chuckled. It was a rusty, dry sound at first, then it was mirthful. "You will never change. Always the quiet before the storm."

"What are you talking about, John?" Elizabeth said with irritation.

"You, Mother dear, you. You will not let Drew languish in some British prison, and you know it. Perhaps you do not yet know what you will do, but can you honestly tell me you are not thinking of going to Cherokee?"

Elizabeth gave in gracefully and laughed. "No, I cannot. I am consider- ing it. I just wish it were a little later in the year. For March it is very chilly —either that or I am aging."

"That is the funniest thing you've said," John said.

Elizabeth walked to the door. She didn't say anything, and she won- dered how long it would be before he dropped the happy flippant façade and read the letter. Just as she couldn't help Joseph, she couldn't help John, either. As much value as she had been able to be to her husband, and she hoped to her grandson, she seemed of little use in helping her sons find their way through life. Perhaps it was just that she was too close to them. Perhaps it was that for all a man's life he had always to fight for indepen- dence from his parents. She didn't know. She went back to her room to consider what, if anything, she might do to help Drew, and if not him, Gwynne and her great-grandchildren. She could help them. They had no need to be independent of her.

Though Elizabeth Manning was for the moment blissfully ignorant of it, the British had already begun the siege of Charles Town. This time they would not make the mistake of trying to take it from the sea. They would come by sea, and they would come by land. On March 9, 1780, the Americans sank eight hulks in the channel between the city and Shute's Folly to prevent the passage of the British ships that had arrived in Stono Inlet one month before. But it wasn't until the twenty-ninth of March that the Mannings were aware of any real danger.

George Manning was returning to the city from having visited Willow-tree, and several plantations of friends, when about twelve miles north of town he saw a sight that made his blood run cold. Crossing the Ashley River, under the leadership of Sir Henry Clinton, were an endless number of British troops. George secreted himself and tried to count the number of men, but it was an impossible task. These were not men numbering in the hundreds, but the thousands. He couldn't see the earth beneath them, they were so thickly packed in formation.

Afraid to move or be seen, he waited until dark, then stealthily made his way back to the road to the city. Five hours later he pelted into the stables at his house and burst noisily through the front door, waking those who were asleep, and demanding they all meet in the parlor. He rushed like a madman into the kitchen, demanding food be prepared for him, then to the liquor cabinet, where he quickly downed two jiggers of whiskey neat. His family and the servants looked at him in awe. No one had ever seen George behave in so erratic a fashion.

Leo broke the silence. "What the hell do you think you're doing bursting in here like this? Are you drunk?"

"No, by God, I'm not, but I wish I were."

"George Manning," his mother scolded. "I won't have such language in my home! I expect an apology."

George ignored her, and told them in rapid-fire language what he had seen. "And that's not all. I visited everyone we know to be loyal within a twenty-or-so-mile radius of here. There's bad news everywhere—nothing but bad news. Listen to this. On the eighteenth that demon Tarleton caught Ladson unawares. He killed or captured a whole damned party of partisans—fifty men in all. Five days later Tarleton showed up at Bee's plantation, killed ten men, and took four more prisoner. And now tonight I see this mass of troops coming over the river. What do you suppose they are going to do?" he ended on a frantic screech.

"Where the hell is the Continental Army?" Leo burst out with. He began to pace the room. "The British do as they please, go where they please!"

"What did you expect from the Continentals?" John asked. "None of you would listen when I—when my brother tried to tell you this was a fool's war! Even if it is won, which now looks like another fool's dream, what have you got? Continental Army! How dare you give it the name? It is a ragtag collection of farmers and shopkeepers. The North won't supply them, won't support them! They damn near froze to death. If you sincerely want to win this war of rebellion, children, look to yourselves, and then you have a chance. That's all I have to say. I am going back to bed."

Elizabeth Manning smiled. It was nice having John back again. She didn't even mind too badly that Sir Henry Clinton was most likely going to ruin her plans to leave.

Eugenia hurried up the stairs after her husband.

George and Leo stared after him. George shook his head. "Boy! I don't think I understand anything anymore! Daddy doesn't say anything for months, and now this. If he was going to give us a boot in the rear, why couldn't he have done it before Charles Town was under siege?"

Elizabeth laughed. "Well, you did understand his message. Good! There may still be hope for the American cause. Good night, boys."

They had little time to celebrate their new determination, or to wait for Clinton's next move. The next day, March 30, 1780, Clinton tried a test probe with the British infantry and Hessian grenadiers. John Laurens stopped the advance two miles from the city in a day-long skirmish.

The days following were move and countermove, with the British making constant headway. They established batteries as they went, and the fleet passed Fort Moultrie and dropped anchor between Fort Johnson and the city.

The Americans strengthened their defenses and made various attempts to stop the British. There were victories, prisoners taken, but none of that was enough to stop the advance. On April thirteenth Peter Timothy, editor of the *Gazette,* watched from the steeple of St. Michael's Church as Clinton and about two thousand Hessian troops crossed the Ashley River on James Island. With the outcome so little in doubt in the minds of the British, they took time to tease a bit. On one occasion they took the time to fill a round shot with rice and molasses and fired it into Charles Town as a bitter-humorous reminder of the short supply of food.

The skirmishes, and the defense of Charles Town, continued, sometimes heatedly, sometimes desultorily, for forty two days. On May eighth the British demanded the surrender of the city.

A few days before, General Lincoln had called a meeting of his generals to discuss the possibility of withdrawing his troops. The citizens, having heard, marched to the council to make clear their feelings. "Leave us to the British, sir, and you shall find that your boats have been cut to pieces, while you find yourself naked to the enemy; for we shall open the city gates for them to better feed upon you!"

Lincoln decided he had better stay and do what he could until the end of the battle. He sent back to the British terms of capitulation, which were summarily rejected. Clinton called them "utterly inadmissible" and warned that hostilities would recommence. The Americans waited, momentarily expecting the next shots and shells to fall, but nothing happened. At the end of an hour the American side fired, and were answered with a huge return of shellfire from the British. The night sky was lit up with the bursting fire of shells until dawn. Cannonballs whizzed past the defenders, and shells hissed as they fell among the men. Powder chests blew up in great coughing bursts, and men cried and groaned all along the lines. It was the last great effort of the Americans to keep the British out of Charles Town, but as more and more of their number fell wounded or dead, the ardor to do battle cooled. On the eleventh of May they gave up the fight, and surrendered.

The Americans beat a "Turks' march." It was over, and few men met the British victors with dry eyes. General Leslie, with the Royal English Fusiliers and Hessian Grenadiers and some Artillery, placed the British colors on the gate to the city, then took possession of Charles Town.

General Lincoln, with a weary ragtag army behind him, walked out to meet the conquerors. The patriots beat a drum, the colors of the colony were cased. On the faces of the more than two thousand militia and Continentals were looks of bitter sorrow and quiet defiance.

George Manning, though he had participated in the fighting, was not officially a member of Lincoln's band, hurried back to Elizabeth's house with the news of what was taking place in the town.

"We've lost?" John asked blankly.

"We may have lost the whole war. What stands between us and the Continentals with Washington? A few scattered pockets of resistance, but there is virtually nothing to prevent the British from marching right up the countryside," George said.

"What about Colonel Buford? He was on his way to join Lincoln . . . maybe he could do something."

George laughed harshly. "I can't say for sure it is true, but I heard that Clinton sent Tarleton after Buford. If he is still coming here, which is doubtful . . . he must have heard the news. He wouldn't walk right into a lost battle . . . he'd have turned tail and gone back north."

"With Tarleton on his heels," John said. "Well, by the Saints, they may be in our city, but they haven't beaten us yet!"

They all looked at him. "John, what have you in mind? Do you know something the rest of us don't?" Elizabeth asked.

"No, you all know it. This has been a bloody, costly war. We have lost friends, loved ones"—he lifted the stump of his arm—"parts of ourselves, we go hungry, our city has been burned to the ground in certain parts, and now we are to endure the taunts and hostilities of the enemy's army in our homes and on our streets. We have only two choices: We shall buckle under and beg to join forces with the King's men, or we shall find we are truly Americans, and if we have to poison them at our own dinner tables, we shall. That is all I know. We shall find out what manner of men we are. Independent, or subjects of a king—any king."

George got up and put out his hand to his father. "I intend to show you what I am, Daddy. I wasn't going to tell the family, I was just going to do it, but I've changed my mind. I am going to try to get out of the city before it becomes impossible. I can't do any good here, but I can if I can join up with Sumter or Marion or some of Drew's Upcountry friends."

"We're most likely going to be put under house arrest," Leo said. "How do you expect to get out? There are British troops everywhere."

"I'll wait till dark and see if I can make it as far as Drew's house tonight . . . then head for the Upcountry tomorrow, or tomorrow night, if I need cover of darkness."

"What makes you think Drew's house is still standing? Most likely it will have been looted and burned. From the experiences of the last few months, we can expect nothing else. The British are leaving nothing standing that they can't use themselves. For that matter, you might run into a regiment using it for headquarters."

"If I do—I won't stop there," George said with a grin. "Actually, if they have looted and burned it, it would probably be better for my purposes, because they aren't likely to come back. Course, Drew and Gwynne might not look too kindly on it."

Eugenia had said nothing while all this talk was going on. Now she stood up and spoke angrily. "Aren't any of you going to stop him? John, isn't one son dead enough for you? Are you going to sit back and listen to this insane scheme and do nothing to try to instill some common sense into the subject?"

"He will be in no greater danger in the Upcountry than he is right here in Charles Town, Eugenia," her husband said. "He may be able to do some good there. We are going to be trapped here."

"I won't have it, George!" Eugenia said directly to him. "If no one else will do anything, I must. You cannot do this! There is nothing for you in the Upcountry. Drew is in prison, and we are conquered. These skirmishes you talk of engaging in are no more than fodder for the British cannon. It is hurling yourself in the face of death! You cannot do it!"

George walked over to his mother and put his arm around her. "I understand your fears, Mama. I share them. I'm not brave—I never have been. But I am more afraid of staying here and letting the British conquer us, and subjugate us than I am of fighting. Listen to me for just a minute. . . . for a long time now we have all fought Drew. We've called him foolish, rash, and all kinds of things, and then a bit after the event, we all end up saying we wish we had listened to him. He told us this war was coming long ago—he said the Regulator movement was a forerunner. He was right. We said he was daft. He told us about Seth and Willowtree, and we didn't listen until too late—much to our regret. Well, he's also told me for a long time that this war will never be won on a classical battlefield, it will be won in the swamps and on farms and in the woods if it is to be won at all. It doesn't make much sense to me, but this time I believe him. And I am going."

Eugenia put her head on his shoulder and cried. George held her, and said nothing until she was finished. She looked up at him. "I suppose you must go, and I suppose I must do my part as well. I am not of much use, George, but I can send you off with my blessings, and my prayers to shield you." She stood on tiptoe and kissed him on the forehead as she had when he was a child, and it had been he who had stood on tiptoe to receive the kiss.

"I suggest we raid the larder and have a celebration meal tonight. If there is great activity in the house of a sort no one will expect, it will be easier for George to get out," Elizabeth said with some of her old sparkle. "The British may think they have conquered Charles Town, but we, the Mannings, know they have just lost the war! Come, Eugenia, we shall dress in our finest. Leo, see to the kitchen, and spare nothing. We shall dine and have music tonight. George, you must just vanish at the appropriate time. John, surely you can find a musician or two?"

"I can be one of them, Great Grandma," Bethany said. "I am always getting left out of everything, and I'd like y'all to know I'm a patriot, too. I am really no longer one of the children!"

The Mannings ate, drank, and celebrated that evening. When a British officer arrived at their door with the information that they were under house arrest, they merely nodded and invited the baffled man in. With his list he asked to see all the known members of the household. He came to George Manning's name and was met with a row of blank faces.

"Why, George doesn't live here," Elizabeth said. "We haven't seen George for well over a month. Last I heard he was visiting friends in North Carolina."

"I was told that he was a member of this household and was seen only today near the city gates."

"I am so sorry, sir," Eugenia said. "Someone has mistaken one of my sons for the other. I am sure it was Leo who was seen. George is not here. If you wish to search the house, as I am told is your custom, you are more than welcome. Shall I guide you?" Eugenia had a glint in her eye no one had ever seen before, and before the man could say or do anything, she had him in tow showing him into every room, opening every closet and cupboard.

When he had left, a little the worse for wear, Eugenia stood in the parlor, hands on hips, and said. "Well! The enemy has been met and defeated in the battle of Legare Street! No casualties. Now, let's have some music. John, I feel like dancing."

No one knew exactly when George had left. The just knew he had. Bethany played and sang, the others danced and laughed and had a marvelous time. The British soldiers who were posted outside the house for the night were not sure what to make of these patriots who should have been mournful over the loss of their city.

32

The letter Gwynne received from Elizabeth, instead of giving her the good news that Elizabeth was on her way to Cherokee, told only of the siege of Charles Town. Gwynne showed it to Ned, who shook his head and smiled. "How do you suppose she got this out of there? She says right here, they're under house arrest, and she's sending letters. It's too damned bad she's not one of our generals."

Gwynne just looked at him. "I hadn't thought of that. How did she get it out? I wonder if we'll hear from her again. Oh, Ned, we may have no contact with them!"

"I wouldn't wager on it. She'll keep writing."

"But how?"

"Don't know, but my money's on Miss Elizabeth."

Gwynne sat thinking for a moment. "Do you know, Ned, the two strongest members of our family are now captive? All of us rely on Drew and on Elizabeth to get us through everything, and both of them are captive. Of the rest of us, only George has shown any real signs of leadership, and now he, too, is in Charles Town, unable to fight or lead us."

"Yeah?" Ned prompted when she didn't go on.

"Something must be done," Gwynne said. "We are going to have to get Drew out of prison, Ned."

"Well, unless you've got an army hidden away somewhere I don't know about, that isn't going to happen."

"We don't need an army. I don't think we could do it with an army. If that is what it takes, I think Jack and Jasper and the others would have done that by now. But I've been thinking . . . one person, someone who would be looked upon as harmless, might be able to do it."

"Is that why you wanted Miss Elizabeth to come here so badly?"

Gwynne gave him a shamefaced smile. "I am not very brave on my own, Ned. Elizabeth is so bold, she spurs me on." She stood up and began to pace. "But Elizabeth is not going to be coming, and I am ashamed of myself anyway. Here she is a woman nearing eighty, and she's just recovering from terrible injuries, and I want to lean on her. Perhaps it is time I make my own way—and if I fail, well, I shall have to see to that when and if the time comes."

Ned looked at her skeptically. "How do you think you are going to do this? I don't argue that they will not suspect you, but that doesn't mean they aren't justified in that. What can you do?"

"I don't know, Ned. I don't know yet. If only Elizabeth were here. I had been thinking of a plan, but by myself, I'm just not sure. I'll think of something."

"Well, I got to see to those men in the fields. It's getting to be that time when we have to start looking for the first ripe leaves, and there isn't a damned fool out there who'll do it on his own. Nathaniel and I gotta keep our eyes on them every minute. That boy is going to be one good planter one of these days, Gwynne. Drew will be proud of him."

Late one night near the middle of June the alarm went up all over Cherokee. The guards Ned had posted rang off warning shots, and the plantation bell was ringing.

Nathaniel came to his stepmother's room, a musket in his hands. His face was pale, but there was little fear showing, only determination. Gwynne hastily put her robe on, and the two of them hurried down the front stairs. Gwynne went to the door, opened it just enough so that she could see the struggle taking place in the front lawn. Five men were shouting and wrestling one man to the ground. As Gwynne and Nathaniel watched, Ned raced from the bunkhouse half dressed, his red underwear showing under his flapping shirt.

He joined the group of men, then with a roar yelled, "You damn fools! Let him go!"

Brushing himself off and muttering a few choice curses, George Manning got to his feet and walked toward the house with an apologetic Ned.

Gwynne threw the door wide, and Nathaniel burst out onto the porch. "Cousin George!" Nathaniel cried, and jumped up and down near George.

George laughed. "It's a damned good thing I didn't meet up with you first. I can see your Mama is well defended."

"George!" Gwynne cried and, despite the onlookers, threw herself into his arms. "We are so glad you are here! Come inside . . . let me get you something to eat and drink. You must be exhausted. I thought you were in Charles Town. What—How—"

"Slow down, little cousin. Let me get this filthy coat off and sit for a minute. It's been a long, dirty trip," he said, and was staggering with fatigue.

Once in the light, Gwynne quickly assessed his condition, and decreed that despite her rampant curiosity, there would be no talking that night. Ned showed him to his room, while Gwynne roused one of the servants to prepare water for a bath, and some hot food for him. For a time after George went upstairs, she and Nathaniel sat in the semidarkness, only one lamp lighting the room. They were comfortable together, the child-man and the woman. After a while Nathaniel said, "Everything is going to get better now, Gwynne."

"I think so, too, Nathaniel. Of course, you know any sensible person would say we are both daft. The situation could hardly be worse, but I think you are right. Things are going to get better now. And we'll get your Daddy home."

Gwynne and George talked the next morning while George wolfed down an enormous breakfast. "I think I could eat a horse and chase the rider," he said, as he reached for another serving of eggs. "You can't imagine how scarce food is in the city. Grandma had a celebration the night I left. She cleaned out the larder. Lord knows what they're doing now, although maybe it is better with the British right there in port."

"Elizabeth was having a celebration the night you left? I thought you said you left the day Charles Town was taken over by the British—surely not a day Elizabeth would celebrate!"

George stuffed a bite of thick slab bacon into his mouth. "Gwynne! I don't believe you said that. Think about it. Tell me a better time for Grandma to celebrate than the very day anyone would expect her to be crying in her soup."

Gwynne laughed. "That's true. That would be very Elizabethish."

"And that made it easier for me to get away. The whole house was filled with music and dancing and the family roaming about. The guards they had posted were so busy peeking in the windows, they didn't even see me leave. I was so close to one I could have reached out and pulled his hat over his nose."

"I wish Elizabeth had managed to get out with you. I'd like so much to get Drew out of that Camden jail, and I thought that Elizabeth and I could manage. But . . . it won't work, so I'll have to think of something else."

"Maybe we ought to think of getting Grandma out of Charles Town," George said jokingly.

Gwynne took him seriously. "Could we? Is there a way? She has been getting letters out of Charles Town . . . we have heard from her twice since the British took it. She must have some means of . . . some contact with someone outside the city." She looked at him with hopeful, pleading eyes. "Could we, George?"

"Gwynne . . . I wasn't serious. I had a hard time getting up here. Grandma could never stand the trip . . . I . . . I had to hide in haystacks in the day and travel mostly by night, much of the time in the swamps."

"But Drew always told me you can fool anyone into thinking nearly anything you want if you're just bold enough. Maybe we shouldn't sneak Elizabeth . . . what if we just drove a carriage?"

"How?"

"Well . . . the Templetons were—are—known as loyalists. I was a Templeton. I could say I am Meg, or even Joanna. Who is to know?"

"I would guess a goodly number of British officers. In case you've forgotten, your brother-in-law is a British officer. A good portion of the men would know his wife by sight. You couldn't be sure. . . . You just couldn't be that lucky, and what are you going to say about Grandma?"

Gwynne shrugged, eyes wide open, then she said, "That she's my grandmother. How simple."

"Not so simple. The Templetons are too well known. Your grandmother is dead. And my grandmother is too well known as well. If I know her she has already established herself as the thorn on every British rose. It won't work."

Gwynne frowned. "I bet Elizabeth would know a way."

"You're probably right, but I am not Grandma. I don't have her nightmarish imagination."

"Then how can we reach her . . . I mean get a message to her? If we could do that, then she could let us know if she could get out of the city. We could manage from then on. No one outside of Charles Town and Riverlea knows about Elizabeth or my grandmother."

"It won't work," George said.

"Why not?"

"It just won't."

"You don't want it to!" Gwynne accused.

"I can't deny that having to sneak Grandma out of Charles Town is not my idea of the best use of my time. But I didn't say I wouldn't try—to get a message to her. That can't do much harm, and it will keep her mind occupied. Of course, you realize, we may be doing the British a favor. If she is distracted from harassing them, they will have far more time to concentrate on the patriots."

"I do wish you'd take this seriously. I am sure with Elizabeth's help I can get Drew out of prison."

"I said I'd try to get a letter in, and I will, but I am not going to take this seriously, Gwynne. The whole thing is impossible. Think about it."

"I have! I have thought of little else. Someone has to get Drew out of that prison. You men haven't accomplished it with all your guns and rebel yells and fighting. What is so much more ridiculous about me wanting to try deception? Is it just because my way isn't violent that bothers you?"

"I'm sorry. I shouldn't have made fun, but, Gwynne, there is so little chance—"

"I know that!" she cried. "Don't you think I know all of what you're telling me? But I want to try! I have to, George. I can't stand thinking of what is happening to Drew."

George later made an attempt to keep his word to Gwynne. He told Ned of their conversation with her. "Got any good ideas?"

"If you really think it is a useless idea, why not tell her you aren't going to do it?" Ned asked.

"It just won't work—at least I don't think it will. If Grandma were younger, maybe . . . but the whole thing is impossible."

Ned shrugged. "Send a bondsman. If he makes it to Charles Town—fine. If he doesn't, then Gwynne will probably accept it as being impossible."

"Have you got a man you can trust not to run?" George asked.

"Sure. He's as slow as a three-legged tortoise, but you can count on him—Old Bill."

George grinned and slapped Ned on the back. "I'll tell Gwynne to write her letter to Grandma."

Old Bill was sent on his way with an old-farm wagon and the precious letter to Elizabeth. "Please, Bill, try your very best. Master Drew needs all of us now," Gwynne said, her hands clasped under her chin.

Toothless and ancient, Bill grinned. "Dis he'p git him outen jail?"

"Yes, it will. God go with you, Bill. Hurry!" Gwynne said.

The old man grinned again and nodded. He clucked at the horse, and horse, old man, and old wagon creaked down the road.

George and Ned had underestimated Old Bill in several ways. Because he was old, they thought he'd be slow, and he was, but he was persistent, and that made up for a lot. The old man snoozed as he rode, his hands easy on the reins, so he didn't have to stop to rest at night as a younger, more ardent man might have. Old Bill made better time rumbling across the old rutted roads than Drew Manning did on his own trips. He passed several encampments of British. Courteously he tipped his frayed old hat and rumbled on, the wheels of his wagon bent inward and wobbling.

He had never been in Charles Town before, but he had heard stories about it. Nathaniel Dancer was a favorite friend of Old Bill's, and they talked quite a lot. He stopped several times when he saw a black woman sweeping a walkway, or a black man tending a horse, to get directions. Just after dark he brought his wagon into Elizabeth Manning's courtyard, just two and one half weeks after he had left Cherokee. He went to the back door and asked for Elizabeth as he had been instructed. Hedy, who happened to be in the kitchen, took the letter from Old Bill and ordered that he be given something warm and nourishing to eat. Having kept calm all through her order-giving, she turned and ran from the kitchen, and all the way up the stairs to Elizabeth's room. "It's a lett', Miss Elizabeth! From Miss Gwynne!"

Elizabeth got up from her bed immediately and tore open the letter. Her brow furrowed as she read and began to understand what Gwynne was asking. "My word," she breathed. "How shall I manage this? If I weren't such an old decrepit thing, I might be able to, but . . ."

She got up and went downstairs to see Old Bill. He stood as Gwynne had taught him, and bowed. Elizabeth sat at the kitchen table opposite him and pulled from him every scrap of information about his trip from Cherokee to Charles Town. No ideas came to her. It had been easy for him, no one was going to pay any attention to an old black man in a farm wagon, but what was she to do? Ride through town in her polished carriage?

Elizabeth stewed and brooded over her problem for two days. Old Bill had tried several times to say his good-bye and be on his way back to Cherokee, but at the last minute Elizabeth tore up every letter she had written and asked him to wait for a bit longer.

Late that night Elizabeth awakened from sleep. She got up and went to her son's room, and told him what she had dreamed and what she was going to do. She asked him to explain to the rest of the family after she had gone. John Manning thought of at least a dozen reasons why his mother should not do what she proposed, but he said nothing. He hugged her, held her close, and wished God be with her.

Before dawn Elizabeth Manning and Hedy were in the kitchen popping corks out of wine bottles and burning them over the stove. Old Bill came in for his breakfast, and finally Elizabeth gave him permission to leave. He packed his cart with blankets and other provisions the Mannings had asked him to take back to the Upcountry. A package of woolen cloth for Gwynne, some candies for the children, and some preserves that Eugenia had been hoarding for special occasions.

Old Bill came in to say his wagon was packed, and he was ready to be on his way. John Manning walked into the courtyard and watched the old man help a bent old black woman up onto the seat beside him, then Old Bill, too, mounted the wagon, clucked to his horse, and the wagon with its wheels bent inward rumbled and creaked off down the street.

George Manning rode with Jack Kimble and the remnants of the group Drew had ridden with, but there was little they could do that was effective against the British. Everyone was waiting to see what General George Washington would do, and whom he would appoint to replace General Lincoln. George kept in touch with everyone he knew in North Carolina and Georgia, and corresponded with a few men in Virginia. In three different letters from different men he learned that Congress had appointed Horatio Gates, the victor of Saratoga, commander of the Southern Department of the war. In another missive George learned that Gates was losing no time. He had gathered what was left of the Continental Army at Coxe's Mill in North Carolina under the command of General Johann de Kalb. Gates gathered as many militia units as he could, including the survivors of Monck's Corners and Lenud's Ferry. As soon as word spread telling of his arrival, he expected others to join him on his march south to Camden.

Among others who heard word of Gates's arrival and intended destination was Cornwallis. Cornwallis had plans of his own. With Georgia and South Carolina subdued, he was ready to move his armies into North Carolina and continue north, using Camden as a base. Lord Rawdon, also alert to any news of Gates, reported to Cornwallis in Charles Town that Gates had an army of seven thousand Americans and was marching steadily south.

Closer to the truth, Gates had about three thousand Americans, most of whom were in no condition to march, let alone fight. Unfortunately Cornwallis did not know this and was convinced that his British troops were outnumbered by about three to one. He came to Camden to take command himself.

George Manning had called a meeting of Jack Kimble's men as soon as he heard that Gates was on his way and was in need of fit men. In short order the men made the decision to gather whatever supplies they could and join Gates as soon as possible. George rode back to Cherokee in all haste to tell Ned and Gwynne of the news and to prepare himself for what would most likely be a long, arduous campaign.

When he rode into the yard, there was a rickety old cart standing in front of the door. Since it was indistinguishable from any other farm cart, George did not recognize it, and thought nothing of it other than it was odd that it should be directly in front of the house. He jumped down from his horse, threw the reins over the post, and ran into the house calling for Gwynne. She answered him from the parlor. He strode in, then stopped dead in his tracks at the vision of Gwynne sitting on the sofa close beside an old black woman. Old Bill stood near the door, hat in hand. George looked from Old Bill to the old woman, then dismissed both of them. "Gwynne, Gates is on his way. Jack Kimble and—"

"Aren't you going to say hello to our guests?" Gwynne asked with a smile, her eyes dancing.

"Gwynne! Listen to me. This is important. It may be *the* most important battle in the war! Jack Kimble and—"

"George!" Gwynne interrupted with some authority.

The old woman got up and walked over to him, standing very near. Without realizing he was doing so, he moved his hand to brush her aside. The old woman made a clucking sound in her throat. "My, my, I have learned a lot in this garb."

George spun on his heel and stared at the old woman open-mouthed. Then he gasped, "Grandma! Oh, my God, Grandma . . . is that you?"

"Oh, yes, George, it is I," she said with a bit of sarcasm. "And now that you know who I am, I want you to reward this man handsomely. He has done an heroic job, and kept me very safe and comfortable."

George stood as though rooted to the floor. Gwynne giggled, and Elizabeth snapped, "Get on with it. The man is exhausted! He has been traveling for nearly five weeks! See that he is comfortable, and I want him given his own plot of land, a mule, tools, and the means to build a cabin. If Drew disagrees, I shall take responsibility, and deal with it, so don't voice the objection I see on your lips!"

"Yes, Grandma," George said, backing up a few steps.

"And be quick about it! I want to hear what Horatio Gates is about."

As George hurried out with Old Bill, Gwynne laughed and laughed. "Oh, Elizabeth, it is so good to have you here! You are priceless! Did you see the look on George's face?"

"I did indeed, and I saw how he treated me when he thought I was an

old black woman. I want to talk to you about that, Gwynne. You did not
do a great deal better yourself, but first things first. It sounds to me that we
had better see to getting Drew released very soon, or we shall find ourselves in the midst of a battle. I wouldn't care for that."

33

On the morning of August 15, 1780, Elizabeth and Gwynne set off for Camden and the British outpost. Elizabeth had managed to bring only one dress with her in Old Bill's wagon, and that black. Dissatisfied with it, she sat in the carriage opposite Gwynne brooding about the dress. "If I am to be Mrs. Templeton out on a loyalist social call to our honorable troops, why on earth would I be garbed for a funeral?" she muttered.

"Elizabeth, you are just not accustomed to behaving as old women do. I know of many older women who wear black. As a matter of fact, I don't recall seeing my grandma in anything but black. I think she remained in mourning for Grandpa for the rest of her life."

"I suppose it will satisfy. . . . I must not have been thinking when I left Charles Town. I should have brought something else."

"You couldn't. It would have been seen," Gwynne said, and leaned forward to pat her hand. "Now, do stop fussing. We know we want the key to the jail, but neither of us has a plausible story to gain it, or a feasible means of getting it."

"We will," Elizabeth said. "Do you . . . would you mind giving me a bit of the ribbon on your hat, Gwynne?"

Gwynne looked blankly at her. "Why do you want the ribbon? Elizabeth, are you all right?"

"I have not gone dotty on you, dear, I just want a bit of ribbon to brighten this up a bit."

Gwynne removed her hat and worked a piece of ribbon loose, then played a bit with it, so that the missing piece wouldn't show.

Old Bill sat atop the carriage, Elizabeth having demanded that George search high and low until he found an old English-type cab carriage. He was dressed in a fine red and navy-blue livery that had been put together from Drew's clothes, the women's capes, and other pieces of material they had been able to find around Cherokee. Old Bill sat rigid backed and proud as he drove boldly into Camden, asked directions to the house where Lord Cornwallis was staying, and then pulled his carriage up near the front door.

Old Bill helped Gwynne, then Elizabeth, from the carriage. Elizabeth stood on the sidewalk for a moment, straightened her dress and her back, then, head high, sailed up to the front door and knocked.

"I wish to see Lord Cornwallis," she said haughtily to the young officer who answered the door.

Being told he was not available for visitors, Elizabeth lifted her head up even higher. "You, man, you will tell your commander that Mrs. Reginald Templeton is awaiting him in the front parlor—you do have a front parlor?"

"Yes, ma'am, but—"

She pushed past him and Gwynne followed, her heart beating so hard it threatened to rise and lodge in her throat.

"Madame . . . Mrs. Templeton, you can't . . ."

"I have, dear boy. Now, do run along and tell your commander that I shall see him." She sat down, arranging her black skirts around her.

Muttering, the young man went to the door, then turned childlike and said, "He's going to have me shot. I have orders!"

"And I am going to have you thrashed if you dare speak one more impudent word!"

The young officer disappeared, closing the parlor doors after him.

"Elizabeth, I do not know where you get the nerve!" Gwynne whispered.

"Hush, dear, I thought I heard someone coming down the hall."

Moments after, the parlor door opened, and an imposing man stood there. He looked at each of the women, an appreciative twinkle in his eye. "Mrs. Templeton," he said bowing to her and taking her hand to his lips. "I was informed that you find it urgent to speak to me."

"I do indeed, sir. As you undoubtedly know, Riverlea Plantation has been a reliable source of supply for your men. My granddaughter and I have taken it upon ourselves to make a tour of the outposts to see how the men are faring, and what might be needed that Riverlea can provide. I would appreciate your accompanying us on a tour of the post, particularly the infirmary. We were informed that you have here a good many wounded."

"Mrs. Templeton, for the King, for the Empire itself, I offer you our heartiest thanks for the superb work you have done, and your loyalty to the cause; however, you have come at an inopportune time. At this very moment my generals and I are engaged in war plans."

Elizabeth's eyes glinted. "There is to be a battle? I'll wager it is that wretched Gates come to harass us!" She waggled a finger at him as though he had been the one at fault. "I quite understand, of course. You must get right back to your strategic planning. We must all do our part, mustn't we? Now, I, for example, have worn black since the outbreak of hostilities, and I shall wear nothing but black until the vulgar rabble have been quelled and punished!" Before he could speak, she moved closer to him, her face only inches from his, if a considerable space lower. "I have but one spot of color on my person! A ribbon in the British colors. The day you have conquered and placed these colonies back into the hands of our beloved King, then and only then shall I burst forth with color and cheer! Back to the war table, sir!"

Cornwallis backed up a step, almost as if he felt compelled to obey her.

"Now, if you will just lend us the services of that young man who answered the door, we'll be off on our inspection of the infirmary!"

"I'm sorry, madame, but that is not possible. As I explained to you, we are preparing for battle."

"Oh, then it is imminent," Elizabeth cooed, her eyes dancing with interest.

"Yes, it is, so I'm sure you understand that I cannot—"

"Of course, dear man! Of course, I understand. My granddaughter and I shall see to ourselves. We will manage quite handily alone. As I said, we must all do our part!" She tapped him on the chest and sashayed toward the door. "Don't you worry about us! We'll find our way around."

Cornwallis jumped to the door before her. "Roberts! Lieutenant Roberts! Show these ladies the infirmary and anything else they want to see!" He took the young man aside. "God's eyes! Make sure they are busy until we have left."

The young man looked at him, real pain in his eyes.

Cornwallis gave him a hearty pat of encouragement on the back and said in a low voice, "Templeton—Riverlea."

"Yes, sir," the young man said, quickly turning to lead his charges out of his commander's way.

Elizabeth seemed tireless. She would not allow Lieutenant Roberts to pass casually by anything. She commented, questioned, and took enormous amounts of time. As the sun began to sink in the west, it was becoming apparent that Lieutenant Roberts was going to get left behind. Already he could hear the sounds that indicated that Lord Rawdon and Cornwallis were nearing readiness to march.

Cornwallis and his generals had decided that with Gates on his way toward Camden with a superior force, their best chance was a surprise attack. Cornwallis had spent most of the day, and several days before that, routing their best line of attack so that Gates could be caught unawares and unprepared to do battle. Knowing that if he withdrew to Charles Town a great many sick and wounded would have to be left behind, Cornwallis marched out of Camden on the Waxhaw Road north.

At about the same time, and for many of the same reasons, Gates decided his best plan was to take Cornwallis by surprise. To that end he ordered his army to march from the mill on August fifteenth, heading south. The spearhead of his army was lead by a French volunteer, the Marquis de la Roverie, Armand Charles Tuffin, who was now in command of what was left of Pulaski's Legion.

Elizabeth was still maintaining a steady and annoying stream of chatter, and unflagging interest in any detail Lieutenant Roberts cared to show her. All that remained of the entire Camden post were the supply wagons, the prison, and the latrines. The young man tried to end their tour right there, gesturing that there was nothing left of interest. He was still managing to be polite and hospitable, and Gwynne marveled at his endurance; even she was finding Elizabeth annoying and terribly tedious.

"I shall look at the prisons," Elizabeth said, when she was certain the troops were out of the town.

Lieutenant Roberts sighed and began to walk to the prison. Elizabeth poked her head into every cell, made comments, and finally found Drew. Both she and Gwynne were hard pressed not to cry out. He was lying against a wall, a dirty bandage still tied around his leg, thin and covered with filth. At first he showed no sign of recognition or movement when they stood by the cell; then, as he listened to the voice that talked on and on, he slowly rolled over and looked into the eyes of his grandmother.

Elizabeth quickly put her hand to her mouth, touching her lips for silence. She turned with equal haste to Lieutenant Roberts.

"Quite a stench, isn't there? Do you suppose it is the filth or the natural odor of the rebels?"

Roberts laughed. "I think the latter."

"Still, it wouldn't hurt to do a bit of scrubbing. I should think the men in the infirmary—it's so near—would suffer greatly from the odor of this pit! It has made me feel quite faint. Go fetch my carriage, young man. I have had quite enough," Elizabeth demanded.

Roberts turned to call to a uniformed man standing a few feet away. Elizabeth's sharp eyes caught the sight of keys at his belt.

"I asked you to see to it!" she screeched. "If you do not, I am certain I shall faint!" And in demonstration, she swayed dangerously, catching herself with a hand on the wall.

"Oh, please! Do hurry! She has spells! Please!" Gwynne cried.

Roberts wasted no more time: he turned, walked a few paces, then ran.

Keeping her crouched position, Elizabeth whispered, "Find something to incapacitate that man with, Gwynne. You must get the keys!" With that Elizabeth let out a terrible moan, and the man moved nearer.

"Is there anything I can do, ma'am?" he asked, and reached for her arm. "Are you in pain?"

Elizabeth moaned again keeping the guard's attention, as Gwynne searched with her eyes for anything to use. She saw nothing and could think of nothing but a pistol, and that was impossible. She jumped as a filthy hand grasped her shoulder from inside the cell. She whirled and looked into the eyes of her husband. In his hand he had the walnut stock of a musket. Gesturing with the broken piece, he indicated she should hit the man with it. Gwynne closed her eyes, then reached for the stock. Hesitating, eyes closed again, she took a deep breath, and brought the stock down on the man's head. She cried in surprise at the hardness of his head and the pain the blow shot into her hands and fingers. Then, to her horror, the man did not fall. He staggered back, his hand going to his head, but he didn't fall! The stock lay on the ground, and Gwynne stared at the soldier open mouthed.

Elizabeth dropped to her knees, retrieved the fallen stock and, struggling to get up, handed it back to Gwynne. "Hurry!" she cried. Gwynne took the stock in both hands and ran at the stunned man, swinging it back and forth like a club, no longer aware of pain in her hands or anywhere else. She hit him repeatedly about the head and neck. The man batted at her blows, but also had Elizabeth to contend with. She hadn't much of a weapon, but Elizabeth was rarely completely defenseless. She had her reticule, which was filled with several medium-sized stones, and began to swing it wildly, hitting him on the back, in the stomach, and on the head. Finally the man backed away from them, shouting for help, until he was against the cell door and too near Drew Manning's reach. Drew's arm snaked out of the cell and wrapped tightly around the man's shoulder and neck. With the help of the two women he soon had a death grip on the soldier. "Get the keys from his belt while I hold him," Drew ordered.

Gwynne's fingers were rubbery. She fumbled at the key ring several times before she was able to release it. Still shaking badly, she had difficulty getting the key into the lock.

"Hurry! I can hear the carriage—that young man may be with Old Bill, and I think we have done quite enough damage without having to harm him, too," Elizabeth said. "Please, hurry! I think for once, I may truly faint!"

Old Bill, as though he had a sixth sense, came wheeling around the corner of the building, the horses pointed north. The unconscious man was pressed against the door. Weakened and thin as he was, Drew had a difficult time pushing the door open wide enough to let himself out. The two women, in response to Drew's shout, ran for the carriage.

Old Bill fidgeted on the top of the carriage, his eyes on the path leading back to the headquarters. "He comin' . . . he comin' fas', Mastah Drew!"

Drew ran with a limping gait to the carriage and flung himself inside. Old Bill clucked at his horses and gave an unfamiliar snap to the reins. The horses bolted forward, unseating all the occupants of the carriage. Old Bill sent the vehicle rocking at top speed north on the Waxhaw Road.

Elizabeth and Gwynne told Drew of everything they had learned about the impending battle.

"Good God, we're going to catch up with the British troops if we keep on this road!" Drew said, and pounded on the roof of the carriage for Old Bill to stop. "Why did you bring this ancient thing? Where did you find it?"

"I wanted to look English," Elizabeth said primly. "I sent George out for it. You'll have to ask him from whom he scared it up."

"I'd kiss you, Grandma, but I smell too bad, and I'm crawling with vermin."

Elizabeth smiled and scratched exaggeratedly at her arm. "I noticed."

"I'm afraid to ask, Drew. . . . Hasn't that wound healed yet?" Gwynne asked timidly.

Drew poked at his leg. "It's healed—as much as it is likely to."

"But it's still bandaged."

He shrugged. "There seemed no point in taking it off." He made a wry, bitter face. "It reminds me of Arthur. There are times when the memory of my brother is the only thing that makes me want to get out of this. . . ."

"Drew . . . you are out of there. Old Bill is waiting for you to tell him what you want him to do. We don't have much time. I am sure Lieutenant Roberts is going to send someone out after us," Gwynne said.

Drew squeezed his eyes closed and put his head in his hands for a second. "God, I am sorry! You don't need to have a crazed man on your hands. Let me think . . . let me think. . . ."

Old Bill got down from the top and came round to the door, peeking in the window. "We gots to be goin', suh!" he said urgently.

"The army is a ways down this same road, Bill. We can't continue on this road, and we can't go back, for Lieutenant Roberts is likely to have sent men out after us."

"How near to the swamps are we, Bill?" Drew asked.

"Mebbe a mile, or two more, we comes to the edge ob de swamps."

"Could you lead us through them?" Drew asked.

Bill shook his old head. "Dis ol' carriage be on its side in no time."

"We'll leave the carriage," Drew said.

"Drew, Elizabeth cannot walk through a swamp! And neither can I," Gwynne said.

"I kin unhitch de horses," Bill said thoughtfully. "Mebbe we git through. Missy kin ride, de res' o' us walk." He gave Gwynne a hard look. "Mebbe you kin ride de odder horse."

Drew got out of the carriage to help. "Do away with as much as you can," he said, then looked away. "Petticoats and the like."

It took fifteen minutes for the two men to free the horses, and the women to free themselves of extra petticoats, frills, and hats. Once they were all standing on the road, Drew looked at Old Bill and said, "Bill, we're in your hands."

Boldly Elizabeth winked at him when his eyes met hers. He grinned broadly and toothlessly at Drew, nodded, and said, "Yas, suh! We be on ouah way home!" He helped Elizabeth onto her horse, and Drew aided Gwynne; then he followed Bill's lead down the road for a bit longer. The old man kept peering into the increasingly thick growth as the road gradually sloped downward. Finally, almost a mile along, he found what he was looking for, and he turned off the Waxhaw Road onto the spongier turf of a path through the dark growth of the swamp. Deeper and deeper they went into damp, muddy lanes that he seemed able to find in the dark.

It was the deepest part of the night when they heard the sounds of horses. The four stopped, standing still, trying to discern if it was the British army, or a group sent after them. "Too many," Old Bill said. "Lots an' lots o' horses."

"There was rumor . . . more than rumor that Gates was on his way south," Elizabeth said. "George went to join up with him, but I thought he was in North Carolina."

Shouts were heard, and a rush of noise as horses and riders moved hastily about.

What they had heard was the Marquis de la Roverie meeting head on with the British advance patrol. In disarray and totally surprised confusion the two patrols tried to sort themselves out in the darkness and get back to their respective commanders to inform them of the presence of the other army.

Afraid to move for a time, the four fugitives stood still trying to figure out what happened and what they should do.

"Dere be a place where de swamp pinch in on de road. We gotta cross ober so's we git home," Old Bill said. "I show you."

They followed as the old man continued his corkscrewing path through the swamp, always keeping them on fairly sound footing, while all around them they could hear the sounds of water, and creatures moving about, but could see nothing. Blindly they followed one another single file, each keeping a hand on the one before him.

Unfortunately, at the spot to which Old Bill was leading them for the crossing, the two armies had lined up an impressive array of forces facing each other.

On the British side were lined along the front the Legion of Irish Volunteers, the 33rd and 23rd Light Infantry, and behind them forces led by Lord Rawdon, Bryan, Cornwallis with the 71st, and Tarleton and his cavalry.

Facing them were the North Carolina Militia, the Virginia Militia, the 2nd of Maryland and Delaware, and the 1st Maryland, men unprepared for a fight, for Gates, unlike Cornwallis, had not laid out any plan of battle.

The Battle of Camden opened with a cannonade and a general British advance in columns. The Americans tried to meet the advance before the troops were deployed, but they were not fast enough, and the British were in position waiting for them, shouting and cheering as they came on.

With the darkness and the numbers of men, confusion broke loose in all directions. Gates's men held their positions, particularly on the right, which was under a furious British attack.

George Manning and Jack Kimble, Jasper Spikes and Nathan Parker, moved closer together after the first surprise encounter and burst of gunfire.

George groped in the darkness, reaching for the man next to him. "Jack? You there? God, don't leave me! I can't see a damned thing!"

"It's Nathan," came the whispered reply.

They moved forward in the water, feeling for footing. Nathan grunted as he crashed to the spongy earth with a splash. All four men stopped as he regained his feet and retrieved his musket and knife.

Before them there was only a tangle of black and dark-gray shadows of growth and the knobby-kneed forms of the tall cypress roots. In their area for the moment it was quiet, but close by they could see the flash of muskets and hear the bark of sporadic gunfire. And somewhere in the blackness of the swamp in front of them they could hear the unmistakable sound of men moving. But they could identify nothing. They had no way of knowing who was ahead, friend or foe.

George moved slowly, carefully, trying to shift from the cover of one tree to another, and keeping as near to the water channels as he could. He and the others stopped again, listening, straining their eyes against the darkness, hoping to see or hear something to guide them.

"I've never been so damned scared in my life," Jasper said. "You see anything? Where the hell's our men? I got the awful feeling we're out here all alone."

Time moved with cruel slowness, and nothing happened. George remembered his complaints to Drew that he couldn't stand the waiting. What a fool he had been! Tonight he would happily wait and wait, provided someone would guarantee him that there was really nothing to wait for. Whatever was coming this night, he did not want to experience.

They had only moved about a hundred yards, not certain of their direction or location, when suddenly the night lit up with a burst of heavy guns and musket fire. The four of them scattered as a shell splashed into the water; then another burst against the trunk of a cypress. George heard Jasper Spikes scream, then heard a thunderous burst and the cracking of a tree. Before he could see or move to avoid it, a huge limb came hurtling down, striking him on the arm. He sank to the ground, tangled in the foliage, his arm a paralyzed agony. Pain shot up the arm from fingertips to shoulder. He tried to sit up, but fell back feeling sick and faint.

George didn't know how long he lay there, or if he lost consciousness, but when he tried to move again, the pain was different, and he could move his fingers. The guns were still firing, occasionally lighting the area. "Jack!" he called in a hoarse whisper as he saw movement some ten yards from him. "Nathan? Jasper? Jack? Are any of you here?"

No one answered him, and he grew rigid with fear, wondering if the man he had seen in a flash of light had been a Tory and not Jack at all.

A hand reached out of the darkness and touched his shoulder. George scrabbled frantically, trying to locate his knife or musket, any weapon. His hands closed on nothing but tree branches. The rustling continued, and again the hand groped in the darkness. "Who's that?" George asked breathlessly.

A weak voice laughed almost in a sob. "Oh, God, George! It is you."

"Jack?"

"Yes . . . you all right?"

"I can't find my musket."

The two of them groped through the branches and waited for the gunfire light to aid them. As they moved on hands and knees, feeling their way, George's hands fell upon the warm unmistakable bulk of a human body. He jumped back. "Jack! Someone's here." The guns burst forth again, and George stared momentarily into what was left of Jasper Spikes's face. He doubled over and heaved up what was left in his already sore and sick stomach. Then a great anger swept over him, and he clambered to his feet.

"We've got to get out of here," Jack said, sounding as sick as George.

"No, by God, not until I've killed one of these sons of bitches with my own hands!" he cried and plunged off into the darkness toward the sounds and flashes of the guns. George, with Jack and Nathan following, found their adversary not twenty yards from where they themselves had been. Coming upon the British troops by surprise, George discharged his musket, felling one man, and then charged forward, knife in hand, to attack another. He lunged at the soldier just as the man was whirling to face him. The soldier lifted his musket, ready to fire; but George thrust aside the barrel of the gun. The two men grappled, falling into the swampy water. The soldier grabbed George's injured arm and, finding the weakness, pressed the advantage, shoving George's head under the water.

For the first time in his life, George Manning faced imminent death. The soldier had hold of his injured arm, and try as he might George could not withstand the pain that came every time he tried to bring his head above water, and the man twisted that arm. He began to black out; his overwhelming need and urge was to open his mouth and breathe in whatever was there. With a scream of agony George reared back with all the strength he had, bursting into the air. He heard and felt the arm snap, but there was in him a deep rage, and a need to live. On his knees now, he lunged at the soldier and drove the knife deep into his chest. His face was but inches from the soldier's. The man grabbed for his throat, a look of horrified surprise and pain on his face. George wrenched the knife from bone and flesh and drove it into the man's gut. The soldier lunged forward, falling face first into the swamp.

George staggered to his feet and leaned against the cypress, trying to rid himself of the dizziness, the flaming pain of his arm that now seemed to be surging throughout his body. He was racked with coughing, and his lungs ached. Then he realized that he could see shapes, and men moving. Dawn was coming. He turned and saw Jack Kimble run from the cover of some heavy bush, a soldier on his heels. George stooped, picked up the dead man's musket, aimed, and shot. The soldier following Jack cried out and fell.

Jack Kimble glanced at the man writhing in the water, and ran to George. "We're alone here—we've got to get out!"

"I don't know how far I can get with this arm, Jack. . . . I don't think I can run."

"You damned well better run—there's more of those red-coated bastards a few minutes away heading right for us, and Tarleton's horsemen are comin'."

"I can run," George gasped. He took a few steps and stopped again. "I can't take this, Jack . . . I got to find something to support this arm."

Jack Kimble gave a wary glance behind them, then saw the bloodied body of a militiaman on the ground. He ran over to it and removed the man's belt. "Here, use this—that fella isn't going to need it."

With Jack's help George fashioned a sling for his arm, and the two men headed deeper into the swamp, guided only by the direction of gunfire behind them. They didn't stop running until the sound of guns was far in the distance. About noon the two of them reached higher ground and collapsed onto the dry, sun-warmed grass. Both men, exhausted, fell instantly asleep, unable to react to danger any longer. It was growing dark again when they awakened. Neither man spoke of Jasper or of Nathan, who had died trying to help Jack. They moved together, knowing, without having to say a word, that they were in search of food. They crept along the road, staying near to the cover of trees, not knowing when or if they would run into enemy troops, searching for a farmhouse, tavern, or plantation they knew to be friendly.

That same night, Drew and Bill conferred, and agreed that they would never get through, and could not stay where they were. "We'll have to go deeper into the swamp, until we can get beyond this action. Can you do it, Bill?"

"Ah 'spec' we gotta. Daylight be comin' soon, dat be a he'p."

They set off again, away from the road and into the heart of the swamp. Daylight made the going a bit easier and considerably faster. Slowly the cannon fire and the gunfire grew fainter. Elizabeth and Gwynne were exhausted to the point of insensibility by nightfall of the next day. Drew was in little better shape. He kept moving, holding himself upright by hanging on to the horse's harness.

Alone, Bill set about gathering dry wood for a fire and fashioning a hut of sticks and leaves that would cover Elizabeth. Again, alone, the old man went into the muck of the swamp and came back with several frogs, which he roasted.

Drew roused himself at the scent of food, then he looked alarmed. "They'll see the fire! Put it out!"

"Nobody see. We too fah away, an' iffen dey do see dey ain't comin'. Dey don' keer 'bout us."

They ate, and then slept. It was nearly noon before the small camp awakened, to find Bill in possession of an animal no one dared ask the identity of, which he intended to feed them for breakfast. They all ate gratefully, and Elizabeth and Gwynne mounted the horses again, and the foursome went on. They dragged into Cherokee five days after they had left for Camden, their clothes torn and filthy, their spirits low with fatigue and hunger.

Ned came out to meet them and immediately called for help. Nathaniel came running round the side of the tobacco barn when he heard the ringing of the plantation bell, and Jane Reston and Penny and Mary came from the house. Well disciplined, and accustomed to reacting instantly to emergencies, each of them scattered in a different direction to see to bath water, food, drink, clean clothes, ointments, the horses, and aid in getting the four travelers into the house.

George Manning struggled into Cherokee the day after Drew and the others had. He had managed to get himself out of the swamp and the battle with nothing more serious than a wound to his left hand and a broken arm. Cherokee quickly came to look more like a hospital than a home. Elizabeth and Gwynne were both in bed, and Ned insisted on looking after the festering sores that were all over Drew's body as the result of filth, poor food, and neglect. George's arm was in a splint of Ned's devising, and he was ordered to remain still until his headaches passed. Angrily he said to Drew, who had hobbled into his room, "I should have expected this! Remember at Ninety Six, when I smashed this hand with one of the swivel guns? That was a warning. The damned bastards shot that same hand."

Drew chuckled. "How's the arm?"

"An insult. A cannonball hit a damned tree limb, and sent it down on my arm and head." He had the grace to grin. "I guess it's better to have a broken arm and a sore head than the other way round."

"You're lucky to have gotten out at all," Drew said. "Jack Kimble's been round. Jasper Spikes and Nathan Parker didn't come back. It was a bloody battle. Gates was routed . . . lost hundreds of men. Jack said Cornwallis has enough prisoners to form a new army. What happened?"

"That damned Gates would have done better to hand us all over to the British! The men he brought from North Carolina weren't ready to fight. Most of them were still recovering from other battles. They weren't rested and they weren't supplied, but that didn't stop Gates. He marched them along the road and made up for lack of food by feeding them corn mush and molasses with some godawful meat and bread . . . do you have any idea what that does to a man's innards? By God, I've never known such pain!" He gingerly moved his arm and hand. "Nothing, compared to what that poison did! We spent more damn time in the woods than we did fighting!"

"We're not going to win with this kind of battle. Our men aren't trained for it, and we sure as hell are not supplied."

"For once you're not telling me something I don't already know," George said. "But I don't have a good idea of what to do."

"We'll give you—and me—some time to heal. Then let's find Marion or Sumter. Of all of them, it seems to me they are the ones with the right idea. You hear a good deal in prison. The trouble is that you can't do anything about it. But—"

"Now you're out and ready to do something," George concluded for him, and smiled broadly. "You know, Drew, sometimes I sit here and think I have gone daft. I'm hurt, just left a campaign that was a bloodbath —a terrible defeat—you are like a ghost, you're so thin and disabled; but I have this feeling of . . . of power. I don't feel defeated. I feel like I'm a victor . . . or am going to be."

"Get some rest now. We're going to have a long haul in front of us before that comes true," Drew said. He got up, preparing to leave for his own bed and sleep. As he opened the door, George said, "Would you mind telling Jane I need a little nursing?"

George had the best of care from Jane Reston, and an attentive ear to all his dreams and hopes for the future. Jane spent every free moment she had with George, and some that weren't so free. When she felt better, Gwynne had come to the room to find George, Jane, and the four children there.

"I'm helping," George said beaming. Adrian is going to be as good a reader as his brother, and Susan is an expert already. Read this story for your mother, Susan."

Later Gwynne said to Drew, "I suppose I should say something to her about the amount of time she spends with him, but I don't have the heart. They both look so happy."

Drew smiled and put his arms around her. "I don't think you'll be remiss in your motherly duties if you let Jane become a little lax in their lessons. I actually think you would be wiser to begin a search for a new tutor. I rather doubt we are going to have Jane's services much longer."

"Do you really think they will marry?" Gwynne asked, her deep blue eyes filled with warmth and curiosity.

"I think they will. . . . I think they had better, or we may have another Manning scandal."

"You have a vile mind." Gwynne giggled.

"I count it a very nice thought. I'd consider another scandal with you if we weren't already married." He kissed her nose, her eyes, then her lips, and the teasing was over. With his strength returning, Drew Manning turned to his wife with all the fervor and love of their early married days.

Drew's hands roved over the lush curves of her body. He kissed her lips, lingering, enjoying the feel and smell of her soft, scented skin.

Gwynne turned to him, a great wave of protective emotion coursing through her. He was so painfully thin, and yet he was Drew, her Drew. She returned his kisses with all the passion of her being. Her hands moved as eagerly as his, touching the hard, muscled, angular curves of his body as he sought the softer, lusher contours of hers. At a moment they both knew from long years of answering the feelings of each other, Gwynne wrapped her legs around his hips and drew him to her. They moved together, renewing each other and their love in a language that no words would ever match.

Drew's and George's languid days of love and recovery were short lived, for the news that came in from around the countryside was bad. The fighting was vicious, and the British committed atrocities in several instances that the patriots could not abide. There had been for some time a phrase used when mercy was denied, "Tarleton's quarters," and now there was word that at Fort MacKay the wounded Americans who had had to be left behind had been hanged and their bodies sent to the Indians to be scalped.

Occasionally, however, good news came in along with the bad. Hearing of the victories, small though many of them were, gave all of them hope.

Something could be done, and the good news supported what Drew had heard in prison. If the war were to be won, it would be won on back roads and in small bands. In the Battle of Black Mingo Swamp, Francis Marion drove the Tories into the swamp for safety. The victory at King's Mountain raised the spirits of all Americans.

George's arm hadn't healed until late October, but as soon as he had use of the arm, he was ready to go. Once again the Mannings said good-bye to each other. This time, however, Gwynne was a little calmer, and a little more accepting of Drew's need to fight. "We'll be fine. Nathaniel is getting to be quite a hand. Ned says he is a big help, so we'll get the harvest to market, and you don't need to worry about food. Ned has seen to that, too."

Drew looked at her, his eyes soft with love. "You're a brave woman, Gwynne Manning. I wouldn't be able to do anything if it weren't for you."

She smiled. "Well, you said I'd have to make it my fight, and I have, but if you notice, I did it through you—just as *I* always said!"

"Noted!" he agreed. "I'll get messages to you whenever I can."

She kissed him again, and walked to the front of the house to watch him and George mount their horses and ride off in search of Francis Marion, who was becoming known popularly as the Swamp Fox.

Gwynne and Elizabeth and the family settled in to wait for the return of the men, expecting that it would be some time before that happened. None of them expected this to be a short foray, but then Christmas came and went, and they had had only one mud-smeared letter from Drew from a place called Fishdam Ford, and Jane had received one letter from George from Georgetown, where he and Drew had finally caught up with Marion's forces.

The three women sat in the morning room reading over again the two letters. "It does not sound as though they anticipate returning anytime soon, does it?" Gwynne said with a sigh. "Why is it that when we—or at least I—think of war, it seems a rather quick thing? No one ever seems to tell you how long it drags on, the months and months that pass between letters and messages."

Jane looked up, her expressive eyes filled with amazement. "I thought I was the only one who thought it would be over by now. Do you really get terribly tired of all the waiting, Mrs. Manning?"

Gwynne glanced at her, then away again, returning to stare out the window. "Call me Gwynne, Jane. It seems silly to be so formal when we are all sitting about talking about and waiting for exactly the same thing."

"And unless I am going blind in my old age," Elizabeth said, "you will be a member of the family shortly after George returns."

"Well, that depends. We've decided we shall not marry under British rule. If George comes back a victor, then we shall marry. If not—we haven't decided yet."

Elizabeth smiled, and said with a tinge of sarcasm, "You could always leave the country—or colonies, as the case may be."

Jane turned bright, light-brown eyes on her. "Yes! That's what we thought. Perhaps Florida—if we are not an independent nation."

"Good heavens! You'd have the Spanish to contend with down there," Gwynne said.

"Well, we have also talked about settling in some of the land beyond the mountains. George says there are vast expanses out there," Jane said, and waved her hand vaguely to indicate land so vast she could not comprehend it.

"You and George have made quite a few plans," Gwynne said. "I do hope, for the safety of both of you, that he comes home a victor. He may be in great danger from his and your ambitions than he is from the British."

All of them were edgy, frightened, and irritable before the next letter arrived. It came from George, and unfortunately did not mention Drew. Mostly he told Jane how much he missed her and in passing said that he was with Francis Marion and had just participated in an ambush at Wiboo Swamp. The battle had taken place March 6, 1781. The letter didn't reach Cherokee until April twenty-ninth.

Gwynne was nearly beside herself with worry. Elizabeth tried to comfort her. "If anything had happened to Drew, he would have said so."

"Then why hasn't he written? I haven't heard from him for three months. He would write if he could! He's probably been captured. Maybe other letters have been written and we haven't received them. Maybe George said nothing because he thinks we already know."

"Gwynne, I am going to fix you some tea with laudanum in it. You must calm down. You are making yourself ill," Elizabeth said sternly.

As Elizabeth hurried to the kitchen, Jane knelt on the floor in front of Gwynne. "He'll write soon. I am certain he will."

"It isn't like Drew. If he could, he would already have written," Gwynne insisted, and blew her nose vigorously.

"It may be as you suggested—the letters could have gone astray. He may have written many times," Jane said.

It wasn't until May, however, that Gwynne's worries were quelled. She then got an enthusiastic letter from Drew describing in detail the eight-day siege of Fort Watson. Faced with defeat after eight ineffective days of trying to breach the fort, one of Marion's officers, Hezekiah Maham, built a tower of logs during the night. He mounted a six-pounder at the top and constructed it so that men could mount it and shoot into the fort. Drew ended with a written hurrah, for they had taken one hundred twenty British prisoners and, most importantly, large stores of arms and ammunition.

Drew and George were not as inconsiderate as they seemed with their infrequent letter writing. Francis Marion seldom stayed in one place any longer than it took to decide upon his next foray. By the time the letter about Fort Watson reached Gwynne and the family, Marion and his men were on their way to Fort Motte, and Drew had been hard pressed to find anyone who was traveling in the direction of Cherokee to deliver his letter.

Fort Motte was a highly strategic location during the war, for it overlooked the juncture of the Congaree River and the Wateree River where they join to form the Santee River. Supplies were sent up the Santee from Charles Town to be stored at Fort Motte, then, as needed, sent along the Congaree and Wateree to British forts and posts farther west, like Fort Granby and Ninety Six.

Aside from the strategic importance of the fort, this was a bitter pill for the patriots, for the plantation which was Fort Motte belonged to Jacob Motte, an ardent patriot until his death. The British had forced his widow Rebecca Motte out of her mansion and into a guesthouse so the Motte house could be fortified. Around the house and the immediate area the British dug a trench surrounded by a stockade and an abatis. The garrison normally consisted of a hundred fifty soldiers under Lieutenant McPherson.

At the time Marion, Light Horse Harry Lee, and their men arrived at Fort Motte, a small party of dragoons carrying dispatches to Camden had been pressed into service.

Lee and Marion were welcomed by Rebecca Motte, and they made the old farmhouse on a hill to the north of the mansion their headquarters. Mrs. Motte, a patriot at least as ardent as her deceased husband, had welcomed the Americans into the farmhouse. The men were moved into position around the fort from the hill to the north. Drew, George, and the others marched through a ravine that ran between two hills, and were set to digging trenches. The object was to inch their way along until they could position themselves near enough to the mansion to launch an assault. They had with them a six-pounder which was to be mounted so that they could rake the north end of the house.

The plan was given up when, on May tenth, Marion and Lee found out that Lieutenant Colonel Francis Rawdon, who had just been victorious at Hobkirk's Hill, feared being cut off and was retreating with his forces to Charles Town. He and his men would be coming to Fort Motte. Not wanting the strength of Rawdon and his troops added to the garrison, Lee and Marion realized that the attack on Fort Motte would have to be done quicker than could be accomplished by digging the trenches and slowly gaining position.

Rebecca Motte, whose family had not been used well by the British, told them to burn them out, if necessary. A Brewton before marriage, Mrs. Motte had had her own plantation made into a British fort carrying her name, and her brother had had his fine mansion in Charles Town also taken for a British headquarters. She was quite willing to make whatever sacrifices she had to in terms of personal possessions, to right that wrong.

Mrs. Motte, a small woman, not only gave the Americans leave to burn the British out of her home, she gave them the instruments with which it could be accomplished. Her brother, Miles Brewton, had been given a gift of some African fire arrows by the captain of an East Indiaman. The arrows were specially treated, and would burst into flame upon impact.

Armed with the arrows, and the six-pounder, the men were sent back to the trenches to shoot the arrows at the dry shingles of the roof.

Drew and George stood crunched together trying to get a good view of the bowman. "What do you suppose they put on those things to make it set fire on impact?" Drew asked.

"It hasn't happened yet," George said.

Drew laughed. "Well, if it does work, you realize the makers of these arrows are the same Africans we are always saying are too stupid to learn anything but the simplest tasks."

"I hadn't thought about it. I don't think I want to. Africans are not my favorite people these days."

Drew said nothing, then nudged George as the first arrow flew through the air and stuck the roof. Nothing happened.

George let out a groan, and muttered, "Africans!"

The second arrow whizzed free of the bow, hit the roof, and burst into brilliant flame. As they watched, the dry shingles smoked, then caught. The flames leaped up and crept along the roof. A cheer went up among the men, then one of them cried out as he saw British soldiers running through the house on their way to the attic. They quickly loaded the six-pounder and frightened the men back down.

For a time the men watched nervously, waiting to see what the garrison would do. Rawdon and his forces had managed to come as close as the far side of the river. McPherson was shortly going to get his reinforcements.

The men kept the six-pounder going, and watched as the fire continued to move along the roof of the mansion. Just at the point when the Americans were thinking that all was lost, that the fort would be aided by Rawdon's forces, a white flag showed at a window. Rawdon, with relief for the fort, was just across the river, but McPherson surrendered.

As quickly as the deed was accomplished, a rarity of spirit in this war occurred. The men, both British and American, worked together to put out the fire on the roof of the Motte mansion. With the house saved, the battle won for the Americans, Rebecca Motte accomplished another small miracle. She cooked dinner for the officers of the British and American sides, and sat them at a table together to enjoy it.

Drew and George, outside with the common military men, shook their heads in disbelief and admiration. "Do you remember what you said to me one time in Charles Town, George? About women?"

"Yes, I remember. But those were the women in our family I was talking about."

"I know, but it does make a man wonder. Do you know of any man who could get both sides at a dinner table after a battle? And happily, if the sounds coming through the window are any indication."

George's face took on a dreamy look. "Yeahhh," he dragged out softly. "They all seem so small and helpless and gentle."

Drew nodded. "That's how they seem." Drew sat on the ground near a tree, his eyes looking at nothing as he thought, daydreamed, and considered. He was closer to Cherokee now than he had been in a long time. "What would you think about taking a bit of time and seeing how things are at home? We haven't been there for a long time."

George nodded thoughtfully. "We can always catch up with Marion a bit later. I'd sure like to get over this dysentery."

As soon as Marion and his men were ready to leave from Motte's plantation, Drew and George told Francis Marion of their plans, and asked permission.

Reluctantly it was given. Marion could not stop in his mission until there was no enemy left in South Carolina, and he needed all the men he could get. These two men were tried and reliable in battle, yet he needed them healthy and willing. It was worth a few weeks at home if they came back to him hale and ready to continue the battle.

George and Drew mounted their horses and set off for Cherokee the same morning Marion and his men went in search of the British.

34

American rebels continued to move in and out of Charles Town, taking back to the Upcountry supplies and vital information about the movements of the British. These activities were possible only at great cost to the patriots trapped in Charles Town.

In Charles Town it was the time of the loyalists, and as they had once been at the mercy of the patriot council, they were now taking full advantage the presence of British troops gave them. The Manning household was a sparse one these days. Nonetheless, Eugenia and Bethany continued to prepare anything they could to give to the Americans in the field, and John and Leo used all available cash for the same cause.

As soon as the town was surrendered to the British, the Tories wanted their pound of flesh, and got it. The patriots were considered, and given the status of, prisoners on parole, and this indulgence was given only because it had been included under the articles of capitulation. Not long after the occupation was an established fact, the patriots status began to change in many ways. Shortly after the taking of the town, the British commander required that the citizens take an Oath of Allegiance to the Crown, a policy that soon made conspicuous the most ardent patriots. As quickly as these rebels became obvious, they also became a constant source of suspicion and irritation to the authorities and to the Tories. The rebels did nothing to help matters, but persisted in spreading news and rumor of every American victory, claiming it to be of great importance. The activity and rumor-spreading increased greatly after Nathanael Greene was appointed to take the place of Horatio Gates in conducting the war in the South.

Several of the patriots were openly defiant and were imprisoned for it. And many of them, including John Manning, harbored patriots who stole into town at night and disappeared again with the morning light. Though the British could not stop it, they did all they could to make life miserable for known patriots. They were forbidden to begin legislation against debtors, and eventually, giving in to pressure from the Tories, the British government forbade avowed patriots from working at their trades or running their businesses.

John called a meeting of all the members of his family. They had all been on short supply for some time, and this last restriction was going to make matters worse. "The British have also said they will not feed the families of these men who can no longer ply their trades. Put at its simplest, it means they will either sign the oath of loyalty to Britain, or eventually starve. No matter how deeply we believe, we cannot ask or expect men to stand by and allow their children to go without food."

"But surely, John, the British would never see such a threat through!" Eugenia said. "They would at least feed the children. No one makes war against little children! They're helpless!"

"I wish I could reassure you, Eugenia, but you are asking too much of a nation at war. Their view is that we can take the oath and go on with our usual mode of living, so it is not their responsibility, but our own. There will be no relief for those who fall under this British policy."

"What will that mean to us, Daddy?" Bethany asked.

"Since we do not keep shop or work in the trades, we will be more or less as we have been, except that the chances that either Leo or I will be imprisoned are increased. But, Bethany, because we get supplies from the fields at Willowtree, we . . . I believe we are obligated to share what we have."

"But we have almost nothing now, John! You and Leo never have enough to eat," Eugenia said.

"We are not starving, Eugenia, and we have only two small children in the house. We can get by on less."

"I don't suppose we have a choice, do we?" she said.

The Mannings pulled their belts even tighter, and continued to harbor the patriots who sneaked into town, and to help their neighbors.

But as 1781 wore on, the British dropped any pretense of honoring the articles of capitulation. The Mannings managed to keep going until the beginning of 1782; then both John and Leo were imprisoned for the period of one week. During that week Eugenia and Bethany had a visitor. John Wells, a Tory printer who was noted for his resentments and his desire for revenge against the patriots, came to the Manning residence, as he had done to many others previously. Wells demanded that the Mannings sign the British addresses pledging loyalty. "Now, I know that you can convince your husband that this is the wise course, Mrs. Manning," the man said with oily sweetness.

"I shall tell my husband of your visit when he is released from your prison," Eugenia said tartly. "I'm certain such a pleasant experience will make him receptive to these addresses."

Wells's eyes turned cooler and harder than they normally were. "I don't think you understand, Mrs. Manning. We aren't playing a party game, little words bandied back and forth in polite repartee. These papers are going to be signed, and that healthy young son of yours is going to do battle against those ragtag fools you've been calling an army."

"You must be daft!" Eugenia spat.

"No, ma'am, I'm not, but maybe you are. Accidents happen to people who refuse to do what is right. Can't ever tell when a fire might start, or a group of rioters get out of hand. . . . They can do a mite of damage to a house."

"You're threatening me! We have children in this house."

"Yes, ma'am, and mighty helpless children are. But I'm not threatening you. You misunderstand me. I'm telling you the wise thing to do, and I'm here to help you. We all make mistakes, but sometimes we're given the opportunity to right the wrongs we have done. I'm offering your family that right. That's the way you should look at this visit."

"You are despicable! You are telling me that if I do not prevail upon my son and husband to sign these addresses we will be harmed, perhaps murdered."

"Is that how you see it?" Wells asked. "Maybe that's not a bad way to see it. I'll be taking my leave now, Mrs. Manning. You talk to your husband when he comes home, and I'll be by to visit again real soon. I'll expect a real reformation in this family's allegiances."

Eugenia was shaking when the man left. She sat in the chair, her head in her hands. Bethany, thinking she was crying, knelt to comfort her. Eugenia raised her head. "I am not crying, Beth. I wish I were a man! I would gladly shoot Mr. Wells, or strangle him with my own hands, had I the power!"

"You aren't going to tell Daddy about his visit?" Bethany asked in amazement.

"Oh, yes, I'll tell him, and we'll have to do something. We cannot risk

John Andrew's and Miranda's life on foolhardiness, but by all that's holy I shall never support the Tory cause! Never!"

John and Leo returned home at the end of the week, full of lice and emaciated. After they had been made comfortable, and Eugenia had provided the most nourishing meal she could manage from their scant supplies, she told John and Leo about the visit from John Wells.

Leo's face was a mask of anger. "Self-important little—"

"I don't think I would even mind you using the word that was on the tip of your tongue, Leo. I am afraid my own sentiments about Mr. Wells match yours. Perhaps, after all, there are people for whom there are no decent names," Eugenia said.

"But what are we going to do?" Bethany asked a bit frantically. "He's coming back, and if we don't sign his papers, he's . . . he's going to do something awful!"

"And he'll do it, too," Leo said. "Wells doesn't issue idle threats. Ask Thomas Elfe or some of the others in town."

"Well, I don't see that we have a choice. . . ." John began.

Eugenia jumped to her feet. "You are not going to sign?"

"Of course not, my dear. If you will sit down and calm yourself, I shall finish what I started to say."

"I'm sorry, John . . . but I am very angry," his wife said, and settled on the sofa.

"Others have left the town, and I think we have no choice but to do the same. It will be a difficult and hungry trip, but if we are of one mind and determined, we shall make our way to Cherokee. We should be safe there."

"Then, we shall go," Eugenia said immediately.

"Not so hasty, my dear. Before any decision is made, we must all be aware of what we face. It is not a simple ride in the country. Between us and Cherokee there are armies, and bands of both British and American troops, not to mention the individual forays made by local Tories. If we take the road we shall be in constant danger."

"What Daddy says is correct, Mama," Leo added. "We may not reach Cherokee. There is the possibility of being taken prisoner, or of being attacked—" Leo stopped midsentence, unwilling to draw the thought to its conclusion. Then quietly he added, "We'll be traveling with children, making it even more difficult."

"And we will not always be able to count on the hospitality of the road that we are accustomed to, for we will have no way of knowing if some of these people are patriot or Tory," John said.

Eugenia was pale. "You make it sound impossible. Is it?"

"Honestly, Eugenia, I don't know. Elizabeth managed it, but that was some time ago. But we shall either chance it, or we shall have to consider signing the oath of allegiance to Britain," John said.

"We cannot do that, John!" Eugenia said.

"Then we must go."

Eugenia smoothed her hand across her forehead. "I don't believe I have ever been so frightened, John—not even during the uprising. I feel . . . so watched, so constantly threatened. When I go out on the streets, I am pointed out, looked at, hear rude comments made about me, and now we shall be hounded and threatened as we cross the colony."

John came to her and held both her hands in his. "I am sorry to have alarmed you so, my dear, but it is my respect for you that has made me tell you the dangers we face. We shall make this decision as a family, so we must all be aware."

"I am terrified, John, but if I have a say, I say that we go," she said, and looked at her daughter.

Bethany looked as though she were frozen in place. Only her large eyes moved. She looked at her father, brother, and mother, then said almost without moving her lips, "I say we go, too."

"Leo? You have the children to consider," John said.

Leo sat for a long time, not knowing what to say. It did not seem right to him to place his children in such obvious danger as the trip would mean. Already they had lost their mother, and while they were still young enough that aunts, grandmothers, and cousins filled in very nicely, that would not always be the case. Yet he could not remain in Charles Town and maintain his patriot loyalty. He would have to sign the addresses, and the likelihood was that he would be ordered to leave the town and fight. He couldn't do that. Nor would it keep his children safe. "I say we go," he said curtly, not liking any of his choices.

"We should waste no time. I imagine Wells will give us a day or two before he returns, but we can count on no more than that."

"We can be ready tomorrow night," Eugenia said. "Bethany and I can pack tomorrow, and be ready by nightfall."

"You must be painfully frugal, Eugenia," John reminded her.

As she passed him, she bent over and gave him a quick kiss on the forehead. "I know, dear. What little we take must be primarily food."

The Mannings left Hedy in charge of the house, and left just before nine o'clock in the evening. Though they had expected trouble, they drove out of the city without anyone even questioning them. They rode in the oldest carriage they owned, and had it packed as full as possible with the items

John and Leo had said they would need. Blankets took up the most space, and Bethany and Eugenia pared their clothing down to what they could wear on their backs. They replaced their petticoats with skirts, enabling them to take three changes of clothing. The blouses were not such a problem, for, being smaller, they could be tucked into other packages. "Of course, I shall smell of pickles and preserves, but I don't suppose that matters too much," Eugenia remarked with a sigh as she nervously went over the supplies in the carriage with John.

The men realized from the outset that this was going to be a long, slow, arduous journey. Though Bethany and Eugenia were willing and brave, neither of the women was accustomed to the hardships or the exhausting hours of travel. Long before the men would have stopped for the night, the two women were weary, and had the cooking and setting up of camp to look forward to. They had traveled for a full week without running into difficulty, but they had gone only a little better than one third of the distance. John and Leo talked, and decided it would do little good to say anything. "I think they are doing the best they can," Leo said. "And I'm not sure Miranda and John Andrew could take the longer hours, either. John Andrew cries all the time now."

John nodded. He, too, was feeling the strain of travel. This was the first time since he had lost his arm that he had tried to do real physical labor, and he was staggering with exhaustion by the end of each day.

They continued their journey for the next ten days with only an occasional scare. Those few times they had moved off the road and into the cover of the forest, waiting for other travelers or a patrol to pass by. For the most part no one seemed interested in them. Once they had been caught and stopped by a disreputable group of six men, who turned out to be patriots looking for Sumter with the idea of joining him. They gave the men some of their precious hoard of food, then went on their way.

Soon after that experience Eugenia said, "John, we are going to have to travel longer each day, or we will have nothing to eat long before we reach Cherokee. I have been trying to keep this from all of you for days now, but I simply cannot stretch our supplies out any thinner."

John and Leo exchanged glances and smiled. Neither of them made comment, except to submit to her wisdom.

John had never actually been to Cherokee, so he was always guessing at distances. He judged them to be no more than twenty miles from it, when Leo came riding back down the road from his scouting post. "There's a British patrol coming!"

John snapped the reins on the horses' backs, and shouted the beast to a near gallop. The carriage, its springs worn, and not particularly well balanced, swayed dangerously.

Leo rode alongside, shouting at his father. "There's a copse about a quarter mile on the left—but it looks like swamp."

They had no choice, and John plunged the careening carriage off the road and into the spongy turf. The carriage tilted, and was saved from overturning only by the tree it slammed into. John pulled hard on the reins, sawing at the horses' mouths, trying to slow the vehicle down. He heard a shrill scream inside the carriage, but couldn't do anything except attend to the panicked horses. The carriage took another bounce as the animals dragged it over an outcropping of rock. A wheel went flying loose and bounced off a tree. The screaming seemed louder to him now, and he had lost sight of Leo some time ago. Finally he managed to stop the horses, his one arm almost numb. He had to force his whitened fingers to release his grip on the reins.

He pried opened the damaged side door of the carriage and pulled Bethany from the floor. She was unconscious, and her face was bloody. Eugenia was not there. " 'Genia!" he cried trying at the same time to tend to his daughter. Tears of frustration ran down his face as with one arm he tried to raise Bethany to the seat. He had finally gotten her on the seat, and was searching through their tangled possessions hunting for the water bottle, when Leo came up supporting Eugenia. Her clothes were in tatters, and there was barely an inch of skin left on her righthand, arm, or her face, but she seemed whole, with no broken bones. John left his daughter to go to her. He put his arms around her and held her, not trying to stay the tears that came. "My God. 'Genia, I thought I had killed you!"

His embrace hurt her more than he could imagine, but she stayed in his arms. "I love you, John. I love you very much."

Leo brought Bethany around, and cleaned the cut she had sustained on her forehead. She was crying, and he was dabbing at her face. "You're going to have two of the biggest, blackest eyes any young lady of quality has ever sported, little sister," Leo said, laughing in relief that she was awake and seemed all right. When she tried to stand, however, they found she was not all right. Her right foot would not support her weight, and she fainted again from the pain.

John and Leo made an amateurish repair of the broken wheel, and Eugenia bound Bethany's ankle as best she could.

"What happened to the patrol?" John asked many hours later.

Leo shook his head. "I don't know. You went off the road, and I followed. I never saw or heard them pass. . . . I don't know where they went."

"All this was for nothing?" Eugenia cried.

"I pray not, my dear," John said, emotion choking his voice. "I don't think I could bear doing you and Beth injury for no cause."

"We had no choice," Leo said. He was seeing to Miranda's cuts and putting a splint on her arm. John Andrew had rolled to the floor of the carriage and suffered no more than a bruised forehead.

They set out again the next day. Eugenia, Bethany, and Miranda were able to withstand only minimal travel, and at a very slow pace. It took five more days before they finally came into the Cherokee yard.

"Stay in the carriage. I'll get help, Mama," Leo said, and got down from his horse. He knocked at the door and was greeted by a surprised Gwynne.

Well accustomed to emergency, Gwynne rang the plantation bell, and men and women appeared from every direction. In minutes each performed his or her well-practiced function, and again, as it had so many other times, the front room of Cherokee functioned as a well-ordered hospital.

For days afterward the story of the John Manning's journey came out a bit at a time. Even Elizabeth was appalled and impressed at what Eugenia had gone through. She smiled at the daughter-in-law she once had thought so little of. "I am so very proud of you, Eugenia. What you did was courageous."

Eugenia held up to her face the hand mirror Elizabeth had given her. "Ummm, and I shall pay for it forever! You and I are quite a pair, Elizabeth. We went to war, and you came out with no hair, and I have no skin!" She tossed the mirror down on the bed in disgust. "John was never a good driver, but with only one arm, he is atrocious! No one is safe with him in the driver's seat."

Elizabeth smiled. "Well, I'm sure John did the best he could. None of us are quite the people we were before this war began, are we?" she said. "But, Eugenia, I am not so certain that what is left of us is not better. As you said, I have no hair, and you have no skin. John has only one arm left, and Leo has lost a wife. Drew will always walk with a limp, and George will never again be innocent and naive as he once was, but we have come through a terrible time, and we have stuck together, we still love each other, and each in our time has met the test given to us. We are a strong family, Eugenia."

Eugenia smiled warmly and took Elizabeth's hand. "Yes, we are, aren't we? And we'll all go home to Charles Town—someday. To an American city, as an American family."

Elizabeth laughed. "With the loss of your skin, Eugenia, you seem to have developed a very sentimental patriotic streak."

"Yes, I have. I do wish George and Drew would hurry home again and tell us this wretched war is over. I do want to be in Charles Town to watch those English devils leave the town with their tails between their legs!"

35

Eugenia had a long time to wait for her wish to come true. There were cheers and hoorahs at the news that Cornwallis had surrendered at York-town, and there was rumor for a time that the war was over. But the war wasn't over, at least not for the people in South Carolina and other parts of the South. With their hopes raised high that the war was coming to an end, even the news that came in daily of new American victories was a disappointment. Even these simply meant that the war was dragging on and on at an enormous cost to the people of the South.

Finally Drew and George returned to Cherokee at the end of September with the news that the British outposts had been abandoned. "This must herald the end!" Drew shouted, and threw his hat in the air. Soon after, he received a letter from his commanding officer, Francis Marion. Marion advised him that Nathanael Greene was engaged in mopping-up operations. "I was told that a party of British foragers were operating near my plantation. I hadn't the stomach for it. I advised General Greene that I would not spill one more drop of blood. The war is over. Let our enemy limp off in peace." Drew looked up after reading that section of the letter. "This is what made him a good commander, and the most awesome of adversaries."

"But do you really believe this is the end?" Gwynne asked.

"If Marion has laid down his arms, it is over. You can trust that," Drew said confidently.

"We can go home!" Eugenia cried, and then insisted that she be there in time to see the British evacuate the city. "If I must walk the whole way, I shall be present!" she exclaimed.

Preparations for this journey were in some ways more difficult, and in other ways simpler, than in the past. They had far fewer possessions to carry, and the heavily laden wagons that had used to carry trunks of beautiful gowns, foodstuffs, bolts of cloth, and other gifts were no longer necessary. Luxury had disappeared long ago. They carried only necessities now. However, all the Mannings were gathered at Cherokee, and that was a large number of people. They made quite a caravan, and called into use all carriages and several wagons.

If it was not the easiest trip Drew had made, it was certainly the noisiest and most cheerful. When they were about two days from Charles Town they heard news that on November thirtieth John Adams, John Jay, Benjamin Franklin, and Henry Laurens of South Carolina had signed the preliminary articles of peace for the new nation. An already exuberant group of Mannings had their spirits raised even higher. They sang around their campfire that night, reminisced about times past, and dreamed about days to come. All the fatigue of the previous days and weeks on the road had fallen away by the time they started out again the next morning.

That morning Drew was aware of another difference in this trip. In his absence his son had grown up. He had passed his thirteenth birthday and become a man. Without needing permission, Nathaniel Dancer had taken his place by his father's side, riding in front of the wagons and carriages watching for poor road conditions, availability of water, and anything else that would be a help or a danger to the travelers. Drew watched his son with admiration and a bit of sorrow. He had really not been present to see Nathaniel become a man. For most of the last three years he had been in prison or away fighting.

The Mannings arrived in Charles Town, and Elizabeth's house, on December 8, 1782. As they went through the streets from which they had been exiled, they waved at old friends, and answered cheers of victory with cheers of their own. Both Drew and Nathaniel were dressed in traditional Upcountry garb, and Drew was reminded of the days when he had first been trusted to bring his father's produce into market, and the people along the street would look in awe at the ferocious Upcountry man. As he had those many years ago, he rode straight backed, his musket at the side of his saddle, a tomahawk at his waist, along with a pouch for his powder.

Beside him rode his son. Occasionally Nathaniel would take a sidelong glance to see what his father was doing, and adjust his own seat in the saddle accordingly, or tip his hat. It was a proud day. Nathaniel Dancer had a sense of pride and power he had never known before. This city seemed as though it were his.

The house was in disrepair, for it had been vandalized several times in their absence. Hedy had done all she could to protect it, but she had not been able to keep roaming Tories from throwing rocks through windows or tramping through Elizabeth's gardens. All of the Mannings, men, women, and children, set about righting the house.

On December thirteenth all thoughts of repairing broken windows or sweeping out cluttered gardens were forgotten. All the Manning children, even the youngest, were dressed in their best, as were their parents and relatives, and taken out to see the evacuation of the British. From all the places where the British were billeted, they marched out through the town, making their way to Gadsden's Wharf to board their vessels at dock there. With them the British took everything of value they had been able to take, loot, steal, from the townspeople, including most of the silver and jewelry. Even that did not taint the joy of the citizens. The town rang with good cheer. After seven years of anxiety and distress nothing could dampen the joy felt at the sight of British leaving in defeat.

Though the Mannings celebrated the leave-taking of the British troops, it was not all joy for them. Among the long lines of British who marched to board the waiting ships were Bert Townshend, his wife Joanna, and their child. Gwynne took Drew's arm and remained close to him.

"It'll be all right, my love. Time will help us all forget. . . . Joanna can return."

"It isn't that, Drew. . . . Joanna and I have been separated many times before. It isn't the distance—it is the bad feeling that exists between us. I wish she weren't leaving with that between us."

"There is nothing you can do about that, Gwynne. Joanna has fostered those feelings for years."

"Would you think me stupid if I tried? I could catch up with her and try to talk to her."

Drew began to move in the direction of the Townshends immediately, steering his wife safely through the crowd of people. It took them some time before they could see Joanna and Bert among the people waiting to board. When he had located them, he took her near to them, then stopped. "I'll wait for you here. My presence will only hinder you."

Gwynne squeezed his arm, smiled at him, and nodded. Then she walked up to her sister. "Joanna—could we talk? I hate for us to part like this. Please."

Joanna Templeton Townshend glanced at her sister as though she were a stranger. Her eyes were hard and devoid of emotion. "We have nothing to say to each other, Gwynne. And I certainly don't want to listen to you gloat. You may think you have won, but what you have won is *nothing!*"

Gwynne looked down. "I don't want to argue, Joanna. I'd just like us to part on better terms we are sisters. That should mean something— shouldn't it?"

Joanna laughed brittlely. "Will you never grow up, Gwynne? We have not been sisters since you chose to sneak behind the family's back and disaffect my fiancé! There is nothing for us to say to one another, Gwynne. Now now, not ever."

"May I write to you?" Gwynne asked, determined not to be affected by the hurt angry words Joanna kept saying to her.

"I don't care what you do."

"Would you answer?" Gwynne persisted.

Joanna looked away from her, turning slightly so Gwynne could not see her face. "One never knows what one will do in the future," she said in a barely audible voice.

But Gwynne heard. And Gwynne knew her sister. Someday, perhaps not for a long time, but one day, Joanna would write to her. She smiled, and turned to Bert. "Good-bye, Bert. I am sorry things are as they have been . . . but perhaps one day we can rectify this. Good luck to you."

Bert smiled at her and nodded, but said nothing. Despite himself, despite the war, Bert liked Gwynne. He took her hand and brought it to his lips, then watched as she moved back through the crowd to Drew Manning's side.

Gwynne looked up at Drew. "Well, it's done. I talked to her."

"And . . . ?" Drew questioned, looking at her. It was difficult to tell, for she was smiling and yet there were tears in her eyes.

"She is so cold, Drew! But I think it is better now than it was. If I am persistent, I think she will write to me . . . maybe the distance will help . . . and then, someday maybe we can visit England . . . or she might visit here. After all, Mama and Meg are still here."

"Yes," Drew said. "And that is something I wanted to talk with you about. Your mother and Meg will be worried about what will happen to them, and—"

"Oh, no! They know they can always live at Riverlea, Drew."

"Now, wait a moment, and let me finish. A great deal has happened since we last saw them, and they will not be able to run Riverlea . . . with Bert gone they will be unsure as to what will happen."

Gwynne looked up at him. "I hadn't thought about that . . . but

George and Jane are going to live there. George will manage it for us, won't he?"

"Yes, my dear, but your mother doesn't know that. I think you had better write to her as soon as possible, welcome her, tell her of our plans and . . ."

"And tell her we will be visiting after the first of the year," Gwynne finished with a smile. "Oh, Drew! I hadn't thought of it before, but now I am free to go to my home without worry! The children will get to enjoy Riverlea just as you and I did when we were growing up."

Drew laughed. "I love it when you turn little girl on me! You sound so happy."

"Hmmm," Gwynne said, looking at him from the corner of her eye. "Does that mean I haven't grown up? That's what Joanna accused me of."

"No, my darling, that means you have retained all the charm of your young life and added to it the charms of a woman."

Gwynne was radiant and smiling broadly when they rejoined the other Mannings.

They returned home and found yet another surprise awaiting them. On the silver tray in the entry hall was a letter. It was addressed to Drew. Eugenia picked it up, looked carefully at it, then handed it to him. "I think this is from your mother, Drew," she said, concern in her eyes.

Drew took the letter, but stood there holding it without making any move to open it. He tried to smile, but failed. "I suppose this . . ." He stopped and rubbed his hand across his forehead. "I imagine Arthur and Mother will be leaving, too." He looked at his cousins and relatives, and again tried to smile. "There isn't much left at Manning. Arthur wouldn't stay. . . . I suppose Mother . . ."

"Drew," Elizabeth said. She placed her hand on his arm. "Read it, dear. There is no point in putting yourself through this. Read it and find out what she has to say."

Drew looked at her. Only she and Gwynne truly knew what this final loss of his mother would mean to him. He nodded almost imperceptibly, then slowly, reluctantly, opened the envelope. He read to himself, fearing what each word would tell him, then suddenly he looked up, amazement showing in every line of his face.

"Drew? What is it? Tell us!" Gwynne cried. "What does she say?"

He laughed, a short, happy sound. "Arthur has gone to New York . . . but Mother is here . . . right here in Charles Town . . . at the Charles. . . . She has a room there. She thinks we wouldn't want to see her, but asks forgiveness, if we can find it in our hearts, and she would like to see us! Grandma! She didn't leave!"

Elizabeth bit back tears and hugged him. "Well, my dear, what are you waiting for? Go fetch your mother. By the time you bring her home, Eugenia and I should have supper ready and waiting."

"Do you think she'll come?" Drew asked.

"Oh, she'll come," Gwynne said merrily. "Nathaniel! Run quickly and get your sisters ready to take a ride. We have to get your grandmother. Hurry, dear, while I get the baby ready." Both Gwynne and Nathaniel hurried up the stairs, leaving Drew to stand alone looking baffled and happy.

The last of the British troops left on December fourteenth, and following their departure the Americans entered the city, raised their colors, and claimed Charles Town for its people once more. All the Mannings had turned out again to watch the doings, but this time Georgina was with them. In her arms she carried her youngest grandchild, and Nathaniel was at her side. Better than anyone, she knew what a deep, wonderful event the return of the Americans to the city was. She, too, had come home. Though there was a deep ineradicable soreness within her at the loss of Joseph and for Arthur's absence, there was also a sense of rightness. She was where she belonged and wanted to be. She smiled at those around her. "I've always been a family person," she said to no one in particular. "It's so good to be home!"

They returned home late in the afternoon, and within minutes of their homecoming, the doorbell was ringing. The Manning house was filled with friends who had come to greet them and rejoice over the peace. All of the Manning women were busy seeing to the comfort of their guests, and catching up on talk and news of marriages and births and deaths that had occurred in the last two years, but none was busier or happier than Georgina. She showed off her grandchildren, and told everyone who had not already heard it at least two other times that she was home for good, and would be living with Drew and Gwynne. With her eyes bright she said, "I shall certainly be needed! Drew and Gwynne already have a large family, and I wouldn't be surprised if it grew larger still."

Drew laughed, and glanced at Gwynne. "Don't encourage her, Mother. I have no defense against Gwynne, and should she get it into her head that we should have another child—we would!"

Georgina blushed. "I should have known better than to say anything like that to you! I had forgotten how willing you are to talk of anything, no matter how improper!" But she smiled, then laughed. How good it was to be able to fuss about such gentle human foibles again!

Georgina was too excited to go to bed after the last of the guests had left. She began to straighten the rooms and clear them of glasses.

Eugenia flopped down into a chair. "Oh, Georgina! Don't! The servants will see to it—and we can help in the morning. Aren't you tired? I am exhausted!"

"I know it is not my place, Eugenia, but would you mind terribly if I just stayed down here a bit longer . . . and straightened? It is so good just to handle the Manning crystal and china again! It truly makes me feel as though I am back—and will never leave again."

Eugenia immediately rose and came to her sister-in-law. The two women stood in a long embrace. "Oh, Georgina, I am so happy you are with us! I have missed you dreadfully!"

Georgina remained downstairs after Eugenia had retired, and one by one in the quiet of the house she was joined by Gwynne, and Bethany, and finally Drew. Mother and son stayed up most of the night talking about the present and future and crying over the past as they laid it to rest.

At breakfast the following morning Mary Taylor, a friend of Elizabeth's, stopped by with a gift of freshly baked sweet rolls. She joined them at the table, smiling and comfortable with this family.

"Since we have missed Thanksgiving, I feel that all Charles Town shall make this Christmas a true holiday of thanksgiving," she said. She looked at Elizabeth. "But, of course, Christmas has always been a favorite time for you, Elizabeth. Oh, my! I remember so many wonderful balls at this house at Christmas time. Shall you have one this year?"

Elizabeth laughed. "It may be a bit frugal, but I shouldn't be surprised if we did."

"I shall expect an invitation, and I will be telling all our friends to look forward to it." Mary stood, pulling on her gloves in preparation for leaving.

After she left, Eugenia came back into the room. "Elizabeth, why didn't you tell her we weren't planning anything so grand? Surely you don't feel up to all that."

"I am just a bit tired, Eugenia. I shall be fit for Christmas, and you cannot argue that we have never had greater cause for celebration than we have this year."

"I am not arguing, dear, but I do not think you are up to it. Gwynne, you talk to her. Perhaps she will listen to you."

Gwynne looked warmly at Elizabeth, then said, "Perhaps what we ought to be doing is making the preparations for Christmas ourselves. Elizabeth has done it for us for years. It is our turn now. Would you agree to that, Elizabeth? You may give us orders, and we shall carry them out."

"I think that is a marvelous suggestion, Gwynne. I am a little tired."

"And I would love to plan this Christmas," Georgina said.

Elizabeth rested, spending a great deal of time in her room, while the other members of the family proceeded with the Christmas plans. The men went out on a turkey shoot, something they had not done for pleasure in a long time. There was the search for the yule log, and the mistletoe, and the toasting, and the singing of carols that went with those festivities.

On the twenty-second of December the Mannings decorated the holly tree that stood in the front parlor of the house. Each of them placed red ribbons, chains of popcorn, and handmade ornaments on the tree. Bethany played the piano, and the others sang as they worked. Finally they were ready to place the candles on the tree. This year they made that a special part of their celebration. John Manning, as the oldest male member of the family, lit each of the candles before its placement, and to each candle he gave a name of one of the members of the family.

As each candle was given a name and placed on the tree, the family thanked the Lord for sparing the life of that person, or asked that He care for him in the life hereafter.

They ended the evening with carols and a toast. John, with the help of Leo, mixed his famous hot toddy. After everyone had his or her mug, he held his own up and smiled. "Ahh, now that is a masterpiece. I would like to propose that we drink to this new country, and that we congratulate ourselves on a job well done!"

"Amen!" George cried, and took a deep, satisfying drink from his cup. Then he got up and walked over to where Jane Reston sat. "Jane and I decided long ago that we would not marry unless we could do it as free Americans. I am very grateful that we won the war, because had we lost I might never have married, or Jane and I would have had to leave the colonies. We didn't want to do that. Now that we don't have to, I would like to announce our coming marriage."

With that announcement George instantly lost a good portion of his audience. All the Manning women turned immediately to Jane. "Oh, Jane, when will it take place?" Gwynne asked. "Why didn't you tell me? You kept it a secret."

Jane blushed and looked at George. "We didn't want to say anything until we were actually here and could see with our own eyes that the war was really over. We have decided to be married in April . . . I like the flowers in April," she added a bit shyly.

"Why, that's barely enough time!" Eugenia said. "This must be a *very* special occasion. You mustn't forget George is my *baby* son."

"Mother! Was that necessary?" George groaned. "Please, don't say that in front of anyone else. I won't be able to hold my head up!"

"I shall not repeat it, George, providing you do not forget it and allow me to plan the most gala wedding Charles Town has ever seen."

"Oh, I will!" Jane said brightly, far more like herself than the shy girl who had just said she liked the flowers of April. "I would love a big wedding!"

They toasted again, and yet again, until they were all beginning to get very sentimental and a little sad as they began to talk about those of them who were no longer there. John finally stood up, sniffing a bit, and wiping the back of his hand across his eyes. "We are getting maudlin. It is time for bed."

On Christmas Eve they all relaxed, visited with friends, and saw to last-minute preparations for the Christmas ball planned for the twenty-eighth.

On Christmas Evening Elizabeth Manning retired to her room early and began writing the letters she would give each member of her family as her Christmas gift this year. For gifts it was going to be a frugal year. There was little cash available to the Mannings, nor was there the normal supply of goods in the shops. The whole city was struggling to overcome the devastation the war had caused to their lives and their businesses.

Elizabeth was still awake, and writing, when Christmas morning actually came. With the first glimmer of the pale rising sun, Elizabeth went to her bed. She laid her head on the pillow gratefully, and closed her eyes.

As was usual, the first members of the household to awaken were the servants and the children. The adult Mannings opened their eyes to a chorus of young voices giggling and whispering that it was Christmas. After the first round of "Mama! Daddy!" had stirred them a bit, the odors of delicious food cooking finished the task. One by one bedroom doors opened and closed and a parade of Mannings went downstairs to look beneath the Christmas tree and to open the few packages that were there.

John took his place beside the tree, as it was his privilege to read the names on the packages and hand out the gifts. He looked around the room to be certain no one was missing. "Where is Bethany?"

"I'm right here!" she cried, and ran down the last few steps, and hurried to a vacant space on the sofa next to Gwynne.

"Are we all here now?" he asked.

They all looked around. "Grandma isn't here," Drew said. None of them moved. None of them spoke. Then Nathaniel got up, and walked toward the staircase, and Drew followed him. Eugenia stood up, then Gwynne and Bethany. One by one they all got up and walked up the staircase, except Jane and John Manning. John remained in his chair, head down.

Drew opened the door to his grandmother's bedroom, and saw what he had expected, and what he had dreaded. Still fully dressed, Elizabeth lay on her bed, her hands neatly folded on her chest, a smile on her face. She looked as though she were sleeping.

They trailed into her room and stood looking at her, wishing that their presence could awaken her. None of her family doubted what they saw, nor could it be unexpected at her age, but it didn't stop them from hoping for the impossible. So often Elizabeth had been able to do what no one else could do. They wanted it of her one more time, and no one was prepared for her to remain lying on her bed. They weren't ready to lose her.

Gwynne was standing nearest Elizabeth's desk. As she leaned against it, her hands touched the stack of letters Elizabeth had spent the night writing. Gwynne glanced at them and, when she saw her own name, picked them up. "Elizabeth has left something for each of us," she said quietly. The others turned toward her. As she read each name, she handed out the letters in turn.

Nathaniel took his and hurried to the privacy of his own room.

In each of the letters Elizabeth had written a special message, but she had requested that all of them go to services at St. Michael's Church as they would have done on any other Christmas they celebrated in Charles Town.

"She knew," Gwynne said softly, and leaned against Drew.

They went to St. Michael's, because she had asked them to, but all of them were thinking more about what she had said in her letters than they were about the sermon.

Drew stared straight ahead, his eyes fixed on the crèche. He kept thinking of the Christmas he and Nathaniel had been traveling back to Cherokee, and he had complained to his grandmother that they could not celebrate the holiday. She had told him then that perhaps he would celebrate it truly for the first time. He thought of other Christmases with Elizabeth. It seemed to be her special time.

Nathaniel's eyes were raised higher than his father's. He was younger, and his memories of Elizabeth seemed to him to have more to do with his future than his past. She had told him in her letter that she would always

Sharon Salvato

be with him. "Life and death are very closely tied, Nathaniel, and you will see it over and over again. Since I shall not be able to tell you this in one of our chats, I want you to see it in this wonderful time of the birth of our new nation. We Americans were born out of the death of British rule. That is as it should be. But, Nathaniel, I urge you not to make the mistake of thinking that the birth of a nation is the making of a nation. What we are as a people is yet to come, and that determination rests in your hands. Have the heart, Nathaniel, to make this a nation of honor and integrity, of justice and high spirit. It is in your hands now, formless, characterless, waiting to be molded and determined. The sins of the fathers are indeed visited upon the sons, but God is not cruel, nor does He judge so harshly or so swiftly as men do. It is in your power to turn the sins of war into the victories of a mighty, righteous nation."

Nathaniel Dancer heard the choir begin to sing, and knew the services were nearly over. He felt a great surge of emotion and hope sweep through him. It was almost as if Nonnie were right beside him. He could imagine he could hear her laughter. And he knew that she had, as she always had, found him just when he thought he was lost. She had found him, and set his foot upon a path. Perhaps better than any of the other Mannings in the church that Christmas morning, Nathaniel Dancer understood what was yet before them in the building of this new nation.

He left the church and looked up into a clear blue winter sky, knowing that with the end of the Revolution the question of liberty had not been answered, only asked.